Earth had everything going for it. Not only was the mother planet top dog in the solar system—her weak colonies hanging on by the skin of their teeth had to heed her every whim.

Her spaceships were tops; her armament invincible; and she had just developed a new method of computerized schooling that seemed certain to develop an army of superminds to do Earth's bidding.

Yet, if all this was truly so, then how was it that the pesty little mining ships of the poorest colonial offshoot of all—the barren rocks of the Asteroid Belt —had beaten Earth's fleet to a frazzle and her homemade strategists were outthinking the best of the whole High Earth command?

Turn this book over for second complete novel

phoenix ship

WALT and LEIGH RICHMOND

AN ACE BOOK

Ace Publishing Corporation
1120 Avenue of the Americas
New York, N.Y. 10036

Lullaby for our Space Children

Parameter, perimeter, and pi—
  There's a trace in the space past the sky that is I
There's a me in the lee of this starred infinity
  That is out to prove the ethic that the universe is free.
We're a shout in the snout of eternities of doubt—
  We're a spit in the mitt as we take our aim to hit—in
                                                the eye—
The multitude of factors that will try to nullify.
  Our parameters, perimeters, and pi.

Astronomy and chemistry and math—
  If you know where to go and your slipstick's not too
                                    slow (don't be slow!)
Where electrons meet the nucleus of mass
  And protons go along the selfsame path
Where the multiples of decimals that mark the whirling
                                              sphericals
  Indicate there may be trouble coming past—
It's a laugh . . . if you're fast
  With astronomy and chemistry and math.

Diameter, circumference, and sphere—
  Space may not yet have noticed, but we're here—Space,
                                              we're here!
With spectrographic dazzle and a certain yen to travel
  And the love of work that brings the concepts clear.
When the know-how got to flowing, we made ourselves the
                                                knowing
  And we left behind the Earthbound who don't care for
                                              the rare

5

*Relativities that measure an incomparable treasure when
you steer
    By diameter, circumference, and sphere.*

*Maneuver is a cone too far to see
    Out where motion's only relativity—
Where inertia is the stronger of the forces, and no longer
    Subject to the biting laws of gravity.
Want to brake? That's a fake! But if planetfall you'd make
    Turn your tail—raise your thrust—you're falling free
Through vectors of a factor known as V
    With dimension governed by your A times T.*

*Now E must equal M times C the square
    If you really think you're headed anywhere
And you care—to get there.
    For a proton or an atom that exists as just a datum
Does not wear—cannot care . . .
    But the manner of his travel to a human who can ravel
Is decidedly a different affair. So beware.
    For that E will always equal MC square.*

I

His NAME WAS Stanley Thomas Arthur Reginald Dustin, and the acronym was intentional, "bought" for him by an uncle at a price. The name had been registered, the price accepted; but when his mother died and his uncle returned to the Belt his father's disapproval had registered as well, and he could be known only by his first name, Stan.

"Ruffians make up the bulk of the planeteers," his father assured him as soon as he was old enough to ask. "Ruffians and ne'er-do-wells who can't make it on Earth and have to flee. There is the occasional adventurer like my brother, but that is the exception," he had added carefully. "Even so, your Uncle Trevor has behaved beneath the dignity of the family."

The red hair, the set chin and the gangling length that he had inherited from his uncle could not be disavowed so easily, but the heritage was offset by a pug nose and freckles; and with that his father had to be content.

There had been friction between the stern, unbending father and the easygoing, carelessly alive boy from the beginning. It was Stan's father's determination that one adventurer in the family was more than sufficient, that Stan should be schooled to the responsible position in his own community that his father had created for him. This determination had nearly obviated the possibility of Stan's entering the school on the Arctic slopes where he now sat in a learning cubicle answering test questions on the computer screen before him.

Interminable questions. They made up almost the entire curriculum of the school. Questions, with nothing on which to base his answers. Questions that leaped from subject to subject; that sometimes centered whole concepts and assumed not only knowledge from top to bottom of the field involved, but, Stan decided, intuition within it.

*Given the lens configuration in the diagram above, speci-
fy the index of refraction required in lens C, and select from
the following list the type and weight percentage of materi-
als required to formulate such a lens for operation in an
environmental temperature range of 220 to 260 degrees
Kelvin.*

Stan glared at the sentence as though it were an enemy,
but it refused to go away. Yet, as though his body had a
will of its own, he began estimating angles by eye and
sliding the slipstick—his sole allowed tool of computation
—while he shifted decimals in his head.

*With a computer and about six months' time perhaps,
I might be able to come up with some sort of answer,* that
part of his mind which refused to be disciplined considered.
The things they expect you to know on a test like this, he
thought ruefully.

It had been a compromise on both his and his father's
part. Stan wanted, perhaps because it was denied him,
abjectly and unreasoningly but absolutely, the training
necessary to ship on the interplanetary lines. At least that
was his stated ambition—to go out in the ships that plied
the system.

What he really wanted, the secret desire that gnawed
his vitals with a deep, unreasoning yearning, was to explore
the stars. But before that became possible, the Einstein
formulas would have to be rewritten; and they'd been
proved long ago and over and over. That desire was hopeless, and, he told himself severely, it was a sign of imma-
turity to continue to harbor it. The fact that his father did
not even suspect its existence was hardly surprising. Stan
hid it from himself whenever possible.

His father was not only adamantly against anything that
smacked of space, but actually anything that smacked of
technical training.

"You shall indeed go to the planets; explore the entire
system," Stan's father had explained carefully, "but as a
tourist, free to explore; free to sample the best of everything that is offered; free of the slave-labor that marks
the life of a"—the word was distasteful in his mouth—"a
planeteer, or a Belter."

The school here was a compromise, his acceptance into
its five-year course a surprise to both of them. And Stan
was not even sure how that compromise had been reached.

The Mentor who had had him called for conference during a late afternoon of his final high school year had been a stranger, and strangely dressed even by the most flamboyant standards. Stan had entered the conference room cloaked in the normal long gray cloak of privacy over his own almost-colorful dark blue singlet and matching hose, to be received by an older man in silken gold tunic and trousers and soft gold kid slippers. It was his face that kept Stan's attention: it was uncreased, smooth, almost featureless.

"I am Katsu Lang," the Mentor greeted him with. "Won't you throw off the cloak? I expect we will be friends, and no privacy between us."

Startled, Stan had removed the cloak and folded it carefully over a chair.

He had been accepted, Dr. Lang told Stan slowly, in a newly organized school set up under rather special conditions, teaching a "newly developed engineering course." Designed, the Mentor had said, to best equip a candidate for a general understanding of the society and possible usefulness in its further technological development.

"Accepted?" Stan had asked, and been assured that the criteria had been rigorous; that he had been found acceptable under the most exacting standards.

He wasn't at all sure how it was that he had quite suddenly become convinced that this five-year course was what he wanted; but he had been quite sure that it was something his father would refuse.

"If you will permit us," the Mentor had assured him, his strange, nearly poreless face without expression, "I believe that this part can be handled for you. If you accept this assignment . . ."

Stan had accepted, and though he was not sure after he'd arrived at the school itself that it was what he wanted—he was here; he had been at the school for over four years.

But it wasn't a school, Stan told himself. It was a series of tests. It was nothing but tests, actually, with occasional lectures that seemed more designed to puzzle than inform. The first day's schedule had consisted of nothing but tests, in this same cubicle, on subjects that ranged from engineering to sociology to anthropology . . . any and every subject you could think of. At the end of the tests he had learned that the next day would consist of a similar series, and that he could study for it or not as he liked.

But study what? There had been several areas in the first tests that had left him blank and curious. He started on those in the tiny library cubicle assigned to him; and he'd found that each tape he'd worked through had led him on to other tapes; and pure curiosity had kept him going, on and on. . . .

He'd fallen asleep in his small room, expecting to be called for the next day's assignments, and had not wakened for nearly fourteen hours.

Without even pausing to find out what meals he'd missed, he'd gone straight to the classroom cubicle, where the impersonal quiz program had simply begun on his arrival and continued until he left.

Famished, puzzled, uncertain, he'd left the cubicle and searched until he'd found an office. His knock was answered and he'd entered to face again the Mentor in the golden suit with a gold belt embossed with entwined snakes.

"I . . . overslept."

"Filing time is important, too," the Mentor had said softly.

"I . . . I haven't eaten. Dr. Lang, I don't know the schedule, I don't know what to study. I haven't met my classmates. I . . ." His voice had run down.

"You will find your classmates in the common room, whenever you care to go there. Your studying seems to have followed a very well selected pattern. The meal schedule is posted in the common room."

"But . . . lectures? Classes?"

"They are posted."

"On what terms will I be kept or dropped? I assume that you don't keep all the students. You said that the course was competitive."

"It is competitive. We expect to drop at least three-quarters of the students to lesser courses within the five years."

"You . . . I guess you're sort of leaving it up to each of us how we study and what we do?"

"Isn't that advisable? In selecting for the best, that is? Those dropped will have fine courses and careers ahead of them."

There was no use asking questions, Stan realized. He took a deep breath.

"Your questions—your tests—cover subjects with which I am completely unfamiliar. How do you expect me to answer the questions? How can you expect us to pass the tests?"

"Have you found it impossible to answer the questions?"

Stan found himself blank for a minute. Then, with an effort, he forced himself to recall one of the tests he'd had the day before. It was a mathematical quiz, and he'd watched himself sitting before the board, the questions arising one from another, across the screen, as he'd answered them. There were long pauses before each answer; pauses in which he'd strained every mental muscle he possessed to . . . remember? Grasp? Analyze? And the answers had come, feebly and unsurely, but they had come. Correct or incorrect, there had been answers there when he'd reached deep and strained to . . . remember.

He felt exhausted, as though he'd been running for miles and was wilting. Standing there before the smooth-faced Mentor, he tried to frame the question that would give him the answer to the school itself.

"If a test selection asks something that you do not know," the Mentor said softly, "you can always answer that you do not know. That would be quite a valid answer, would it not?"

I've come this far, Stan told himself grimly. *I won't be licked by the prospect of endless examinations. And I won't be one of those relegated to merely fine courses and careers.*

"You have had your inoculations?" Again the soft voice carried no inflection other than the question.

Stan was startled. Inoculations had been part of the entrance proceedings. He nodded, mutely.

"You will have them weekly," he was told. "They will . . . help."

And the answers had come. Almost invariably, if he reached hard enough. The answers seemed to grow out of the pyramidal structure of the questions—and yet, they didn't. He was calling on information he had not known he possessed, and it puzzled him; and yet the catholicity with which he pursued information during the free hours of the day must be the source, he told himself.

The hours between exams—and outside the sleep that seemed to claim him willy-nilly and occupy far more hours than he liked to waste this way—were in the nature of a race. He never had any idea what the next day's tests would cover. So he found himself grabbing for information in those off-hours in so helter-skelter a manner that he was attempting everything and acquiring nothing.

Five years was a long time, he finally decided. If a subject was dropped today it would probably be resumed in the forseeable future. And he began following the subject of each day's tests in that day's studying. It seemed to pay off.

It was the sleep that he continued to fight. After that first night, it hadn't been a normal sleep, not for a long time. It had been a feeling of sleep that built an increasing tension within until it would seem as though he were bursting; and as it seemed inevitable in his dreams that he would burst, he'd wake; he'd fall asleep again almost instantly and go through the increasing tension again hour after hour; and he'd wake exhausted.

He found himself increasing his study hours to avoid sleep; found himself fighting to keep his attention on the library tapes to the point of exhaustion. But exhausted as he might be, at the moment he fell asleep the tension would begin to build and build . . . until one night he didn't wake and there was what he remembered later as an internal explosion that had continued for some time as a series of minor explosions. They wafted him forward and back, forward and back, as on a constantly reversing current, until he drifted peacefully with it, no longer fighting, no longer tense.

Waking, he'd felt refreshed for the first time since coming to the school. That night he'd returned to his sleeping room expectantly and had fallen asleep to the old tensions, but almost immediately an explosion had occurred—a lesser explosion this time. Then came the forward and backward motion that was as restful as a rocking chair.

The process had gone on for a week, until finally the tensions and the explosions had dropped out, and the rocking motion had begun the instant he'd fall asleep. He looked forward to it now: to the refreshment, greater than any he'd ever known; to the soft currents themselves, and the satisfied feeling with which he'd wake.

His life had taken on a similar alternating-current rhythm. The tests were a flow in one direction: if he relaxed and let his subconscious work, the answers came easily; whereas if he strained they seemed to be stopped.

Studying was an alternate flow, a pursuit of knowledge that was a furious, instinctive demand he found within himself for knowledge that came from his conscious and pursuing mind. It was a competitive urge that claimed him daily as he left the testing cubicle and took him direct to the library and its concentrations.

The race left him little time for the common room, though there were games and conversation to be had there. On the occasions when he did appear, it seemed to be full of students, uncloaked and informal as Stan now was, in variations of the dark singlets and hose that were stylish. He rather assumed that the other students were taking the same hours he did for studying, and didn't worry about it. What they did was their business, he decided.

Mostly, though, when he allotted himself time off—and no one in authority seemed in the slightest interested in setting hours or schedules except for the occasional lectures, meals, and weekly inoculations—he went topsides. He'd discovered the entrance to the outside once when he went determinedly exploring the school plant, originally an oil refinery complex abandoned when the age of oil ended. There'd been heavy outside wear—quilted boots and trousers; hooded and gloved tunics—in the small room beyond the door that was marked simply OUTSIDE; and he'd helped himself and gone out into the arctic wastes.

That first time he'd not intended to go far, but the empty spaces beyond the small entrance held an enchantment. The sun was on the horizon, bright and small, and making a gold path across the white expanse. He followed the path almost blindly, drinking in the lonely sweeps of snow; a loneliness that he'd never found before; that created a hunger in his entrails. The cold air bit into his lungs, and he fastened his hood to cover his mouth and nose and went on.

Abruptly the sun was gone, and a wind rose violently to sweep snow into his eyes. He kept on for a bit, but the wind gusted harder; he turned to find the white expanse on all sides, his tracks covered, and no sign of the entrance through which he'd come. A near-panic gripped him, and he stood stock-still for a minute, feeling it wash over him, feeling his body react to panic, the urge to run pulling at his legs.

Then he laughed. This, he'd thought, must be what it was like to be in space. And he looked at the whiteness reflecting back the remaining light and stretching to infinity in every direction, and felt an urge to throw out his arms and embrace it.

Turning then in a complete circle, he had tried to determine the direction from which he'd come. It was then that he saw the small figure approaching and recognized it instantly by the golden padded suit, shaped like his own, but glowing in the reflected light.

Bracing himself against the gusting wind, Stan went to meet the figure. "Dr. Lang," he shouted through the wind when they were near, "have I done wrong to come out?"

The face that he knew to be broad and expressionless was hidden behind the hood, but as the wind lulled between gusts, the voice was unmistakable. "I think, Stan, that we shall give you a special inoculation. No, you have not done wrong. Should it be wrong to come out into the open?"

A question for every question, Stan thought. But, "No," he answered. "This is peace. It should be sought."

After that, he'd gone out for at least a little while almost daily. He'd never gotten lost again, and he'd never met the Mentor again. But the trips topsides had come to mean a relaxation and a cleansing, more effective than a shower.

Stan had missed his home and friends at first as the strange course went on; but more and more the trips home had come to seem like visits to a foreign land, the people to speak an alien tongue.

And then, in one short week, his home became enemy territory.

He had barely arrived for Christmas vacation when the news broke on 3-D: ships of the Belt had attacked Earth Fleet; had attacked and destroyed a few of the mighty vessels that controlled interplanetary space.

And the Belt forces were led by Trevor Dustin.

The shock was felt everywhere. It was impossible. The tiny, weak population of the Belt taking on the might of Earth?

But as the hours passed and the 3-D marshaled its on-

14

the-spot coverage from space itself, the shock became greater.

The screens showed the huge battleships of Earth, light-colored to reflect back the impinging rays of the sun; long cylinders more than two hundred feet across, spinning slowly to give gravity when not under thrust. Mighty ships. Their hulls held six feet of water for radiation shielding over the entire surfaces; water that served as a major part of the life-support systems for the crews and the two thousand Space Marines that were the normal complement. They were armed with powerful laser beams for space warfare, with projectile and atomic cannon for planetary warfare, though the ships themselves would never come nearer to a planet than a two-hour orbit. Massive monsters, capable of maneuvering at up to a two-G thrust. . . .

And darting among and between them like a flight of stubby crossbow arrows, black so that they were nearly invisible, the tiny ships of the Belt.

"The Belters have dropped their freight doughnuts, and they're using the central control-cabin/thrust-tube segments of their freighters as fighting ships!" an excited commentator explained. "They've painted them black so they can't be seen by eye . . . a useless gesture. They can be seen by ladar."

Breathless, he went on, explaining to an Earth audience that had never considered the problems of Belt shipping. "The Belters load their freight into doughnut-shaped containers, the way freight used to be loaded on Earth into the trailer end of a trailer-tractor truck. Their control cabins are directly attached to the ion drive tube that centers any spaceship, and that control cabin is the only part of the ship that needs shielding, since the freight travels in vacuum. When the freightnut is loaded, the control-cabin/drive-tube combination is fitted into its center and the Belter accelerates it into a Hohmann orbit toward its destination, then lets go. The freightnut is picked up at the far end of its trip by a similar ship/drive-tube.

"Those drive-tube ships are *fast*," he went on. "With no shielding needed except for the small living section, they're long and fast and maneuverable. They can get thrusts up to any G's a man can take; and the system of dropping the freightnuts makes almost every ship in the Belt a fighting ship."

Then the head of Earth's Space Commission was brought on to reassure the vast listening audience. "The Belters," he said solemnly, "are getting too big for their britches. Of course they haven't any fire power at all, comparatively speaking; and this uprising should be over in a few hours. They have been listening to the traitorous leaders who have quarreled with Earth's very light and reasonable control measures from the beginning. When this is over, the traitors must be weeded out, and restrictive measures taken.

"It may hurt a parent to spank a child," he went on in a kindly tone of voice, "especially an insanely brave child. However, it must be done for his own good. The very act of attacking where there is no possibility of winning shows the extent of the delusions of grandeur from which the Belters must be rescued."

Yet time went on, and the predicted spanking became more and more remote.

The tiny ships of the Belt were everywhere, black mosquitoes diving onto light-colored elephants and pulling out again. They didn't even try to match fire-power with their prey; just dove almost onto the Earth ships, then pulled into steep climbs that flicked their tails toward the hulls of their enemy and sprayed them with the full jet streams of their drives.

A few were swatted, but very few compared to the numbers that were diving again and again. The mighty laser guns of Earth Fleet had been built to focus sharply at distances of one hundred miles and better, and were having trouble with their accuracy in this in-fighting. The Earth gunnery officers did hit their targets, as demonstrated with fair frequency by minute sparks of light on the target hulls. But the targeting sparks seemed to be without effect except when a spark hit the control-cabin end; and even then it was usually followed by only a tiny puff of steam that was gone almost as soon as it appeared, while the Belt ship arrowed on instead of exploding.

Not so with the stings of the myriad Belt mosquitoes. As the tail of the Belter lighted the hull of its prey with the ghastly blue glow of its jet stream, a great gout of steam would pour forth, and continue to spout. It did not take many hullings before the giants dissolved from hydrostatic shock in great soundless blasts of steam and debris on the viewscreens of Earth.

They were strange battles to watch, as the two fleets came together time after time: the ponderous ships of Earth maneuvering majestically, while the tiny Belt ships dove in and out among them, dancing like fireflies at punishing accelerations and decelerations, in patterns impossible for the heavily manned, heavily armored leviathans of Earth.

"Guerrilla ships," the Belters were called by the astounded commentators. Guerrilla ships that were showing a technological invincibility that had not been suspected. Guerrilla ships that were recklessly, impossibly, remaining on the attack—and winning.

It was over in three days; three days in which neither Stan nor anyone else left the 3-D; in which food was something to be gulped between battles; in which sleep was out of the question.

Stan watched the last and crucial fight. The Earth fleet had been maneuvered into massing; and the guerrilla ships were diving through the mass, one after the other, picking off the central ships while the firepower of the Earth ships was limited for fear of hitting their own. It was a daring thing to watch as the one-man Belt ships threw themselves, unhesitatingly, into and through the mass of monsters.

Stan was watching too, when the flagship of the Belt fleet, "Traitor Dustin's ship," the commentators called it, as tiny as the others, took a hit and spun out, exploding slowly in the fantastic silence of a space war. But with that ship went the giant of the Earth fleet, the main battleship, *Earuna*.

It was over. Earth Fleet had withdrawn to "regroup and study the situation," the commentators said, though the euphemism was obvious to even the most chauvinistic. Earth was defeated, and the Belt independent.

And Uncle Trevor dead, Stan added to himself, while the commentators talked excitedly of the unexpected technological abilities of the Belt, which were matched (they emphasized) by the technology of Earth, though that technology had not been thought necessary to the control of the spaceways. . . .

Stan left the 3-D, but instead of going to his den to sleep, he took the elevator to the top of the sky-rise, to the park-area where he could look into the sky and think beyond it.

As he left the elevator, a familiar figure, tall and heavy under its flapping cloak, was approaching it.

"Hi, Tom," Stan said, preoccupied.

"Traitor Dustin!" was Tom's only greeting, and Stan found himself ducking a roundhouse right cross that barely missed his nose, the broad sweep of Tom's cloak sleeve slapping across his face.

What happened next was as much a surprise to Stan as it was to Tom. He had been attacked. The attack had missed only because of his own quick reflexes which, almost of their own accord, now had Tom engaged in a half-nelson, Stan's left arm gripping a pressure point at the back of Tom's neck.

"What shall I break first?" he heard himself asking in a mild voice. The overstimulation that should have resulted from a flood of adrenalin to the circulatory system in the standard fight-or-flight response wasn't there. There was none of the raggedness of heavy breathing that would formerly have accompanied any fight. The automic responses hadn't been needed or triggered. He hadn't even had his attention on the fight. He was still debating his own fierce pride that the Belt had won. He should be loyal to Earth —or should he. Somehow there was a feeling of justification, both in the war and in his own personal battle that he neither understood nor wanted to question.

The next day he had gone to the tailor's and had himself fitted for tunics and trousers—of a light gray silken material that held a gold tinge. Then he'd selected a tunic belt of gold—plain gold—though he knew that the tailor, his family and friends would find the clothes, the color, even the fact of the belting, distasteful.

He'd made his visits home as infrequent as possible after that, and now he felt almost a stranger there; and the feeling was mutual. The pug nose was gone; the freckles gone.

"You look too much like your former uncle for comfort," his father had remarked on his last trip home. "If I were not assured that this school is training you for one of the higher governmental positions, I would suspect . . ."

Stan punched the last figures into the board before him,

and to his surprise saw it clear completely. Then the questions were replaced with a terse summons:

Student S.T.A.R. Dustin. Report to Professor Mallard in Office 201.

Stan jerked out of the daydreams that had more and more accompanied his tests over the years as he had relaxed to let the answers come easily.

The almost hypnotic rhythm by which he had worked for more than four years lay shattered around him, and he felt as though he were stepping over its shards as he left the cubicle.

II

PROFESSOR MALLARD stood, cloaked but unhooded, behind his desk as Stan entered, his piercing eyes seeming to X-ray the student and his pursed lips seeming to find what he saw unpleasant.

Stan drew himself up. "Student S.T.A.R. Dustin, reporting as ordered, sir."

The professor's face relaxed, and he allowed a small smile to superimpose itself on the disdainful expression.

"Star Dustin," he said in a clipped voice. "Perhaps the name is prophetic, General."

Startled, Stan turned to find a uniformed figure seated casually behind him, beyond the door by which he had entered.

"So this is the young man." The general eyed Stan from his carrot thatch to his new gray-gold slippers, then nodded to himself and rose, a big figure in a carefully tailored uniform. "This your somewhat independent but exotically educated guinea pig, eh? Well, have no fear, Professor. We'll tame him. We've tamed the likes of him and better before. After that we'll see whether he performs to specifications." He nodded briefly to the professor, ignoring Stan, took cap and gloves from the table beside his chair, and left without another word.

As the door closed behind the general, Professor Mallard almost let the precise smile slip, then replaced it carefully. "You have brought yourself to important notice, young man," he said.

Stan felt an internal stillness that held every sense alert, waiting. There was a sure knowledge of danger beneath the stillness, but it was the lesser of the two emotions. There was a dislike of the professor so intense as to be nearly overwhelming. *Why the professor?* he asked himself. *Why not the general?* And he found no answer except the fact.

"I haven't flunked, have I, Professor?" he heard his voice asking and knew himself to be asking for time to get his balance, to sort out the emotions that threatened to flood his system.

"Flunked?" Mallard considered for a moment, then shook his head from side to side. "No. Not that. A bit too . . . self-motivated, perhaps. But as the general said . . ." He decided to leave the sentence hanging.

A silence lay between the two then. The professor stood immobile, his eyes boring into those of the student.

He expects me to speak first, to look away, Stan thought. *He's determined to force me. Why?* His chin lifted and firmed.

At the gesture, the professor's smile deepened. "Ah, yes," he said with the casual triumph that comes with winning a personal bet. "A bit too self-motivated. However . . ." He slowly dropped himself into the desk chair, tenting his fingers on its surface, each action deliberate. Then he began to speak, lightly, as though discussing a subject of no possible import.

"You will be apprenticed as a Marine in the Earth Space Service," he said. His eyes still did not leave Stan's, and the effect removed any casualness engendered by his tone. "You will be in that post for perhaps half a year. When your . . . obvious eagerness is thoroughly under control, and because you have shown yourself rather exceptionally bright, you will be transferred to more and more responsible positions. By the time that we are ready to re-subdue the Belt, I expect you to be among the squad leaders of the effort. By then you should have a squad completely composed of personnel who have been molecularly trained as you have been, who should prove—"

"The Belt?" Stan heard his voice ask. "The Belt is independent, sir."

The professor brought himself up crisply. "The Belt is temporarily independent. It is, you will realize, a condition that Earth cannot tolerate."

"Sir." Stan paused, marshaling his words. "I should prefer another assignment. I have loyalties. . . ."

"Ah." The professor nodded. "Trevor Dustin's memory. The traitor mythologized into a hero. Trail Duster. And your nickname is Star Duster? What a mistake your parents made! I should have realized." Then, fiercely: "You know, of course, that he would be captured and hung if he were not dead already? That he has been hung in effigy?"

Then the voice relaxed. "Well, the first inoculations you get before going to—never mind." He clamped his mouth with a sudden snap, then smiled again. "We can understand your misplaced loyalties, young man. We can also handle them. You have been accorded a high honor, and it is not one that you will be allowed to refuse. It is an honor that has already been accorded you in part, for you were accepted into this school although your IQ was at first thought to be too low and—"

"Sir. If I may interrupt. I should like to talk the matter over with Dr. Lang."

The professor's face showed another of its abrupt changes. "Professor Lang," he said distastefully, "is no longer with us. He has not been with us now for almost three years."

Stan felt himself sinking, as though a support had been removed from beneath him, and the feeling startled him. He'd barely known Dr. Lang, but he'd trusted him. And Dr. Lang was no longer here? Somehow Stan had thought of him as . . . well, as standing in the wings, watching and waiting. It was an odd thing to have thought, he reminded himself. He'd seen the smooth-faced Mentor perhaps four times, and exchanged very few sentences with him. Yet the feeling of trust, of familiarity, of . . . Dr. Lang had represented to him what he thought of as the school. And Dr. Lang had not been there for most of his schooling.

The professor's voice was continuing, and he brought his attention back to it. "At any rate, young man, you have very little choice. The results the school is obtaining must be demonstrated to the military in no uncertain terms and as immediately as possible. We have convinced them the-

21

oretically that with molecular training we can put the wisdom of an older man into the resilient body of a young man on a stimulus-response basis. But theory and demonstration are two separate items. Therefore the demonstration must take place. Once they are convinced, we will be able to do this work on a mass production basis.

"You have no choice, as our top pupil, but to be the demonstration agent—and you will not fail us." Over the precisely composed face a slight smile was allowed to appear and the voice that continued was more kindly now. "We have made an investment in you of well over a magacredit. That is an obligation that you cannot disregard."

Stan was startled. "A *megacredit*, sir?"

"That is correct. Later, mass production will bring the costs to a reasonable figure, but experimental work comes high."

"I . . ." Stan paused. Then: "You keep saying 'molecular training.' May I ask, sir, just what sort of training I have had? I thought . . ."

"You thought! You were not supposed to think!" The professor's voice was almost a snarl, but immediately he brought it back under control and allowed the slight smile to recompose itself over his severe features, in spite of the annoyance that threatened his composure.

"The training you have had did not *require* thinking; and the insistence you have placed on independent study has gone far toward nullifying the results we had every right to expect. However, it has also enhanced the results, and the nullification can be itself nullified. But you must not forget—you must not be *allowed* to forget—that it is the molecular training that has given you the education and the abilities of which you find yourself possessed."

"Am I allowed to know," the boy before him was choosing his words carefully, "just what this molecular training is—of what it has consisted?"

"You will be questioned on the subject, and you must know enough to answer those questions intelligently. Yes." Mallard leaned back in his chair and his voice took on a lecture-platform quality.

"You have been trained by molecular memory transplantation. The inoculations you were given were of memory molecules, produced originally by minds thoroughly schooled in each of the disciplines to which you have been subjected." He leaned forward again, and again tented his hands on the desk before him. This explanation was a familiar one. He had used it effectively on the military, on prospective donors. It came easily to his tongue.

"These memory molecules are extracted from trained and dedicated persons in each discipline. They are then duplicated in the laboratory and returned to the original donor; any of the duplicates may be substituted with equal success. The donor loses nothing but a few blank days during which a majority of his memory molecules are sorted and duplicated and then reinstalled. And even should the reinstalling, by some misfortune, not be complete, the infinite filing system of the body's biochemical processes can reduplicate and replace throughout the donor's system from the molecules that have not been extracted in only a matter of weeks."

Stan listened in growing amazement to the statements, recalling the memories of the tests, the search for answers that seemed to be right there but not quite within reach, and their sudden appearance. He thought he was drawing facts and abilities from his "subconscious," but . . .

"But, sir. I understood that memory was an electronic, not a molecular function. That it was a function of the brain itself . . . ?"

"Ah, yes. The electronic brain function as against the biochemical body function of memory storage." The professor was pleased with himself now. Stan might not be the student he would have most wished to see succeed, but the work of the years would be demonstrated, and his efforts culminate in the recognition that he—yes, *he* deserved. There was pleasure in his voice as he went on:

"The research is new. As far as we can tell, the old educational system of study, which required information to be filtered through the five senses into the electronic brain system, gave the student conscious control of the knowledge and abilities he acquired. Whereas our molecular training implants, introduced directly into the biochemical information-filing system of the body, produce a stimulus-response basis on which the knowledge is available. And," he added, the pleasure in his voice becoming more pronounced, "it is the stimulus-response reaction to information-need for which we are training."

The professor paused, nodding his head slowly. "You

can see that the normal response of an older person to any situation calling for his knowledge and abilities would be quite different from that of a young man. What we need is youngsters, primed with knowledge and trained abilities, who will use those knowledges and abilities the way an old man would use them: with caution, with due regard for accepted methods of operation, with due respect for his superiors.

"With this molecular training system, we will be able to fill the action posts of government and the military with young men who will dependably react to almost any situation not only with the most extensive knowledge and abilities that experts have achieved, but in the manner that would be dictated by those same elderly, disciplined minds!"

"In other words," Stan said slowly, "what you are doing here is creating educated robots?"

Mallard found himself jerked back to the realities of the moment, and he stared at the boy. "That's a harsh term," he said finally. "But, yes, in its way. What we are doing is putting the education and discipline of mature minds into young bodies. You may find this emotionally upsetting at first thought," he added kindly, "but consider. You have an education and abilities that could have been given you in no other way. You have a spread of knowledge that no one person could have attained in one lifetime; and you have acquired this while you are still young. If the knowledge and abilities are not exactly under your control, why—in the military no one is under his own control anyway, so what loss?"

Stan found his emotions chaotic, fear predominant; but was not convinced. If he was, in fact, a robot, why must it be for the military?

Then anger surged. Their puppet, was he? But he'd studied—for himself and by himself—and that was not puppetry. There had to be a way to find out whether, essentially, he was indeed what they supposed him to be. But it would take time.

"I . . . I'll need some time to think this whole thing over," he said weakly.

"Of course you will, my boy." The professor nodded to himself. "You have had a strenuous course, and will need a bit of relaxation. So you are being given a two weeks' leave to return home and enjoy yourself. Then you will report back here for a short pre-induction training, and will be taken to Greateryork for your first assignment. You've not been drawing against your student's credit balance, so you have in excess of two thousand credits to spend any way you wish before you report to your new post. Enjoy yourself. You will be quite busy for a while after you return, so enjoy your leave."

Accepting the professor's smile and nod as a dismissal, Stan left the room. *Pep talk's over and I'm to swallow the fact that Authority has made me a guinea pig without my knowledge*, he thought, *and I imagine without my father's knowledge either. I'm supposed to swallow it with pleasure and feel obligated to go right on being a demonstration guinea pig for the rest of my life.*

The bitterness of the thought surged through him. *But,* he asked himself honestly, *would I change the situation if I could? Would I forfeit having had the course?* And he knew he wouldn't.

The resentment was there; but the knowledge was there too; knowledge in fields that had each taken a man his entire lifetime to acquire. *The knowledge is there,* he told himself, *and I got most of it from Professorburgers.* But he found himself fiercely glad that he'd studied as hard as possible; that there was knowledge there, too, which he had gotten by himself, for himself.

His thinking was still caught between resentment and pride by the time he was aboard the tubecar that would whisk him through the vacuum tunnel system. Having inserted his credit card and dialed his destination, Stan would be delivered direct, in this same tubecar, to the tubeport beneath the sky-rise that was his home in Elko, Nevada, more than two thousand miles away, in under two hours.

Home. He'd thought of it through his childhood as open and free, with its sky-rise buildings separated by several acres of trees and playgrounds and fresh air; with the vistas of distant mountains giving the feeling that there was some real space in the world, even when you knew the mountains themselves were thoroughly inhabited.

A nostalgia for the open wastes of snow and ice topsides at the school shook him, and he drew his cloak of privacy more tightly around him, though he was alone in a two-seater. He'd always had privacy. It was the factor given top priority in a crowded civilization. But space—that was another factor, and a different thing entirely; and he'd found himself drinking it in in his daily trips up and out into the intense cold and intense aloneness topsides at the school.

Suddenly he knew he was not going home; not just yet. Five percent of the credits given him as student aid were spent; but the other credits were untouched yet, and they'd take him where he wanted to go, keep him for at least a few days—a few days in which he could watch the tugs that took off for space.

He looked at the map of the tube-network on the screen of the car before him, saw by the tiny light that marked his position that he was already in the main Alcan-Europe Tubeway that carried most of the traffic across the Pole; and nearing Anchorage.

He leaned toward the small keyboard beneath the map and pushed the button marked CHANGE OF DESTINATION. Then he inserted his credit card into the slot beside the keyboard.

With a click the keys of the board loosened so that they could be used, and he punched out carefully: *White Sands.* Then, glancing at the map, he added the coordinates given there.

The action put the invariable record into the computer for anyone who cared to ask through Information Retrieval.

But who would care to ask? He was a student, with two weeks and a fist full of credits to spend as he pleased.

III

STAN ARRIVED at Termdock, White Sands, and made his way to a visitor's gallery from which he could watch the vast tarmac on which the space tugs landed and took off.

For an hour he watched in fascination as the stubby-winged aerodynamic needles, skirted like old women for their ground-effect takeoff, ran through their twenty-five mile ground run. The real activity of the port was invisible to him here, restricted to the mile after mile of underground warren that subsurfaced the field itself. There would be mountains of freight being fed up to the waiting tugs through moving belt loaders. There would be the few passengers and the many workers. There would be rebuilding and repair, bargaining and sweating: the varieties of activity that backgrounded trade between Earth and the system.

Above, Stan had seen two takeoffs and three landings while he watched; and it had left him unsatisfied.

Why had he come here, anyhow? he asked himself. To think. To think—and to be near the ships that were reaching out; to be near the fact of space.

But he felt shuttered from it; felt as barriered as . . . as a robot, he told himself.

Abruptly he straightened away from the rail. He had plenty of credits to his card, didn't he? And seven hundred of those credits would get him freighter-tug passage, round-trip, to Orbdock. At least there he'd be in space itself, or nearly. At least there he'd see the real freighters, the ships that went into the system, not just their servicing tugs.

Stan entered the freight tug with his hood up so that the excitement boiled in him would be disguised, but all the pilot saw was another privacy-mad stupe of a suburban Earthie. He gestured to the acceleration couch beside his own.

"And keep that damned cloak out of my way," he said, not bothering to hide his casual contempt.

The boy's flush was not completely hidden by the hood that shrouded his head, but he only asked timidly, "Don't planeteers wear cloaks?"

The question didn't merit an answer, the pilot decided, and only replied, "Hmmmph," then busied himself over the controls.

Stan restrained an impulse to throw back his hood, contenting himself instead with studying the pilot.

He was perhaps thirty-five, with a mobile face over a wrinkled uniform; his every gesture was alert and intent on what he was doing. The gestures were quick and sure; the hands . . .

Stan's eyes followed the hands to the controls they were

manipulating, and a feeling of familiarity tugged at his senses. Alert now himself, he leaned forward. That would be the skirt control; there the dials indicating atmospheric density; that the rate-of-approach indicator; there . . . His hood fell back and his cloak loosened without his noticing the fact.

"Belt in. We're taking off." The pilot didn't even look at his passenger as he strapped himself into the padded chair.

The surge of acceleration was less than that of a tube-car, but it thrilled along Stan's every nerve, and he watched the great tarmac move past, then fly past, and finally flash past as the tug reached mach speeds; felt the surge as the needle-ship went through the sonic barrier as though bursting a brick wall with a karate blow, and flew beyond it, free. He saw the pilot's sure hands flash first to the vanes which angled them suddenly upward, and then to the skirt controls which withdrew those ground-effect wrappings into the belly of the craft.

Earth fell away, and Stan, who had seen it fall away in this manner a hundred times in 3-D dramas, exulted in the difference of the fact from the fantasy; saw, eventually, Earth like a ball to his vision and himself the still center of the blackness of space. They were an ecstasy of factors, those differences. *A robot, am I?* he thought. *I'll get my own experiences!* But it was a small thought, far at the back of his mind as his senses drank in the facts of flight.

Orbdock is mile after mile of interlocked gridwork of air-stiffened tubing, floating in space. The zero-G plastiplex is centered by a two-thousand-foot plastic doughnut that spins slowly to give gravity to the offices and restaurants and trading halls, the repair shops and maintenance and living facilities that are the nucleus of the dock.

Freight and passengers arrive here from Earth via space tugs which dock at one side of the complex. They tether there to the longest tubes of the grid, tubes which string out from the grid itself like loose spaghetti.

The freight is transferred through the tubes by fan-powered pneumocars directly to the interplanetary ships that berth on the far side of the complex. Spherical, with ion-drive tubes through their centers, the ships look like huge balloons with sticks through them; or like some form of alien insect which hangs, as though disdaining the complex itself, at the very tips of the tubes through which it is fed its tonnage of food, air, water, freight and people.

The passengers are transshipped through the tubes by pneumocar, too, but usually go first to the spincenter doughnut.

Stan stepped out of the pneumocar into a shrub- and flower-bordered area that held a restaurant on one side, an information booth on the other. He made his way into the restaurant and chose a small table near the wall, his eye caught by its clear plastic and the aquarium beyond. He knew the water was for shielding from the strong radiation of the sun out here beyond the atmosphere; that it also served as a major part of the air and waste recycling system, and that the fish were part of that system too. He knew that the water was flowing past in six-foot-deep rivers, its motion creating the spin of the doughnut he was in, that gave him gravity. But the serenity of the fish, of the plants stirring in the river's motion, belied the fact.

There could be no viewports as such within this shielding, but huge screens showing the complex beyond gave the illusion of windows; though the scenes were all still, the arrival and departure of tugs or ships was almost the only visible activity, and those might or might not occur while he watched.

He turned his attention to the people around him. They seemed to be mostly ships' personnel or dock workers, in uniforms of various styles and kinds—some neat, others looking used and rumpled. He felt conspicuous. There were cloaks to be seen, but very few, and those obviously tourists. Earth tourists, Stan thought, surprised at the distaste that went with the thought; and realizing with revulsion that the category included himself and that his cloak was the mark that categorized him.

He sat for hour after hour and let his senses simply absorb the scene: the light gravity, the complex, the space beyond and between its network; the smell of recycled air, the movement, the talk around him, the soft music—the feel of an orbital station. He felt drugged with the new sensations, drugged and content to sit, unthinking.

And then, as though a switch had closed, his mind turned on; his emotions, held in leash since he had left the school, would no longer be denied.

Over a megacredit the school has spent on me, and I am obligated for that, he found himself telling himself. *Or am I? I didn't bargain for the investment, though I'm glad I've got it—extra knowledge, be it robot or my own.*

But shall I be a guinea pig for the rest of my life? Let them manufacture me into a complete robot? A megacredit. Is that what a lifetime is worth?

And while he talked to himself, he felt the tug of the ships he had watched all afternoon. *Man will never reach the stars,* he thought. *That's been shown by the equations. But . . .*

But oh, the free, untrammeled spaces between the planets! Yet, was the Belt a free man's area? He didn't know; he had no way of knowing. The Belt had won its independence in a daring and individualized fight; his uncle had fought to win that independence and died for it. Yet had the freedom he had won survived the hazards of necessity the Belt itself imposed? Survived the fact that to stay alive a man must be enclosed in atmospheres built and designed for man? And was that so very different from being enclosed in a privacy cloak, the only protection against an environment too crowded to be meant for man?

The 3-D told of slaves in the Belt, working and sweating because there was no "outside," no "topsides," to which they could escape. The 3-D told of hardship and privation. But Uncle Trevor—Trail Duster Trevor—he'd been a proud man and a strong one, with a strong laugh. . . .

Stan remembered the only time he'd seen his uncle after he was old enough to remember the details. He'd been tall and strong, swinging the youngster into the air and then onto his shoulders, as though physical contact were not something to be avoided. Stan had been scared at the time, but he'd responded after a minute to the hard hands that lifted him; to the feel of flying through the air; to the height of his uncle's shoulders; to the exhilaration of roughness and . . . yes, to the physical contact itself.

You don't make slaves of that sort, he told himself now.

He remembered the taste of fear as his uncle bent down, and the rough hands took him up in the delicious freedom of flying. *Freedom and fear,* he thought now; *would freedom always carry the connotations of fear?* He supposed it would, for freedom was bought by a man at a price, and only a stupid man refused to recognize the price as he demanded the commodity.

"Get yourself an education, boy," the big man had told him, roughing the red hair so like his own. "But don't let 'em make you a sissy while they're giving you an education. Do your own thinking while you get the information you need, boy. Then come on out to the Belt. I'll have a berth for you; but you're going to have to get yourself there, you know." Then he'd added, half under his breath, "And you not even old enough yet to properly remember."

The small boy had remembered; and the twenty-four-year-old remembered now with a nostalgia that was overwhelming.

Guinea piggery; and for the military at that. . . .

With a rejection that was almost bigger than he could contain, Stan flung himself to his feet.

At the gesture a man at a nearby table looked up.

"Where's the hiring hall? Here or on Earth?" Stan asked him abruptly.

The man, hard-faced, hard-muscled, in rumpled coveralls, looked Stan up and down—the soft student's hands; the quiet student's face; the crisply cut hair; the cloak. . . .

"It's up here. Level five, quadrant three," he said disdainfully. "But a fat lot of good it will do the likes of you."

Stan nodded his thanks curtly. "You might be surprised, sir," he said, and was himself surprised at the title he'd given the surly spacer, though he felt justified in giving it.

The hiring hall turned out to be in a much lighter G area, a barn of a room filled with figures of every description: uniformed and coveralled; neat and slovenly; none cloaked. All had what Stan had come to think of as the spaceman's look, a hard, almost blank expression. An inner absorption, or just blankness?

High on the walls, constantly shifting lights listed the names of ships in dock, their destinations and their needs in the way of personnel. Occasionally a loudspeaker called a name and an office number, and a figure would rise and make its way to one of the cubicles.

"Where do you sign up?" Stan asked the nearest figure, a small man with a wizened face and sharp eyes that surveyed him again disdainfully.

"Application boxes there," the man told him after the survey, nodding toward a series of booths against the wall behind him that closely resembled the test cubicle in which he'd spent so many hours at school.

Inside it was nearly the same—a seat, a desk, a scanner; except that the seat was of air-support plastic; the desk a harder plastic; and instead of a keyboard into which you punched your answers, there was a glass plate on which you wrote, on which you pressed your fingers for printing; a scanner for retinals.

Name and number. Fingerprints. Retinals. Main area of training. Stan thought a minute, then entered: *Engineering*. Preferred destination. Without hesitation Stan wrote: *Belt City*. That was all.

There was a pause, then the screen cleared and a metallic voice came to him through a tiny speaker: "Take a seat in the hiring hall. You will be called."

He found a seat near the application booths and waited. From this part of the spincenter there were no viewscreens. He watched the crowd. He slept. He woke and watched the crowd again. He grew hungry, but he ignored the hunger.

He was asleep again when his own name, coming from the loudspeaker, woke him. "S.T.A.R. Dustin," the voice was chanting. "Report to office seventeen."

The office he entered was tiny and bare except for a desk and two plastic puff chairs. Behind the desk sat a heavy man, erect even in the sagging softness of the pneumochair. His face held a hauteur that spoke of authority. He was cloaked, but the hood was back. Stan was relieved. At least his own cloak—he had thought of discarding it but had lacked the courage—wouldn't be held against him.

"I'm Stan Dustin," he introduced himself.

The man looked him over carefully. "I gather you want to work your way to the Belt?"

Stan nodded and remained silent, standing.

"Sit down, sit down." The man gestured to the chair by the desk. "I'd have recognized you even if your identity hadn't been checked quite thoroughly," he said. "You resemble your late uncle Trevor Dustin quite remarkably." Stan started but remained silent. "I gather your decision to go to the Belt is irrevocable? Have you notified your parent?"

"I haven't notified anyone," Stan said, his heart sinking.

"I rather thought I'd let my father know after I was gone. I hope it won't be necessary to your hiring—"

"Probably wise from your point of view," the man interrupted. "I assume that any sane family would discourage you."

"I hope that it's not to discourage you, sir, from—"

The man looked at him quizzically. "It is not my business to be encouraged or discouraged," he said. "I have the quite dubious honor of representing your late uncle. Did you think I was a hiring hand?"

Stan nodded, crestfallen.

The lawyer shook his head in annoyance. "A lack of perception that will not get you far," he said cruelly. "However, that is not my purview. Young man, your uncle left instructions that if you decided, quite on your own, to go to the Belt, and initiated action in that direction, I was to see to it that you got there. So I've taken passage for you on a Mars freighter that raises within the hour. Naturally, you can't go to the Belt directly, relations being what they are, but Mars is a free port. At Mars you will transfer to a Belt freighter. I have the passages here."

Stan found that he was both pleased and disappointed. Why disappointed? he asked himself. Was he trying to prove something?

The lawyer looked at him distastefully, as though he could read the other's thoughts. "Perhaps you could sign on as a member of a ship's crew. Probably not. But most certainly the technicalities of signing on would alert your family and any others that might be interested in delaying or preventing you. Which is why," he went on dryly, "I have seen fit to drop everything, charter a space taxi, and get here, preferably before you left Orbdock, for the privilege of seeing you off at the earliest possible moment and before you involved yourself in some mess from which I must extract you. However I may feel personally, I am professionally charged with getting you to your destination, and I should prefer that the charge did not involve us together in legal technicalities that might associate our names for years."

Stan said stiffly, "I did not mean to seem ungrateful, sir. I—"

"But you wanted to run away on your own? Well, it's a fine fat attitude with little that is practical to recommend it. However," he went on before Stan could interrupt, "I am quite sure that I am not doing you a favor in assisting you in getting to the Belt.

"You will have to leave your Earth credit balance as it stands. If you draw it down to zero, or even draw heavily on it while at Orbdock, the computers will automatically be alerted and start an investigation, which will delay you. When you get to the Belt you will find that Belters are an intolerant breed, not given to lightly accepting gifts, such as yourself, from Mother Earth. Neither is Earth apt to accept you back lightly, should you fail in the Belt. You will be very much on your own. Do you still wish to go?"

"I'll take my chances," said Stan defiantly.

The lawyer harrumped. "Well, traitor's blood is traitor's blood, and you are like your uncle in looks as well as actions."

Stan flushed and started to speak angrily, but the lawyer gestured him silent. "This business is as unpleasant for me as for you. Let us get it over and done with. There is also a bequest here for a thousand shares in a small Belt enterprise which your uncle founded. Whether it still exists, I do not know, but I do not think you should build any hopes on it. Your uncle's death left the corporation in the hands of two partners who may or may not be surviving themselves; and it is an enterprise which may or may not have survived. The shares are yours, for what they may be worth. The corporation is called Astro Technology."

Having finished his business, the lawyer abruptly hooded himself and left the room without a farewell.

Stan stood gazing at the passage vouchers and the shares of stock lying on the small desk. Then he pulled his travel-case from the greatpocket of his cloak and stuffed the papers inside, zippering it carfully.

It was as he started to put the case back into the greatpocket that the realization came.

The Belt, he thought. *I'm going to be a Belter now.*

A grin came over his face; his chin lifted; and with a huge shrug he dropped the cloak from his shoulders, letting it fall to the floor; stepping over it as he walked out of the office.

IV

STAN REACHED Orbdock, Mars, still preoccupied with his own chaotic emotions and the changing vectors of a lifetime of habitual thinking and reaction. The change had been accelerated and made easier by the fact of being in space, and by the new sensations and information that his senses were absorbing; but his real attention had been on finding out just what his own basic precepts were, or could be; and the experience and the information flowed by, almost unnoticed to his preoccupations.

Spincenter at the Mars Orbdock was small compared to Earth's, the doughnut a mere two hundred feet in diameter, the gravity at the rim only .15 G; but Stan, who'd been in a tenth G acceleration all the way, was used to it by now and stepped confidently from the pneumocar when they reached the rim.

It was more barren here than on Earth, although the walls were clear plastic and showed the same aquarium beyond.

Beyond the usual restaurant he could see what must be the information center sloping sharply up from him, a big board on its wall with changing names and numbers on it. He turned in that direction to see a man coming toward him in red skintights with matching red kid slippers; his waist was belted in gold worked in the pattern of a snake.

The outfit fascinated Stan, and he found his eyes returning again to the figure as he made his way toward the big board in the distance. To his surprise, the man was approaching him.

"You Dustin?"

He was larger than Stan, blond, and apparently of about the same age. Perhaps a little older. Heavy in the shoulders, slender of waist, and lithe in his movements as he approached. His face looked puzzled.

35

"Yes, but how did you know?"

"Well, your ship's in, and I've been waiting for you. You're not Mars-clad, but you're not Earth-clad either. It was a guess. I understand you were from Earth?"

Stan felt minutely proud of his gold-tinged gray tunic and trousers, which were more in the nature of the red-suited man's clothing than either Earth or Mars style.

"I'm Dustin," he reaffirmed. "Stan Dustin."

"I'm Paulsen. Skipper of the *Sassy Lassie*. I reckon you're my passenger for Belt City. I've been waiting for you, ready to scat, for the past three hours. You ready? That all your duffel?" He nodded at the travelcase Stan was carrying.

"That's all of it," Stan answered.

"If you have a yen to look over Marsport, you'll have to catch the next freighter. The *Marjorie* is due in a couple of days. You want to wait for her and see the sights?"

Stan grinned. There was an air of defiance in Paulsen's attitude. Or perhaps intolerance? Whatever it was, he was obviously prepared to shake Stan at the slightest excuse.

"I'm ready," he said quietly.

"Okay. I'm tied up at Tube 109."

Paulsen turned and strode swiftly to the pneumocar that Stan had just left. Stan entered in time to see him punch out a destination on the controls, and the car started accelerating up through the doughnut, through its spoke to the hub, then angling off on an increasing acceleration toward the tip of the tube where Paulsen's ship would be anchored, some six miles away. Deceleration caught him unexpectedly, and he found himself swaying forward in his seat.

The pneumocar stopped, and Stan was floating in null G. Grasping the seat ahead of him he pulled himself behind Paulsen to the opening of the car which was locked onto the *Sassy Lassie*'s air lock.

He saw Paulsen pause a second, then push himself through the opening, and as the skipper moved from before him, he could see two extra figures in the air lock, each hand-held into place from one of the straps on the cylindrical walls. Stan pushed himself in, carrying his travelcase, to join them.

The situation seemed eerie and unreal to senses schooled to gravity; but the two grim-faced men in the lock with them were very real indeed.

"This Dustin?" one of the two asked Paulsen.

"Yep."

"You just lost a passenger. He's wanted on Earth."

Finding a handhold, Stan held himself immobile, watching Paulsen, who glanced at him briefly, glanced at his belt, then turned back to the other two.

"Charges serious?" Paulsen asked.

"How should I know? Some school on Earth sent orders."

"School? Dustin, what's the problem?"

Stan found himself answering in normal, unhurried tones: "I guess the school I left doesn't like the idea that I prefer the Belt," he said quietly.

"Still want to go?"

"Yes."

Paulsen turned his head again to the other two and his voice was grim. "You interfering with a Belter in the normal pursuit of his business?" he asked.

"Dustin's no Belter."

"He's my passenger."

Stan grinned to himself. Then, releasing his travelcase, which continued to float inconspicuously at his side, he said pleasantly, "I sure wouldn't want to cause you unnecessary trouble, Skipper. Come on, boys." And with that he pushed back through the entrance to the pneumocar.

Just inside, he held himself out of the way so that the two following him could reach the control panel. Then, turning his head, he noticed the travelcase still floating in the air lock.

"Oh. My duffel," he said happily, and pushed himself into the air lock again, angling his motion toward a large red handle marked EMERGENCY PRESSURE RELEASE.

His fingers grasped the handle before anyone could react, and he used it as a lever to set his feet against the side of the lock and pull against his own leverage.

Abruptly the air spilled from the lock, and with a *thwummp*, the tube bulkhead closed. Stan, timing the lowering of pressure by a feeling of internal expansion, had just released the handle when Paulsen reached him.

"Get your hands off that dump switch. You'll have us in vacuum," he said with a snarl.

Stan pushed away to the bulkhead handle, tested it. It refused to budge.

"But they're on the other side and the pressure's triple out there."

Paulsen looked at him in complete disbelief, then a smile crept over his face. "Well, there's not enough pressure in here for comfort very long," he said, and began cycling them through into the ship proper.

The trip to Mars hadn't prepared Stan for the control cabin of the *Sassy Lassie*. It was clean, but it had a used and battered look. It had been repaired and re-repaired, and it very definitely had the feel of being lived in. There were two decks for living quarters beneath this cabin before you got to the ion-drive tube, Stan realized; but it was normally a one-man ship and the skipper probably spent most of his time up here.

The freight doughnut around the ship below was useless to them except in spacesuits. It was vacuum and unshielded; so that this thirty-five foot tall, approximately twenty foot wide extension of the rocket tube was the "ship" as far as people were concerned; and of that space, the hull shielding left only a cylinder twenty-three feet tall and with an eight foot radius for living quarters.

Stan pulled himself over to the acceleration chair beside the pilot's without waiting to be told, and strapped himself in. Paulsen was already busy releasing the ship from the docking tube so that it would drift off, "Before we get boarders," he said lightly.

"Thanks for the backing, Skipper," Stan said carefully in reply.

Paulsen answered, "Your air dump used up a lot of air. Since we don't want to stop for it here, I'm traveling at low pressure, just to be on the safe side of our emergency supplies."

There was silence then as Paulsen warmed the motors, nursed small pulsed thrusts to give them distance, and finally cut in power to the drive to give them the normal one-tenth G acceleration. Then he pulled the log toward him and began to write.

Stan let his eyes wander around the control cabin, and a sense of familiarity tugged at him. His interest was so intense, though, that it triggered the study habits he'd lived by for so many years, rather than the quiz habits; and the more he concentrated the more the familiarity faded, to be replaced by a need to learn, to discover each dial individually, each effect of the ship's motion as a separate effect.

With a start he recognized the symptoms and forced himself to relax, to let his eyes wander over the dials without any conscious attempt to interpret them, to let his senses absorb the small cabin and its smells and feels and informations.

This was a Kinco Sixty freighter, better known as a K-class, its capacity about half that of the big Earth-Mars freighters. It wasn't a question. It was a fact that he knew.

The circular wall of the tiny control cabin was a checkerboard of insulation squares, except that most of them were covered by instruments. These ships didn't spin to give their crews gravity; thrust was the only gravity they offered. So the river system of hull-shielding which gave Earth ships their spin-gravity could be replaced by compartmentalized shielding in hull sections. The squares would give individual access to the many sections of shielding behind.

The air lock was directly behind Stan and Paulsen as they sat in the acceleration chair-couches that could be lowered nearly to the horizontal for high-G thrust. Between the couches and the air lock was the tiny well that gave access to the decks below; and in a small opening built into the wall above the air lock bulkhead was the emergency medical kit.

The instruments before them were plainly visible from both seats, and the controls were double so that either he or Paulsen could maneuver the ship. Their tenth-G acceleration would continue for half the trip, and would build them to tremendous velocities on an exponential curve; then they'd start decelerating for the second half of the trip, to come into relative motion with the asteroid that was known as Belt City.

Paulsen could, of course, accelerate the doughnut into a Hohmann orbit, then drop it and take them at higher accelerations and decelerations to their destination; but since he was shepherding this load and would probably pick it up himself, the chances were he wouldn't bother. But he could. And that brought up the possibility—the probability—that the *Sassy Lassie* had been one of the ships of the Belt Uprising. Had Paulsen . . .

Excitedly Stan turned to the skipper, but his thoughts

were cut off by a thunderclap which hammered his body. Instantly the explosion was followed by a high-pitched whining scream that echoed on each nerve, and the internal feeling of bursting that meant rapidly falling atmospheric pressure. Instinctively he opened his mouth and yelled, expelling the pressure from his lungs.

Paulsen's lips were moving, his fingers reaching out to a control—the control that would cut the motors, Stan realized, even as he released the straps and pushed his own body out of the deep seat beneath it, twisting with the push to bring his hands into line with the small opening in the wall above and behind their seats. His fingers found the opening and began groping, since his eyes refused to focus. The scream was fading, then cut off abruptly just as his fingers found the syrettes they were seeking, grasped two, and reached one toward Paulsen.

The skipper was almost beside him, a hazy figure, and Stan groped for his hand, forcing one of the syrettes into it.

Now Stan brought the remaining syrette to his leg with a slap that forced the needle in and injected its contents into his system. Pulling the syrette carefully out, he pinned it to his tunic, his eyes now barely making out the most gross objects in the cabin swinging lazily about him as he spun slowly in free fall.

The dioxo solution from the syrette spread a warm glow through him. Stan opened his mouth wide and expelled the last of the air that was doing its best to strain out of his lungs. The pressure in his ears let go with a loud pop. The cloudy look of things before him and the burning sensation in his eyes caused him to squeeze his eyes tight shut, and as he did so, pain shot through them, tiny crystals of ice grating across the tender surfaces; and as this was followed by a sensation of cold, he realized that the boiling tears would freeze in the vacuum around him and freeze the lids shut.

Something grasped him, and he struggled momentarily, then realized it was Paulsen and slacked off. There was a feeling as though someone was trying to stuff him into a bag, but no sound.

Then he felt drawstrings pull tight at the shoulders and across his chest, and suddenly there was pressure around his face again. The bag was then slid quickly down over

Stan's arms and tied at each joint; then down over the torso with a repeated lacing. Blinded by the tears, he opened his eyes nevertheless to see clear plastic standing only inches ahead; and, as he began to breathe again, Paulsen's voice came to him over a tiny speaker somewhere in the hood.

"That's right, Dustin. Work your jaws and the swallowing mechanisms. Keep blinking your eyes."

As Stan became more aware of his surroundings, he saw that he was in a loosely fitting plastic bag, tightly belted at each joint.

The tingly sensation in his throat came to his attention, and he realized that the "air" he was breathing was not air but carbon dioxide quickly developed from a small plastic pack of acid and soda. It was a device that could not have been used except for the diox which would supply his oxygen requirements for the next hour.

The pressures removed, Stan found a handhold and turned himself toward the control panel.

Paulsen was in his seat now, checking the space around the ship for enemy craft—and the guy *wasn't in a spacesuit.* Unbelieving, Stan stared. Paulsen had on a hood, but just that, over his regular red pilot's suit. But of course. That pilot's suit *was* a gas-proof spacesuit; and the hood that had obviously been unzipped from a pocket at the back of the pilot's suit collar had a similar pressure gas generator packet.

Stan sighed his relief, then let his attention wander to the deep hole in the checkerboard wall centered above the control panel.

The hole was a full two-foot square that had blown through to the outside hull and was now crushed there, a mess of metal and foam plastic insulation, at the bottom of what seemed to be a square tunnel into the hull structure. The water shielding from the compartment had obviously been blown on through into space, followed by the air from the control cabin; but the hole through which they had blown could not be seen past the mess of metal and plastic.

Paulsen was through with his check now, and his face looked puzzled, but he only said, "I'm going to put us under drive to get gravity, then we'll see what the damage is."

The return of even the light tenth-G gravity was grate-

ful to Stan's senses, and the cabin reoriented quickly a-
round him.

"If we can work fast," Paulsen's voice came to him abruptly over the tiny intercom, "we can save having to pres-
surize the bunk area to get you into a tightsuit. I've got
plug-in compartments aboard, of course, so it shouldn't
take more than half an hour to clear up this mess. Do you
think you can take the bag for that long?"

Experimentally, Stan flexed his arm and found that it
responded stiffly. The veins that had been standing out like
cords against the taut skin were beginning to recede. The
rapid breath induced by the one hundred percent carbon
dioxide atmosphere was exchanging nitrogen out of the
blood at a rapid rate, and pressure was equalizing between
himself and the suit.

"Seems okay," he said. "A little stiff and a few cramps,
but yeah, I can work like my life depended on it."

Paulsen chuckled, then without another word crawled
into the tight tunnel.

It was several minutes, while his squirming legs were
the only indication of motion within, before his voice
reached Stan again.

"I think I've got it more or less in one piece. Pull me out,
but slow and easy."

Stan took hold of the ankles, braced himself against the
pilot's seat, and started the slow tug, following instructions as he pulled, unable to tell what was going on.

"Harder. Oops. Hold it. All right, pull. Damn it, lost it.
Push me back an inch. Not more than an inch."

It only took about ten minutes, but they seemed long.
Finally, shoulders past the edge now, Paulsen pulled his
head out. "You can hook on and get it the rest of the way,"
he said. "My muscles are cramping."

Stan reached his arms, head and shoulders in, and felt
around until he got the positioning of the package of
crushed metal and foam plastic, found jagged handholds,
and began to inch the mess out. Then, with a jerk, the
wreckage let go its final hold and dropped him, jagged
package in his lap, into the pilot's seat. He sat there a
minute, panting, then looked around.

He was alone in the cabin.

For a minute he stared in panic around the small room,
then the skipper's voice came to him: "You all right?"

"The wreckage fell and sat me down in the pilot's chair," Stan said.

"Don't touch anything," was the only answer.

Stan was suddenly amused. *"Don't touch anything," the man says. I whop back into the pilot's seat, carrying a package that spills onto anything and everything around, that would have knocked anything fragile in spite of me, and he says don't touch anything.*

Before he could do much cautious maneuvering there was a thump as something was levered up from the cabin below; and the skipper's voice said, "Wait." A minute later Paulsen was at his side, carefully lifting the wreckage from his lap.

"Stay right there. I'll be back," he said, taking the wreckage into the freightnut access lock.

Stan relaxed, content to be the inept passenger for whom the skipper must care. Twisting his head he could see the plug-in unit Paulsen had brought—a ten-foot plastic bag filled with water and what looked like white noodles.

He turned back to the square tunnel before him. By craning his neck he could see down the six-foot tunnel to the hull at its far end, and he easily located the hole by which the water and air had escaped—a circular hole, about two inches across and bulging smoothly outward.

Paulsen had patching material in his hand when he returned and, Stan estimated, they had about ten minutes left to do a patching job. Without pausing, Paulsen wriggled into the tunnel and was busy for several minutes. When he had wriggled back out, he reached for the plug-in unit, and with Stan's help fitted it slowly into its niche. When the tip of the ten-foot bag reached the hull, they applied pressure, squashing it slowly to fit its compartment. Then, while Stan held the square of inner hull and cabin insulation in place against the water pressure, Paulsen snapped its bolts into place, and the section was sound again.

They still had time to spare as the skipper fed air back into the control cabin, though Stan could feel the slightest touches of cramp in his muscles.

"Even lighter pressure this time. We sure been getting rid of the air this trip," Paulsen said over his suit speaker before shucking the hood.

"That hole didn't look like an accidental rock coming in to me, Skipper," Stan said cautiously, removing his own emergency suit. "It looked more like an internal explosion."

The other looked at him queerly. "Yep. It sure wasn't any accident."

"But it was so easy to fix up! No real sweat. Why in hell would anyone bother?"

"That's what I was going to ask you," Paulsen told him tartly. "And since we're sharing this one together, maybe you'd better let me know at least how serious it's likely to get."

"But this is *your* ship. Somebody must have been after *you*."

"I thought of that. I thought maybe the Earthies had started sabotaging Belt ships at Mars. But anybody who set out for a systematic system of sabotage would have taken time to find out how Belt ships are built. It wouldn't have been a hasty, ineffective job like this one. Then I thought maybe you were an Earthie spy, and somebody in the Belt was after you. But in that case, I'd have been in on it. So either of those is possibly the reason, but not probably."

Stan stayed silent, and finally Paulsen went on, "On the face of it, I had a chance. Not much of one, but a chance. But you didn't.

"You're an Earthie. You're an Earthie passenger. You wouldn't have been expected to know about diox. Even if you knew about it, you wouldn't know where it would be found. Even if I'd been the one to get it and hand the syrette to you, you wouldn't know what to do with it without waiting for instructions, and that would have been too late.

"You're supposed to be dead, Earthie. Which tells me somebody wants you dead real bad. Which also tells me that I'm a sitting duck as long as I'm with you, and maybe you'd better give with a little info."

As Stan stayed silent, the other shrugged, then started to pull the log toward him. His hand hesitated on the book itself, and slowly withdrew. Then he leaned back, clasping his hands behind his head.

"Look," he said conversationally, "I'm not a prier. And I'm not asking many questions. And who you are and what you are is not, essentially, my business. But when a High-G

Earthie—that means rich—is on my ship—and I risk the *Sassy Lassie* without knowing I was going to—by taking you aboard; and you hadn't warned me one word—and when you ignored my question . . . I'm not a prier," he added defiantly, "but by God—"

"You don't have to pry. I'll answer any questions you want to ask. I'm as puzzled as you are," Stan admitted. Then he asked, "But why shouldn't you pry? It's your ship, and—"

"I reckon," Paulsen said slowly, "that's another difference between Earthie and Belter. On Earth, everything about you is in the computers, and anybody can find out anything they want to, like what you spent and where you spent it, and probably if they're interested, why.

"But in the Belt, the only think anybody else needs to know about you, unless you want to tell 'em, is what job you're doing—which they can tell by the color of your suit; or what kind of training you have—which they can tell from your belt. Those are useful bits of information for you to have other people know. If you don't want 'em known, you change to a plain suit and a plain belt. Inside your belt is your credit rating, which automatically changes as you spend or get credited—but that's private information unless you want to display it; and though it goes through the computer nobody else can get at your credit rating in the computer but you.

"So a man's not subject to interrogation by computer or by anybody else, unless he wants to be. And it's . . . well, you just don't pry into a man's business. It's his business. If it affects you, you stay with him or you leave; but you don't pry."

"Well," said Stan. There was a lifetime of training behind that "well." It was a lifetime habit that anybody could know anything about you at any time, except for the privacy cloak and the immediate moment, and it took time to digest the fact of his obvious freedom from that sort of—yes, prying. Then:

"Would it be prying to ask why you took on the Mars guys when they wanted to arrest me?"

Paulsen leaned back his head and laughed, a loud, long, tension-relieving laugh, and Stan found himself smiling in return.

"You can ask, but I don't think I rightly know the answer

to that one," he said at last. "I wasn't looking forward to an Earthie passenger, but—well, you got off the ship without a damned privacy cloak. And then there was the belt. Out here a gold belt means AT training; and the level of training is indicated by the workings of the belt. I didn't think your belt meant anything but it . . . well, it might. Then you walked straight, and you talked straight. You didn't sort of *slink*, like most Earthies. And anyhow," he added defensively, "Marsers and Earthies just aren't *allowed* to interfere with a Belter. We don't let 'em."

Stan thought a minute before answering. Then: "I don't know why anyone would be after me," he said slowly. "I was as surprised as you were—probably more so—that those guys had a warrant for me from the school. I'm supposed to be home for a two-week leave; and I'm supposed to report back to the school. But it's just a school," he added, and knew himself instantly for a liar. He'd always thought of it as just a school, until the day he'd left. But that wasn't something you could explain, even if you wanted to.

"I'd say," Paulsen was speaking in a slow drawl now, "that, if it's the school, they want you back, dead or alive."

"Yeah," said Stan. "It—well, it just *can't* be the school. But it can't be anyone else, either."

"You said I could ask anything I liked. Okay. It may be important. Damned well could be important to you; and it is to me as long as you're aboard. So I ask: What are you doing out here anyhow?"

"I guess I'm running away from the school. They were training me, I just found out, for the military. I didn't like the idea."

"Oh? So you just up and ran away? You must be *really* High-G to afford it."

Stan grinned. "I only had enough to get to Earth Orbdock. I was trying to find a job on a ship, when a guy came and said he was my Uncle Trevor's lawyer, and that I'd been left some stock—a thousand shares—in something called Astro Technology. He also left me passage fare out, so . . ."

At the look on the other's face, his voice ran down. What could he have said to cause a reaction like that?

V

THE SILENCE went on and on; and Stan waited. Finally Paulsen spoke:

"Your name's Dustin," he said. It wasn't a question. "And your uncle was Trevor Dustin." He looked over at Stan in awe. "Do you have any idea who Trevor Dustin was?"

"He . . . he was nicknamed Trail Blazer Dustin. I've been told," Stan said, "he was killed in the Belter Uprising. . . ."

"He was the biggest hero of the Belter War of Independence," said Paulsen reprovingly. "He was the guy who—well, he was Mr. Belt. He was the guy who invented ship-guerrilla; who invented ship-freeze. He had us paint our hulls black to radiate the heat out and freeze the hull shielding water so we didn't blow open when a laser beam bit into the hull. He was the one who invented putting soft plastic noodles into the shielding water to absorb freezing expansion and to take up the hydrostatic shock from those laser hits.

"He was the one who taught us to sting the Earthies with our tails, since we didn't have the fire power to hurt them. . . . You're *Trail Blazer's* nephew?"

Stan nodded dumbly, his mind racing.

Paulsen was continuing slowly. "And you've got Trail Blazer's shares in AT?" At Stan's nod, he went on: "One of his partners is dead; the other's sort of in retirement. AT's in the hands of—well, they're different now. Powerful and power-hungry. They're taking over an awful lot of the policy-making out here. AT's different than it used to be but . . . but look. This belt." He thumbed at the gold belt he wore. "It means I've been trained by AT; it's the most valuable possession I own.

"The school's been going down since the partner that ran it went into retirement, almost four years ago; but the belt that says you're AT-trained will give you top priority on any job they say you've been trained for. It's going downhill, but it's still better than the best."

He looked at Stan again. "If you've got a thousand shares of AT stock, I don't have to ask who's trying to kill you. Nor whether it's serious, either. I think the AT partner who died—not your uncle; the one who died shortly afterward—well, the scuttlebutt is that he was murdered to get him out of the way of the guys who took over at AT. It's been hushed, but he probably was."

"So what do I do now?"

"Damned if I know. But you're fast on your feet and you've got an amazing amount of knowhow, even if there are some pretty astounding gaps in it that take a guy unexpected. I think I'm on your side, at least for this part of the action. I haven't liked the way the school's been going recently—the kind of kid they've been turning out. Seemed more like zombies than AT-trained experts. I don't know much about the rest of AT enterprises, except they're rooting for war with Earth, which doesn't make sense to me. And maybe if you've got enough Dustin blood in you, you'd be better than what's there now. I damned well better be on your side, at that, if I want to keep my hide; 'cause somebody sure doesn't want you around. So I reckon we better figure how to keep you and me both alive until you can do something with those shares."

"But we're on a ship that they know I'm on, which puts your ship at hazard. And—"

"First thing we do is see if there's a beacon on this crate. Then, when we get de-bugged, if we're bugged, we put the doughnut on a homing course . . ."

"Does that mean a Hohmann orbit? It sounds as though it should."

Paulsen laughed. "Right. We put it on a Hohmann orbit for Belt City. Then we turn on its beacon and let it coast on in, while we cut loose and get there a bit before they expect you. Or you want to change course for AT's own asteroid? It's about two weeks away."

"I think Belt City. It might be a good idea to find out—"

"Well, at any rate, we'll land there at an unexpectedly early time. You're probably right. AT's a small pebble; you'd be conspicuous. At Belt City, with about six million people around, we can get a little lost. We'll land at a docker I don't normally use. And once we're docked, we'll skip into the tunnels so fast they won't know where we got to. What do you want to do once you get there?"

"Why . . . I was going to look for a job."

Paulsen looked at him in disbelief, then threw back his head and guffawed. Then, "With a thousand shares of AT in his clip, the guy wants to go out and look for a job! Well, well." More soberly he asked, "Do you realize that with those shares you could practically buy the Belt? A fair slice of it, anyhow."

Stan's thoughts were chaotic as he began to grasp the implications of what the other had been saying. Finally, "Well, maybe it's . . . What would you do?"

"Actually, I don't know just what I *would* do."

The two sat silent for a minute. Then Stan said, "Maybe I should get a job until I find and speak to somebody that my uncle trusted."

"I know who the retired partner is that ran the school. I think he's even at Belt City. You oughta be able to trust him, I'd think. Lang. Dr. Katsu Lang."

Belt City had originally been a chunk of nickel steel approximately twenty-five miles in diameter. In terms of planets, this was practically microscopic; but in terms of the size of particles in the Belt, it was relatively large.

At first it had served as a base for small technological operations, mainly because of its mass. Later it had served those who were interested in the mass itself, and the nickel steel had been carved off in chunks and pieces and carted away; while other chunks and pieces of it had been drilled and bored on the spot to fashion crude reaction vessels for this or that in the line of chemistry.

It was then that Alfibe had taken over; the Alfibe Corporation was using the vacuum of space to make boron into microscopically thin fibers of tensile strengths far higher than any of the metallic alloys. Boron fiber was not new; it was just that space vacuum made it newly inexpensive to manufacture. On Earth, mass production had brought the costs down from seven hundred credits a pound to seventy credits a pound. Here the fibers could be made for seven microcredits a pound—and a pound was a lot of fiber.

The boron fiber was a major trade item with Earth; but

for use in the Belt it was combined with aluminum from asteroids that were towed in for mining, to create a metal of tensile strengths fourteen times stronger than steel, pound for pound—and a pound went a lot further.

So Belt City grew. Port facilities that had been built for the boron fiber trade were enlarged for Belt trade in Alfibe; were enlarged again as corporations were formed to build Alfibe ships for the Belt.

Where port facilities are available, every form of manufacture for trade will move in. It wasn't long before the surface of the planetoid, as well as its mined caverns, were crowded.

That was when the Belt City Corporation was formed, its board of directors made up of the heads of the corporations that supported and were supported by the planetoid; its major duty was overseeing the G-swing and the balance of industry—in this instance, the *weight* balance of industry.

The terms "gravity" and "G's" were commonly used, but the weight effect was by centrifugal force, and the G-swing necessary to keep that force evenly applied was constantly being upset by new heavy industry moving in, by new construction that failed to take into account the balance and counterbalance necessary to prevent wobbles. The wobbles were not only upsetting to the manufacture going on, but had proved several times nearly disastrous to the vast hydroponic farms and the "ranches" where meat was grown in vats, the necessary core factors to any Belt habitation; and the swing-weight of the city was shown to be too critical a survival factor to be left longer at hazard to unplanned activity.

The first and gigantically expensive but necessary act of the BC Corp. was the construction of an even flooring over the entire scalloped-looking built-up portion of the planetoid, a section around the equator that extended roughly thirty degrees to the north and south. It was flooring, not ceiling, since centrifugal force applies outward, and the floors of the existing structures were toward space, the ceilings toward the planetoid core.

The second and concomitant—and quite as necessary—act was the contruction of hull-style river systems immediately over the new floor. The rivers were for inertial control of rotation with huge tanks to provide for balance and counterbalance; they also served as the medium for growth of sea life and plankton as an additional source of food, and as a far superior method to the simple hydroponics one for recycling air and waste products.

That was the start of the planned growth of Belt City; and because of the planning it was now possible to really grow. New overall floors were needed and constructed almost immediately, always as a unit, surfaced with built-in rivers. Transportation systems for freight and people intertwined through the growing structures in an orderly and efficient manner. The internal ecology was protected from sabotage by unthinking corporate or individual action.

And always, as the city grew, the growing hydroponics farms moved outward to the rim where the plants could take full advantage of the highest accelerative stress. There were plants that would grow with practically no gravity; there were others that wouldn't grow without at least three-quarters G; but almost all grew best where the gravity was most nearly Earth-like. So the G-swing was set to maintain a full gravity at the rim, leaving the lower areas to their proportionate heights; and the plants that were the city's sustenance were given top priority on that best-growth potential section. People-comfort was never more than a secondary consideration, though the schools were kept on the rim, which gave the children a full G during part of the day; and enough credits could buy you space between the farms.

Now Belt City hung in space, a wedge-shaped wheel around the central nickel-steel core that was itself caverned and structured for man's use. The floors that made its rim extended now more than twelve miles out from the original surface; and where the original sixty degrees at the equator had given the first flooring a width of twelve miles equal to its radius, the outside rim was now nearer twenty-four miles across.

From the north and south poles of the planetoid, taking advantage of the null-G at these axes, the long strands of docking and transportation tubes of a space-dock complex were strung out. The tubes extended a good thirty miles beyond the non-rotating caps by which they were attached to the rotating asteroids; and each ship that docked was tethered and serviced by several of the tubes.

Fan-powered strut-cars traveled the tubes from ship to

planetoid-cap, then dived across to complimentary tubes in the rotating structure of the planetoid itself.

There were parts of Belt City that gave the impression of being crowded; and there were places where people were likely to be only once a year, or perhaps even less; other places people went only to work. All of the areas were served with air and heat and power and freight and transportation by the tubes and their strut-cars that efficiently serviced the entirety of the inside-out asteroid that was Belt City.

"The docking tubes look like a man-of-war's tendrils, with the ships its prey," Stan said softly, watching the planetoid enlarge on the *Sassy Lassie*'s viewscreen. "Or like a net for invaders."

Paulsen looked at him in surprise. "I reckon they do look a bit like that," he said finally in satisfaction. "The docking tubes are the green ones. The passenger tubes are yellow. The freight tubes are the red ones. And the orange ones are the smaller tubes in which liquids can be carried without being loaded into jungle-gyms."

"Jungle gyms?"

"Boy, as much as I've been educating you, there are still gaps!" Paulsen smiled ruefully. "Tubecars you use on Earth, because that's an induction-repulsion linear motor vacuum system. Pneumocars you have at Orbdocks, where the tubes are air-filled, and the cars can run on battery-powered fans. But pneumocars are built for comfort, and they're a luxury we haven't gotten around to out here. Here we have the air-filled tubes and the battery-powered fans, but the cars behind the fans are just . . . well, jungle-gym affairs that you can strap freight into or people can ride sitting on the bars. They have floors and skirts for use in G fields, but the rest is just a batch of struts. They're formally called strut-cars."

Expertly the skipper matched orbits with the asteroid, then maneuvered slowly until the *Lassie* hung at the tips of a ganglion of different colored tubes. He reached over and flipped a switch marked MAGNALOCK, activating powerful magnetic coils at various spots on the hull, and with a soft *thump* each of the green tubes reached out and sucked onto the coil-area that matched its code-pulse.

"We're docked," he said succinctly. "Now to air lock us into the passenger and freight systems."

While Paulsen worked over the controls, Stan watched on the screen as a great yellow tube bent slowly and unwillingly, stretched a bit, and then made contact with the magnetic coil around the air lock, its internal pressures resisting every motion but being slowly overcome by the magnetic attraction between its head and the coils. The action was repeated with one of the red tubes, which was made to seek its own type of pulse-code and fall into place over the access lock that would have led into the *Lassie*'s missing freightnut.

"Okay, bud," Paulsen said, unstrapping himself almost as the red tube thumped into place, "here's where we get lost. You think you can fly the tubes? Now that you can see how far out we are? Or had we better take a chance on the strut-cars? We could go freight. . . ."

"I can fly," said Stan shortly and unstrapped to push his way in the null G toward the freightlock where they'd already prepared their wings and fins.

He was wearing one of Paulsen's bright red pilot's suits now. "You better be in spacemen's outfit," Paulsen had said. "Wear mine until we can get you some of your own." "But they're pilot-red," Stan had objected, "and I'm not a pilot. How do I get to be one?" "By flying a ship," said Paulsen. "Here, fly this one and do me a few navigation problems." It had been as simple as that. Once he had proved to a competent pilot his ability to fly and navigate a ship he was entitled to wear pilot-red. His gold belt, though, was his own.

The wing and tail outfits they would wear, flying the tubes, had been blown up in advance, and Stan had practiced getting into them, had been instructed carefully in their use. They hung now in the air lock, ready: two stubwings, scarcely longer than his arms and shaped somewhat like a bee's wings, and a seven-foot tail that would run from his waist to well below his feet.

In the null G he had no trouble slipping his feet into the foot-grips about halfway down the length of the tail, belting it to him with the belt that went around his waist, then reaching down and pulling the wing-straps across his shoulders, slipping his hands into the handholds of the wings. Gently and experimentally he moved a wing, and found himself caroming into the air lock side.

"Save it for the tube," said Paulsen shortly, palming open

the air lock bulkhead before slipping his hand into his own wing-grip.

Before them the tube stretched out, an eerily glowing red diminishing to a point in the far distance; infinitely long, infinitely fragile, seen from here. Stan made an involuntary motion and found himself flying into Paulsen, who swung out his arms in counteraction and was propelled out of the air lock into a long glide down the tube. But he kicked his feet up at the knees, and then snapped them down to come to rest spread-eagled across the three-yard diameter tube, wings and tail touching the sides.

"Watch out for those unintended movements," he called back. "Did you see the stop I made? Do you get the idea?"

"I think so. Every slightest movement sure counts."

"Yep. Tail motion is the most important part, though, remember. A gentle up-down swish of the tail with the arms held rigid will give you plenty of speed. The arms can propel too, if you're in a real hurry. If you want to stop, just flip yourself over like I did, but don't forget to straighten out, or you'll keep right on tumbling. I'm going ahead. You come on along."

With that, Paulsen pulled his wings down toward his body, flipped them, straightened them out, and dove off down the tube, tail undulating in a smooth powerful stroke that had him diminishing down the tube like a bird in flight.

Poised on the lip of the air lock, Stan tucked his head down to line it with the direction of flight and slipped his wings open. His head scraped the tunnel, slid along it. He kicked his tail, found himself twisting, and brought his wings into play again. He was moving rapidly, but his head was scraping first one side then the other.

In automatic reflex, he pulled up his feet. The tail flipped over, flipping him end over end in a wall-to-wall passage down the tunnel. Frantically he pushed his feet out, pinioning his wings. His head buried itself deeply into the soft wall of the tube. He threw his arms and legs wide, and found himself stopped, spread-eagled across the tunnel.

Dizzy, he looked around. There was the tube, stretching away from him. His wings looked a bloody red in the eerie light. And Paulsen would be far ahead by now.

Carefully, he pulled in his wings, gave a light flutter to his tail. He was moving down the tube, but scraping from wall to wall. Experimentally he balanced his wings, flapped them gently. The motion, tried gently, centered him more or less in the tunnel, so long as the tail flapped evenly and slowly. The walls of the tube were moving past at a fair rate, and he was scraping them very little. He increased the motion of his tail. His speed increased violently—and his head rammed firmly into a hard surface.

Summoning every bit of presence of mind he possessed, he flipped his tail, then straightened it, threw out his wings, and landed spread across the tube—facing the closed bulkhead of the *Sassy Lassie*'s air lock.

"Damn," he muttered, "I'll never get to Twelfth and Main this way."

Very cautiously now, Stan fanned himself around one wing, aimed himself down the tube and flapped his wings gently once. It worked. Slowly and smoothly he took off down the tunnel. With care he added a tail motion, but the two legs moved not quite in unison. His speed increased, but the slightly uneven motion added a vector of steering for which he had to compensate rapidly. He was caroming from side to side, but he found himself compensating with more and more efficiency.

His speed was remarkably high, he noted, as the walls of the tube seemed to wobble past his erratic motion; but he was tiring. It was hard work. He knew that once he got into a good, stable glide headed along the center, he could rest; inertia would keep him going. But he was still awkwardly wing-and-tail tipping the walls when he heard a shout in the distance.

"Halloo," he answered.

"Junction here. Can you follow me?" The voice was coming much louder now, and by craning his neck he could see the rapidly nearing figure spread across the tunnel.

"Move or I'll run you down!" he shouted.

"Pull up your knees, then straighten out," was the reply, too near.

Stan pulled his knees up, then straightened them violently, and found his head thrust firmly into the plastic wall, while his tail scraped to a rest on the opposite wall.

"That's how you stop." Paulsen's noncommital voice was only feet away. "You get started like this."

Paulsen drew his wings in across his chest, ducked his head and allowed the tail to give him a slight kick forward, snapped the wings open again and was off down the tunnel.

Stan started to try it, found himself confused, stopped. Suddenly he couldn't remember the first motion.

Abruptly he let go, relaxed, and let his arms and legs take over. With relief, he let natural motions replace the forced ones he'd been using; slow motions that didn't demand strength, only gentle undulations that took him faster and faster.

In the near distance he heard a call: "Right turn. Kick only your right leg when you get here." It was a Y-branch, and his turn was not smooth, but the compensations were coming naturally now.

Cautiously he craned his neck and sighted Paulsen not too far ahead. There were tiny lights further ahead, too, and Stan quit kicking, allowing himself to glide along at a speed he guessed to be in excess of fifty-five miles an hour.

"Stretch your legs apart and slow down."

He stretched his legs as far as he could force them, and was rewarded with a fluttering, vibrating sensation from the tail fin, and a simultaneous rapid slowing of his forward motion. The stiffening tube members in the tail had been pulled flat by his action, allowing the plastic between to wrinkle and flutter in an action that absorbed energy rapidly.

"Okay. Park. Or are you going to run me down?" came the call.

Stan kicked both legs up and back, and once more succeeded in ramming his head into the soft plastic wall, but this time he was going too fast. The tail scraped the far wall and snapped open again beyond it, leaving him still sailing down the tunnel, but feet-first, a direction of travel for which the device hadn't been intended. The flexible wings bent and tried to wrap themselves around his arms, buffeting him madly first against one wall and then the other. The tail bent, too, and forced his legs into a crouch position; and then—snap—he was headed down the tunnel head-first again, but with most of his momentum gone. Again he tried to brake, and this time was successful.

"Fanciest stop I've seen yet," Paulsen greeted him.

Stan was about to give a short reply when he looked beyond Paulsen to a large open chamber full of moving tube-

PHOENIX SHIP

cars that looked like they'd been stripped for action. Freight was fastened haphazardly into the frameworks.

One of the strut-cars—an object sized to fit neatly into the tubes, its three-yard fan covered with a mesh grille, its rear simply a tubular jungle-gym—was heading straight for their tube. The monster fan looked lethal for all its grille-mesh protective covering.

"Look out!" Stan yelled. "That freighter wants in. It's going to try to chase us back up the tube."

Paulsen turned in a leisurely fashion as the huge freighter came to a snarling halt about three yards outside the tube, and hung there buzzing at them like an angry, oversize bee.

"It can't come in while we're here."

"Oh . . . good. Hey, could we reprogram one of those to take us where we want to go?"

"Could. But it wouldn't be a good idea. The dispatcher would get hep to us. Those things have a tracer on them, in case they go wrong and somebody has to come out to correct them. It's easier to hitch a ride on one that's going our way. You think you can handle an open space like this? Fly it, I mean?"

"Should be easier than running into the walls of a tube all the time," Stan answered, "as long as you're sure one of those outsize bees out there won't try to eat me for a rose."

"You haven't got enough oil for that kind of bee to worry about." Paulsen dove gracefully from the tube and Stan followed. They'd barely cleared its mouth when the big strut-car, with a final angry buzz dove in and accelerated off in the direction from which they'd come.

The fact of flying this time seemed almost familiar; and to Stan's surprise he managed it with fair ease. Was this one of the familiarities of the molecular training? he wondered. Surely it hadn't been an intentional part—or just possibly it had.

Ahead of him, Paulsen had come to a hovering stop over one of the dark tunnel mouths that led into the city, identifiable only by its code name; he now settled gracefully onto the very lip of the tunnel and divested himself of his wings and tail. As he was deflating them Stan shucked his own wings and settled himself precariously; there wasn't enough G-pull to feel safe.

The cavern in which he sat was dim, lighted only by

57

the reflected red light of the transparent tubes through which they had come, and by the faint glow of the signal lamps lighting the various tunnel entrances on all sides of him, up and down.

It's unsettling, he thought. *You have to become accustomed to thinking in odd directions.*

The strut-car traffic above him and to his side seemed to be sorting itself out in a haphazard manner, each vehicle searching slowly for the pattern of lights that would satisfy its own equations, then diving into the tunnel that matched its code. The freighters were large and awkward in this space, moving very slowly; and since it would be quite impossible for any one of them to pass another freighter in a tunnel, one of the code signals must indicate, Stan decided, whether the tunnel was occupied or not.

Following Paulsen's lead, Stan folded his deflated wings and tail assembly into a small packet that fitted into a pocket, and fastened it to his belt.

"Why don't we just fly on in?" he asked.

"Ever try flying in a G-field?"

"Well, no. I guess it can't be done. Leonardo da Vinci even failed at that, didn't he?"

"Oh, it has been done. On Mars. Even on Earth. But you need bigger wings and a lot more room to maneuver in. These wings wouldn't hold us up in a tenth of a G. Right here"—Paulsen patted the floor on which he was sitting and almost dislodged himself—"we've got less than a thousandth of a G. But it picks up as you go down—or rather, across. And from here on we get heavier. I think that's our ride coming now," he added.

Stan looked up at an angry buzzing overhead to see a freighter hovering there, waiting for them to get out of its way.

"This part is tricky. We have to stay in its way until we get in position to jump after it right after it goes by. But don't grab any struts that might pinch you into the wall. These walls aren't plastic. Incidentally, this thing has no sensor circuits on its backside."

Carefully Stan worked his way back in the very light gravity field to just beyond the edge of the tunnel. Paulsen was doing likewise, holding only one hand in front of the big buzzing freighter to bar its passage.

"Let it go all the way in—it'll be downward from here—

then fall in after it. We'll catch up quick enough." Paulsen pulled his hand out of the way and with a snort of fans the freighter surged forward and dived into the hole. As soon as it had cleared the mouth, Paulsen slipped in behind it feet first, and Stan followed.

Sliding out over the emptiness was like sliding into a soft pillow. He was moving downward, but slowly.

It was pitch dark in the tunnel, and for a minute Stan wished that the Belt City Corp. had used the translucent plastic tunnels on the surface, at least until the tubes reached the built-up areas and went inside. Then his eyes began to adjust, and he could see the faint emergency glow from his buttons—the spacemen's last protection against utter darkness in enclosed spaces.

He looked down and could see tiny glows that meant that Paulsen was there ahead of him in the pitch black; and beyond Paulsen—near or far, he couldn't tell—the code lights of the freighter. If the freighter had accelerated, as it was quite capable of doing, it would be far ahead of them. Could they catch up? But it would be moving at a steady pace, possibly fairly slowly, and they were accelerating.

By the faint illumination from his buttons he could see the wall of the tube moving gently toward him, and he reached out and pushed himself away. By the feel, he was moving fairly rapidly now. The next time, it was his back that was scraping the tunnel wall, and as he pushed away again, to fall free, he found his speed quite impressive.

"Look out. Don't land on me."

Stan looked quickly down. The glows that were Paulsen were moving beneath the code lights on the back of the freighter, and those lights were rising beneath his feet. Slowly at first, then faster; and the illumination they provided gave him a true sense of falling for the first time. Then he was down and onto a package of freight at the back of the strut-car.

"From here on in things get heavier," Paulsen said. "We're still on the surface, but we're coming away from the axis into the gravity areas. It's about a half-G at the surface at the equator. Then the car will dive on out to whatever level it's dialed to. We'll change to a car for the area we want when we hit the equator shift-space.

"Find a comfortable seat on this side," he went on. "The

tubes tilt gradually, so the side of the freighter that drags is the side that has the ground-effect air support; and that's the side that will be dragged by gravity to the bottom when the tube flattens out into a cross-G slant. These cars are designed to go almost anywhere—up, down or across G. They stay in the tubes mostly, but they can go out of the tubes for unloading, in half-barrel shaped runs."

Just when the freighter shifted from fighting the force that caused it to cling to one wall of the long down-tube, to the fight against the centrifugal force that substituted for gravity here in Belt City, would have been hard for Stan to say; but now it seemed to be gliding down a less and less steep slope, and slowing as it came to a shift-space between tunnels. This shift-space was different, Stan realized. It was dimly lighted, and there was a definite gravity. The cars hugged the floor. They criss-crossed their way about the low-ceilinged cavern, searching out new codes, but always gliding only a few inches from the floor.

Paulsen was examining a card attached to a package beside him.

"Do we change here?" Stan asked.

"Nope. We're in luck. This one is headed for a shopping area."

The hunting period for their own freighter was brief, and it dived into another tunnel. But this time they weren't falling. The tunnel felt level, and for a while it continued that way. Then they were going downhill again—a sensation, Stan realized, rather than a fact. Actually, they were slanting up-level toward the rim. Now the walls were lighted, and numbers began to flash past; numbers that were blocked out both in the binary code that the strut-cars could read, and in common decimal figures. But it was still code as far as Stan could tell, and he felt no familiarity with it.

Occasionally and briefly there would be a widening of the tunnel as the freighter passed a platform level with its own floor, each such dock area causing a *thwop* of changing air pressure as they passed it.

And then they began passing an occasional terminus of a different type; a place in which the car could be halted to shunt sidewise and pass through a lock. Stan was about to ask the advantage of this configuration when a surge of deceleration thrust him forcefully against one of the packages ahead of him, and the freighter came to a halt next to just such a system, moved slowly sidewise, and passed nose-first through a lock.

Immediately beyond the door was a lighted area, with freighter-troughs leading out between unloading docks. There were two men on one of the docks unloading a freighter, but most of the docks were empty.

Their freighter nosed its way into the empty dock next to the one being unloaded. The men from the crew straightened and one called over, "Hey, there."

"Hi," Paulsen answered laconically. "We hopped a ride in. Our freighter was too loaded and we didn't want to wait for a yellow-belly. This is twelve-thirty-two, forty-seven south fifth, isn't it?"

"Yep. Area one, seventy-five, sixty-third."

Stan felt his stomach wrench. As the man had straightened to accost them, one had shown himself to be long and willowy, arms hanging out of proportion to his height; the other to be short and stubby, out of proportion the opposite way. He kept from averting his eyes.

"Which way to the walks?" Paulsen was asking.

"Through that door. Shops."

"Thanks."

They went through the door into a walkway, mall-centered, shop-lined, its ceiling perhaps sixty feet above them, and five levels of walkway between their own and the ceiling. The flowered and shrubbed mall served as the well to the multileveled walkways of the shopping area; and Stan could see stairs leading from one level to another at intervals.

His first impression was of color—a riot of color. There was color in the luminescence that flooded from the far ceiling; from below the walkway above his own; from every partition between the shop windows along the walks. There was color in the flowered and shrubbed mall; color in the display windows of the shops; color in the costumes the people on the mall were wearing.

There was an air of gaiety to the scatterings of people around, and the gaiety and color were infectious.

It was several minutes, as they strolled along the mall, before Stan could sort out individual impressions; and then it was with an empty feeling at the pit of his stomach that he realized that under the color, under the gaiety, something was very wrong. The Mutt and Jeff of the freight dock were not isolated cases, if the people he was seeing were any sample. The willowy, gangling form was predominant, the shorter, squat form less in evidence; but almost everyone, male and female, presented some grotesquerie.

There were burns and scars to be seen. That you would expect of a pioneer society, he thought. But the differences in build and structure of the majority from the norm he was used to . . . It was like a hydroponics farm not properly tended, missing some of the essential elements, or grown without proper light, or with poor G considerations, Stan decided, and knew he had the answer.

There were a few normally formed persons like himself and Paulsen; but they were so far in the minority that he knew himself to be quite conspicuous.

Paulsen was leading them into a restaurant, and as they sat down he didn't wait to be asked. His voice was gruff, held a bitter note of defiance.

"Space is unforgiving," he said, "and the sins of the parents *are* visited upon the children unto the third and fourth generations. Sins of omission, and sins of commission," he added. "And ignorance is no defense."

He paused for a minute while his eyes sought through the people at the tables around them and then returned to Stan, who sat silent.

"As a matter of fact, ignorance not only isn't a defense, it's the one unforgivable sin out here. Unforgivable by space, that is. Ignorance kills, and it kills right now. Or it maims. Ignorance and stupidity.

"You're seeing the small ignorances and stupidities when you look at the people here at Belt City. Not enough provision for this; not enough attention to that . . . little errors. The big errors—their results are death. Even so, this is a protected environment, here at Belt City. A freak can still stay alive. Outside Belt City, a small error in judgment is sure death.

"You can't be just an average joe, and survive in the Belt. You can't let anybody else do your thinking for you, and expect to survive. We each live our own lives and do our own thinking out here—and we each pay our own price for our own inabilities. We don't do it because we figure it's a good way to live, to be independent and stay on your toes; but because if you don't you *don't* live.

"And any one of the joes you see out there—the ones who

got metabolically unbalanced and grew beyond their strengths, or the squat ones who got G-squashed, maybe before they were born, or the burned or the deformed—any one of them is still brighter and more able to take care of himself under any circumstances—any single one of them is a better man than any molly-coddled puppy dog of an overprotected Earthie, and don't you forget it. If they weren't brighter and more able, they'd be already dead; and the death rate's high. Because space hits you where you hurt if you act ignorant or stupid even for a little while; but it hits to kill if you stay that way.

"Space doesn't forgive," he ended.

Then he changed—expression, manner and voice—and Stan knew that this subject was dropped, now and forever, as far as Paulsen was concerned.

Looking around the room in a casual manner, Paulsen said lightly, "There's a telescreen over there. You go screen Dr. Lang. I'll order us up some rose-hip tea. Then we'll see what gives from here."

The screen was normal Earth-style, and Stan had no trouble with the controls. He kept the screen dark while he dialed computer info for the code for his old friend. Then, as he was about to dial Dr. Lang's number, the screen before him suddenly cleared, and he found himself looking at a heavy face with tiny, porcine features. The small, alert eyes riveted his gaze, and the man spoke without preamble:

"Mr. Dustin, I am Jonathan Weed of Astro Technology. Your activities since the *Sassy Lassie* docked have been reported to me from no less than five different sources. Your current position is pinpointed as twelve-thirty-two, fortyseven south fifth; area one, seventy-five, the restaurant at fifty-eighth.

"Your call to Dr. Lang will not be accepted. Since AT is only one of several parties interested in your current activities, and since you must know that your interests lie with AT, I suggest that it would be to your advantage to report to my office immediately, before your life becomes unduly complicated by others. You are, as I hope I have impressed you, easily monitored in our society.

"I am at thirteen-oh-two, eighty-one north sixth, and any of the area directors will bring you to me. Your friend Paulsen can get you to the area."

Stan started to speak, then changed his mind. As his mouth closed, the man on the screen rose slowly, so that the intricately woven gold belt he wore dominated the screen. His hands went to the belt, and framed it from the sides.

"In the name of the Belt," he said in a voice of authority, "I command you to come. Immediately. Unobtrusively but rapidly."

Abruptly, Stan cut the connection, rising from the seat in the same motion. He turned to see Paulsen standing behind him, evidently having heard the conversation.

Paulsen was smiling gently.

VI

"THEY'VE SPOTTED US," Stan said furiously. "Let's jet."

Paulsen nodded, still smiling, and turned toward the walkway, taking long strides that would appear unhurried but would cover a lot of territory fast.

Stan fell into step with him and continued talking: "The guy said he was Weed of AT, and that he'd had a tracer on us since we left the *Lassie*, but I doubt that last. They simply spotted us when I tried to call Lang. Must have his phone monitored. That Weed character! He was trying to give me some sort of hypnotic command or other, to get the hell up to his office. What a dullie!"

Paulsen was leading them back to the freight loading area behind the shopping center through which they had come, apparently thinking to take the same freightways.

"You going to double back on the same trail?" Stan asked, worried. "Now they've spotted us, it should be easier to tracer us. Maybe . . ."

"Doesn't matter. Mr. Weed just said to be unobtrusive. I don't think any of the others have spotted us yet."

"Any of the others?"

"He warned you that others were looking for you too,"

PHOENIX SHIP

said Paulsen impatiently. "We're to be unobtrusive about getting to his office, but I don't think we have to hide exactly. It will be just as well if AT *can* tracer us. Then if anybody else stops us, they can get to us to help."

Stan came to an abrupt stop, and Paulsen, of necessity, turned to see what had occurred. It was then that Stan got a good look at Paulsen's eyes. They held a strange blankness.

"Where are you taking me?" Stan asked.

"To Weed's office, of course. We're to hurry."

Stan stood stock still, estimating his chances. Without Paulsen he was indeed a stranger in a strange land. But with Paulsen?

Why hadn't it occurred to him that the AT school was a molecular memory training school? Katsu Lang had headed each; and each had turned out—robots. If he had needed any demonstration of what Mallard had been talking about, he had it now before him.

But why wasn't he, himself, reacting in the same manner as Paulsen? The command had been "in the name of the Belt." And it was quite obviously a phrase that keyed in a hypnotic condition. But there'd be another command phrase for use on Earth; and that hadn't been used. Okay, he was safe until somebody started using whatever phrase had been selected to key in his own robotic responses. He shivered violently, knowing his own vulnerability to be as great as the one he was witnessing; then, with an effort, he pulled himself back to the immediate problem.

He and Paulsen were facing each other just inside the door to the unloading area. From the corner of his eye, Stan could see the Mutt and Jeff freight loaders straightening, beginning to pay attention to what must seem a disagreement—a disagreement in which they would take the part of the Belter against an Earthie.

Idly he let his fingers go to his belt, then glanced down at it. Paulsen's eyes followed his own. When he was sure that Paulsen was looking directly at his belt, he said softly, "Wait here." He started to use the command phrase that Porky had used, but stopped. If he got it wrong, he'd trigger the wrong reaction. Anyhow, it was not a phrase he could bring himself to utter.

Paulsen was looking confused. "We are to hurry," he said.

"Wait here. Then we'll hurry."

65

Not daring to pause any longer, Stan turned on his heel and went back through the door onto the walk. Turning away from the direction of the restaurant, he lengthened his stride toward the nearest byway.

Behind him he could hear light running footsteps, obviously not far behind, or he couldn't have distinguished them among the numbers of people about. He was just yards from a byway, but the runner was not many more yards behind.

Abruptly, he turned into the byway. No sooner had he made the corner than he flattened his back against the wall of the shop he had rounded, hands loose and ready.

As the figure came around the corner at top speed, he reached, reflexed, half caught her on the withdraw, and ended up supporting his quarry to keep her from falling.

He was looking down into a pretty Oriental face, topped with mussed dark hair, flushed from running, and completely startled so that the mouth was still open in an "oh." She was wearing a gold belt over tunic and trousers.

In spite of himself, Stan began to smile. "Every day in every way," he said happily, "the robots get prettier and prettier."

The flush that mounted her cheeks this time was not from running. She pulled away from him in fury, then softened again.

"You're Star Duster," she said breathlessly, "and you've got to trust me quick, because I can get you out of here. I'm Sandra Lang. Will you trust me?"

"Yes," said Stan, surprising himself. He would rationalize later that he couldn't get out by himself; that trusting her was the best gamble available. There would be all sorts of reasons, but when it came right down to it, he trusted her because he trusted her. It was that simple.

She nodded at him, but remained still, thinking. "They'll have all the strut-cars monitored, so we can't go by car," she said hesitantly. "Freight cars, too . . . Oh, I know."

Back onto the mall she led him, down a ways, across the mall, into a foodstore. Through the store to the back through a door to the delivery area, looking in every direction, then breaking into a run to catch a man stopping over some newly unloaded vegetables on a platform.

"Mr. Jim." She stopped beside him, panting. "Are you returning anything to the rim right now?"

The face that turned up to hers was graying, lined, a bit grim, but the expression softened as he looked up. "What sort of trouble you in today, Sandra? I thought you'd out-grown hide and seek."

"This one's for real, Mr. Jim," she said solemnly. "This is Star. We both need to get out to Gramps's, fast and inconspicuous like."

"Those crates over there," he said, smiling at her fondly. "They're going back out to Rosie's. You get in them and I'll dial you to Katsu, then you tell him to dial them on to her. Hop in. How serious if you're caught?"

"Plenty." She didn't amplify the statement, but her tone left no doubt.

"Don't you get yourself mixed up in politics, Sandra," he told her severely as he opened two of the biggest crates for them to climb in. "It's not a game for sweet youngsters like you. A pretty face is no protection when it's power politics that's being played," he went on as he replaced the covers and checked the lashings to the strut-car, "and they're playing it rougher every day." Then, "Here you go," he ended, and Stan felt the strut-car begin to move as he lay curled in the dark in a crate on a freightcar near a pretty girl who was the granddaughter, obviously, of the man who had made him a robot. *And perhaps I'm a fool,* he told himself, but there was something inside that re-fused to believe the statement.

Katsu Lang sat at the keyboard of the symphony master, taking out the tensions that had been building within him in thunderous, rolling tones of barbaric style, harnessed to an insistent violin concerto theme. The contrasting elements delighted him, and took his attention from the chase he knew to be going on, matching the demanding insistence of a violin *rampant,* he thought, to the overpowering bru-tality of a cadenced bass viol clawing at the understructure of the racing theme. The two musical forces were harmo-nized by a patterned form that included within itself the warring elements—and he found himself quite satisfied with the resultant dynamic stability.

He had turned on the recorder, and he knew that the tensions had given him a body of music which, with a few months spent in organization and handling, could be made into a great work.

Lifting his fingers from the keys, he leaned back in the maestro's great seat and flipped on the recording of what he had just played. It washed over him in rolls of movement and countermovement, and it almost drowned the tiny wrist receiver that told him that Sandra, at least, was back. And young Star Dustin must be with her, he decided, for if she had lost him she would not return until she found where he was taken and what could be done—and that would necessarily have required more time.

Muting the recorder, he rose to meet his guests, approaching now through the apple orchard beyond the bays of the music stall. The grass carpeting beneath his feet felt resilient; the glow of late afternoon filled the air. He wondered idly if the Earth boy would recognize the programming which kept the light of the enclosure that was his home tuned to the Earth-light sequence for any time of day. Or the need for that programming: the changing colors within the atmosphere modulating a changing of body reactions, preventing the hypnosis that is a single-light-frequency response.

We have so much to learn of artificialized living, he thought; *and,* he added to himself, *so much to learn of learning itself.*

The two coming through the orchard made a graceful contrast to the stubby-fingered grace of the trees themselves, now in full leaf with tiny apples budding.

Paulsen was not with them. It had been some years now since he had seen Paulsen—one of the hopefuls of the program that had turned out to be so flawed. Sandra was light and graceful beside the tall figure of the now grown young man that was Star Dustin. The young man's stride was easy, his head high, the hair a deep flame beneath the trees. He was graceless in contrast to Sandra, but his stride held a strength that was a grace of its own. *How very like Trevor,* Lang thought.

He watched Stan's face as the young man stepped through the bay into the music stall; watched his slight catch of breath as he noticed that the grass over which he had been walking continued as carpeting of the stall; watched his glance as it went to the acoustically designed canopy.

Then the boy's eyes met his own, and he felt the warmth of pleasure with which the other responded; and, like a slap in the face, the fear and fury which shuttered it almost instantly afterward.

He bowed his head in reaction to the mental blow, then managed to make the gesture into one of greeting.

"Welcome, Stan Dustin, son of my late partner and very true friend," he said formally.

"Son?" Stan's voice was startled, and there was hope behind it.

"You are Trevor Dustin's son, Stan. The other was a fiction of convenience, and in the Belt such fictions are not necessary."

"Then, if I am the son of your true friend, why did you let them make me into a robot?" The words seemed torn from Stan, but he looked straight into the older man's eyes as they poured forth.

"Would I have made my own granddaughter into a robot? It was an unforeseen flaw in the program, Stan; and one that was enhanced and emphasized by those who killed the third partner and forced me out."

Stan's face crumpled from the fierce anger it had held, and the hope and pleasure slowly returned to it. Holding the younger man's eyes with his own, Katsu Lang continued softly, "It is my hope that if you will work with me, as Sandra has, we can find the key to changing the responses."

The work began next morning, work that was based on tests in a cubicle like the one in which Stan had spent so many hours for so many years on Earth; and he threw himself into the tests with a fierce, exultant hope that was overridden only by the need to eat and sleep.

The tests went on for three days, but in the afternoon of the third day Katsu Lang came to call him from the cubicle into a small study, where Sandra served them tea.

The older man waited until the tea was served and the three were relaxed in deep pneumochairs. Then he said slowly:

"Stan, you are not a robot. You do not show any of the robotic reactions."

The sentence hung there between them for a long minute, while Stan looked at him, trying to stifle the hope that flooded him, hope that would surely be dashed. . . .

"I do not understand, sir. I was trained, with the others. I saw Paulsen's reaction. . . ."

"Nor do I understand, Stan. But I have given you every test of which I can think. I have used every hypnotic command I know that has been trained into those who attended either the Earth school or the one in the Belt.

"Then, in case I had not known the ones to which you might be keyed, I have tested your reactions to the information patterns to which you were trained molecularly. And even to these, you respond as you yourself would respond; not as the donor of the molecular patterns would have responded. You respond as a young man would respond, armed with vital knowledge from many fields—not as the person would have responded who had spent a lifetime acquiring the one set of knowledge, with his reactions necessarily shaped by that knowledge alone, and with the thought habits of such specialization.

"Further," he went on slowly, "your information depth is not limited to what one man in each field might have acquired in one lifetime; but is infused and colored with factors that must have been transmitted genetically from generations back, for it includes accurate and detailed information on factors which have not been in use for generations."

"What do you mean by that, sir?"

Lang took his time before answering, sipping his tea thoughtfully. Finally he said slowly, "For instance, when you flew the tubes. Your reactions, I gather, were structured in an accurate, detailed, seat-of-the-pants knowledge of small-plane flying; of flying of a type that hasn't been done since the very early Twentieth Century. . . ."

Stan broke in excitedly. "You're right, you know. I could almost feel the flimsy structure of a . . . a flying machine around me; and a stick in my hands with which to guide her; and someone shooting at me. . . ."

"So detailed? I had wondered. Yes, I think it is undeniable that you have picked up genetic recordings along with the molecular memories with which we were training you."

"Sir . . . Dr. Lang. *Why* am I not a robot, and what about the others?"

Again Lang paused and sipped his tea. Then he leaned back and half-closed his eyes. "The normal method by which a person acquires information," he said, "is through the five senses. Information is fed into the brain by electronic signals from each of the five senses. In the brain that information is assembled by the intelligence, analyzed, sorted out, and readied for storage—for filing. The intelligence is the analyzer.

"Reason," he went on, "is the function of the intelligence. The information input is electronic, is analyzed by the intelligence, and is filed in the biochemical body which acts on it *without further analysis.*

"Now, when you hypnotize someone, you remove the intelligence from the circuit, and the responses you get are purely logic-circuit responses—backed by an eidetic 'memory,' or complete access to the near infinite information filing system.

"And when we put information into the body through a molecular memory training system, we are filing the information biochemically without putting it through the electronic brain/intelligence system. It is therefore filed without analysis or patterning.

"The only way that this information can be properly correlated and patterned by the intelligence is for it to be brought back to the cerebral circuits for review.

"Now it is possible," and here excitement crept into Lang's voice, "that, in insisting on re-studying every subject to which you were trained by molecular memory patterning, you forced the brain to call up all relevant information for review, so that the new information you had acquired could be patterned in with the old information already in the system.

"If that is true, then the 'alternating current' effect that you spoke of feeling while you slept would be the electromagnetic recall and refiling mechanism at work."

"If that's true, sir, then we can retrain Paulsen and the others?" Stan's voice held a hope so great as to make his voice shake. "We can . . . put the robots under their own control?"

"Let me think how it would work." Lang paused for a long minute, then began speaking again in a distant voice. "It would be necessary for them to seek out, on their own, information with which they had been inoculated. And then . . . we must find a way to inoculate the sleep-review system.

"I think that, with your experience in mind, we shall be able to handle the retraining of the molecularly trained students—once we remove the influence of the basically

71

hypnotic command-responses that have been driven deeply into them; and if we can get them where we can work with them for . . . I'd say at least several months."

"That's a pretty big *if*, sir."

Lang smiled. "That is an *if* we shall have to find the means to accomplish," he said softly. "And perhaps, with your cooperation, we shall not find it impossible."

VII

STAN WALKED into Weed's office with his head held deliberately high, his shoulders squared, as though the trepidation that might be expected of a younger man faced with the awe-inspiring might of the AT Corporation was forcing a defiant reaction. He held the pose as Weed slowly rose from his seat and extended his hand, which Stan ignored.

"Ah," said Weed, "I see that you are unconvinced, though sensibly coming to see what AT has to offer."

Stan nodded curtly.

"Very sensible of you." The porcine-faced man before him nodded his head solemnly. "Very sensible, though somewhat insensitive to retain this obviously recalcitrant attitude. However . . ."

Weed reached into a drawer, pulled out a large signet ring, placed it deliberately on his finger, and stood twisting it, watching Stan to be sure that the younger man had fixed his attention upon it. Then, in a voice of command, he said: "I, the trainer, speak. You obey."

Stan felt the slight tug at his senses that recognized the old command, discarded it instantly, and then forced his eyes to take on a glassy stare, his shoulders to slump slightly, his head to lose its defiant lift.

"Ah," said Weed, and the sound carried a world of satisfaction.

Stan stood immobile, waiting. This was going to be quite tricky, he realized.

"Now, young man," Weed was saying, "we will get to the business at hand. I made a mistake earlier in not using the correct symbolism, but then I had two of you to control. Hereafter," he went on, "you will respond either to the Earth command I have just used, or to the phrase, 'In the name of the Belt, I command you.' Do you understand?"

Stan nodded, slowly.

"Then tell me," said Weed, "to what you must respond, and what response you must make?"

"I must respond either to the ring or to the belt, and I must respond with complete obedience," Stan said, keeping his voice flat.

The other looked at him sharply. *Oh oh,* thought Stan. *I should have said to the phrases backed by the objects. Have I been caught out?* But he maintained his glassy-eyed stare, and it seemed to satisfy Weed.

"Now, young man," Weed said slowly, "I must have your shares in Astro Technology."

Stan let his hand move as though toward a pocket, then hesitate, as though a stronger force was working on him; then move again to the pocket and hesitate again. Finally, he let his hand rest immobile halfway between his pocket and its former position by his side.

"Oh?" Weed puzzled for a moment. "I gather that the shares of stock you possess hold an attraction nearly as strong as the command under which you respond to me?" There was silence and he finally added, "Answer."

"Yes, sir. They do."

Weed sank back in his chair and waited a moment. Finally he said, "Give the shares to me."

Stan made the gestures of trying to obey again, again let his hand rest immobile in a halfway gesture and stood silent.

"Why do you not give them to me?" asked Weed.

"I cannot, sir. They were given to me in trust."

"Um." Then, "I could have them taken from you forcibly."

"You could, sir. That would break my conditioning. Then I could fight you." The voice was still a monotone, and Stan waited, forcing his eyes to remain unwavering. This was the crucial point. Would Weed believe that Stan could produce this much independent reasoning, while still under control? Lang had thought that he would. Weed

73

was not a fighter; he was a weasler. He would have to figure this one out, but if he figured it out in terms that were normal to him . . .

"I was told that you were independent. However," Weed said softly, "let us reason together." Stan kept himself from breathing a sigh of relief. The pig was going to go along with it.

"The shares—the trust—are, I gather, from your uncle?"

"Yes, sir."

"And what would your uncle's wishes in the matter be?"

"I am not sure, sir. It is a trust. It is a trust to see that his projects at AT are finished in the way in which he intended them."

"Ah." Weed began to relax now. He'd been given a bargaining point, and bargaining was something in which he felt secure.

"And just what were his projects?" Weed asked, almost happily.

"That the Belt become and remain independent, sir."

"It is, and AT is seeing to it that it will remain independent. If that is all, you may sign over your shares to me."

"That I could not do, sir. I was given them in trust. I might be able to give you proxies."

"Very well. I shall have them drawn up."

"No, sir."

"No?"

"No. The independence of the Belt was not my uncle's only project. I must carry out his projects."

"What, then, were the others?"

"That AT remain technologically advanced over Earth."

Weed's voice lost some of its aplomb. "That's being done, son," he said impatiently. "If you want proof . . ."

"Your word is sufficient, sir."

"Then you have my word. That is being done. Anything else?"

"That the colony on Jupiter's moon be established."

"That is being . . ." Suddenly Weed paused. This was too easily checked, and the boy had mentioned that the "trust" under which he'd been placed was sufficient to break his conditioning if it was forcibly thwarted.

The name Dustin was one to conjure by in the Belt, Weed knew. If he could get this boy's wholehearted—at least apparently wholehearted—cooperation, half his troubles with the Belters would be over. The Jupiter colony ship, the *Phoenix*, was a useless hulk; and perhaps this would be a method by which he could get the youngster's open cooperation, as well as getting him out of the way. It would take some cash and time to get the old hulk actually out into the system with Stan aboard, but the time could be utilized for propagandizing the Dustin reassociation with AT; and the expense would not be too great.

A smile crept over his features. "Your uncle wanted you to see to it personally that these projects were properly carried out?"

Stan nodded.

"And you recognize that the first two have been implemented in the proper manner?"

Again Stan nodded.

"Then why don't I assign you as, say, a vice president of AT, to take the *Phoenix* and carry out the project of the Jupiter moon?"

Stan kept his voice dead with effort. "Yes, sir."

"Do you know what the *Phoenix* is?"

"She's a ramjet scoop ship, sir, that was readied to pirate air from Jupiter and to ferry personnel to Io to prepare the colony site, sir."

"Very well. We will make you vice president in charge of the Jupiter project, and commander of the *Phoenix*. And for your part, you will sign over those shares to me."

"No, sir."

Weed's face fell and his voice showed the short leash on which his obviously childish temper would be held.

"What now?" he asked with restrained fury.

"The *Phoenix* will have to be rehabilitated. I will have to have a crew, and they must be trained. Then I can give you the proxies of which I spoke."

Weed sat back grimly. But it was a perfect plan; and obviously, except for this evidently strong loyalty and compulsion, the boy was under control. Well, he could have an "accident" any time that he went out of control, once it was publicly established that he was enthusiastically with AT. The expense would be justified. They would actually save money by buying the loyalty of the Belters at the price of refurbishing the old hulk. And the boy might even get the project far enough underway so that it became commercially feasible as a corporate project, in the long run, after the coming war was over.

"Very well," he said. "You will announce your loyalty to the AT Corporation as now set up, and will proclaim it widely and frequently." He watched the boy closely for reaction, but the glassy stare and the solemn nod were his only answer. "We will refurbish the *Phoenix*. It may take several months, and I shall demand your complete cooperation during that time."

Stan nodded again, and again in the flat voice said, "I will pick my crew immediately, and set up quarters for training them. I will announce my loyalty to AT as now set up. You will see to it that the *Phoenix* is properly refurbished, and I will inspect it occasionally. When we are ready to take off, I will sign proxies for my shares to cover the time in which I shall be absent."

Weed nodded to himself. Not a bad bargain at that, he decided. And, that "accident" could occur. . . .

Tobey Olsen had started work at the Ace Sector Shipyards of AT the day that the hunk of ungainly nickel-steel asteroid that was to become the *Phoenix* was towed into the yards.

He'd been cable jumper during the laser-milling of the asteroid, when they put her into a free fall spin and milled her just as though she were in a lathe. He'd listened to the jokes about Trail Duster's Folly, and he'd laughed with the crews, but he'd believed in the hulk, and it had been pure magic to him, seeing the rounded, wad-cutter bullet form take shape.

They couldn't do *this* on Earth, he had exulted to himself, watching the jutting crags and the jagged irregularities cut smooth by the knifing of the huge laser beams as the hulk rolled gently and smoothly in the "jaws" of its inertial lathe, and the steel-strong, smooth squat form of the hulk that was to be a scoop ship began to seem strangely akin to his own squat form. Squat but powerful. The changing G's that his mother had met while she carried him had formed his own body, smooth, blunt and powerful, as the lasers were forming the shining irregular chunk of nickel steel before him. The squashing he had undergone had not squandered the strength inherent in his structure, any more than the lasers were squandering the strength of the asteroid they milled so delicately. *We both came out better for the treatment,* he told himself, and to him the *Phoenix* became the symbol of all that was powerful, though misshapen by Earth standards, in the Belt.

By the time the *Phoenix* hull was formed and the milling began that would make nests for 144 K-class ships at her back—the power structure for the bullet—Tobey had been made foreman of a small crew, doing part of that milling. The waffle-like structure that would nest the K-classers was to him the epitome of beauty; a powerful nesting that would give the *Phoenix* a 144-ship boost into high acceleration. The ships would cut loose just before they hit Jupiter's atmosphere, would cut around, and would catch her on the far side, nesting in again to take the scoop ship on to Io.

The tanks that went into the otherwise solid steel of the nose area, and the plugs that would open or close those tanks, were the work of other men; but the tanks were small in diameter and deep in length, and the delicate job of milling the interconnecting tubing from tank to tank was Tobey's; for by then he was one of the most skilled of the laser-lathemen of the Belt. During the building of the long corridors, cabins, common rooms and life support systems that filled the *Phoenix* backsides, Tobey was crewmaster.

It was when the *Phoenix* was almost finished that Trail Duster had made him supervisor of the project. It had been a proud day; but it had been less than a week later that he and the crew had been called off.

"The *Phoenix* has got to wait," the red-headed director of AT had told him. "Earth is interdicting the rest of the system to Belters; we've got us a war to fight."

Instead, he'd been supervising the reworking of every K-class that could be called in—the 144 scheduled to power the *Phoenix,* along with most of the privately owned ships of the Belt. There'd been little time and great fervor, and he'd worked the crews until they dropped, given them a bit of rest, and started them back on the job again.

It was when he said "ready" that Trevor had said "go," and the Belter War of Independence had been underway.

Things had changed then, with Trevor Dustin dead. Things had changed and stayed changed; and the old *Phoenix* had drifted there in the yards, fifteen miles from the nearest ship, a sort of stationary anchor point that defined one back corner of the yard—too big to move and too tied up in corporate policy to use; a vast, monumental junk pile, according to the new powers-that-be at the Ace Shipyards of Astro Technology.

Now Tobey stared from the orders in his hand to the man who had brought the orders to him.

"You're Star Duster," he said fiercely. "I heard you'd gone all-out for the new AT setup."

"Yep," said Stan. "I reckoned you'd heard."

"And you're going to refurbish the *Phoenix?* Finish her?"

"Yep," said Stan. "I reckoned you might have heard that too."

"Okay." Tobey's voice was far from friendly. "I'll get a foreman and a crew together. How fast a job you planning?"

"A couple of months. Maybe three."

Tobey whistled. "Well," he said slowly, "she was nigh onto finished when we dropped her. We might could. Where you going to get the K-class? One hundred forty-four of them?" he asked, his voice soft, not dangerous, just soft.

"Don't reckon we'll get more than fourteen," Stan said, and waited.

"Humph," said Tobey, and stayed silent. Then, "You won't boost her very fast with fourteen," he said cruelly. "I'll get on her, Mr. Dustin." He turned to the door of his small office, opened it, then flung back over his shoulder, "You sure are trying on big britches for an Earthie."

"I sure am trying on big britches for the son of a Belter," Stan said softly.

Tobey stood with his hand on the door for a long minute, then turned slowly back into the office and closed the door softly behind him. He came to stand beside the slender, red-haired figure seated in the chair beside his desk; his powerful hands hanging limp at his sides.

"I haven't given you a fair, have I?" he asked.

"No," said Stan. "I didn't really expect you to; but I was hoping." Then he added, "I guess you're giving me a fair now. Will you talk a minute?"

Tobey nodded and seated himself at his desk. "Trail Duster," he said, "was . . . well, he was Mr. Belt. And I guess I didn't like it when they called you Star Duster."

"That was the propaganda machine at AT," said Stan. "I gotta let them keep it up, too."

"Gotta?"

"Gotta. If we want . . . Tobey, let's start out by scotching some of the rumors you've heard. Not the propaganda. You can scotch that or not as you like. It's a machine product and most buy it, but some don't. I don't think you buy it. But the rumors—that's something else again.

"All right. Rumor number one: The *Phoenix* is a rich boy's play toy. That one's true. If I weren't rich, I certainly couldn't have it. Trevor made me rich by giving me his shares in AT. But the *Phoenix* is going to be used. Not just as a base here, or for scooting around the Belt having fun, but to go out and do the job she was intended to do. As soon as you can get her outfitted, we'll be taking off for Jupiter; and we'll be taking a complement of science personnel with us. If you find that you can go along with an idea like that, I'd be glad to have you aboard."

"Not with fourteen K-class for power, you're not going to do the job. Takes a hundred forty-four K-class to boost the *Phoenix* at three-G, and you'll not be safe around Jupiter with less than a three-G drive. Fourteen K-class would give you about a point-three-G drive."

"Couldn't do it with that, hunh? Yes, I know we couldn't. However, we *could* run a scoop operation that way if we took our bloody time about it. It's velocity that counts around Jupiter, not necessarily drive thrust. If we wanted to take, say, a hundred and thirteen to slow her down, and take a chance that our aiming was just right, we could do a dive with fourteen K-class." He watched the other narrowly.

Tobey nodded, his expression still hard. "You could," he said coldly. "That what you're planning?" Then he went on without waiting for an answer: "You're right that speed's the important thing. And you figured that time just like out of an Earthie textbook. But you got to do better'n that. There are a few other vectors to add in. Like original velocity, old Jupe's orbital speed, and whether or not you want to come to a complete stop relative to whatever you pick out to come to a complete stop relative to."

Stan grinned to himself while he kept his face stern. The guy was hopping mad now, but at least he was listening. "And if I planned to do it that way, then that's how I'd figure," he said. "However, I was only pointing out that it would be possible, so I made the figures more or less arbitrary. From the pragmatic point of view I *don't* think that's a possible method, because I'm quite sure that AT won't play ball. I figure on getting fourteen K-class all right—and that's all I figure on. But I don't figure on keeping even those fourteen, because I expect that the powers at AT plan to let those K's boost me into a Hohmann orbit, and then they plan to yank them back. All of them. On that schedule, if they figure a true Hohmann orbit, I should get to Jupiter in about six years and, if I do, I could consider that I was a lucky son of a . . . a Belter. One way or another, though, that would serve AT's purpose and get me out of their hair quite effectively for a bit, wouldn't you think?"

Stan eyed the other speculatively for a moment. "And now," he continued coldly, "I have just put my life in your hands."

Tobey's face was slowly losing its hard lines as he chewed the problem over before answering. Then, slowly, a grin crept out and his eyes began to twinkle. "Yep," he said, "I guess you have at that—if the story reads the way you're telling it. If AT is using the *Phoenix* to get you out of their hair, and you're on to it, then if I tell 'em you're on to it . . ."

Stan grinned back at the square-set yard supervisor. "Now let's try rumor number two," he said quietly. "The one that says I'm happy with AT. That one's true too. I'm happier than hell with AT. I'm not very happy with how it's being run, or where it's going under present management—but AT isn't going that way much longer, nor will it be run by those boobs much longer."

Tobey slid down into his desk chair and leaned back happily. "Hell," he said, "I could get killed in an accident just for listening to you. I hear you good, Star. What's the plan?"

"Well." Stan picked up pencil and pad. "Obviously the *Phoenix* has got to have her own power system, independent of the K-class. And obviously it will have to be installed without AT knowing she's got it."

Tobey raised one eyebrow. "She's a one hundred twelve gigaton mass, Star. If you've got a drive for her, you've got what they *know* to be impossible You could install it in front of their noses and they wouldn't believe it. Don't know as I would either," he added.

"Then take a look and see what you think." Stan began sketching rapidly. "While you're refitting the *Phoenix*, could you whomp up a Tesla coil system like this"—he continued to sketch—"that reacts with the first nuclear resonance level of a lithium hydrogen reaction?" Swiftly he drew lines on a skeletalized outline of the *Phoenix*. "We could feed hydrogen in here . . . and lithium through . . . here. The plasma reaction center will be contained by an alternating field effect. And we sweep the reaction products out by supplying the hydrogen under pressure. We should wind up with a tight little fusion reactor which would put out plenty of power, I'd think. Plenty. Even for a gigaton mass like the *Phoenix*."

Tobey was staring at the sketch. "I'll be damned," he said, slowly. "Well, I'll be damned." He looked up at Stan with respect. "Now why couldn't I have thought of that one? A Tesla drive." Then his face clouded. "But look, a drive like that will sure push the *Phoenix* around the system. But, Star, it sure will be lethal to anything that gets in its wash. And the yards—they'll be the first things in that wash."

Stan nodded. "That's why we've got to get those K-class aboard. We've got to hold this—well, you're right; it's a Tesla drive—until we've got distance. Use the K's to boost us away from the Belt."

"But, look, Star. With that drive, you ought to be able to pick up your own fuel on the way, if you had a magnetic pickup system. There's plenty of fuel in the solar wind to be picked up with a proper focusing mechanism. You could use this drive as a matchstick, say, to light a little hydrogen fusion candle at some distance behind your tail, which would be held in place by the focusing coils that collected the protons. It would make a real good ramjet."

Stan frowned, then his face cleared and brightened. "By damn, you're right. And you could make a magnetic lens, set up external field coils like this. . . ." He sketched rapidly, pulled more paper to him, sketched some more, Tobey following his outline and sketching in details of his own. Finally, *"That,"* he said, "should set us up a magnetic effect that would trap all the hydrogen a drive could use, and funnel it into a nice little hydrogen reaction sun at about twenty-five miles off the stern. Right?"

Tobey went over the sketch again, drawing out the fields with his finger, seeming awed even at the touch of the sketch. Then, "It works," he said. "With that nickel-steel hull for a core, I expect we can get plenty of magnetic field for that system. Why, you could drive anything with that. Not just the *Phoenix*. You could . . . you could drive a small planet with that, and keep its sun right handy behind it . . ."

Stan leaned back, staring at Tobey. "A planet," he said softly. "A small planet. With its own sun. Tobey, that's the answer to the quasars. Some people said they might be planets with their own drives, going space-hopping. And they were right. Tobey, we're going to the stars. Not just the system. The *stars*."

"With the *Phoenix*?" Tobey seemed nonplussed.

"Hell, no, not with the *Phoenix*. There's one little point in the Einstein equations that makes it pretty damned important to take a good-sized ship load when you go, you know; and to take along conditions under which a man can lead a fairly normal life. With a drive designed like this, we could get to Galaxy Center in twenty-one years. Take a year to build up to light speeds, then we cross the galaxy in no time. But that's nothing, shipboard time. If you go out one hundred thousand light-years in a ship and then come back . . . Well, there's two hundred thousand years of history has happened between you and the time you left. It's fun to think about. But without enough people along that speak your language, and without a home base that you can tolerate to stay on, it might get pretty damned upsetting.

"No, Tobey. This makes it possible, and we're going to the stars. But not on the *Phoenix*. We were going to set up Io as a colony—shucks, we'll set her up as a good-sized Galactic Scoutship. With what you might call a Tesla Tesseract drive. Call it a Teslaract drive for short . . ."

Tobey considered this quietly for a long time. Then his face creased back into a huge grin. "A Teslaract drive—and a planet for a ship. Yep. I buy that."

Then he leaned forward. "Now," he said brusquely, "I reckon that takes care of the long-range planning. But before we get to Jupiter to get to Io to build our Scoutship, we need the *Phoenix*. And we need to get her ready before AT gets hep or changes its mind. So we can . . ."

It was several hours before the two of them drew back from pages of sketches, satisfied that the preliminary work for the immediate project was well underway.

Leaning back in his chair, Tobey nodded to himself,

watched the satisfied expression on Stan's face. "I'll start getting that crew together tonight," he said.

"Picked crew, Tobey. All of them information-tight. But just in case there's a spy . . ."

"There won't be any spies, Star."

Stan looked at the other, realized he meant it, nodded. "Okay. But, Tobey, take my word for one thing: no gold belts. Not on your crew. Don't trust a gold belt unless I give you the word to trust him. Okay?"

"I know about gold belts, Star. What I don't know is why you're wearing a gold belt."

Stan looked down at it ruefully. "Yeah," he said. "I'm wearing one. And it's going to be a proud thing to wear one of these days. I think I've got some answers. But until I'm sure I'm right, don't trust a gold belt. I guess that's got to include me, too, doesn't it?"

They both laughed, but Stan thought there was still a hollow sound behind that laugh.

VIII

TIME. Time was the factor both at the Ace Yards and in the rim area at Belt City where Lang and Stan were putting forty of AT's top gold-belters through a system of study that was more strenuous than any of them had ever thought he could attempt.

Weed had almost laughed when Stan brought him the list of the gold-belters that he wanted prioritied to his project; had spent long hours using the strongest command techniques he could dream up, but Stan had been adamant, and the theory of the "stronger loyalty of the trust I hold" overrode the other's objections.

"He's getting his money's worth in loyalties from the Belters," Stan told Lang grimly. "The propaganda's working. But I don't think he'll let the gold belts I've picked actually take off with the *Phoenix*. Not without a fight. I guess that gives us the timing of whatever move he plans against us."

Retraining the gold-belters was a touchy question in itself. That they were being questioned in their off-hours by Weed and his gang, Stan was sure. Therefore they could not be allowed to know what was being done, nor why; nor could the hypnotic commands themselves be touched, for those would be specifically tested. They could not be touched until after they were aboard the *Phoenix*. Not even in Paulsen.

What they could do was reclaim the straight educational information the students had been fed, put it under the students' own control. So the schooling this time was thorough, but of an opposite form to what they'd had before. The gold-belters were put through a system of personalized study as intense as it could be made; and the testing that ended each day demanded of each facts from the areas in which he'd been studying that day, brought out in questions which were designed to draw on background facts that had been molecularly transplanted into their memories during the old schooling. Over and over Lang insisted, "Give us as much background information as possible with your answers."

Only in Sandra could the hypnotic commands be pulled and canceled; but the work with Sandra was sufficient to make Stan and Lang feel sure they had the techniques by which it could be done for all the students as soon as it was safe to do so.

Between trying to resolve the technical details at the school and the technical details at the yard, Stan felt as though he was putting himself through a course of study more intense than he'd ever attempted in his own education.

Once he carefully invited one of the gold-belters that he knew to be questioned by Weed to go with him to the *Phoenix*. "I've got to go over her stem to stern," he told the man. "Want to go along?"

The idea had worried Tobey, but it worked out as Stan had hoped. "He's got the preconceived notion that we're K-class powered. He won't be looking for a drive. He won't see it."

As it worked out, the man obviously looked at the obvious, unobtrusively looked for the unobvious, and asked questions that were intelligent enough, but that could be answered quite truthfully. By the time they reached the nose, Stan quit worrying and could put his own attention on an actual inspection for himself.

Time. The three months originally predicted passed, and the work went on. Two more months passed, and although everybody was at stretch, both jobs nearing completion, the work was not done. Then in the middle of the sixth month, Stan got Tobey on a tight beam channel.

"Tobey," he said, choosing his words with care, "it's gotta be go. Now. Say, three days."

Tobey chewed his lip. Then, "Yeah," he said. "I'm getting the signals too. Okay, it's go. Three days. Make it seventy-two hours from now."

"Right. And, Tobey, clear your crew from the B for baby crew area as of now. And seal it off from the A and C areas, but leave the corridors from the locks and officers' country open."

Tobey raised one eyebrow quizzically, but all he said was "Right," and without another word Stan signed off. Then he called Paulsen up to the monitor's desk from which he was supervising the work going on in forty cubicles.

"Is the *Sassy Lassie* fueled?" he asked, knowing that it was.

"Sure, boss," said Paulsen.

"Fine. So is my *Erika Three*. I'm canceling classes. Can you lift twenty-two out to Ace Yards?"

"When? Now? Give me a couple of hours to get food aboard and duffel . . ."

"No food. No duffel. Right now. The *Phoenix* is just twelve hours from here."

"Fourteen with a load like that."

"Fourteen hours from here. Our gold belts have never seen her. Thought we'd just jaunt over and take a look. You take Dr. Lang and half the class. I'll take Sandra and the other half."

"Just jaunt over, take a look and jaunt back? Thought you'd wait until we were ready to move aboard, then spend a couple of weeks aboard familiarizing."

"Yeah." Stan leaned back in the monitor's seat, relaxed and smiling. "That's what I plan. But a looksee in the meantime . . . I don't know. I figure they're getting a little stale and a little impatient. A jaunt out there would break the monotony. Where you tied up?"

"Tube one-eleven."

"Okay. Don't even tell them where we're going. Let it be

a surprise. Call them all in here, cancel all classes. I'll order up enough strut-cars, and we'll take off."

Stan, with his half of the class, reached the *Phoenix* first, sent Sandra to the bridge, the gold-belters along to Common Room B.

Having seen that his part of the class was safely in the common room, Stan stationed himself by the nest assigned to the *Sassy Lassie*. As soon as that ship was maglocked in, he made his way through the air locks.

"Turn off all circuits now," he told Paulsen.

Paulsen started to obey in reflex, then his hand hesitated on the switch. "Hadn't I better leave her on standby?" he asked.

"Not this time," said Stan in a voice of authority, and before Paulsen could object further he'd pulled himself back out of the air lock into the corridor.

When Katsu Lang and Paulsen, with the first of the gold-belters immediately behind them, pulled through into the corridor, Stan was waiting.

"Dr. Lang," he said, "you go on through to the bridge. Sandra's waiting for you there. Paulsen, you and your men gather in Common Room B. It's right down that corridor," he said, pointing.

Then he waited again until the last of the gold-belters was into the corridor before turning and closing the bulkhead behind them, activating bolts that would seal it off until someone released them from the bridge. Following the men, now, to the common room assigned them, he quickly counted to be sure they were all there, then climbed on a table, gesturing for them to gather around him.

"We are leaving," he told them firmly, "almost immediately." There was an instant clamor, which he silenced with a raised hand. "We will have two weeks on board to become familiar with how this ship works. By the time we reach Jupiter orbit, we will either know that we have around us a good sound ship and a good working crew, or that we should turn back. I have no intention of turning back," he added. Then, "If we win, we will be opening a colonly about the size of Earth's moon, and our next step will be the stars. If we lose—well, that won't mean much to anybody but us.

"I brought you aboard by surprise," he said into a quiet

that was the first reaction to shock, "because we have enemies. Those enemies will try to stop us. You are aboard and will stay aboard. I will talk to you again before we go under thrust."

With that he jumped down from the table and made his way to the bulkhead toward officers' country. He had crossed the bulkhead and secured it behind him before anyone had recovered sufficiently to try to stop him.

Now they were locked in. The best brains of AT kidnapped right out from under Weed's nose and secured in a nickel-steel prison in space.

Stan reached the bridge to find Tobey and two of his crew waiting with Sandra and Katsu Lang.

"Have you got two men who can handle a K-class?" Stan asked Tobey without preliminary.

"Any one of us can, Star," Tobey answered.

"Okay. Put them on the *Erika* and the *Sassy Lassie*. We've got to use them to swing the *Phoenix* so she's at right angles to the yard. We may have to take off on own drive power, and I don't want to crisp the docks."

Tobey looked at him quizzically. "I just got word that our fourteen K-class are on their way," he said. "I gather ETA about eight hours."

"In that case, let's get the *Phoenix* swung just as fast as we can. It may take a few hours to position her right, and I want her swung and the men onboard before those K's arrive."

"You really think Weed will make a move to take over the ship instead of letting us take off?" Lang asked.

Stan looked at the Mentor in surprise. "Of course. He's got to. He's not planning to lose his forty top goldies! He'd do it even to keep from losing Tobey's crew, but it hasn't occurred to him they're vulnerable.

"No," Stan went on, "he's got to make his move now. We took him by surprise, loading the belters aboard, and he's off balance, but he'll move. I expect those fourteen K's are loaded to the gills with soldiers, and we'll be in the middle of a first-class war in about eight hours.

"But meantime, Dr. Lang, you and Sandra can start setting up Common Room A for the de-hypnosis techniques. You can't start the actual work until after the war, but, assuming we win, I can free up a few men then to help you. You can get the place ready now, and you'll have two weeks on the way to Jupiter to do the job."

When the fourteen K-class ships showed, flying a tight pattern, it was Tobey himself who talked them into the nests, assigning each one its berth and berthing time, yakking informally but with authority to the pilots, screening each one of them as he gave them instructions, and getting each one into a pattern of communication as he worked.

As the third ship magnalocked in, he switched his screen off and spoke to Stan, who was carefully out of range of the video.

"The pilots are alone in the control cabins," he said, "but I rather think you're right that there are other men aboard. Probably fifteen to twenty per ship."

Stan grinned crookedly. "It's a fair bet there are," he said.

"And, Star . . . these men are Earthies. There's not a Belter pilot aboard."

"Oh?" Stan paused. "You sure?"

"Hell no, I'm not sure," Tobey said. "But I'd lay odds on it."

Stan nodded. Then said, "If you can spot the command ship, bring it in last."

"I think I've got it spotted, and it even seems to be maneuvering to be last in. Okay."

Paulsen switched the screen back on and the process of talking the ships in continued. As the last ship was berthed there was a long pause, then Tobey's screen lighted to show the pilot of the final ship.

"Control officer," the man said grimly, "the locks aren't opening. What is the problem?"

Tobey raised his head to the screen as though from concentrated effort. "I don't know," he said. "I was just trying to find out. I seem to be having some trouble with the magnalock system."

"Well, get it fixed and let us out," the voice said sternly.

Tobey left the screen on while he busied himself over the control console, biting on his lips in a gesture of vexation. Then he turned again to the screen.

"Have your pilots shut down all circuits for a minute," he said. "I'm going to send a power surge through the magnalock system to see if I can free it, but it might be enough to blow a weak circuit in a ship, and it'd be better if they were off."

"Who are you?" the man on the screen demanded fiercely.

Tobey looked at him in surprise. "Tobey Olsen," he said finally. "Supervisor of the Ace Yards. Who are you?"

"Is Dustin aboard?" the man asked.

Tobey raised one eyebrow as though considering whether to object to the brusque treatment, then shrugged his shoulders. "I believe Mr. Dustin is with his crew and scientific personnel. They are"—his voice held a very light sarcasm—"familiarizing themselves with the ship. If it will make you happier, I can have him called to the bridge."

"No. No, leave him to his toys. Very well. I'll have my men come off standby for a minute."

"Fine," said Tobey. "I'll give it a shot. If that doesn't work, I'll have to send a man down to open the locks manually."

There was a pause while the pilot on the screen spoke into an intercom system. Then, "Very well, Olsen. All ships except this one have shut down, and I'm doing so now." There was a click and the screen went blank.

Instantly Tobey threw the switch that would send a surge of one hundred thousand gauss through each of the magnalocks to which the ships were joined—enough locking energy to hold the ships against a ten-G thrust; and enough stray magnetism to prevent the operation of any radio or electric motor on board. The fourteen K's were locked on, silenced, frozen in place, and helpless.

Then Tobey turned to Stan. "Your birds are secure, Star," he said. "Sure you don't want to just leave them aboard their ships? For a little, anyhow, until they learn who's boss?"

"No," said Stan. "Best we continue the operating procedure and get them the hell out of our way." Taking his seat at his own console, he activated a screen in the corridor outisde the locks. Tobey's twenty men were standing there, fully armed and at the ready.

Tobey had already activated his own screen and was speaking to his men. "Looks like what we've got aboard those ships is about twenty Earthie soldiers per," he said. "Think you can handle 'em?"

He was greeted with a roar of pleasure.

"Okay," he said. "Start with Lock Two. And boys," he

added, "leave lock one-forty-four until last. That one's got the command personnel aboard."

Stan watched, forcing back the tension that threatened to keep him from a clear head, as Tobey's crew began hand-manipulating the inner lock. This one they opened all the way, then five of them disappeared within. The outer lock would be opened only far enough for one man to squeeze through, according to plan, and . . .

He could hear shouts and mumblings and a long time passed, but finally one man stumbled out of the lock into the arms of the waiting crew, followed a minute later by a small arsenal of personal weapons. The man was frisked again in the corridors, then shoved toward C section by one of Tobey's men, who held a gun to his back. Watching the man closely, Stan realized that Tobey had been right: these men were Earthies. He wasn't sure just what small clues gave the man away, but the Earthie background showed plainly.

Another followed, and another. It was a slow process.

When fifteen had come through, one of the crewmen came out and called toward the screen: "They say that's all of them."

"Don't believe it," Tobey answered. "Tell the rest they've got just three minutes to come out, then we're going to sleep-gas their ship and seal it. They'll be there for at least two weeks, if they want to spend that long in suits."

There was a pause, and Tobey began timing it. At the end of the three minutes he called again: "Come on out, boys. Then sleep-gas that one and seal it."

Emptying the second ship was a similar task, but it seemed to go faster. Tobey's crew was getting familiar with the operation. There were sixteen out this time before word came that that was all.

This time Tobey changed his command. "Take the last man out of that ship, send him into the other to see that we meant what we said. Then send him back for any more men that may be in his ship."

The last man out, disarmed and disheveled from a thorough search for small arms, was brought up, given a low pressure suit and a diox shot, and the lock on the first was unsealed. Five crewmen disappeared into the lock with him. Several minutes passed, then the Earthie came running from the lock, holding his arm, followed shortly by the five crewmen. One addressed the screen while the others sealed the lock.

"They thought he was one of us," Tobey was told succinctly. "They shot at him."

"Good." Tobey's voice was grim. "Now send that man back into his own ship, and let him tell them the story."

Shortly, from the second lock, men began appearing again, until the ship had disgorged twenty. When word came that that was all, Tobey instructed his men to use the wounded man as a shield, and go in to search the ship. It was all clear.

It took hours, but the crews came out, until they reached the final ship.

"Before you tackle that one," Tobey instructed, lines of strain showing around his grim mouth, "have one of the men from the first crew write a note. Get it shoved through the lock to the men in the first ship. See if they want to take advantage of a final offer, or if they prefer to stay where they are at our convenience, which will be a long time coming."

This time the remaining five men capitulated, and the only ship still unsealed was that one nested in 144.

"Now," said Tobey, "bring out the wounded man from that second ship. He's had first aid? Good. Send him through, alone, into the command ship, and have him explain the situation. If they want to capitulate, they can come out the way the others have—one at a time. If not, they stay where they are, and we sleep-gas the ship."

The man went in and the minutes passed. It seemed to Stan that time stood still. The inner lock on the 144 stood open; five of Tobey's crew were inside the lock. The outer lock was, presumably open enough to admit one man.

Finally the wounded man came out, was searched and sent on to Area C. Stan found himself holding his breath until a second man came out and the former process was on again.

The twentieth man out this time was in full Earth uniform, and Stan caught his breath as the men of Tobey's crew turned him this way and that, searching him as thoroughly as the others but, Stan noted, with a care that showed a deference for his insignia.

It was the general, Stan realized. The general that he had

met once before, in Professor Mallard's office in the school on Earth.

"Bring the general to the bridge," he heard himself saying.

IX

THE GENERAL was seated on the far side of the desk from Stan; Tobey's man, Jarl, was lounging in the doorway with a stun gun, where he could keep a close eye on him. Tobey himself was seated against the wall.

If the general noticed the guard he gave no indication; he merely began to raise the hand that held a signet ring, to place it on the desk where Stan could see it. Stan let his own eyes follow it. Then, in a voice of authority, the general spoke: "I, the trainer, speak. You obey."

From the corner of his eye Stan saw Tobey jerk forward, Jarl draw himself up, but he gestured to them both.

"Never mind," he said. "It doesn't work on me." Then, to the general: "Remember? I'm the robot who refused to robe."

The general smiled, twisting the ring on his finger. "It always did seem a little too pat to me, Dustin. Very well. For the present at least, it seems to be your move." He looked up, the smile gently twisting his lips.

Stan found himself admiring the man. A professional to the fingertips. "What do you mean, 'for the present at least'?" he asked.

The general relaxed into his seat, but the motion in no way decreased the basic military exactness of his bearing. "I could, of course," he said genially, "stand on my right to give you my name, rank and serial number and to refuse other information. But that seems hardly justified in"—he stared slowly around him, at Tobey, at the small cabin—"congenial circumstances. Instead I should prefer simply to tell you that I am authorized to give you clearance to Jupiter to continue your mission."

Stan nodded to himself. "That's why you brought two hundred and eighty men to board me—fully armed?" he asked.

"Oh, we didn't plan to let you take the gold-belters along. But I think we might have spared you fourteen pilots to K-boost you to orbit. Then you and Dr. Lang and the young lady could have remained aboard. Paulsen was to be allowed to remain as well."

"Thanks," said Stan. "Kindly of you, I suppose."

"You'd have had the *Sassy Lassie*. You could possibly have made something of the trip."

Stan laughed. The general looked at him thoughtfully.

"I think, however, that under present circumstances . . ." He allowed his voice to drop, then continued. "Since things have taken a different turn from that which we, ah, expected, I have sufficient authority to allow you to proceed with your gold-belters, and to keep the K's, once you have put my men"—he paused, and sketched a glance at Tobey, over his shoulder at the guard—"and Olsen's, down at the docks."

Stan smiled gently. "General," he said, "I must admit that you have gained my sincere admiration. It takes real guts, sir, to sit here in my office, my prisoner, and try to make terms that will set you safely back in the Belt. Earthies in the Belt," he said softly. "Earthie soldiers in the Belt. You took off from Belt City," he added.

The general looked at him speculatively. "A small garrison," he said nonchalantly. "Available. So we used them."

"We?"

The general shrugged. Stan's face grew hard. "Weed," he said at last. "He took over AT so easily. I should have guessed. A tool of Earth?" The general's face remained bland, and Stan went on, "And he is the one who has been beating the drums for war with Earth—a war that the Belt was scheduled to lose. A fleet war that would be backed up by a fifth column in the Belt."

He waited, but the general remained silent.

"A small garrison, you say. Then you'd have been depending on a certain number of gold-belters in key points of control . . . hmm. I *did* upset your plans by kidnapping this particular forty, didn't I?"

He stared at the general, who had fixed his attention on the ceiling.

"Well," said Stan. "Well." Then he leaned forward and keyed the intercom to the bridge. When the screen lighted, he said, "Get the Belt News Service on the wire and ask where Earth Fleet is currently maneuvering." Then he leaned back and waited. The general's face had gone from red to white and was now coloring again.

It was several minutes before the word came through. "Last reports, sir, believed correct to about twenty-four hours ago: Earth in Gemini Sector and the fleet is reported maneuvering Beltward of Earth."

Stan switched off and turned to Tobey. "That puts Earth Fleet a bit over two weeks from Belt City at top acceleration. We should have at least that long before Weed is convinced that the general and his forces are irretrievably gone. He'll think that the general is using the K's to boost us to a Hohmann orbit as planned before coming back. It won't occur to him that we could knock out a force of two hundred and eighty Earth soldiers, especially when he thinks our goldies are under hypnotic control of the general, and that you're just aboard, Tobey.

"So I'd think we have at least two weeks before Weed can be convinced and can convince Earth that their schedule is shot to pieces, their cover is blown, and that they'd better scrap their timetable and attack on a crash priority basis; plus two weeks to get to the Belt. That gives us, say, twenty-eight days, plus or minus a few to go to Jupiter, and get back to intercept Earth Fleet."

Suddenly the general's voice rose to a bellow: "Surely you don't think this"—his voice choked off and his arm waved around to indicate the ship—"this *ramscoop* hunk could take on Earth Fleet? What do you think you are, a one-ship Goliath protecting the entire Belt orbit with a nickel-steel canister that doesn't even mount a cannon?"

Instead of answering, Stan turned to the guard in the doorway. "Jarl," he said, "quarter the general in one of the officer's suites under constant guard, one outside the suite, one inside with him. Take even the door to the fresher down. He is not to be by himself for one minute. It'll tie up some men," he added, "but I think it's a good idea."

As the guard left with the general, Stan turned to the plug-heavy figure in the chair by the wall. "Tobey," he said, "we'll get going as fast as you can assign your men to jobs. The *Phoenix* is a ramscoop . . . uh, canister," he added grimly, "and it's time she started cannoning."

Tobey nodded, grinning. "It's a picked crew, Star. They can handle."

The banded face of Jupiter was glaring in the control cabin screen, its fluorescence like a varicolored neon sign, with not one whit of surface detail visible from whatever might lie below the neon glow of the upper atmosphere.

The hoot that sounded action stations went out over the intercom, dulled to a distant murmur in the control cabin.

"Main drives off. Relative velocity to be monitored continuously. Inertial guidance . . ."

The ship was now on its own. Without drive, it was falling like a rock toward the huge planet below, aimed nearly directly for the equatorial belt and just toward the edge of the disk in a plotted flight that would take it around the curve to the east. The chunk of nickel-steel that was the *Phoenix* would penetrate the atmosphere with a fantastic velocity, until the craft was gradually slowed in the thick friction of the hydrogen gas.

The G-needle climbed and climbed, and the droning voice that had been counting the seconds and the relative velocity had now switched over to reading G's.

Without moving his attention a hair's breadth from the control panel before him, Stan ordered, "Close the valves and activate the repulsion field."

"Aye, sir."

In the nose of the ship the huge tank plug was snapped into place by a magnetic field; and the gases forced through the radiator surface of the first compression tank began trickling out as liquids into the subsidiary tanks.

Then, almost as suddenly as it had come, the G-force dropped, the control room swung slowly on its gimbals to take up a new position oriented toward the planet they had passed. The lightest of tidal forces, less than a tenth of a G, was still tugging them back; but they were clear of the atmosphere and back in space.

Another G-force appeared as the drive tubes went into action and the control cabin swung once again on its gimbals, oriented now stern-drive in the normal manner of drive acceleration.

Stan smiled grimly. "And now we have a tight ship with a proved crew and full tanks of compressed liquid gas. We can go hunting."

X

STAN COULD only guess at Earth Fleet's course. It was purely a guess, and like a game of chess, the number of other moves that Earth Fleet might make formed an astronomical figure. Yet, like chess, those moves were limited to the area of the board, as long as the goal was Belt City and a war to destroy the independence of the Belt.

And it had to be Belt City, for the Belt would be won or lost there; and Belt City was where the Earth garrison of troops would be hidden.

Yet searching space by guesswork to locate the blinkers that would identify a fleet in motion was playing tag blindfolded in the dark, Stan knew. The search would have to be narrowed to a comparatively minute sector for there to be any hope of success.

When he took the problem to Tobey, the answer was immediate.

"Hell," said Tobey, "me and the crew, we know almost every skipper in the Belt . . . and Belt ships are all over the place. I'll send out word we want to know where Earth Fleet is. We'll get it."

"But Tobey! The fleet will be on radio silence and deep secret maneuvers."

"Won't make a nevermind," Tobey snorted. "There's no fleet made that can keep its whereabouts secret if you've got enough eyes watching from enough places."

But as the *Phoenix* sped on its swift flight sunward, the queries that sped ahead of it brought no satisfactory results. Rumors came back by the dozen; rumors that placed Earth Fleet all over the system. But no hard facts. Nothing on which to focus a camera.

Yet as the reports came in, the cameras went into action; and each sector named was filmed. After the twentieth report, Stan gave up sitting personally and looking at the blinking pattern of stars. Blinkers they spotted time after time, but blinkers that were normal Belt debris, either asteroids or ships, but no fleet.

And velocity and vectors, the basic factors of space flight, were drawing the deadline closer for any course change that would intersect—if the fleet was actually readying to attack Belt City.

Stan held himself calm on the bridge, but off duty he paced his office. Suppose Earth Fleet was refusing to react to the factors that *dictated* immediate action? he asked himself. No. They had to react now, or sacrifice the build-up of their garrison in Belt City. They had to react before the *Phoenix* returned to alert the Belt to the entire plot. They *had* to react. And the only sensible reaction was immediate attack. . . .

Then came an almost laconic message from a Belt prospector: "Bogies on my screen. Too far to be more than bogies. Could be a whish of asteroids out of orbit. But could be your fleet." The message was addressed to Tobey, who brought it instantly to Stan.

"Reckon that's them, Star?"

Stan stared at the message. "Who's your man, Tobey?"

"Prospector. A good one. He doesn't spook easy. When he says bogies, there are bogies. When he says they could be our fleet, he means there are enough of them and the characteristics are there. But he has no info on why they should be there; and they could be something else. So he's not about to commit himself."

"You think it's them?"

Tobey grinned. "I know damned well," he said. "Jim knows asteroids don't go out of orbit."

Hope surged through Stan as he and Tobey set up the computer for a view of the prospector's sector. As Tobey manipulated the computer, Stan manipulated the camera, swung it onto the target area and matched the stars on the videoscreen as projected by the camera against the stars on the videoscreen projected by the computer.

Blink, blink. For a few moments they were all blinking. And then with the fine controls of the camera, they phased gradually in until the stars burned steady and clear.

There were many blinkers left after the background steadied out, and then those began to disappear as the computer picked off and identified the normal orbits of asteroids, leaving only the non-standard orbits of ships.

Many of the ones that were left, Stan could disregard. They were obviously K-class, identifiable as much by their winking patterns as by their size. But there was one group left, unidentified; and these he magnified up to the very limits of the camera's ability, and then again up to the very limits of the ability of the electron screen to magnify the camera's image. The ghostly shapes were still mere pinpoints, but it was a group of at least twenty traveling in unison, and that, for Stan, was enough information.

For the next two hours, the *Phoenix* shifted back and forth across a line drawn from itself to the moving targets. The range was found, and the velocity; and it was very definite that its velocity would bring Earth Fleet to Belt City in fourteen days.

"We can just make it," Stan said, "with maybe two days to spare."

"Now hear this. Now hear this. All hands secure for high-G. Fifteen minutes."

Stan's eyes roved across the bridge as Paulsen's voice continued over the all-channel intercom, and his chin set slowly. He would have preferred to have Paulsen at the control officer's console. But not yet, he told himself. The hypnosis had been yanked; he was sure of it, and Lang had reassured him. Yet, not until there is absolute certainty, he told himself.

The other gold-belters thought themselves free now of confinement; but he had given orders to Jarl that once they had secured for high-G the bulkheads were to be secured without their knowledge, and the action reported to him.

"Area B secured, sir." It was Jarl's voice on his personal intercom.

"Thank you. Best you secure yourself for high-G now," he answered. Then to Paulsen, "Turn on screens and speakers throughout the ship so that every man, prisoner or crew, can watch and hear the action."

"Yes, sir," said Paulsen.

The minutes passed slowly, and the *Phoenix* hung directly in the course of the oncoming Earth Fleet with an orbital velocity that matched her fairly well to the Belt, though she was inside it.

Stan now addressed his first mate: "Mr. Barnes. Are they closing satisfactorily?"

"Yes, sir. They were all bunched up, but now they're beginning to spread out as though they plan to pass us in a ring pattern."

"Are they still decelerating?"

"No, sir. When they smoothed out into a ring, they began to let 'em drift."

"And we're still nose-on?"

"Yes, sir."

"Very well, Mr. Barnes. Operate the external proton beams to bring us up to ten KV negative charge." That would make the *Phoenix* negative in respect to Earth Fleet. Any metallic vapor discharged would be attracted to the fleet. Turning to the navigator's console where Tobey sat, relaxed, Stan saw him smiling, a grim smile with a fierceness tugging at the corners of his mouth, but a smile. Stan nodded quietly to himself and put his full attention on the screen before him. "Laser range?"

"Five minutes to laser." The voice became taut as Earth Fleet seemed to leap toward them.

"Count down to their range of firing, Mr. Barnes."

"Estimated countdown, sir, is four minutes; three; two; one. In seconds . . . thirty. Twenty. Ten. Nine, eight seven six. . . ."

The countdown passed zero and went to minus one, then minus two. . . .

There was a swirling glare that covered the forward viewscreens, but Barnes held the controls steady and Stan watched the second hand of the chronometer. Three seconds. Then a slight jar.

"Damage control, sir. They all bracketed the same center of the bow and penetrated number one tank. We've lost approximately fifteen hundred cubic feet of hull from that area, and tank pressure is falling over toward zero."

On the screen the cloud of roiling metallic vapor that had been solid nickel-steel was drifting away from the *Phoenix*, racing ahead of them. Then, at first mistily and then more solidly, Earth's fleet appeared, pulling through the cloud of vapor, but scattering wildly as though they had attempted to miss its outer edges.

But there had been no misses. Each ship emerged from the cloud as shiny as a newborn nickel. The viewscreen showed no damage, only a bright, shiny mirror-surface which had been plated on the normal dull-white of the Earth ships by the metal vapor in vacuum.

"Mr. Barnes. Put us on a braking course and maneuver as necessary to match velocities with the Earth Fleet. Set the course to maintain this distance."

"No ladar signals, sir." Paulsen's voice was strained as he handled the console above his couch.

On the screen, the circle of ships was drifting past them, and then seemed to rotate as Barnes brought the *Phoenix* around in a match-course maneuver.

Stan flipped his microphone onto another channel. "K-class pilots. Get your ships warmed up. You will be dropped as soon as we match orbits with Earth Fleet, and you will each guard a section of that fleet. Take no action unless an attempt is made to remove the mirror plating on those ships. If such an attempt is made, sting 'em till they blow."

"They don't seem to be operating very well, Star, those Earthies." Even Tobey's heavy-muscled throat seemed to be having trouble with the now constant four-G maneuvering thrust.

"Few ships operate well with all viewscreens, navigation equipment, and aiming devices out of service," Stan answered in what he had intended to be a dry tone, but what came out as a croak.

"That was the damnedest suckering move anybody ever pulled on them, Star." There was a satisfied note in the croaking voice. "I wouldn't be surprised if it didn't even seal their air locks."

"How about common old radio, Boss?" Paulsen asked. "Does it bother that, too?"

"It'll have plated out over the antenna insulators too, and grounded them to the ships." Stan frowned in concentration. "They do have a system which uses the whole ship as a half-wave dipole. They might still be able to get through on that. Mr. Paulsen, see if you can pick up Earth Fleet on the four-ninety to four-ninety-five kilohertz band."

Paulsen began twiddling the dials and snapping over switches, and after a few moments was rewarded with a thin, scratchy voice. ". . . peat. S.O.S. Flagship *Aurora*. We have been hit by a mirror bomb. Our circuits are . . ." The voice scratched and grew fainter, then came in more strongly. ". . . screens blank. We cannot maneuver. . . ."

"Very well, Mr. Paulsen. Break in on them."

"*Phoenix* to Earth Fleet. *Phoenix* to Earth Fleet." Paulsen's voice had reassumed the crisp duty-tone of the bridge.

There was silence elsewhere as Paulsen's voice intoned the call, a little louder than necessary, Stan realized, for the benefit of the intercom. *Listen good, you guys aft,* he thought. *Listen real good, all of you.*

Abruptly the speaker on Paulsen's console came to life. It was a weak life, and the voice was scratchy.

"Commodore Rimes to *Phoenix*. We read you."

Stan pulled a microphone to him, nodded to Pauslen to switch the call over. Then said, "Commodore Rimes, this is Star Dustin, Belt Commander. You are now blinded, and therefore I must warn you: you and your ships are safe only as long as you make no attempt whatsoever to send men onto the surface of any ship. Any ship on which figures appear will be blasted out of space. Otherwise, you will not be harmed."

"Commander Dustin, I hear you. We will give you our answer shortly." The voice was stronger now.

Stan grinned to himself. "Commodore Rimes," he said, "while you are considering your answer, you might consider the fact that it is within my power to hit you with a megaroentgen second blast from my drive tubes that would kill everything on board and sterilize your entire fleet. I do not plan to do so."

There was a pause before the answer came back: "Commander Dustin, I have no choice but to take you at your word when you say that you will *not* sterilize this fleet."

"There would be no point to senseless slaughter, sir."

"Then I accept your terms. We will send no men to the surface until further notice. However, Earth cannot be too long patient with piratical actions. I hope, Commander Dustin, that you will come to the *Aurora* immediately to discuss the situation."

"Commander Rimes," Stan said grimly, "Earth Fleet was on its way to take over the Belt when we intercepted. The Belt has no quarrel with Earth. It is Earth that is quarreling with the Belt. We will discuss the matter at our convenience, and will at that time ferry you over here. In the meantime you will be safe *only* as long as you keep your men inboard."

After he had switched off, Stan leaned back in his chair and rubbed his hand wearily over his eyes. Then he turned to Tobey. "Your K-pilots are not to harm any ship unless and until a man comes to the surface to repair damage. We don't want anybody taking out their desires for personal retribution."

Tobey nodded, his eyes on Stan.

"And, Tobey. Belt City will have to take care of Weed and whatever Earthie garrison he has stashed there. Can you alert them?"

"We'll take care of the cleanup job, Star," said Tobey quietly. "With Earth Fleet out of the way, there won't be too much of a problem in that. They'll be knocked out as soon as the boys on Belt City find out they're there. But, Star . . . I don't guarantee there won't be what you call personal retribution in that operation."

The general, Commander Rimes, Stan and Tobey sat around the small desk in Stan's office. Paulsen, Sandra and Dr. Lang sat silent against the walls.

The general, Stan noted, had lost none of his military bearing, and Stan found himself irrelevantly pleased with the fact. *There's a dignity about professional military men,* he told himself hopefully, *and perhaps some common sense. I'd hate to be dealing with Weed or Mallard,* he thought.

Then he turned to Commander Rimes and silently retracted the idea. Rimes was quite a different breed of cat, even though probably a professional. His bearing was arrogant rather than military; and he was carrying it to the point of insolence. Frustration, Stan decided; and guilt. Both show.

"You understand what has happened, gentlemen?" he asked, opening the conference.

It was the general who answered. "No," he said. "Not really. We know that you have knocked out a small army and then Earth Fleet. I am not trained as a physicist, Mr. Dustin; but I expect that the military will do well in the future to put physicists into prominent posts. It has been

—well, technological thinking, I suppose, by which the Belters have caught us by surprise each time."

Stan smiled and shook his head. "You don't need physicists, General. You need individualists. Mallard and Weed were trying to give you robots; and that was the worst sabotage anyone could have perpetrated upon you. It takes a man who has had to fight and win against his own hostile environment to be able to fight and win against the far less serious opposition of an army or a space fleet."

Commander Rimes spoke up brusquely. "Whatever we may need, Commander Dustin, you may be sure we will put our attention to it. Our question is, simply, what do you hope to accomplish now? With us?"

Stan looked him over carefully. "I hope," he said, "to accomplish bloodless cease-fire and surrender terms in which Earth admits the Belt's sovereignty and withdraws all future claim to control of the solar system."

The commander snorted. "You have, sir, in a rather simple technological maneuver, blinded Earth Fleet and now hold it helpless. You fooled me, Dustin. You won't fool us twice, of course. You have also, I gather, captured and now hold a small force of Earth soldiers, captured no doubt by some other unexpected system. But Earth herself is neither stupid nor helpless; nor do I think you can dictate surrender terms to her."

Stan raised one eyebrow, looking at the commander quizzically. "Earth is not helpless? Well, no. Earth is just scared," he said quietly. As the commander started an angry rejoinder, he continued, "Earth has been afraid of space since the first Sputnik back in the mid-Twentieth Century. Earth's establishment has used every weapon at its command, from the top secret label to murder and sabotage, to keep man *out of space* . . . because Earth is afraid of spacemen. And rightly so.

"But, gentlemen, *we* are spacemen. And Earth may fear us all she likes; she can no longer control us. The Belt will accept Mother Earth as an equal, but Belters will be no man's servants. Neither, as free men, do we wish to force Earth to her knees, although we are quite capable of doing so."

"Force Earth to her knees? Why, you pipsqueak commander of a one-ship armada, Earth does and must control the solar system. She—"

From the corner of his eye Stan saw Paulsen stiffen, saw Tobey half rise from his seat.

Quicker than either of the other two, he leaned forward and his voice overrode the commander's, his eyes fiercely boring into the—yes, frightened eyes, he realized—before him.

"You don't control any animal but a tame one, mister," he said, and his voice held the grimness of space. "And take this as a dictum: the men of the Belt are not tame—not to you, not to anybody. You don't tame space with tame men, mister.

"The Belt," he added slowly, "the Belt will not now, nor ever again, accept as much as a single gesture of domination from the tame men of Earth. And we have the means to back up our refusal."

Commander Rimes opened his mouth to answer angrily, but the general silenced him with a gesture, and it was the general who spoke quietly to Stan. "You have the means?"

Stan turned with relief to the professional calm of the other. Slowly he nodded. "We have the means," he said; and then he added bleakly, "It is a brutal means. We will not use it unless we are forced to do so. But neither will we let the weaklings of Earth use our ethical sense to enslave us. If Earth forces the question, we will not hesitate to be brutal."

Stan paused a minute, noting that the commander was holding himself in check only by obvious effort, then turned back to the general. "You've seen the *Phoenix* dive through atmosphere? On Jupiter, where the escape velocity is much higher than that of Earth?"

The general nodded, and Stan went on. "If this ship was taken to about five thousand feet and orbited Earth, only once, at say the forty-five degree parallel, do you know what would happen?"

The general answered slowly: "There would be a rather major disaster from shock wave, I assume; and the forty-five degree parallel would, of course, take you across the major population and governmental areas. . . ."

"Yes," said Stan. "Shock wave. But not just major shock wave damage, General, at the speeds at which this ship travels. Say a shock wave sufficiently deadly to kill anyone within five hundred miles on either side of the ground path zero. We wouldn't be breaking any nuclear test ban treaties. There would be no nucleonics involved whatsoever, other than the nucleonics of our drive. But the effect would be much the same.

"Where that shock wave touches ground, over a wide band, well . . . How much of Earth do you think would withstand a blast of upward of a million degrees of temperature? At that temperature, the very rocks would melt. And the ground zero path beneath that shock wave would be as sterilized as any desert you now have.

"I doubt very much that Earth is prepared to pay for attempted domination of the solar system by such a disaster."

The general's face had gone quite white.

The glowing veils of neon light with which Jupiter hides her face from the rest of the solar system danced and shimmered before them as Stan and Sandra stood outside on the nose surface of the huge wad-cutter bullet that was the *Phoenix*, staring up at the still distant but approaching planet.

"I knew it would be worth coming out to see it, but oh, Star, I didn't realize how truly beautiful it could be!" Sandra's voice, even over the speaker in his suit, throbbed with a joy that brought a catch to Stan's throat. Then she added, "It seems a shame to dive into that. Are you sure we won't spoil the beauty?"

"Not much." He looked down at her trim figure in the P-suit tights that outlined every curve and detail. "We'll just look like a big streak of lightning—and be gone about as quick."

Her voice was hesitant. Then, "But, Stan. Why should we bother? Why have we come back? We've won. You're in control at AT. The Belt is free. Earth is whipped."

"What do you mean, 'won,' *liebchen?*" Stan slipped his arm around the slender figure, holding her lithe suppleness close, though the bubble helmets kept their heads apart, and the heavy cloth of the P-suits made a wall between them.

"Why . . ." She looked up at him, her face showing through the bubble, doubtful. "We have won, haven't we?"

He laughed, looking down into the bubble of her helmet, separating the blazing reflections from Jupiter on its surface from the stubbornness of her face beneath the clear plastic.

"In words made famous long ago, we have just begun to fight, you know," he said happily, a deep pleasure suffusing him. "Sandra, Sandra—can't you see that we haven't won? Not yet? There will be tensions between Earth and the Belt for as long as there are only the two terminals—two groups of men with different ideas. The only answer is for us to go to the stars, so that there are lots of groups with lots of ideas; then those ideas and groups will be so spread out that it's impractical, ever again, to get man bottled up into one little system where his only way to let off steam is to clobber his nearest neighbor."

"The stars, Stan? I thought that was just . . . just the stuff of dreams. Just talk. Can the *Phoenix* . . . ?"

"No. Not the *Phoenix*. Not to the stars. But see that spark of light over there? That's one of Jupiter's moons. That's Io. And Io falls just within the mass limits necessary to make a planetary starship. It'll take a few years to stock that ship, to get a colony going, to set up the necessary radiation belts and atmosphere, to build the small 'sun' that will be the focus of the magnetic vortex that will power and light our ship. It will take a few years to build her right. But we can do it. The equations are all there. They've been there since the mid-Twentieth Century. And it's time somebody put those equations to work.

"Sandra," he said softly over the speaker into her helmet, gazing up into the glory that is Jupiter, "Sandra, we can't stay planetbound or Beltbound, or systembound. We're going out to where we'll be a quasar on Earth's telescopes. We're going out to join the other quasars that Earth has spotted in her telescopes.

"We're going to the stars."

Though Standard was his name, he was anything but standard.

He was in the country without the all-knowing computer knowing it.

He was listed as slain in the last war.

He had no credit and no means of establishing it.

He was fitted with a non-standardized artificial arm too heavy for comfort and with insufficient control for good usage.

He knew too little of his own background.

He was wanted by the official police, by the secret police, by the underground, and by the ever-growing mysterious world-wide cancer known only as the Rim.

Standard was his name—saving the world was his game.

Turn this book over for
second complete novel

EARTHRIM

NICK KAMIN

AN ACE BOOK

Ace Publishing Corporation
1120 Avenue of the Americas
New York, N.Y. 10036

I

"ABOUT THAT SHOULDER," the doctor was saying. "You've had a bad wrench there, but it should heal up with no particular problem. Of course, it may be a little stiff, but that's not bad unless you're a Quod player."

"I gave up Quod when I had my arm replaced," Standard said dryly. He was still feeling uneasy from the nerve block and swung his feet gingerly off the examination table and sat swaying on its edge. The block was diminishing slowly and he could feel the growing throbbing in his shoulder.

The doctor was rewinding his probe. "What's that about your arm?"

"I said, I had my arm replaced." Standard looked up warily. "Or didn't you notice?"

"Of course I noticed. I couldn't very well patch up some torn nerve endings in your shoulder without noticing the splicing work you've had done. Rather unusual arm, isn't it?"

Standard glanced up suspiciously. "Oh? In what way unusual?"

"Well, I just meant that large amount of metal in it. Vitallium, is it? It's awfully dense and heavy for a prosthetic, especially with the synthetic bone and cellular plastic available. There's nothing wrong with it, mind you. It just seems a mite awkward, considering."

"It was a foreign job," Standard grumbled.

"Don't worry about it," the doctor said. He finished rewinding the probe cord and stood resting his arms on his paunchy belly. "They did a good job matching your flesh tone and you seem to have sufficient neural response in it. Perfectly adequate. But don't try to use it too much until your shoulder heals. That arm can put quite a strain on your muscles, heavy as it is."

5

"I'll try to be careful," Standard said. He flexed his arm, testing the fingers. He had a strong dislike of doctors, and a glowering distrust of doctors who found it necessary to use an anesthetic with a simple probe. That was the whole idea of a probe. To allow internal surgery without going through the messy procedure of cutting. Any doctor who had to use a knockout block with a probe was a sloppy technician.

He did the important thing and made a fist. A fine line of quivering traveled from his shoulder to his hand. He tried it again and the hand jumped uncontrollably.

"The reason it's metal, see," he said coldly, "is because I was afraid plastic would break every time I socked some idiot in the mouth."

The doctor's face flushed. "That's very interesting. Do you make a habit of going around hitting people?"

"Only on occasion," Standard said. The hand spasmed again, this time without his applying any effort. "Right now, this seems as good an occasion as any."

The doctor stepped back slightly and pressed the recorder button for his desk computer. "Well, now what seems to be the problem?"

"My hand, you moron!" He held it up and watched it tremble like a leaf caught in a rocket's wash. "You fouled up my hand with your dumb probe."

"I don't think that's terribly likely," the doctor said. "I only worked on your nerves in the coracoid region, not in your hand."

"For Pete's sake, where the hell do you think the nerve response comes from to operate this hand? From my *shoulder*, meathead!"

"You do have a point there," the doctor said absently. "But you can't blame me if your arm is a weird foreign contrivance. Now if you had a normal Series J prosthetic, that'd be a different matter. Those function directly from the central nervous system. Apparently, you have a rather antiquated model there, using a servo bypass from your shoulder. You really would do well to have that replaced with a newer model."

"Don't you check anything before you go chopping around with that damned probe?"

"Now there's no reason to become agitated," the doctor soothed. "After all, it's pink. It looks like a normal prosthetic.

I *thought* it was normal. How was I to know you had an offbrand?"

"Oh, Lordy," Standard moaned. He could see he was getting nowhere this way, but his instincts were welling up to a dangerous level. Now that was not particularly smart, because the last thing he could afford to do would be to make a big antisocial scene and get labeled as an Unstable by Policontrol. That would really be cute. A secret agent running around with a social stigma and a listing with the area psychologist.

He pushed himself off the table and stood uneasily, slightly sick to his stomach. Man, that was *some* nerve block. He waggled his hand in the doctor's face and said, "All I can tell you is that you'd better damn well fix this arm."

The doctor cocked an eyebrow and yanked the probe out of its cabinet. Standard blinked. For a pudgy old guy, the doc could move pretty fast.

"Don't you threaten me," the doctor said. "You come one step closer to me and I'll give you a touch with this that'll make your wrenched shoulder feel like a pimple."

Standard stared at the doctor. Quivering or no quivering, with thirty-odd pounds of steel from his elbow to the cosmetic nylon hairs on his fingers, he estimated he could at least eliminate a jowl or a collarbone with the first blow.

He wanted to; he wanted to pulverize the fumbling doctor all over the shabby office.

Instead, he stood smoldering.

"Look here," said the doctor, his voice slightly less than frenzy. "It was an accident. It happens quite often with steel prosthetics. All it takes is to get the tiniest margin out of line with the probe and half the neural responses can be polarized. That's why everybody prefers plastic nowadays. You really should look into it."

"That's fine for the plastic factories, but at the moment I happen to be connected with this metal relic you call an antique and I've grown attached to it."

"That's very good." The doctor smiled. "Grown attached to it. Rather clever. I'll have to remember that."

"Meanwhile, why don't you remember that you're the one who fouled this arm up, and why don't you do something about it?"

"Oh, I wouldn't say that I necessarily caused any difficulty in your arm. No indeed, I wouldn't say that. That

fall you took on your shoulder may very well have started it."

"It wasn't quivering before I came in here this morning," Standard said defensively.

"That's what you say. For all I know, that arm may have been acting up for months and you're trying to stick me with a free repair job."

"I'll tell you one more time." Standard shook his head. "You fouled up my arm with your goddamned electric probe, and you damned well better fix it."

"Don't forget," the doctor pointed out testily, "my 'goddamned electric probe,' as you so lovingly call it, fixed your shoulder."

"Baloney," Standard said. "I told you just to yank it back in place."

"That would have been most painful."

"Painful? What kind of favor are you trying to give me? You think this jumping hand is a big treat? Good God, with the size of that nerve block you gave me, you could have amputated my spine and I wouldn't have felt it!"

"That's really not too bad an idea." The doctor grinned sarcastically, the lines of mirth rippling across his cheeks. "We'll save that for next time. Meanwhile, why don't you give your card to the front desk on your way out."

"Not on your life, you blubbery butcher. You're not getting paid until you get my hand fixed."

"All right, all *right!*" the doctor said, exasperated. "If you're going to be that way about it, the desk will make a new appointment for you. But I say that it will go away when your shoulder heals. Nevertheless, if it makes you feel better, you can stop back. Now, leave. I have other business to attend to, and you're wasting my time, young man."

"I certainly don't want to make you late getting to the slaughterhouse."

"Leave," the doctor bellowed. "You're not the only patient I have."

"If I was, it'd be the most merciful thing for the world," Standard grunted, lurching drunkenly out of the examining room. The waiting room was as vacant as it had been when he came in. *Other patients, my foot,* Standard thought.

The desk computer accepted his identity card and regurgitated an appointment slip. "I hope you are feeling better, madam," the computer's unctuous voice said.

Standard gave the desk a dirty look and staggered out.

The doctor watched him leave and waited until he heard the closing doors of the pneumolift. Then he walked into the waiting room and deftly kicked the desk. "Can't you tell a man from a woman, you simpering screwball? Good heavens, that's what I get for buying the cheapest model on the market."

"Although I am economical, I am polite and punctual," the desk said with a touch of wounded pride. It did not like being referred to as cheap. "Besides, it is not my function to differentiate among illnesses. As a physician, that is your function. Unless, of course, you would like to trade me for a complete diagnostic and answering service, splendidly encased in genuine chromium plate and simulated reptile skin. I would make an excellent trade-in."

"I don't need a diagnostic machine," the doctor said. "And furthermore, a person's sex is not regarded as an illness."

"Of course, that is your own biased opinion, since you suffer from the same malady," the desk answered. "Now a Mark XIV would ease your schedule and afford you completely objective viewpoints."

"I'm not interested, I told you."

"Allow me to contact our regional sales director. I'm sure he would be able to give you the facts much more succinctly than I."

"I don't doubt that. A garbage disposal could deal with facts better than you can," the doctor returned. "I don't want to talk to your sales rep, and I don't want to buy a new machine. What I do want is to be connected with Policontrol."

"If you really insist," the desk said airily. "But Policontrol can't make you nearly as attractive an offer as we can."

The doctor kicked the desk again and the wall screen reluctantly lit and flickered on.

"Policontrol," drawled a bored voice.

"This is Doctor Graystone. I was talking to one of your people earlier and we were interrupted. I would like to finish that conversation."

"Who were you talking to?" So far no image except the mailed fist insignia had filled the screen. Graystone realized it was another computer talking.

"I don't know. I may have been talking to you. Why don't you check your records. That *is* your job, you know."

The Policontrol computer grumbled. "Okay, here it is. You were complaining that someone impersonating a Control officer was bothering you."

"Not exactly bothering me. I wanted to get in touch with him so that I could give him some information, but then you told me that he didn't work for you."

"That's right, and he still doesn't work for us."

"I'm not concerned about that. This had to do with the man this phony officer wanted me to examine."

"What's this patient's name?"

"Wait a minute, I'll check." Graystone kicked his desk. "What was his name, dummy?"

"Standard," the desk said. "Michael E. Identity number 40936-15699, region UW 71."

"Thank you," the Policontrol computer said. "He doesn't work for us, either."

"I *know* that," Graystone said. "At least I was reasonably sure of it. I have some information to report about him that I think is important."

"Go ahead," the computer said and chuckled at an inaudible joke between it and Graystone's desk about the bushbeating of humanity.

"It is my civic duty to report that I believe the man to be Unstable, grade five, and make formal recommendation that Social Adjustment Seriously is Suggested."

That did it. The SASS code automatically shifted the Policontrol computer into a different circuit. A businesslike voice, authoritative and blunt, replaced the bored computer.

"We have noted that information, sir. Every effort will be made to readjust the patient as soon as we locate him. Please excuse me for a moment as I converse with your desk. I would like to scan its optic recorder for visual identity of the patient. Do I have your permission, sir?"

"Naturally. Help yourself."

There was a muffled click as the desk retrieved one of its storage crystals and fed the information to Policontrol. The click was followed by more clicks.

"Pardon me, sir, but have you been trying to adjust your desk by yourself?"

"Of course not," Graystone said. "Is the thing malfunctioning again?"

"There appears to have been some tampering. Our records verify that you called us earlier today, but there is no record of that call in your desk. Your desk indicates that you had only one patient today, a Mrs. Keiller, who was suffering from a dermal condition; there is no record of your having treated a patient named Michael E. Standard."

"That's ridiculous," Graystone said. "Mrs. Keiller was here yesterday. Mr. Standard was here all day."

"And he was the only person in your office the entire day?"

"He was my only patient. That phony officer I called you about was here, too, of course."

"There is no record of him, either," Policontrol said. "It may be that he was responsible for the tampering with your desk's crystals."

"Dummy," Graystone said, looking at his desk. "Maybe I should replace you after all."

"Do not blame your desk," Policontrol said. "It was unable to defend itself. Rest assured that this entire matter will be investigated thoroughly. We thank you for your assistance and cooperation. Because of you, we may be able to help not one, but *two* socially unstable citizens."

"That's quite all right," Graystone said. "I *am* a doctor, you understand, and I am concerned with the health of *all* people."

"That's very noble, Doctor. Thank you again for your unselfish act."

"That's very nice of you," Graystone said. "I wish my computer had your manners."

"Don't be too critical of your desk, sir," Policontrol said. "Please realize that I am a Mark XX and vastly superior to your desk even though it is adequate for menial tasks. As long as we're on the subject, I might advise you to invest in a Sentinel Service, available through Policontrol for a nominal lease charge. It would eliminate precisely the kind of tampering your desk has been subjected to, plus the reassurance that you are personally guarded by the largest and most effective police force in the world."

Graystone pressed his eyes shut. "Thank you. I'll think about it."

The screen blanked and Graystone stood in his reception room, slightly numbed. What a day this had been. Rudely awakened in the middle of the night, dragged down to his

office at an unnaturally early hour, frightened half out of his wits and insulted by a man with all the intelligence of a Neanderthal. All for a silly mechanical arm and, as though that were not ridiculous enough, now his own desk computer was on the blink.

The more he thought about it, the idea of a vacation became more appealing. He gave the desk one more kick for good measure and locked the front doors.

Standard stumbled off the streetwalk and into the nearest restaurant. Lord, he was hungry. Breakfast had been nothing to shout about (and that girl said she knew how to cook), but it was barely into the morning yet and he was starved. He glanced at his watch before he remembered that he had smashed it in the fall last night. It didn't matter. The doc's fooling around couldn't have taken more than a couple of hours at the most. More like an hour, probably. But he was hollowly hungry.

He found an empty stall and propped himself against it. A few more nerve blocks like this one and he could kiss the rest of the day goodbye. Crazy doc must have probed too deep and hit the spinal column. Standard guessed he was not too far off the track when he had sarcastically mentioned that the doc could have removed his spine.

He squinted at the menu card, annoyed that the breakfast list had already been removed. The choice was on the sparse side: fried soya mash or cellumeat. He pushed his credit plaque into the menu box and punched the mash selection.

Clunk, went the vendor. Standard peered at it. Nothing came out. No fried mash. No returned credit plaque.

"Come on," Standard grumbled and slapped the machine.

Clunk, it went again. Nothing. It hung on the wall, silent and impassive, mockingly illustrating its food promises. Standard glowered sullenly. He hit it. The nerve block was still eroding his timing and his metal fist jumped spastically. He hit it much harder than he had intended.

The faceplate caved in and splinters of plastic littered the dining shelf. But still no delivery of food and his plaque was still locked inside the recalcitrant box.

He was bending back a piece of plastic when he felt the hairy paw clamp onto his wrenched shoulder. He winced.

The bouncer stood a good foot taller, with large masses of muscle that had begun to turn to fat.

"What the hell you doing to my machine?" the bouncer said.

"Nothing came out," Standard said.

"I'll tell you what is going to get out. You. You can't come barging in here and start busting up things."

"All I wanted was some mash. I put my plaque in and nothing came out."

"That's no reason to beat up the little thing," the bouncer said. "It's just trying to do its job, wotthehell."

"It's doing a pretty lousy job," Standard volunteered. The bouncer tightened his grip. "Maybe it's stuck. And maybe you better take your hand off my shoulder."

The bouncer looked at the broken machine. "Yeah, I guess to hell it's stuck. I think maybe you should pay for it. What'dya think about that?"

"I can't pay you anything until I get my plaque back," Standard said. He sure was getting pushed around a lot lately.

"Now that's really tough. Why don't we just leave your plaque in there and when we get that box fixed we'll just deduct the cost and send your card back."

"Up your nose," Standard said. "I don't care much for that idea. By the time I get my plaque back, the entire Shore Drive will be charged to me. By the way, you still haven't taken your hand off me and that's beginning to make me nervous."

The bouncer considered the alternatives and slowly released his grip. "Okay. You get your card out of there and we'll settle up right now. A good vendor like that is probably going to run you a hundred, hundred and fifty."

Standard looked into the vendor's innards. "I may have to bend it a little."

"Sure, buddy." The bouncer chuckled. "That's a tamper-proof machine. You just go right ahead and bend it to your heart's content."

"You sure you're not going to mind too much?"

"For a hundred and fifty, you can do anything you want, buddy."

"As long as you don't mind too much." Standard tapped it lightly and the faceplate landed on the floor. He began

poking it with his fingertips, denting braces and shearing rivets.

The bouncer watched apprehensively. "You know, maybe it was getting kinda run-down."

"They sure don't make them like they used to," Standard agreed. A small corner of the clear plastic credit card was visible under the tangled metal. He backhanded the machine. The side crumbled and disgorged the card, with assorted shreds of metal.

He withdrew his card, brushing away pieces of aluminum and cast iron. "There's the little devil," he said.

The bouncer gazed at the pile of rubble hanging from the wall, stroked his chin and pushed his hands into his pockets. "That thing must've been rotten. Why don't we just settle up for fifty, buddy?"

"Fifty, huh?" Standard blew the dust off his card.

"Make it forty. I can pick up a used vendor for forty."

"I never did get anything to eat. Let's call it at thirty-five."

The bouncer sighed and recorded the amount. Standard weaved toward the door.

When he had left, the bouncer turned to the crumpled wall vendor and jabbed it with his fingertips. A sliver of torn metal laid open his thumb and he stood sucking it as he watched Standard aiming across the street.

Standard had nearly forgotten his hand until he reached the streetwalk. When he grabbed the rail, the hand jolted instantly and sent a ribbon of pain dancing into his shoulder.

"Lordy, I can't take this very long," he mumbled, drawing raised glances from the commuters jammed around him. He dug into his pocket for the appointment card the doctor's desk had given him. The appointment was two weeks off.

He wished he had gotten something to eat.

Now that's sweet, he thought. *That's really sweet.* The military had sunk fifteen thou into the metal pross, it had taken him two years to learn to use it, and now some quack messes it up with a dimestore probe.

Of course, Standard argued with himself, it *was* his own stupid fault. After all, he *had* suggested experimenting in the bathtub and how did he know she was actually going to bring a bar of soap with her? Doing a brodie on the tile floor had been dumb enough, but he really tied it when he

14

agreed to go to *her* doctor. Lord, what more could he have expected?

He spotted the phone booth and hopped off the street-walk, which caused his knees to buckle and almost landed him on his face. *Yessir, that was some nerve block,* he mused.

In the booth, he fumbled with the appointment card. There was no phone number, just the good doctor's name. He pressed for the operator.

The booth computer scanned him and provided a pleasant blonde on the screen, nude to the navel. The utility companies, Standard reflected, were sure using more imagination.

"Your number, please," the reconstructed voice said.

"I want to reach a Doctor Graystone. Doctor Westport, uh, Graystone."

"Thank you, sir." The blonde smiled inanely as the computer ran through its listings. "That number is 8274/22-4088. You can punch that dial directly or I can place the call for you, sir."

"Place it," Standard said.

The blonde faded and was replaced by a facsimile of a glossy male from a muscle camp, as visualized by the doc's cheap desk computer. "Doctor Graystone's office. May I help you?"

"This is Michael Standard. I want to change my appointment."

"Oh, yes, you're the lady who was in this afternoon. To what date would you like that changed, dearie?" Big show of flashing teeth and heavily lashed eyebrows.

Standard looked at the ceiling of the booth and swore. "Just as soon as possible."

"Sorry, but your present appointment *is* as soon as possible."

"I want it sooner."

"Sorry, but your present appointment *is* as soon as possible."

"Says you. Let me talk to Graystone."

"That is not possible. Doctor Graystone is out of the office and will not return for two weeks."

"Malarkey. I just left him a couple minutes ago."

"Doctor Graystone is out of the office and will not return for two weeks."

"Then contact him."

"I can't do that. Doctor Graystone does not wish to be disturbed during his vacation."

"Look, you get hold of Graystone and tell him if he doesn't talk to me, I am going to track him down and *permanently* disturb him."

The muscle man hesitated. "If your intentions are serious, what you are suggesting is a criminal offense and I will be obliged to place this information immediately with Policontrol."

In truth, of course, at the mention of Standard's name, Policontrol had automatically taken full control of the phone booth and was relaying the entire conversation directly into its computer complex. Naturally, there had been no outward sign. Simply a rechanneling of data with all the booth systems intact.

Standard's irritation had not been salved. His first impulse was to bury his fist in the muscle man's computerized teeth. On second thought, there was no reason to break up the communication system's equipment. On third thought, there wasn't much sense in getting angry with a computer, either.

Machines weren't bad. They did pretty much what you told them to do. It was the cretins who built and programmed the damn things that made them so smartassed. One of these days, Standard promised himself that he would find one of those programmers in a dark alley.

"I was speaking figuratively," Standard apologized. "Cancel my request."

"Thank you, sir. Goodbye." Muscles broke the connection.

"I hope you rust," Standard grumbled and punched for the operator.

The blonde reappeared. "Your number, please."

"I have had a lousy morning. Give me Dial-a-Joy."

"Thank you, sir." The screen scanned Standard's chunky body and scar-lined face. It inspected his clothes. A week old, off the rack. A sensor detected his metal hand and, unsure of it, interpreted it as "weapon, probable."

The booth made its analysis. There had been a long legal hassle when the analytic phone booths were first designed for public consumption. Constitutional rights or privacy versus the comsystem's concept of public service. Policontrol ignored both sides and wanted all personal analyses made by the booths piped routinely to the National Security Central, for

rather obvious reasons. What better way to keep track of the populace?

The comsystem argued that the analyses were only superficial and not legally binding; the constitutionalists said the whole concept was a violation of privacy, not to mention decency, since half the population's ids were considerably more raw than the late viewings on the home screen; and Policontrol just wanted the analyses, period.

They compromised. The booths analyzed only when the person requested a psych service and Policontrol received the information only when it had made a prior request for data on that particular person. The constitutionalists suspected they were not satisfied by the arrangement, but their squabblings were drowned out by the martial law imposed less than a year later.

After the Eastern war, when the threat of espionage and the ogre of sabotage diminished, and it appeared that the federal government had at last blown its budget for all time and was wallowing around in the dregs of bankruptcy, the comsystem succumbed to the final but weakened constitutional amendment to the franchise. All computerized analyses were deemed inadmissible in a court of law. The constitutionalists went home happy.

The comsystem announced the benevolent phone booths, with all the attendant therapeutic and emotional allegations, were finally available to the public, and quietly raked in the proceeds. The Fed tactfully reminded the utility companies of their profits and collected its share. With everyone nominally satisfied, each congratulated the other for a very sensible solution.

Which it was, on the surface. The legal limitations were meaningless to Policontrol, because Policontrol rarely bothered to bring its cases to court. Legal entanglements simply ceased to exist when Policontrol handled a case. Policontrol did away with all those little inconsequential matters, like warrants, arrests, trials and the like. It did away with its suspects just as efficiently, too.

The booth made its analysis. Normally, the tape would have been destroyed, but by this time Standard's name had already reached Policontrol's dossier with Graystone's social maladjustment complaint.

There was a momentary flicker as the computer constructed what it felt was an appropriate imagery.

"I hope this will give a *big rise* to your morale, sir," the booth cooed. The view angle dollied back as the blonde operator stood up. Still topless, she was wearing fluorescent tights that were only marginally higher than her legs. A stocky nebulous figure entered the screen carrying an old automatic. "This gun makes a *big bang*, baby," he leered. He pulled the trigger and covered the blonde with green paint. He continued to spray the stage with the squirt gun and, with his free hand, began shredding the fluorescent tights, while thoughtfully standing to one side to allow a clear camera angle. The blonde giggled and began running around a couch which suddenly materialized. The gunman clouted her over the head with the pistol, which sent her into fits of hysteria. She took the gun from him as they wrestled on the floor, and clouted him. That brought even more laughter and the gunman began tearing off his clothes.

"Operator," said Standard, "give me something else."

The screen froze. "I'm sorry, sir, but your personality profile indicates . . ."

"I don't care what it indicates, give me something lighter."

"Thank you, sir." The computer reorganized itself. The screen dissolved to a troupe of water nymphs balleting to an upbeat version of "The Blue Danube." The operator was now a peasant girl and the story line seemed to have something to do with hiding potato stompings from a herd of Cossacks.

He was certainly getting an interesting analysis, Standard thought. He had been out of the country longer than he realized. The really unsettling thing was that the booth had analyzed his hand as a weapon, and that was getting just too close for comfort. If this tape got into Policontrol's hands, he was going to be in big trouble.

As the music droned on in his ears, Standard sorted his thoughts.

To begin with, he had to have his hand repaired. He was not entirely sure why, but he did know that the most important part of his mission was centered around his prosthetic limb. He wondered if Graystone had noticed the incongruities when he was recircuiting and aligning the nerve patterns.

Could Graystone have guessed? Was that why the doc had cleared out of his office so quickly?

The real question, Standard decided, was whether to kill Graystone now and abort the mission, or take a chance, kill

Graystone after the hand was fixed, and proceed as planned. Whatever those plans were.

Speaking of taking chances, that had been a childishly stupid display he had put on in the restaurant. Why had he done it? Because he had been hungry, almost starving, that's why. Sure, breakfast had been less than satisfying at the girl's apartment, but why so enormously hungry this early in the day?

An insidious thought came charging in. Standard punched the operator button, breaking the ballet in mid-step.

"Operator," Standard snapped. "What time is it?"

"The time is precisely 1628:32."

"Oh, damn," Standard moaned and slammed his credit card into the slot.

"Your charge is nine dollars and eighty cents, sir." The booth recorded the amount to his balance, returned the card, and unlocked the portal. "Please Dial-a-Joy again whenever you feel the need for stimulation or relaxation, sir. This is a franchised service of the Bay Shore Communication System."

Standard stepped out, shaken. Four thirty P.M.! He had been at the doctor's office when it opened in the morning, and had been the first patient admitted. Come to think of it, he had been the only patient admitted. But he had been in there all day! Lord, what a dunce he was. That had been no ordinary nerve block. That had been a total, fall-down, roll-over-dead mind arrest.

He had been unconscious for more than six hours.

Graystone must have had a reason. Probably the same reason that had prompted him to leave his office for two weeks.

Which also meant that the girl last night must have had a reason for sending him to Graystone.

There was a chance the doctor was still in his office and just refusing to answer the phone. Or he might have gone over to the girl's place.

Either way, Standard calculated, it looked like it was adding up to a couple of necessary eliminations.

II

SHE HAD BEEN sitting at the bar when he entered and she watched him because new faces were rare in Harold's place, but even so he seemed familiar. She tried to place him as he unfolded himself into a booth, outlining his coarse, thick back.

He was an inch or two under six feet, heavily built with hunkering shoulders that seemed to precede him as he had half-walked, half-shuffled into the bar. His face had been patched by plastic surgery and from the scar tissue that laced his cheeks she guessed it had been a rushed wartime job. The ready-to-wear vendomat clothes hung loosely and ill-fitted and he used a sleeve to wipe off the booth table.

She shivered as his eyes struck her, lingering for a moment, then bolting away as rapidly as they had fallen. Beneath the drooping, sleepy eyelids his eyes were pale, nearly colorless, darting like albino lizards.

His eyes continued to flit, gauging the distance to the door, to the bar, to the rack of decanters. She imagined that he saw not bottles, but bludgeons, and quickly told herself to be rational. Otherwise she could see, too clearly, the sharp corners of the picture frames and the weighted lamps on the tables. It was surprisingly simple to visualize him tearing off the bar stool seats, hurtling them around the bar, acting like the animal he resembled.

She disliked the man on sight, and she disliked her job for putting her in the proximity of the man. Thinking of her job, she recalled where she had seen the man.

He was one of the suspects shown during the last hologram briefing session. One of their British Columbian agents had noticed him at the customs inspection. At the time, he was carrying an Australian passport. Shortly afterward, he had crossed the American border, this time with a Canadian passport. Even so, he was still a curiosity, a man to be watched. Until, of course, he had walked into the bar. That was difficult to accept as coincidental.

"Care for a drink, Jeannine?" Harold had been watching her study the man and had noticed the revulsion in her face. He tried to run a clean bar and take care of his girls.

He flicked his towel imperceptibly at the man in the booth. "You don't have to wait on him," Harold said quietly. "I'll take care of him."

She smiled stiffly. "No, that's all right, Harold. Thanks, anyway."

"You sure? I think I can manage without his business."

She forced herself to laugh and pushed away from the bar. "Maybe so, but I can't."

As she walked toward him, his eyes stopped their incessant movement and fastened onto her. The impact was frightening, almost physical. With the other trampers who came in here, she could sense them trying to undress her with their eyes. This one was different. This one seemed bored and irritated with her intrusion.

But she said, "Hi, stranger. What would you like?"

The eyes relaxed, withdrawing under the dark brow, sinking slowly over her. He looked back up slowly. "Now that you ask, I guess *you*. Why don't you sit down?"

"Just for a drink," she answered.

He shrugged. "Anything you want. Booze, trips, or wipeouts. I don't care what you want, so long as you get it and not some tea sneaked in by your bartender friend that's going to cost me twenty bills."

She frowned. He had noticed Harold's mother hen attitude in the time it took him to find an empty booth, and it angered her that he knew.

"Don't worry about that. Harold will serve me whatever you order."

He shrugged again.

It would be easy to walk away from him. All she had to do was to report his presence and that would take care of her duties. She could say that he rejected her and she was not able to follow him, and let someone else worry.

They would probably reprimand her, but it would not be the first time. They were as callous as this brooding man and failure was disregarded as though it did not exist. They would relieve her of the assignment, but then in a few days she would be back here under orders again hustling another brooding degenerate.

Providing there was no other agent in the bar. Since she

had never met her superiors, except Quinn, she knew little of the organization, had never even knowingly met another agent. For a while, she had wondered about Harold, but as time passed she had ceased to speculate, ceased to think, and did only as she was ordered the infrequent times her phone rang. Otherwise she was simply one more bar girl.

But if Harold *was* an agent, things could go pretty hard for her. She had slipped up on a few of her past assignments, and Harold might be watching her closely to see how she handled this one.

She sat at the booth. "I'll take you up on the drink. A grain mash."

He glanced at her, then pressed the order button. "The lady will have her usual grain squeezings. I'll have a cup of coffy."

Now why did he do that? To prove that Harold would not serve her a watered drink, she had ordered something hard enough to floor a longshoreman. Was he trying to throw her off balance by ordering coffy? Careful, she told herself. There may be more here than an immigration violation.

"You have a little tiny bit of an accent," she ventured. "You aren't English, are you?"

"Nope."

"Maybe you're Canadian?"

"No." He glared at her. "I was in Australia for some time. I probably picked up a twang down there."

"Were you there during the war?"

He grimaced, the scars forcing his mouth open at one side. "Yep, during the war."

"That must have been terrible. I remember seeing some of the newscasts when I was just a little girl. They kept saying how we were winning, and they'd give the number of how many enemies had been killed, but they'd never tell how many of our men were dying." She let her words trail off as he began drumming his fingers on the table.

"I'm sorry. I shouldn't be talking about something like that, but it's just that it seems so long ago."

"Nine years now when it started. Four years when it ended. That's not very long."

"It's a long time if you weren't even twelve when it started."

He nodded. "Yeah, I guess so. Look, my name's Mike. Mike Standard."

She smiled. "I'm Jeannine. Jeannine Brochet."

"Nice meeting you," Standard said.

Harold brought the drinks to their booth. He looked questioningly at Jeannine and then shrugged and turned away when she didn't answer his look.

Standard sipped his coffy. Jeannine noticed that he was left-handed, and the details of the briefing session came back. He was not really left-handed. His right arm was artificial. For some reason that had interested Quinn when the Canadian report had come in.

"How's your drink?" he asked.

"It's all right. Actually, it's pretty strong. I don't drink this very much, but I wanted to prove to you that Harold doesn't water his drinks." She coughed slightly and cleared her throat. "How is yours?"

"It's okay. Coffy's coffy."

"Not quite," she said. "That's not just plain coffy. That's coffee, with a double E, the real thing. Harold uses real coffee beans. He has one of the few places on the shorefront that does. One of those espresso shops went out of business after the war and Harold bought one of those funny machines. He put it in storage until the embargoes were lifted and now he has real coffee. Lots of the big restaurants don't even have it."

Standard tasted the brew again. "To be honest, I can't tell a whole lot of difference. It's all the same to me, as long as it's hot. I guess it's a good sales gimmick, though."

"Harold says it adds *classy past* to the place."

He looked at her lightly. Now that she was close to him, his eyes no longer seemed reptilian, only hollow, as though something were missing from within them. "I don't think it's the coffee so much that adds class to this place. You have a nice face."

She smiled. "Why thank you, Mike. That's nice of you."

After her initial revulsion to him, he did not seem all bad. Was she beginning to feel pity for the man? She wondered how much of his body had been destroyed, how much had been glued and sewed and grafted back together. How many of his emotions had been burned out?

She thought of herself. How much of her was left after

working for a faceless, enigmatic presence that ordered her to meet strange men?

Perhaps she could have loved this man if she had met him years before. Somewhere in his past before the war had taken its toll there must have been someone who could have broken through his sullenness. Or had that elusive capacity for love been destroyed also? How much emotion was left in a man who had already lost part of his body?

She was daydreaming, wildly romantic. Love had nothing to do with her job.

But the thought of it, even the remotest possibility, would make it easier for her to take this hulking man home with her.

"How long have you been in the States, Mike?"

"Not too long."

"Do you plan to stay?"

"I'm not sure. That depends on how things go."

"Are you job-hunting?"

"No, not exactly." He looked up and gestured toward the order vendor on the table. "You know, it's funny. For years we were always saying how great things would be in the future. So now the future's here, and things, all those fancy promises, are still waiting. Everything seems so damned much tinnier than when I left. The war hit the Aussies pretty hard, but they still seem to hang onto some of the basic things down there."

"Things always change after a war."

"Sure, things change. But this time, things haven't changed that much. Everything looks about the same as it did when I left for the war. The food is bad, and there may be a few less people running around, but otherwise, everything's about the same."

"Then why did you say things seemed tinnier?"

"I guess I didn't mean things so much as people. It's like a different attitude, like everyone is just shuffling around, not really going anywhere in particular. I don't know. Things just seem different."

He bent over his coffee cup, knowing his words were awkward.

"Some things aren't so different, Mike," she said and sloshed her drink around. "I still like some of the old basic things."

He looked over his cup and slowly grinned. "Is that right, Jeannine?"

"I mean, lots of things are the same." She dipped a finger in her drink and traced a circle on the booth table. "Things like life, death. Love."

He leaned back. "And money."

She smiled and nodded. "And money. That, too."

"Good old basic things." His grin broke across his face and made his pale eyes seem even lighter. "Jeannine, what's a nice girl like you et cetera?"

"I'll ignore that," she said and motioned toward his cooling coffee. "Wouldn't you like something more stimulating than that?"

He mulled the suggestion. "No, you're stimulating enough. I'll just finish my coffee to make sure I stay awake."

"Then give me a minute to call my roommate. I'll tell her to go out to a vidi tonight." She had to contact Quinn.

Standard stopped her as she started to rise. "Why don't you tell your bartender friend to transfer the call here in the booth."

"Why, Mike, don't you trust me? And I thought we were going to get along so well."

"Trust has nothing to do with it. I thought I'd save a pretty girl a few steps."

Silly of her to have asked that. Why plant a seed of suspicion if none existed?

"By the way, how long have you worked here?" Standard asked.

"A couple years. Why?"

"Then the barkeep knows your number." He punched the order button.

"All this seems like an awfully elaborate way to learn my phone number," she said. "If you want it, I'll tell you."

"Oh, if I want you again, I'll know how to find you," Standard said.

Harold's face appeared on the screen. "You wanted to order?"

"Jeannine wants to make a call to her apartment. Plug it in here to the booth."

"Sure enough." Standard saw him make the connection behind the bar and heard the soft click as it was patched into the order call box. The number rang. Jeannine knew it would continue to ring. There was no roommate at her apart-

25

ment, only the ghost of one. Double closets, double ward-robe, twin dressers, all furnished by Quinn to create the il-lusion of a second occupant for the benefit of the men she was ordered to meet.

The arrangement had benefits. Quinn wanted it that way to discourage any of her acquaintances, as he called them, from becoming permanent lodgers. Besides, it gave her a second set of clothes.

For a moment she nearly panicked. What if Quinn was waiting at her apartment? What if he answered the phone? Would Standard believe that Quinn was one of her fictional roommate's friends?

The phone continued to ring and Standard jabbed the order button. "Thanks, but forget it. There doesn't seem to be anyone home."

"Maybe she had a date tonight," Jeannine said and hoped the relief was not audible in her voice.

"Maybe," Standard said. His eyes picked her over. "She's probably a popular gal."

"She is," Jeannine said. "You might like her if you met her."

"I might at that," he said, studying her. He seriously doubted that the girl had a roommate. Few of the girls along the lakefront did, but most of them claimed to have one. The fantasy gave them security, he speculated. Like a shadow replacement for a marriage partner.

But there was nothing to be gained by pressing the matter. "Maybe some other time," he said, "but not tonight. I just want to be undisturbed with you."

"Don't worry about that," Jeannine said. "I'll leave a note for her."

Standard grinned. "Sort of a quarantine, huh?"

"Something like that. I'll paint a big red cupid on the door."

"That's what I like about you," Standard said. "I admire subtlety in a woman."

"I have many admirable qualities." She hesitated. "There is one thing, Mike. It's cash. And in advance."

"Fair enough. How much?"

"Oh, a hundred."

"Oh." He rubbed the side of his nose where the scar terminated, and chuckled. "Well, Jeannine, we've just en-countered the first obstacle in our budding friendship."

"I'm worth it, Mike," she said.

"That could very well be. But I'm not arguing price. I just don't carry that much cash with me."

"Harold accepts credit plaques. He'll convert if you like."

He thought for a moment. "Okay. I'll get the tab. Did you want to visit the powder room, or something?"

She shook her head and smiled. "My apartment's not far. I can wait." He was practically handing her an opportunity to call Quinn, but it seemed too perfect. She decided to keep any of Standard's wariness at a minimum.

"Well, let's see. That's about five," Harold said as they stepped to the bar.

"I need some cash, too," Standard said and dropped his plaque on the counter. "The lady says you accept these."

Harold picked it up. It was a United plaque, clear and featureless except for the embedded identification number. "Let's give it a try," he said and pressed it into the register.

Standard pressed his thumb to the window and the register compared his print and number with the information stored in Geneva. The feedback indicated a balance of over fifteen thousand.

Harold counted out the bills, a small rainbow of multi-colored chits the size of playing cards. "Hundred seventy-five. Five for the drinks, and twenty for the conversion charge."

He caught the sudden glare in Standard's eyes and added, "There's a helluva tariff on foreign banks, you know."

"Well, at least you don't serve watered drinks," Standard said.

He peeled off five pink twenties and handed them to Jeannine as they left. She accepted them matter-of-factly.

The street was glittering with the signs of the lakefront clubs and bars, adding their blaring to the muffled sounds of the people and trampers and the wheezing whisperings of the steam cars. Chidyland was the same city it had always been before he had left. Jammed, stinking, and hot. Only one thing seemed to have changed in the nine years. People rarely spoke while they were on the street.

"Which way?" Standard asked.

"It's only a few blocks. Do you feel like walking?"

"You mean an honest to God walk? Not one of those moving rubber bands?"

"Sure. I like to walk. Anyway, the streetwalks will be closed

in another hour. They stop running at two o'clock. It *has* been a long time since you were in the country, hasn't it?"

"They didn't let me out very much," Standard said. "The 'walks used to run all night before the war. Then they put a curfew on them to conserve power for the factories."

"I didn't know that," she said.

The night air was thankfully cool. On warm nights, the stench from the freighters and the sewage treatment plants would blow in from the lake, bringing the rotting odor of the algae that scummed the shorelines.

Standard had seen fish in Australia, but could not imagine that fish still lived in this slimed lake. He could not recall having seen any except the bloated gray things that scavenged along the pipelines. The great inland sea was now a cesspool for the sprawling cities complex.

"You're a funny guy, Mike," Jeannine said. She was balancing herself on the edge of a gutter as they walked.

"Why do you say that?"

"Oh, I don't know. You're sort of a throwback."

"Thanks a lot. That's a hell of a thing to say."

"I didn't mean your looks." She giggled. "Now that you've mentioned it, you do look kind of like one of those old cavemen on the vid."

"Thanks again."

"I was just a kid before the war. Were things really any different then? Tell me more about them, Mike."

"Things weren't all that different. People worked, people argued, people dropped over. They had put the second colony on the moon and were starting to go out to Mars, and that was pretty exciting. When they said they planned to go public on the Mars colony in five years, I remember thinking that's where I wanted to go. But then the war broke out and everything came to a stop. So I enlisted and got shipped over to Australia. Got busted up a little, but it didn't seem to matter very much. Everything else seemed to be going to hell anyway."

"You don't like the vendors, do you? And you don't like the streetwalks very much either?"

"I don't like a lot of gadgets cluttering up the place. They slow you down. It's been four years since the war and things still seem to be running at half speed. There's nothing *happening*."

"What do you like, Mike?"

"I'd like to see things get moving again." For an instant, she thought she could feel his memories and remembrances being sorted, examined carefully. Then, abruptly, the temporary thaw froze over again. "What I'd *really* like is to get into that bed of yours before I fall over from fatigue. There's something to be said for those lazy streetwalks."

All right. He had reminded her that this was strictly business. And she still had to make that call to Quinn.

But under that careless, rude exterior, she thought, there really did lurk a man. Without fully understanding why, she was determined to root out that vestigial shadow.

Her apartment was in one of the mid-century's vacation housing units that had sprouted up along the shore drive. The silver horizon was now replaced by the opaqueness of the greenish mist that curled around the stilts of the city. The vacationers had long since moved farther north. The rich who still could afford it sojourned along the Amazon in the Brazilian jungles.

The area was not yet a slum. They were too far out of the city, which lay fifty miles to their south. Standard gave the area ten years before the center of the city grew and ingested it.

They walked through the lobby, past the darkened shops that sold hallucinogens and questionable aphrodisiacs, to the center column that housed the self-serve elevators. A pay slot had been installed and Jeannine dropped in a credit chit. The doors slid open and the ancient machinery creaked them upward. The indicator light was out and Standard amused himself by counting the floors.

The elevator stopped on the top floor. Standard had counted ten, including the lobby. The doors opened to a dimly-lit hallway, shaped like a squashed doughnut. Her apartment faced the column, its doorway decorated with a fading mosaic that blended into the ragged lounge chairs in the hall.

"Home sweet home," Jeannine said and touched on the lights. The rooms glowed a pale purple.

Standard glanced around automatically, a reflex action. The apartment had been remodeled extensively with bulbous organic furniture that seemed to swell out of the floors and walls. Velour carpeting covered everything, changing colors as it mushroomed into the pod shapes and shallow bulges

that formed chairs and tables. There was not a straight line or clean edge of demarcation in the entire room.

"Do you like it, Mike?"

"Reminds me of a padded womb," he said.

"It can be more comfortable than that," she promised. "At least it's not cramped."

Cramped it wasn't. Standard wondered how she was able to keep this much room for herself alone. Or even for a family. Somewhere she had an unusual amount of political pull, or knew someone who did.

He kicked off his mocs and wandered across the room, parting the fleece curtains at the balcony window. The lights of the city were small pinpricks in the night haze, stretching out and bending around to the south until they were lost on the horizon.

He watched Jeannine's reflection in the glass as she undid the clasp at her waist and pulled the blouse tails out of her slacks.

"The city makes me feel grimy. Would you like a shower, Mike?"

"Good idea."

She pointed to a curtain. "In there. I'll make some coffy while you're cleaning up."

Standard grinned. "More of that real bean stuff?"

"No, just plain old concentrate. Or whatever it is that comes out of the tap."

Funny, he thought. *Funny how the old becomes new and the new becomes old.*

He listened to her fuss about, punching the kitchen buttons, as he lathered himself. Distastefully, he realized that the soap was heavily creamed and perfumed and, he guessed, loaded with hormones. He did not care for the thought of washing with a bar of gland secretions. Truthfully, the thought chilled him. He did not trust glands, not after what happened in Australia. He let the water run long and cold, rinsing hard. The towels were pastel and downy and he ignored them, drying himself under the air blast instead.

He was pulling on his tunic when he noticed the second toothbrush in the holder. It was used, and he wondered if by client or if there actually was a roommate.

Jeannine was bending over one of the bulbous shapes, pouring the coffy, when he pushed the curtain aside. He stepped behind her, encircling her with his arms, pulling

30

her toward him, and unfastened her blouse. She pressed back into his chest and he cupped her breasts.

"Ouch!" she recoiled.

He released his hands as though she had bitten him. "Huh?"

She was laughing. "Your hand, Mike. It's like ice."

He stared at his hand and began to chuckle also. "You know what they say: cold hand, warm heart."

"In that case, you must be the most feverishly passionate man in town." She turned and took his hand. "I'm sorry, Mike, but it did startle me."

She ran her fingers up his forearm. It *was* artificial, as they had told her, and well-done at that. There was no scar, no seam, where the plastic skin joined the real flesh. They had even reproduced the cuticles on his fingernails.

"That's okay. You surprised me, too. For a minute, I thought I had the wrong idea about you."

"No, it was silly of me. Was it the war?"

"Yeah, it was the war." He held his hand away until it warmed and drew her close with his left arm. She kissed him lightly.

"I still have to take a bath, Mike."

"Maybe I'll come in and scrub your back."

"Maybe I'd like that." She kissed him longer and pushed away. "I'll call you when I'm ready."

She let the blouse slip from her shoulders as she stepped through the curtain. Standard drank his coffy slowly. He finished half the cup, then lifted the blouse, noting the label. It seemed a grade above the general vendor brand, in keeping with the obviously expensive furniture. Business was good, he mused. Possibly too good.

Jeannine soaked herself, sinking deep into the lukewarm water. This was the man, she knew. A man with a metal arm. Perfectly designed, but poorly insulated. Why, unless there was not adequate room for better insulation? It must be agony for him, she thought.

The constant shock of conducted temperature, one moment freezing, the next scalding, must rack his entire nervous system. Without tactile sense in the hand, he would be unable to avoid pain and intense heat until it was transferred through the arm to the living nerves in the remaining stub.

And then it would stay burning there until the metal in the arm dissipated the heat.

Why would Rim be interested in a man with a prosthetic arm? Did they know he *had* a metal arm? Intuitively, she knew the arm was the center of interest for Rim.

She had to contact Quinn.

A phone was in her bedroom, another in the kitchenette. The kitchen phone was ruled out, but perhaps she could slip into the bedroom.

Until Standard stood in the bathroom, leaning against the basin, naked.

"I thought maybe you'd like that back scrubbed now."

She forced herself to smile and made room for him in the tub. "You have excellent timing, Mike."

Standard grinned and stepped down into the frothy suds. He shouted once as his foot hit the bar of soap. The soap ricocheted off the tile, throwing his legs out from under him. One ankle caught under the girl's knees, almost somersaulting her. He twisted in mid-air, landing heavily on his shoulder in a shower of water and foam.

"Dammit!" he swore and rolled woodenly on the floor.

"Are you all right, Mike? Is anything broken?"

"How the hell should I know? No, I don't think anything's broken. What the hell did I step on?"

Jeannine spluttered out of the tub and sprawled beside him. She wiped some of the suds from her face. "I think it was the soap bar."

"A soap bar? What the hell was that doing in there?"

"I *was* taking a bath, remember?" she said petulantly.

"She was taking a bath," Standard repeated under his breath. He looked at the ceiling. "You know, this isn't exactly the prone position I had in mind for the night."

"You're too impatient," Jeannine said. "Can you stand?"

"Yeah, I think so." He grasped the wash basin and hauled himself to his feet. He let his arm hang limply. The shoulder was beginning to swell already from the weight of the artificial hand.

"Are you all right?"

He massaged the joint and grimaced. "I think it's wrenched."

"That's terrible, Mike. I'm really sorry."

He tried flexing his hand. It was dull and unresponsive. "I

don't mind a little pain. What worries me is I might've jammed a nerve in my hand."

"Can a doctor fix it?"

"Sure. Just a matter of getting my shoulder back in place."

"Oh." She was nearly speechless. What a fantastic opportunity to call Quinn! And how easy it would be for Rim to put him under surveillance. The coincidence all but stunned her.

"Don't worry about it, Mike. I'll call my doctor and he'll look at it right away."

He stopped her as she stood. "No, not right away. Morning is soon enough. We have better things to do tonight."

"Are you sure? I mean, can you . . . ?"

Standard grinned. His gray eyes were very pale again. "What the hell. I can't say my shoulder ever particularly helped a whole lot before. And there is that little matter of an advance."

She smiled. "All right." She ran her fingers through the hair on his stomach. "And I promise you won't even have to move."

She led him from the bath to her bedroom and let him collapse on the inflated floor. The lights dimmed automatically, drenching the room in dark orange. He pulled her down to him.

"Let me call the doctor, Mike," she said. "At least let me make an appointment for you."

"Later," he said. "The doctor needs his sleep. Let him wait."

III

Quinn answered the phone.

"Hello, Doctor," the voice said. "I'm sorry to bother you at this hour of the night, but there's an emergency."

He tried to adjust the contrast but all he could see was a dark silhouette in the screen. "Who's calling, please?"

"This is Jeannine Brochet," the voice said.

"And what is the emergency, Miss Brochet?"

"I have a gentleman here in my apartment. Mr. Michael Standard." She paused and gave Quinn a moment to place the name. "I believe he has a wrenched shoulder."

Quinn arched his brows. He recognized the name immediately. In fact, Rim had given him a personal directive to be on the alert for the man Standard.

"That's hardly an emergency," he said, playing the role.

"Not by itself. But Mr. Standard has an old war injury, an artificial arm. The wrenched shoulder is causing him some difficulty of control."

Intriguing, Quinn thought. He had almost given up hope for Miss Brochet's usefulness. Perhaps she was redeemable after all.

"I see," he said. "Do you want me to come right over?"

"That won't be necessary. He is sleeping right now. Can I make an appointment for him to see you in the morning?"

Quinn thought rapidly. Standard might be too cagey to allow just anyone to get near him under the guise of a doctor. Quinn would have to locate a legitimate doctor, one who would not object too strenuously to an unorthodox request. That shouldn't be too complicated a task.

"I can't say offhand," he hedged. "I know I have a rather busy schedule tomorrow, but let me check my appointments and I'll call you back shortly."

"Thank you, Doctor. I'd appreciate that very much," the girl said.

He broke the connection. There was no time to contact the Rim. He knew the Rim was interested in Standard from the briefing session, and especially interested in the artificial arm, but Rim's reasons had been vague, as always.

Quinn punched for a medical listing, concentrating on the fringe area where respectability might be at a minimum. He selected an address close enough to the girl's apartment so that Standard would not lose himself in the city going there, but far enough away in case Standard should suddenly become suspicious.

The number rang several times before a disheveled, middle-aged man answered it in his pajamas.

"Hello, Doctor Graystone?"

"Yes?" the doctor said groggily.

"I hate to wake you, but a friend of mine had a small

accident and we wondered if he could stop by your office tomorrow morning?"

"Well, uh, let's see." Graystone tried to collect his thoughts. "Uh, what sort of accident?"

"Fairly minor. Just a wrenched shoulder. But he is quite uncomfortable."

"Yes, of course. I imagine so." The doctor was blinking his eyes, trying to shake the sleep out of them. "That can be most painful and, uh, especially so if not properly treated."

"Precisely. That is why I called you, Doctor," Quinn said. "Then you'll see him? First thing in the morning?"

"Well, now, there are other patients who have appointments, you know."

"Naturally. I understand completely. I certainly would not want to cause any hardships for your regular patients. Nevertheless, if you *could* manage to accept my friend early, I'm sure he would be, as they say, *most* appreciative."

"Ah, I'm so glad you understand. Under the circumstances, perhaps I will be able to fit him in later in the morning."

"I hardly think so," Quinn said. The doctor had taken the bait. Now to draw the wire tighter. "The truth is, my friend was spending the night at a young lady's when he slipped and hurt his shoulder. I'm sure you can appreciate how awkward this could be to explain later."

"Mm, yes." Graystone smiled. "Well, since it is *that* sort of an emergency, I think I may be able to see him early in the morning. Perhaps before my regular hours. I know how feisty some employers can be about this type of thing."

"Many thanks, Doctor," Quinn said. "About eight, then?"

"Eight will do nicely."

"Very good. And thank you again."

Quinn broke the connection and punched Jeannine's number. It was one of the few subagent's numbers he had bothered to memorize. There had been a number of occasions to use it, not all necessarily official.

Standard heard the phone ringing. He yawned and watched lazily as the girl answered it. Someone was speaking, but the set was turned obliquely to his line of vision and he could barely distinguish the hawkish features of a lean, dark complexioned man. He tried to prop himself up to get a better look, but his shoulder twinged and he settled back to the pillow floor.

"Miss Brochet," the image was saying, "concerning the appointment you requested, I'm afraid I won't be able to see your friend in the morning."

She frowned. "I see. Is there anyone else?"

"Yes, I've already taken the liberty to make an appointment with a colleague of mine, Doctor Westport Graystone. He has agreed to see your friend at eight o'clock tomorrow."

"Oh, that's good." She sounded genuinely relieved.

"All the arrangements have been made. If I can be of any more help, call me," Quinn said. "I'll be seeing you shortly."

They broke and Standard cleared his throat. "What was all that about?"

She turned quickly. "You startled me, Mike. I didn't know you were awake. I was talking to my doctor about an appointment for you."

He watched her cross the room. "You sure are concerned about me."

"You were moaning in your sleep," she said, sinking beside him. "If I don't get you fixed up, how will I ever get any sleep myself? You have an appointment at eight in the morning with Doctor Graystone."

He nodded. "Okay. I'll see him, but only to let you get some sleep."

She sat beside him and studied his nakedness. "You know, you really are an animal. All hairy and your face looks as though it's been chewed on by some other animal. But I think I like you."

"I think I like you, too," he said. "Why don't you slide over here and we'll make sure of it."

She pressed beside him, careful not to jar his shoulder. "I can do a lot of things, Mike."

"Somehow, I've already gotten that impression."

"Besides that. I can cook. Did you know that? Not many girls can cook nowadays. A lot of them don't know how to even add water to the powders, but I can cook. I really can, Mike."

"That's nice," he said. "You can make me breakfast when we get up. Or is that an extra charge?"

"Don't be silly," she said.

The pink light of the sunrise splashed into the apartment. Mixing with the orange fluorescents, it transformed the bedroom into neon. Standard woke and glanced at his watch. The crystal was broken, the read-out digits fixed on the

moment he had fallen on the floor. From the angle of the sunlight, he guessed it was close to seven; then he noticed that the girl was not beside him on the bed.

He heard her moving about and started to sit up. The pain in his shoulder nearly pulled his breath out. He managed to twist onto his side and push himself up with his good arm. Dressing was a slow process of tugging his tunic over his shoulder, now swollen and shiny with blue blotches.

Jeannine was making breakfast, boiling water for the dehydrates and taking great pride in stirring. She had a bowl of soya gruel waiting for him when he entered the living room.

"Breakfast is ready," she said, placing the bowl on a rounded table.

He poked at it with a spoon, separating the undissolved lumps.

"What kind of cooking is this?" he snorted. "This is the same trash that comes out of the vendors."

"No, it's not," she insisted. "I mixed it myself. I thought you'd like a home-cooked meal."

He tossed down his spoon. "The only difference between this and the stuff that comes out of the wall is that the wall is a hell of a lot faster."

"I'm sorry," she said. "But—"

"And the wall stuff isn't so damned lumpy."

Suddenly she was irritated that she was on the defensive. "Well, I don't think you have room to complain."

"What's that supposed to mean?"

"If you must know, you make love like a wet sock."

She saw his neck muscles tighten. "You seemed to like it last night."

"Last night was business," she said. "Now it's checkout time and I don't have to like it any longer."

Standard stood up, nodding angrily. "I'll buy that. The service around here is getting a little lousy anyway." He turned and walked to the door.

"Mike," she said. "What about the doctor?"

He wanted to slam the door and get as far away as possible from this girl, but his shoulder *did* hurt. He stopped. "Yeah. Well, where is he?"

"I don't know," she said sheepishly. "I'll have to check." She found an old directory and began leafing through it.

"Lord, what a display of efficiency," Standard grumbled. "Why don't you just ask for information?"

"If you know so much, find out for yourself," she said.

"Hell, I don't even know his name."

"I told you it last night. Don't talk to me about efficiency," she retorted.

He squeezed his eyes. She had told him, but he couldn't remember. "Just give it to me," he said.

She tore the address out of the directory and handed it to him. He took it without a word and stalked out.

"Stay out of bathrooms in the future, Standard," he heard her call as he pressed the down button. "I'm not sure if you're toilet trained, yet."

She waited until she heard the elevator door close and then reached for the phone. From the haggard darkness under his eyes, she guessed Quinn had spent the bulk of the night planning strategy.

"Standard left here a few seconds ago," she said.

"Is he going to the doctor's?" Quinn asked.

"I think so. I'm not sure."

Quinn frowned. "What do you mean *you think so?* Why aren't you sure?"

"We had an argument." She gesticulated. "He may decide to go somewhere else. His arm seemed to be bothering him, though, so I *think* he'll go there."

Quinn glowered at her without speaking. She hated it when he did that. It made her want to hunch her back and cover her head.

"Okay," Quinn finally said. "Now stay out of the way. Don't try to see Standard again. We have good reason to believe he may be dangerous to the Rim. And we wouldn't want to see you get hurt," he added, almost as an afterthought.

"Why should I want to see him?" she said. "He's a crude, dim-witted animal."

"Crude he may be," Quinn said. "But don't gamble on his being dim-witted. Just stay out of it from now on. Were you able to learn anything more about that arm of his?"

"Only that it's metal," she said. She was not particularly fond of being told what she could and could not do. "Also, that it's badly insulated and I think the fall did something to it. He was complaining that it wasn't operating properly."

Quinn squinted with concentration. "On the surface, that

38

seems somewhat contradictory. Anything as heavy as a metal arm would have its own independent servo motors. Bumping his shoulder shouldn't affect controlling his arm. The lack of insulation is interesting, too. We'll see what this Doctor Graystone can learn, if anything."

He relaxed a fraction. "You've done your job well, Jeannine. Lately, I've been concerned about your performance. You can be assured that Rim will be satisfied with this information."

"Thank you," she said. She had never questioned Quinn or the ways of the Rim before but, for the first time, courage or exasperation prompted her. "Quinn, do you know what this is about? Why does the Rim feel Standard is dangerous?"

Quinn stiffened. "You've done a good job so far. Be content with that. I'm sure the Rim has adequate reasons for whatever it does."

He broke the connection and Jeannine watched the blur of light diminish and flick out in the center of the screen. She had never understood Quinn, but knew she had to remain loyal to him. He had, after all, been responsible for taking her out of the orphanage. But it was increasingly difficult, she told herself, to work for the savior of the world.

Quinn saw the portly man enter the lobby and cross the terrazzo to the elevator. It was still early and, except for the two of them, the building was vacant. Quinn stepped to the elevator as the doctor was pressing his floor button and adjusting his jacket.

"Doctor Graystone?"

"Yes?" The doctor turned his jowly face. "Oh yes. You're the one who called me last night. Is your friend here?"

"Not yet, but he should be here shortly," Quinn said. "I'd like to talk to you about him, if you don't mind."

"Not at all," Graystone said. They stepped off the elevator into his waiting room. The desk computer greeted them and began its day of clerical work. "But I can assure you, it is a quite trivial matter, taking care of a wrenched shoulder."

"It's not that simple," Quinn said. He burrowed in his tunic and extracted the plastic identicard he had supplied himself with earlier, and held it briefly before Graystone's face. The clenched fist insignia of Policontrol glittered on the card. "To begin with, the man is not my friend. We

believe he is a foreign agent and I'd like to request your assistance."

Graystone's lips parted. "Really! Are you quite certain?"

"Not entirely. That's why we need your help."

"I don't understand." Graystone bustled nervously about the office. "I don't see how I could possibly be of any help to you."

"It's really quite simple," Quinn said. "This man was wounded in the Battle of McDonnell Range during the Australian conflict. Now he has appeared in this country illegally, with an artificial arm."

Graystone scoffed. "Does that make him suspect? A great many veterans have artificial limbs of one sort or another. You seem to be rather confused, young man. This sounds like a matter for the immigration authorities."

"Ordinarily, yes. But we think there may be a weapon built into this artificial arm. That is where you can help us."

Graystone coughed. "In other words, you want me to examine his arm."

"Yes, thoroughly."

"Won't that be rather obvious? Surely the man would become suspicious, and then where would that put your security?" Graystone was growing uncomfortable with this talk of secret agents, particularly ones with built-in-weaponry.

"Not if you knock him out first," Quinn said calmly. "I want X-rays, neutrographs, whatever it takes."

They heard the front door open and the desk greet the visitor.

"That's him," Quinn warned. "Do I have your confidence, Doctor?"

"Yes, yes," Graystone said confusedly.

"Good. Then admit him." Quinn disappeared down the hall as Graystone looked out into the waiting room and at the hulking man who stood there impatiently.

Quinn waited until Graystone and Standard were behind the examining screen, then returned to the waiting room. He scrutinized the desk computer. A cheap model, he decided. Capable of answering and taking messages, programmed by direct voice control—Graystone's voice.

He bent to his knees and located the component slab under the desk. He yanked it out, inspected it briefly, then

plucked out a crystal, bypassing the voice identification system.

"I want you to cancel all my appointments for the rest of the day. Tell them that I'm taking a vacation and can't be reached," Quinn said.

"Yes, Doctor. I'll begin immediately," the unctuous voice answered.

"Another thing," Quinn said. "Obliterate your recall for today."

The desk hesitated. "If I obliterate *all* my recall, I will not be able to function."

"That's true," Quinn said. "Very well. A man entered the office with me this morning. Do you recall him?"

"Yes. Dark man, thin. Monotone voice."

"That's him," Quinn said, mildly displeased with the description of himself. "Obliterate that recollection."

"Done."

"A few minutes later, another man entered. Heavier set, with a damaged limb. Obliterate that, also."

"Done," the desk said.

Quinn exhaled slowly. He was not positive this would work, but it might be sufficient to throw off any inquisitive questioners later.

"The thin man and the heavier man will be leaving sometime today. Since they do not exist in your memory, you will not see them leave. Is that understandable?"

"Of course," the desk said. "That is perfectly logical."

"Very good. You're remarkably intelligent for a Mark VI," Quinn cooed.

"Thank you, sir. I appreciate that."

"Now obliterate all recollection of this conversation," Quinn said.

The desk was silent. Quinn watched it for a moment, amused with having made it wipe out its memory of his compliment. He replaced the identification crystal and strode down the hallway to the examining room.

Graystone motioned him inside. Standard lay spread out on the table, eyes closed, bare from the waist up. He was breathing slowly and regularly.

"What did you do to him?" Quinn asked.

"I told him I was going to give him a nerve block while I worked on his shoulder. I gave him a total anesthetic instead." Graystone was perspiring heavily, wringing his hands.

"Drug or electrical?"

"Electronic. A mind block."

"Too bad." Quinn frowned. "That rules out using hypnosis now." He saw Graystone cringe and hastened to soothe him. Unfortunately, the doctor was still necessary, but already he was beginning to come apart. "No matter. Can you examine here or will we have to move him?"

"We'll examine here," Graystone said quickly. "All my examining rooms are fully equipped."

Quinn glanced around the room. There was an ancient X-ray, a well-used probe, and shelves of unclassifiable lotions.

"That is a matter of conjecture," he said. "Get on with it, though."

Graystone swung in the X-ray and exposed several frames, pausing only to let the machine develop them. He pulled the prints out and spread them on the light table. From the shoulder to almost the elbow, they showed normal tissue.

But from there, to the fingers and including the elbow, the film had been virtually unexposed.

"Extremely dense," Graystone whistled. "There appears to be a foam packing around the prosthetic to shape it out, but everything inside that seems to be entirely sheathed."

"Shoot it again. Up the exposure time."

"It will take an awful long exposure to penetrate that. I'm afraid it may burn his natural flesh. Besides, this isn't an industrial X-ray. Even at full power, I don't know if it will penetrate."

Quinn considered. "Very well. Concentrate on the arm below the elbow. That's all artificial there. Try it again at full exposure and we'll see what we get."

Graystone propped the insulating pads around Standard's body and spun the timer dial. They stood behind the lead shield and exposed again.

The prints were only marginally better. Graystone could pick out the artificial radius and ulna bones connecting to the elbow and the joining of the metacarpus bones in the hand, but most of the forearm, from the wrist upward, was again unexposed.

He ran the negative again, punching for an enlargement, and peered at it.

"Well?" Quinn asked.

"Offhand, I would say there are a number of inconsistencies."

"How so?"

"That will take a bit of explanation, first," Graystone said. "You see, there are two ways to control a prosthetic. One is by tapping the nerve impulses directly at the central nervous system. To do this requires a separate power source in the prosthetic, because the muscles remaining are used only to hold the device on, not to control it. The other method is to manufacture artificial muscles and tie them in with the original muscles. This way the prosthetic is controlled by the same immediate impulses that controlled the original limb. That is the preferred way today, incidentally."

Quinn nodded. He was no cybernetist and cyborgs were entirely out of his realm, but he could understand simple mechanics. "What is unusual about this arm, then?"

"It appears to be a combination of both," Graystone said. "If the blow to his shoulder is causing him difficulty controlling the arm, it would seem to indicate that it is operated by the immediate impulses. But this solid mass that's unexposed on the print must be a separate servo motor, which may mean it's controlled by his brain and not by nerve impulses in the arm."

"Now wait a minute," Quinn said. "I thought the brain controlled all the body movements."

"Essentially, yes. But, in practice, there is an intermediate step." Graystone was feeling more secure now that he was doing the explaining to the pushy, ignorant policeman. "Let's say you want to move your finger. Your brain sends out an impulse along the nervous system. When the impulse reaches the receptor area, a minute amount of a chemical called acetylcholine is produced, which causes muscle contraction. By regulating the amount of this chemical and the muscles which receive it, you move your finger.

"Now, the old way of making prosthetics was to take this original brain impulse and pick it up with an artificial sensor. Then it was amplified and directed to an assist motor of some kind that was implanted in the prosthetic. That opaque area in his arm that we can't penetrate must be the motor and sensing unit."

"That's the old way," Quinn said. "What about the new way?"

"Well, that's simply a duplication of nature, except the nerves, the muscles—everything is artificial. And that's the paradox, you see. With this kind of system, a blow on the

shoulder could cause the same paralysis as it would in a natural arm. But it shouldn't happen in a servo-assist arm, and especially not in one that was obviously designed for rugged use."

"What do you mean, rugged use?" Quinn asked.

The complexity of the arm both intrigued and delighted Graystone, and even more now that the cocksure man bending over his back was no longer giving orders, but was as ignorant as a first term student.

"Try lifting it," Graystone invited.

Quinn lifted it. "Good Lord, it must weigh forty pounds!"

"More like thirty, I imagine," Graystone corrected. "The question is, however, why would anyone elect to build such a heavy arm when it could just as easily be built at a fraction of that weight?"

Quinn pondered. "Good question. Anything else unusual about it?"

"One minor thing. Notice that there appears to be an artificial ulna and radius bone. These are two separate bones, like sticks. At one end, they're attached to the elbow, and at the other end they're attached to the wrist. That's how you are able to turn your wrist. The radius and ulna bones twist over each other, something like torsion bars. Do you understand?"

Quinn twisted his wrist, watching it. "I'll take your word for it."

"Our patient has those bones, but look here." Graystone pointed to a fine line on the X-ray print that seemed to circle the artificial wrist joint. "In addition, he seems to have some sort of ball and gimbal arrangement for his wrist. Why have both? One or the other is all that is needed."

"You are posing questions that are completely beyond me, Doctor," Quinn said. "These are precisely the questions I had hoped you could answer."

"I have no way of knowing," Graystone said. "Unless I can see what is in that mass within the arm."

Quinn turned his back to the doctor and the examining table and pondered. He was not sure what he had expected, but this did not appear to be it. An internally concealed laser, or an anti-matter charge would not have surprised him. But this—this appeared to be no more than a curiously refined prosthetic, no less, but possibly more. Based on its sheer weight, it *could* be used as a weapon, of course. In

hand to hand combat, it would be deadly. But beyond that, how could this man be a threat to the Rim? Did Standard intend to rush in and strike everyone dead, swinging his arm like a metaphorical jawbone of an ass. Yet Rim was convinced that he was dangerous.

It could still be argued, Quinn thought, that there were enough unknowns to add up to a total contradiction. The complexity of the arm ruled out an average wartime graft. The double systems, almost a back-up in case one failed, meant that the intent was serious. Someone very talented had spent a great amount of time and money on Standard. But still, why, with all that skill, all that necessary precision, why in the name of everything that was scientifically sacred, why make it so heavy?

Maybe the Rim knew what it was doing when it labeled this man as the agent of a sinister underground. Extremely sinister, to be exact. Because, obscured in that impenetrable shielding was a lethal purpose.

An atomic bomb? Was Standard a walking furnace of devastation? Quinn rejected the idea immediately. There was the simple physical limitation of size. An atom bomb could be designed to fit into a briefcase, but enough fissionable material to form a critical mass could not possibly be concealed in a forearm. What then?

Quinn made his decision.

"How long can you keep him unconscious?" he asked, turning back to the doctor.

"As long as you like." Graystone looked up from the prints spread out before him. Very obviously, he was fascinated by what he saw. "Although, after six hours, we should begin intravenous feeding or else he may dehydrate considerably."

"That won't be necessary." Quinn shook his head. "I'll be back before then."

"You're leaving?"

"I have to report this to my superiors," he said, collecting the prints, much to the consternation of Graystone. "I'll be in touch with you later."

"How long will you be? I have several patients scheduled for today."

"I've already taken care of that. Your appointments have been canceled for the day." He shoved the prints under his tunic. At the door, he turned and added, "I think it would be most wise if you stayed in your office."

Graystone stared at the door after it had closed, then slowly turned into his waiting room. He stepped to the desk and looked at it. It was the same simulated wood, the same chromium talk box it had always been. But he knew it was different the moment he talked to it.

"Who is my next appointment?" he asked.

The desk was confused. "You have not yet given me that information, Doctor. I had assumed you would reschedule your agenda when you returned from your vacation."

"I see," Graystone said, and did not. "And I have no other appointments for today?"

"I have already informed your patients that you would be out of the office," the desk answered. "You did tell me to do that, did you not?"

"Hm," Graystone said. Uncomprehending, he walked back to the examining room and stared at Standard. He felt a small measure of sympathy for the man now. Any organization like Policontrol that could reshuffle a man's day was too powerful to fight.

It had never occurred to Graystone that there might be an organization beyond Policontrol. An understandable oversight, because the suspicion had never occurred to Policontrol, either.

He passed his time organizing his instruments, not knowing when Quinn would return, and glancing at the first set of underexposed prints. The intriguing arm remained on his mind. As the hours passed, he returned to the prints and squinted again at them.

Here, there was a hazy blotch visible like minute spiderwebbing where the natural flesh had grown into the porous plastic skin and made an almost perfectly intermeshed seam. Here, at the edge of the opaque mass, he could detect the intrabone staples that held the artificial limb.

Graystone looked at the man on his table. He may have been handsome at one time, before the war had scarred and gnawed at his body. Not old, but of an age that was difficult to guess because of the extensive surgery. Well muscled, with curious lopsided effect, the right side of his torso noticeably heavier and coarser. That meant something, Graystone knew, and the thought nagged at him as he busied himself around the office.

The answer came nearly an hour later as he was reading over a case history of a woman with an atrophied leg.

Standard was lopsided because the muscles on his right side had grown to accommodate the added weight of the prosthetic. Which meant that the artificial arm was *not* servo-assisted, and the opaque mass in the forearm was *not* a servo motor.

Excited, Graystone returned to the examining table and unraveled his probe. There was still the matter of soothing the muscles in the wrenched shoulder, but the probe was useful for more things than that. It could, for instance, be used to trace the nerve patterns.

He watched the platen as the probe charted the nerves and muscles, nudging and prodding the bruised muscles into position. Within minutes, the swelling subsided. A few more minutes, and he had dissipated the black and blue surface clots. Then he began exploring.

It was complicated and frustrating. Nerves seemed to go nowhere. They began where they should not have been and ended in blind alleys. It should be like an electrical schematic, Graystone kept reminding himself. Cause and effect. Follow a lead long enough and it had to end in a wall socket. All the while, be careful not to trip over a wire and pull out a plug.

Except that it did not work that way. Some of it made sense, but not all of it. It was definitely an advanced transplant, controlled by the local, immediate impulses. But there seemed to be a direct override to the brain.

Worst of all, and sweat broke out on his forehead when he realized it, there was a whole congelation of nerves and musculature that was totally isolated somewhere within the arm.

He lost track of time, recharting, reanalyzing. Every person has muscles that are not used. But the muscles are there, nonetheless, waiting for the correct impulse to goad them into action.

How many people can wiggle their ears, or curl their tongue into a tube? Or wag their tails? Nobody had a tail, but the muscles, feeble though they might be, still remained. Some women used them. Somewhere back in man's evolution, all these unused muscles must have had a purpose.

The muscles were still there, and no matter how specious, the ability to use them was still there also, buried under eons of sophistication.

But even vestigial muscles had to have *some* connection

with the central nervous system. Not isolated. Not independent, not like a separate living entity existing inside another body.

But it was there, a bundle of living, healthy nerves and muscles inside Standard's artificial arm, connected only by a few blood vessels.

And suddenly, like a rush of numbing chill, Graystone understood.

"My God," he whispered and stared at the man sprawled on the table. He had looked right at it with Quinn. Right in front of them all the time and they had not seen it. The irony shook Graystone and left him with a mild euphoria. Pushy young men who flashed identicards under his nose irritated him, and especially young men who were wallowing in ignorance.

"So, secret policeman," he chortled to himself. "You couldn't wait to rush out to your superiors and tell them how stupid you were instead of waiting and using a little brain power."

The initial shock passed quickly. A few questions remained, such as *why* and who, but he had no doubt now of *how*. More than anything, he was cheerfully fascinated. After all, there was little difference between the psychological composition of a scientist and an artist, and this artificial arm was a work of artistry. No matter if it had not been designed for a museum; artistry nonetheless.

Michael Standard was a walking cannon. Armed, ready for firing, waiting only for the correct touch on the trigger. Standard had been created for one purpose: to kill. Sooner or later, the correct signal would trip the firing mechanism and five pounds of steel-fingered hand would crush anything in its way.

That was *how*, but *who* would send that signal? Because the firing mechanism, that opaque mass in Standard's arm, was not connected to his nervous system. And there was no evidence of any electrical transmitter or receiver. It was a gun without a trigger.

Finally, *why?* Why go to so much trouble to kill one man, because it *was* a one-shot affair.

Graystone had no love for the federal police, but he punched for the operator, requesting immediate contact with Policontrol. The screen filled with the fist insignia and a toneless facsimile voice answered.

"Policontrol. Please state the nature of your call."

Very businesslike, Graystone thought. The way a national security force should be. "This is Doctor Westport Graystone. This morning one of your agents was in my office requesting aid. I would like to speak to that agent, please."

"What was the agent's name?" The computer's question surprised Graystone. He had assumed that Policontrol knew where all its agents were at any given moment.

"His name was Quinn," Graystone wavered.

There was a pause as the computer sorted through its memory banks, simultaneously locating each of its agents. Central returned.

"Can you be more specific?"

"That was the only name he gave me. It was on his identity card," Graystone said, perplexed. Surely Graystone's own name should give the computer ample clue as to which agent he wanted. Where else did the agents receive their assignments?

"Did this agent require medical aid, Doctor?"

"No, he requested aid in examining a suspect. I gave him what aid I could and he left to make his report. I have some additional information for him. If I can't talk to him, can I give someone else the information?"

"One moment," the voice said. The insignia on the screen flattened and was replaced by a heavy jawed man wearing the black uniform of Policontrol.

"Doctor Graystone." The voice was obviously human and cautiously skeptical. "What seems to be the trouble?"

"There is no real problem. I would merely like to talk to an agent of yours named Quinn."

"Yes, I gathered that from the summary the computer just gave me. You say this man represented himself as one of our people and requested your assistance in examining someone he termed a suspect. Is that correct?"

"Yes, that's correct. What is the problem? Didn't Quinn arrive at your headquarters?" Graystone had a sliding feeling what the problem was.

"The difficulty," the controller said quietly, "is that we do not have an agent named Quinn in this area. I'm afraid you have been misled, Doctor."

Graystone started to object, then stopped himself. It made sense, in an oblique sort of way. No criminal group would

have constructed a technological achievement such as that arm. Perhaps it was the other way around.

"I'm afraid you have been taken, Doctor," the controller said. "It was probably a con game to get some free medical attention. We can't reimburse you for your time and expense, but you can file a complaint for tax purposes if you like."

Graystone shook his head. "No, I don't think that was the purpose."

"Well, don't worry about it. These things happen. Sometimes we get complaints of men impersonating our women agents. You don't know what some people will do for kicks."

The elevator doors hissed open and he heard Quinn enter the waiting room. "Thank you," Graystone said, breaking.

Quinn looked suspiciously at Graystone. "Were you talking to one of your patients, Doctor?"

"Yes," Graystone said quickly. "It's an experimental drug. I have to check the progress regularly."

Quinn was satisfied. "Sorry if I took longer than I thought I would. There were several points we had to consider before we could reach a decision. Were you able to learn anything more about our patient?"

"No, not really," Graystone lied. They walked back to the examining room. "I spent most of the time working on his shoulder. By now the trauma should be alleviated. Beyond that, I learned nothing new. It appears to be no more than a rather elaborate prosthetic device."

"My superior does not agree," Quinn said. He studied Standard's slowly breathing body. For a moment, panic closed around Graystone. He was not going to allow himself to underestimate the thin man.

Quinn's hand sunk into his tunic and Graystone caught his breath.

"All that is irrelevant, however," Quinn said. His hand emerged with a plastic chit. "We'd like to demonstrate our appreciation for your help and the inconvenience we have caused."

Graystone accepted the chit as though it were a coiled snake. If there was any doubt remaining in his mind about the illegitimacy of Quinn, it was dispelled as he glanced at the card. Government agencies did not casually hand out unmarked credit vouchers for ten thousand dollars.

"This strikes me as especially generous," he said.

"We suggest you spend it on a vacation," Quinn said. "Preferably a two-week vacation. Beginning now."

Graystone looked up from the chit. "I suppose it's ridiculous of me to worry about my other patients?"

"They have already been notified," Quinn said coolly.

"I thought as much," Graystone murmured. He contemplated it and then placed the chit in his pocket.

"We are only concerned with your safety," Quinn explained graciously. "Sooner or later, Standard will realize that several hours of his day are missing. When that happens, we think it would be best if you were unavailable. We'd hate to see you become an innocent bystander, if you follow me."

"I follow you," Graystone said and forced a smile. He understood only too well what the thin man was suggesting. "Now that we've taken care of the payment, what *about* our patient? Shall I wake him, or do you people plan to place him under arrest?"

"Wake him after I've left," Quinn said. "We have no real evidence to arrest him. But he'll be under surveillance."

I'll wager on that, Graystone thought grimly. They shook hands and Quinn disappeared down the elevator.

The day was a mystery to Graystone. He knew Quinn was an impostor, but where did that place Standard? Whatever the answer, he decided to wipe it from his mind. He had a two-week vacation in store and felt he could definitely enjoy it. There was a beach far up the northern coast that he had been meaning to explore for years now. As soon as he cleared his office, he would arrange for that lazy trip.

Standard was in good condition, Graystone reflected. He came out of the mind block immediately.

"About that shoulder," the doctor said. "You've had a bad wrench there, but it should heal up with no big problems."

IV

STANDARD GLOWERED and weighed his trembling fist in his hand. The lift refused to stop at Graystone's floor. He must have locked up right after the so-called examination. As though he expected Standard to return pretty damned soon. Things were sure stacking up against the doctor.

He punched the down button and tried to think on his way to the ground level. It was difficult. The mind arrest was still fuddling his brain, like soft vanilla syrup clogging up the processes. Sluggish reactions were disastrous, but what really bothered him was the chance of pulling another stupid move before the arrest wore off of its own accord.

He had accomplished objective one, that of meeting someone connected with the Rim. He had done that, all right. In spades. The first time out, he had met one of the bar girls who was responsible for the Rim's "recruiting." Not too much doubt about that, nor that her doctor friend on the vidiscreen last night was a partner. It was a pretty simple technique to find out if someone was working for Rim. Use the same technique for finding lions. Stick your head in its mouth and if it bites off your neck, you know it's a lion.

Subtlety didn't work against an enemy who could infiltrate a mind and turn it inside out. How do you sneak up on someone who can feel you coming from two thousand miles away? How do you fight an enemy when nobody believes there's an enemy? How do you set up an ambush when he knows before you do what you're going to do?

Easy answer. You don't.

Instead, you stand up and wave your arms and yell, *Here I am, come and get me,* and hope he takes the bait. Then you hope like hell you get the first shot in before he pinches off an artery in your brain with his mental fingers. And *that* was the big catch.

Because Rim could sense the nerve impulses, the total thought, the action before it happened.

Standard vaulted onto the main loop. It was close to rush hour and the streetwalk was jammed with people shoving and jostling to gain elbow space. He pushed his way to the speed lane and let the fetid air run over his face. He was close to the lake and that meant he was close to the girl's apartment. And with the girl, he would be one step closer to the Rim. Then what?

Bluntly, he did not know. He knew that there was enough explosive charge in the arm he wore to fragment anyone standing in its way, but he had no idea of how to fire it. Clever, cunning Condliffe had seen to that. Condliffe had made the arm automatic, independent of Standard. It would choose its own time and place. Standard was only the carrier, like a fat cow stuffed with a killer parasite.

He did not want to know. In fact, he could not afford to know. The moment he learned how the arm worked, the mission was scrubbed. Because if Standard knew, then Rim would know, and Rim would make sure the arm never got its chance to operate. Condliffe had spirited all of his engineers and surgeons off to Lunar Nine to be sure that no stray thoughts would be accidentally intercepted by Rim.

It was a risk building it on Earth to begin with. If Rim had chosen to leave the States at any time they were building it, there was an outside possibility that he could have gleaned a random thought connected with the project. But Rim had stayed put, building his rudimentary empire, gathering a cadre around him. Even though Rim's ability was growing, halfway around the world was still too much for him. So Australia, in Condliffe's rehabilitation hospital, had still been safe.

But not for long. Rim was growing. Superficially, he was influencing half the North American continent. In another year, Condliffe estimated that Rim's influence would be out of the superficial realm. Rim would be affecting major policy decisions. Within five years, he would have half the world. And nobody even knew it was happening. Rim was too smart to make any sweeping changes as he was growing. But there were indications already.

Even Condliffe did not know what was happening, or how, or why. But it was a slowing-down process. The birth rate was declining rapidly, in all opposition to the post-war feelings to rejuvenate the country. People were maturing later. Infancy lasted until four or five. Teenagers were not

reaching puberty until their late teens. Nothing that the Bureau of Statistics could put its finger on, but something was there, insidious, creeping, sapping the vitality from an entire country.

And it would spread until it was global. A contagion, a disease that was putting the brakes on life itself.

It had to be stopped. Now, before it became stronger. Before it became resistant to every cure.

Standard was carrying the cure stitched to the stump of his arm. The only cure left in the world. Condliffe and the entire Opposition Group, as they half-jokingly called themselves in the earlier stages, were waiting on the moon to see if Standard could deliver the panacea. They were all up there, sitting and waiting. And if Standard failed, they would not return, because if Standard failed, it meant that Rim would know the plot and Rim would systematically eliminate the plotters.

Standard was a pawn. They had chosen him because he rarely bothered to think ahead, but acted on the spur of the moment, reacting to the situation rather than attempting to plan in advance and avoid danger. He knew why they had chosen him and it neither angered nor pleased him. There was no other way. Condliffe had not needed a thinker. He had needed a delivery boy. A delivery boy with a fine instinct for survival.

He was feeling better. Hungry, but steadier. He hopped directly off the speedwalk without bothering to go through the step-down stages. The gutters, the odors of the rotting fish, the amplified noise from the cafés were familiar to him. He cut down an alley that opened on the dirty beachfront with the girl's apartment building on it. She had taken him around in circles, which could have thrown him off if he had taken her up on her suggestion of a drink in the bar.

He paid the elevator and let it creak him to the top floor. Her door was locked and he pounded on it.

"Hey, Jeannine. You in there?"

"Just a moment," he heard. The door clicked. Remote lock, Standard thought and pushed the door open.

The thin, dark man was leveling a metal rod the size of a pencil directly at his head as he halted abruptly. The rod was connected to a looping strand of wire that coiled into a briefcase at the man's feet. Standard knew what it was. An electron gun, the kind used by archaeologists to melt

through six inches of solid rock in a microsecond. He had a healthy idea of what it could do to his head.

"Nice of you to join us, Mr. Standard," Quinn said.

Standard's eyes narrowed. Through the sheer curtain, he could see Jeannine pulling on her slacks.

"Sorry if I'm interrupting a private party," Standard said.

"Don't worry about it. The night's still young," Quinn said.

Standard cocked his head at the thin man. "Seems I've seen you somewhere before. Like last night on her vid. How's the medical consulting business going, Doc?"

"Don't pretend naïveté, Standard. Even you know better than that," Quinn said. "Come in, won't you? Close the door behind you. Carefully."

Standard stepped inside and pushed the door closed with his heel. "Hope I haven't kept you waiting."

"I apologize if I borrowed your girl friend," Quinn said. "But I have known her for some time, you know."

"Yeah, I'll bet. No argument there. Finders' keepers, I guess."

Jeannine slipped past the curtains, draping a blouse over her shoulders. Standard noticed she was holding a stun pellet in her fingers.

"Hi there, Jeannine." Standard smirked. "You're looking rested."

"Hello, Mike," she said. She walked across the room and fired the pellet point-blank in his face.

God, that stuff works, he thought just before he collapsed. He crashed into the floor as though his knees had been slashed. Jeannine tossed the exhausted pellet on one of the mushroom seats and finished clasping her blouse.

"What are you going to do with him now?" she asked.

"Simple." Quinn shrugged, dialing power on the electron gun. "I'm going to take that arm off."

The runway was as immaculate as it always was this time of the evening. It was alive in light and the soft murmurings of the computer banks as they churned through their days of sorting and filing. DeAmico walked the length of the long hall leisurely, basking in the simulated sunlight that filled the subterranean headquarters of Policontrol. Behind the concrete walls, the multibands of the answering desks handled the routine of the deluge of complaints that evening brought. Trivial complaints of supposed injuries, gripes that neighbors

were keeping someone awake, store owners reporting a shop-lifting in the drug department. The minor complaints and anxieties that occupied twenty hours a day of a police force. The kind of inconsequentialities that machines could handle with ease.

He said, "How's it going?" to Tilloson as he entered the console room. Tilloson grunted, absorbed by his printouts. Most of the second shift had already arrived and were replacing, or had already replaced, the day crew.

He squirmed behind his console and flipped through the sheaf of papers waiting for him, looking for the red printouts that signified a problem the answering computers could not easily answer. A computer could be programmed to arrest, prosecute, and sentence. They could handle anything that stemmed from an established precedent, but it was the un-expected occurrence, the ability to circumvent a crime before it happened, rather than cope with it afterward, that required human judgment.

"Good evening, Sergeant DeAmico," the desk said as he settled himself.

He thumbed through the stack of papers. There were less than a half dozen red imprints and none of those appeared urgent.

"How about some coffy?" he asked, leaning back and locking his fingers behind his head.

The desk obliged and slid the cup to DeAmico's accustomed spot. He spent several minutes drinking the coffy and looking at the papers. Nothing especially exciting, thankfully. Peeping Tom complaint from an old lady; someone else had had his aircar vandalized. Mark that one for Traffic. What was it doing here in Criminal, anyway? He made a mental note to mention it to Programming. Vandalism on a transportation vehicle simply did not fall into his jurisdiction.

Impersonation complaint. Attempted rape, and a success-ful rape. An ordinary enough day. Take care of those rape cases first and then attend to the small things later.

"What's the status on this rape case?" he asked.

"He has been apprehended and is presently in the inter-rogation room. Two previous convictions, both on moral charges. One, seducing a minor. The second, an attempted rape on his sister which was unsuccessful."

"Why is he still loose?"

"He is a juvenile, on probation since his last conviction. Do you want his name?"

"No, I'll take him cold. Let me speak to him."

The screen opened on the four-by-four interrogation room. The boy was huddled against the far wall, looking up at De-Amico's image as it flashed on the room screen.

"This makes you a three-time loser, kid," DeAmico said.

"Tough shit," the boy said.

"You're lucky you're still a juvenile," DeAmico said. "Do you know what would happen if you were an adult?"

The boy looked sullenly at DeAmico's image. When he did not answer, DeAmico continued.

"You'd have your choice of prison or surgery. You would be examined, your problem analyzed, and a cure recommended. If you choose surgery, that could mean anything from a frontal adjustment to castration. Unless you feel your trouble is a double Y chromosome."

"What if it is?" the boy shot back. "You think your cutters can fix that?"

"If that's your problem, we wouldn't even try to correct it. That would mean mandatory exile to a lunar prison camp. Consider that. The rest of your life in a shell. Most of them don't last very long up there. No guards. Any time you want, you can take a walk outside. The only catch is that there are no pressure suits. So you don't walk very far."

The boy spat defensively. "Don't give me that crap. If you're going to do something, why don't you do it, cop, instead of flapping off?"

"For now, you are going to sit in that room," DeAmico said. "You'll be released in the morning."

"What's the matter, cop? No evidence to hold me? Think you can't make it stick?"

"We won't even bother. You have already received two hearings. As far as we're concerned, that takes care of your rights for a jury trial. We brought you in to tell you the playing's over. Next time, no interrogation, no hearing. You'll have your choice of prison or surgery. You may as well start thinking about it now."

He blanked the screen, bored and dejected. He would see the kid again, he knew, and he would be called on to make a recommendation. He finished his coffy, brooding about the young offender.

"What do you think about him?" the desk asked. "The

chances are approaching maximum that he will be arrested again. Do you think you will have to make a judgment?"

"I suppose so," DeAmico said, looking at the thick coffy sludge remaining in his cup.

"That's unfortunate," the desk said. "Personally, I would consider a circuit change in his brain pattern. How do you feel about that?"

"I haven't really considered it. Offhand, I think I would be against any surgery in this case and recommend imprisonment with a probation guarantee. I hate to see a kid that young receive an irreversible sentence so early in life."

"You're probably right. But I was thinking of the possible future consequences on society in general. If he is released at a later date, there would still be no assurance that he would be stable."

"No," DeAmico agreed. "There's no assurance. But that is a matter of judgment and foresight. Enough of this. I'll have to consider it more carefully when the occasion arises. Now, what about this attempted rape?"

"The victim was unable to give an accurate description of the assailant and we have not yet turned up a suspect. We're working on it."

"Mm. How is the victim? Is she all right?"

"Not she," the desk corrected. "He. It's in the report."

DeAmico paged through the report. "Disregard this unless we receive more like it from the same area. And in the future, route these complaints to Social Counseling. They're better equipped to handle homosexual disturbances than we are."

"Very well. Would you care for more coffy?"

"No, thank you. Tell me about the next item, this impersonation."

"This may be rather interesting. We received a call this afternoon from a doctor who claimed one of our agents used him to examine a suspect. At that time, we attributed it to a trick to gain free medical assistance. Then the doctor called later requesting an Unstable classification for the patient."

"What's this patient's name? Anything on him?"

"His name is Standard, but there is a difficulty in identification. The doctor's desk had been tampered with and we were unable to find any visual identification of the man Standard."

"That is interesting," DeAmico said. "Any criminal record?"

"No. We list a Standard, Michael E., who may be the

same man. Our last report indicates that he is recuperating in an Australian hospital from a wound or wounds suffered in the war. If this is the same man, he is in this country illegally. That is curious in itself, because there is nothing in his record that may have caused him difficulty in obtaining a passport."

"We have no visual identification of him, then?"

"We were able to receive nothing at the time. However, after the Unstable was listed for him, we intercepted a phone call, apparently placed by this same man. It's not positive, but we believe we are accurate."

"Okay." DeAmico pointed at the printout. "What about this other man? The impersonator?"

"He is known on the waterfront area by various informers as Quinn, but beyond that we have nothing."

"Nothing?" That was unheard of. How could a man exist without *some* identification in Policontrol? "Is he an alien?"

"Unknown. We don't know how he managed to escape census, but he has."

DeAmico chewed his lip. "You're absolutely right. This is very interesting. Give me everything you have on these two men."

He leaned back and began riffling through the printout as the console disgorged it. It took him several hours to form a judgment. When he reached it, he cupped his forehead in his hands and thought carefully.

Something was happening in his collection of scattered reports. Not the cold facts the computers had compiled, but something more.

He punched the com button and Captain Szamual's face filled the screen.

"I have something here on Station Four," DeAmico said. "Would you connect in please, Captain?"

Szamual glanced over his facsimile copy of the printout. "How do you read this, DeAmico?"

"It's an underground movement of some kind. Two opposing factions. One may be carrying an internal weapon, the other is curious about it. It doesn't fit in with our crime patterns, so it's something else. My guess is that it's political. Someone is going to get hurt, regardless."

"Do we have any ident on either of these two?"

"Nothing at all on this Quinn with the exception of a possible address. Tentative identification on Standard, though.

There is an isolated complaint of a man wrecking a vendor box with his bare hands, and a phone call presumably placed by the same man. If it *is* our quarry, then we have a visual and we know the weapon is probably carried in his arm."

Szamual nodded. "We'd better head this off before something blows. Do we have a present location for either of these men?"

"Negative. We have an informer who claims Quinn is known to associate with a waitress in the waterfront area. We have her name and address, with firm identification."

"Good," Szamual said. "Feed all your information to Interception. I think I'll have a few men drop by this waitress's place."

"Right," DeAmico said and made the computer transfer.

He pressed his knuckles against his forehead. That took care of three cases tonight, but four more had come in while he was trying to untangle the last one. "How about another cup of coffy?" he asked.

"Are you certain you want it?" the desk asked.

"Why, what do you mean?"

"It's nearly quitting time for you," the desk said.

He glanced at his watch. It was almost midnight and the morning shift was reporting into the console room already. He had an instant idea and punched Szamual's button again.

"Yes, what is it, DeAmico?"

"I'm going off duty now, Captain. I was wondering if I could go along with Interception on this last problem."

"Sure. Why not? But you'd better hurry. They're about ready to pull out now."

"Thank you, Captain," DeAmico said.

"Good night, Sergeant," the desk said as he pushed away.

V

STANDARD WAS SUFFOCATING in a fine brown haze that stung his nostrils and pummeled his skin. His eyes were rheumy and filled with congealed tears from staring at the rocks and sand strewn before him. A persistent insect was making a home for itself by burrowing into the soft flesh around his crotch. He ignored it stoically, not daring to move.

A saltbush had been slowly, almost imperceptively, changing positions for the past hour. Since bushes were not known to pick up and take walks, it intrigued Standard. Right now, it was a good three feet from where he had first begun to watch it.

The movement was no steady creep, but a series of jerks, each only a fraction of an inch long, too rapid for the eye to follow in the chiaroscuro of the intense light patterns of the desert.

He watched it carefully, blinking the crud from his eyes and letting the insect gnaw happily. The bush was a scanner, he decided. Out there somewhere, the enemy lay dug in as himself with their electronic scouts reconnoitering their line of advancement before the mass of troops came surging forward. They were playing it carefully. Now that the brunt of the allied defensive had been broken, they could afford to take the time.

So far, the scanner had taken no notice of Standard. He was half buried under a rubbish pile of sand and gravel, the snout of his impact rifle barely protruding from under his belly. The valley was fringed by the burnt desert, sloping up to his ridge until it was lost in the undulating foothills of the McDonnell Range.

The war had been coming for two decades, seething and boiling in southern Asia. It had ignited in northern China; then, while the attention had been drawn, broken through the Indonesian islands, expanding in volume.

It was no pushbutton war. Australia learned that when the northern coast became a holocaust within a week under the onslaught of the first wave.

The rise of nationalism that had overtaken the seventies had immobilized SEATO years before and before the alliance could realign, the battle of the mid mountains had been fought and lost. Two-thirds of Australia fell with more than half its population under occupation.

Some mornings Standard would tell himself it was all a grand farce. If he could just clear his eyes and get the goddamned sand out of them, it would go away like a drunken nightmare. The Battle of McDonnell Range had been a rout. Outbackers and 'roo hunters were no match for the Chinasian invaders. SEATO was outclassed, outmanned, outgunned.

The alliance was pulling back to mount a massive defensive along the Bering Straits, the next and, Standard thought bitterly, the last final assault the Chins would make before they poured into the Western Hemisphere.

And as sure as the saltbush in the valley in front of him was an enemy relay scanner, he knew the final defensive would fail. There was too little time left. The Chins were moving cautiously, but rapidly. Too rapidly. In a week, they would be descending in mass into New South Wales. The retreating alliance would be chopped off in a giant scissors movement.

So he had volunteered for this duty, to implant himself as a rear guard to mark the progress of the enemy to his retreating army. He had preferred to die alone in this wasted expanse of rock rather than to watch his own country in its death throes.

In a way, Standard felt privileged. Few men were able to choose their exact moment of death. Standard could. Once he switched on the dove, his life could be counted in seconds and a few seconds one way or the other was close enough for him.

The small white plate of the dove was pressed against his breastbone. Once he pressed the first actuator, it would fix its position by the polarized light of the sun, just as a honeybee. With the second button, it would blare out a steady stream of location and time data. The allied mobile command post would receive the signal and note it on its charts as the southernmost advancement of the enemy. It

was crude and simple. It was about all they had left that could break through the Chins' jamming.

And it was deadly. In theory, so the classroom drill had gone, Standard only had to deactivate the dove, retreat further south and wait until the enemy caught up with him again and mark that new position. Realistically, he knew the enemy could zero in on the dove's position as instantly as headquarters could. That added up to another statistic. Him.

Apparently, their scanner had not relayed back any indication of heavy ambush armament in their path. On the horizon, he could detect the dust being churned and guessed their arrival time around dusk. He still could not afford the luxury of swatting the gnawing insect, so he waited motionlessly.

He woke from a fitful sleep and peered into the darkness. Dimly he saw movement before him in the valley. He dislodged himself carefully from the rubble and pulled the dove from under his shirt. Here goes nothing, he thought, and pressed the first stud. Hoping there was enough sunlight left to make a fix, he jabbed the second stud.

He tossed the dove to the sand and dodged as quickly and silently as he could away from it. The gravel splayed out from under his feet, clattering down into the valley. A garbled cry drifted up to him. They were aware of him and he scrambled for the outcropping of rock to his left before the mortars began lobbing down.

There was a flash from the valley. The mortar explosion threw him off his feet, landing only a few yards from where he had left the dove. The second round was less forgiving. Scores of rock splinters needled his face.

Now what the hell? he thought. *Go drop your shells on that dove!*

A line of bullets smacked across the outcropping. *Oh Christ.* He realized they weren't even bothering to locate him by triangulating the dove's position. They were on to him with direct infrared visual, watching him scurry among the rocks. Now that was a kick in the head. They weren't even giving him the niceties of a technological death.

The next round confirmed it. He rolled in the sand to extinguish his smoldering fatigues and crawled back to the edge of the ridge. Bright, tiny bursts of flame were joining the fireworks of the mortars as the Chin troops were using him for target practice.

He flipped the safety from his own impact rifle and aimed

into the encampment and began squeezing off shots. When the clip emptied, he reloaded and methodically continued. That was the last time he was going to do any planning ahead. If he had just stayed with the dove, they probably wouldn't have even noticed him.

There was no way of knowing whether he was hitting anything. The cad batteries for his own scope had given out weeks before, along with the bulk of his ammunition. He felt like laughing, ridiculously ineffectual. The rifle butt punched into his shoulder and he thought playfully of Horatio at the bridge defending Rome against the invading barbarians. *Yessir, baby, gonna save the world from them Chins. Yessireebob.* Except that he did not feel particularly heroic and did not feel he was making any notable change on the world tonight.

It was a game. A great big game with a spin-around pointer a mile long, and when it came around and pointed at you, it was all over, babes. You were home free for all time after that.

One of the lights was not an intermittent flash. It glistened with a single, seering glow.

Laser! his mind recoiled. His random shots must have been taking effect, because they were pulling out the serious stuff and putting an end to the game. The rock wall was suddenly incandescent. A gush of incredibly intense heat and the stench of molten rock engulfed him.

He kicked, driving himself backward down the slope, flinging his rifle out of the way, hitting the gravel on his side.

He almost made it. The laser cut through his outstretched wrist like a powersaw through lard.

The pain was an uncomprehending thing that rammed down his throat, gathered his stomach and tore it out of his mouth in a ripping howl. Half blinded by the fury of it, he saw his severed hand with great gouts of black blood arching in the air. Fascinated, he watched it land inches from his face, the fingers twitching and grasping in the sand until the cascading darkness drowned out his howling.

The first day was bad. The Chins found him on the ridge after the rock had cooled and dragged him into their encampment. They decided they had better use for their medical supplies than to waste painkillers on a prisoner who looked as though he had all the life expectancy of chopped

liver, so they tied his back to a scrub bush and let him alternate wildly between a thrashing semi-coma and a red-hot consciousness.

The second day was worse because he managed to stay awake more and consequently screamed more. One of his captors found his first aid kit and squirted jelfoam in the gaping facial wounds the shards of rock had cratered. The first aid kit disappeared among the Chin troops, as did his boots and his fatigues. His rifle had been sliced in two. They did not notice the dove under the gravel. It remained broadcasting.

At first, his screaming did not overly annoy the encampment. The Chins screamed back at him. By noon they had tired of the serenade and landed a few well-placed kicks to quiet him. By afternoon, two of his ribs were cracked and he was screaming more quietly. Since the stub of his wrist had been nearly cauterized by the laser, the wound was left raw. Sandfleas and dirt began to accumulate and infection crept up his forearm. Blood and lymph oozed down his neck as the jelfoam was assimilated.

The third morning was the best. He was babbling incoherently. The platoon leader listened to him carefully. Luckily, the lieutenant could not speak English, because otherwise he might not have called in the helicopter and had Standard transferred to their base hospital.

He woke, feeling the moist salt air and knew he was on the northern coast. A Chin doctor in a dirty smock was bending over him, examining the arm. The infection had swelled and festered beneath the glazed skin. The doctor reached for a scalpel and jabbed it into the stub to let it drain.

Thanks a lot, Standard thought, and passed out again.

They packed him full of antibiotics. Standard had an allergic reaction to their brand of myocillin and died twice. Each time, they managed to restart his heart. Each time, his babbling became more intense. He had no idea of what he was saying, but he knew it had to have been worthwhile because he dimly became aware that the treatment was gradually improving.

One day he found his forearm several inches shorter, the sloughing gangrenous flesh completely trimmed away, and the arm sutured and bandaged. The pain had rescinded to

a dull throb. The plasters held his rib cage securely and the dressing on his face was changed every morning.

He retched, aware of all the things he must have told them to warrant the treatment.

"Don't give me any more of those goddamn shots," Standard said. He had been punctured, pricked, and pumped full of so many drugs he was worried he was becoming a junkie. The shots kept him confined to the bed, wiping consciousness from him. He wanted to move about, to walk farther than to the john, and even though he knew he would not be allowed to wander down the halls of the hospital, he felt that even a concentration camp was preferable to his isolated confinement.

The nurse smiled and squirted the excess air out of the hypodermic.

"What are you doing, Lotus Blossom? Now why do you want to give me any more of that stuff? I've told you people every goddamn thing I know by now, anyway. It's just a waste of time."

She beamed and expertly guided the needle into his vein.

"Go tell Lin Sang this is violation of the something or other."

She nodded pleasantly, inspected the glucose bottle and left the room, still smiling.

Time was an ocean for him. He felt it wash against him incessantly, eroding him, but like an island, he was rooted to the room and the waves that broke on his shores passed over him and left him undisturbed.

He watched the glucose drip down the intravenous tube. As he studied the molasses flow, the drops began to splash outside the tube. They trickled down in a thin rivulet until they fell off and dribbled on the floor. He was hallucinating, knowing the splashing drops were still contained in the bottle, but life was too boring to overlook a single diversion. He settled back to enjoy the spectacle. Anything to break the monotony, even if it was his own imagination. He was curious to see how far the buildup of drugs would take him.

Each splash left a tiny blue filament in the air after it. The lacy filaments intertwined and grew until the entire tube was covered with blue lint, fuzzing up until it encompassed the glucose bottle in soft flocking. Experimentally, he looked away and watched a fly crawl up the opposite wall.

When he turned back to the bottle, the blue fuzz had increased by the same amount that it would have if it actually had been leaking outside the tube. That surprised him. The hallucination was continuous, a separate band of reality all to itself.

No wonder some of his buddies in training camp had been druggies. It was hard to tell where reality ended. A man could lose himself pretty easily in his own mind.

He timed the droplets and estimated the probable growth of the blue moss per drop. Then he counted off the time with his eyes shut. When he looked again at the bottle, the growth seemed to be consistent with the amount he had estimated.

He marveled at the apparent reality of the hallucination. The big question, of course, was whether the hallucination was *really* consistent with reality. Maybe the fuzz had grown at the rate he *thought* it should. There was no way to tell if it would have grown that much if it was really happening.

But he enjoyed it, nonetheless. Fascinated, he watched until a movement caught the corner of his eye.

A gnome was clambering through the window, dressed in khaki bush fatigues with a tennis racket in its hand. Standard considered that. It had to be an illusion. There were bars over the window, but a gnome would be able to find a way through those. No, the telltale sign was the tennis racket. Nobody, not even a gnome, would play tennis in a hospital. On the other hand, there was no guarantee that he was in a hospital.

The gnome passed like vapor through the wire strands of mesh that blocked the window until it materialized on the floor. With a sweeping flourish the gnome turned a dial on the wall (strange he had never noticed that dial before) and the window lit up like a tridimensional teleview screen. Standard frowned.

It was obvious the gnome knew more about this place than he did. Miffed, he watched the window screen. The action was taking place outside the mesh, but Standard could see it clearly enough. It was a musical of sorts, the participants all dressed in fatigues that were spangled and sequined, dancing to a soundless noise.

The dancing became progressively more frenetic until it became an all-out burlesque with slapstick comedians and

winking girls who kept shedding iridescent battle jackets, which were magically replaced as soon as they had been removed, to keep the gnome censors happy. Standard was enormously pleased, although irked by the prudity.

Slowly he became aware of the tempo and imagined he could hear the chords. But that was strictly his imagination, because he was finally able to hear the music after straining. It wasn't music after all. It was machine gun fire, machine guns roaring from a dozen different pillboxes. And they weren't dancing. They were being hit. All at once, from a dozen machine guns, over and over. They were pirouetting, arms flaying, a frantic mincing step as the slugs jostled them back and forth, not letting them fall.

The gnome was standing on the ceiling now, motioning with a gnarled finger to his purple lips for silence. Standard realized he had been humming in time to the dance steps. The gnome put a hand to its ear and listened intently, so Standard listened, too. He heard whispering voices from down the hall. The voices were emanating from a laundry closet, clandestinely occupied by two people in hospital smocks.

"He has told us everything he knows," a voice was saying and Standard recognized it as Lin Sang's. He was talking to his nurse, the one with the constant hypodermic; for the first time, Standard noticed that she too wore an enameled star on her breast. Look out for star-spangled hospitals! It was lucky for Standard that the gnome had let him look through the walls.

"Not only that," Lotus Blossom said. "This afternoon he told me he did not want any more shots." *Damn*, Standard thought furiously, *she can speak English*. She had been holding out on him all along.

"What?" Lin Sang erupted. "Who does he think he is, trying to tell me how to run my hospital? If I say he gets a shot, then he's going to get a shot. I don't need some white-eyed sonofabitch telling me what to do. *Nobody* tells me how to run this hospital."

"That's true, Doctor. That's absolutely true. That's absolutely, gloriously true."

"Betcherass, it is. He's beginning to suspect, anyway. As a matter of fact, I think he's trying to listen to us right now," Lin Sang said, his narrow eyes squinting even more.

Standard tried desperately to pull back his ears, but they were held firm by the gnome.

"Hey, whose side are you on?" Standard yelled at the gnome.

"His usefulness is at an end," Lin Sang said.

"What shall we do?" Lotus Blossom asked.

"We'll teach him a lesson he won't forget. We'll give him another injection. *That'll* teach him!" Lin Sang gloated and exposed a vial of fuming fluid. "A good belt of this and he won't be telling me how to run my hospital."

This is no hallucination, Standard thought, panicked. *My God, this is real!* They were getting ready to kill him because he knew too much. What the hell did he know? Of course! He knew how to hear through walls. Lordy, lordy!

The gnome was not on the floor. It had stolen away. No, there it was, on the ceiling. It was hanging by its feet from the ceiling, hanging right over him, both hands clutching a hypodermic as long as a carbine. Standard could see the gnome's muscles strain as it tensed the needle over its head, poising it directly over Standard's belly.

"Oh, ho," Standard yelled. "Now you reveal your true nature!"

"Bonzai!" the gnome howled.

"The hell you say!" Standard screamed. He grabbed the glucose bottle, tearing the tube from his arm, and flung it at the gnome's face. The gnome sidestepped gracefully and the bottle shattered against the wall, spraying the room with glucose. The gnome brought the needle slashing down and Standard twisted frantically, throwing his weight sideways. He felt some tube tear loose.

The gnome's glittering rapier knifed into the mattress, igniting the sheets with the fulminating fluid. There was a dull ripping sensation in his arm, and blood—his or the gnome's?—was staining the bed. Or maybe it was the blue flocking that was drifting through the room from the broken bottle. Standard had no time to investigate.

He careened across the room, ramming into the night stand and tipping the water pitcher. The gnome was on his back instantly, digging its talons deep into his face. He drove his elbow into the gnome's chest, driving it backward. The gnome crumpled, gasping for breath.

Footsteps were pounding up the hallway and Standard knew his only escape was through the window. He kicked the gnome under the night stand and yanked at the window grillwork, but it was rigidly fastened. How the hell did that

gnome manage to get in? The dancers on the other side weren't much help, either. They were watching him curiously. When they saw that he was watching them, they went back to their machine gun dance, this time with the addition of landmines. *Nuts*, Standard throught peevishly, *I'm going to miss it.*

He dived for the door, reaching the hallway. A guard was rushing to stop him. Standard swung, seeing the flecks of blood pepper the guard's face, and missed him completely. He forgot that his arm was almost half a foot shorter. The momentum of his swing drove him to his knees, leaving him wide-open and vulnerable.

I think I've just killed myself, Standard through lucidly, and the guard's clubbed hand came clipping down to the back of his neck.

Lin Sang finished replacing the drainage tubes and said something unintelligible to Lotus Blossom. She nodded agreement and they left Standard with the gnome standing on the ceiling. Since they seemed to take no notice of it, Standard decided it was a figment of his imagination, but he wished they had taken it with them.

He discovered one amazing bit of information. No matter how rational he was, no matter how hard he tried to make the gnome disappear from his mind, the hallucination remained as real and true to perspective as the bed was. The information was not overly comforting. It was a blow to his pride to learn that mental control was only a textbook phrase, not a governable actuality. He mulled the scanty knowledge of psychiatry he had and sneered. By God, there *were* demons and possessions and no couch or notetaking or regression theories would ever get that gnome off his ceiling.

The gnome stayed there until morning. Standard did not dare sleep, partly to be prepared in the event that the gnome would find some new diabolical plaything, and partly from the hope that staying awake might raise his metabolic level higher to help disperse the accumulated drugs in his system in as short a time as possible. He stayed awake, watching the gnome's every movement until the dawn crept into the room.

With the tentacles of light, he cautiously turned his attention to the window, still warily keeping the gnome in the corner of his vision. The ballet troupe was still going through its motions, but now sleepily, and some of them

were even picking up the clothes they had shed. Even the faint staccato melody was fading. He watched the lazy acrobatics until noon, when the gnome lifted (dropped?) itself from its yogi position and scrambled down the wall. Bracing himself, Standard watched it bow to him and switch off the scene in the window. Standard forgot to notice where the control knob was hidden. With a gracious smile, thanking him for an extremely entertaining evening, the gnome stepped out the window and vanished.

Slowly the blue moss drifting around the room collected itself on the new glucose bottle. By evening, it had disappeared and the fluid was not splashing outside the tube.

He received no shot that day or the next. After a week, Lin Sang and Lotus Blossom were satisfied that the wounds Standard had reopened were healing and they stopped making regular visits to his room. They seemed slightly disgusted with his behavior. An armed guard brought his meals. Sometime later, they wheeled another bed into his room.

"What's this?" Standard asked Lin Sang, who was supervising the installation of some rather exotic equipment.

"We have decided to give you a roommate," Lin Sang said. His English was flawless, with an amused singsong lilt to it. Sang's singsong, Standard thought.

"That's nice." Standard grimaced. "I suppose you're putting him in here to watch out for any more tantrums I throw."

Ling Sang smiled gently. "Possibly."

"What's his problem? Another drug addict?"

"No," Lin Sang said. "Brain damage. He won't cause any problem for you."

"Good. I hate complainers."

He watched Lin Sang and the orderlies prepare the bed. Lin Sang was wearing his customary smock and face mask bunched under his chin, with the enameled star medallion pinned to his chest. Sang's duties ran beyond medical and he was willing, if not eager, to talk to Standard.

"Hey, Sang," Standard said, "what day is this?"

"Close," Sang answered.

"Close? What do you mean close?" Standard frowned.

"Close to victory," replied Lin Sang.

"Oh, Christ. Besides that, dammit. What day is today?"

"What difference does it make to you? You have no purpose for the information. Soon your government will capitu-

late and time will begin anew from the day of the glorious victory. The entire freedom-loving world will rejoice and will begin a new calendar. That is what is important."

"Until I start rejoicing, what day is today by the old-fashioned decadent figuring?" He had long since learned not to take Lin Sang too seriously in his conversational moods and often questioned whether Lin Sang himself took the whole glorious revolution very seriously.

"If I told you that this was the Year of the Ox, would that have any meaning for you?"

"Not much. How about telling me in respect to the year of Our Lord?"

"Since I do not recognize your 'lord' that would be difficult and meaningless to me. We are struggling to create a new world in which all men can attain their true nobility and democracy without the oppression of lords and serfdom. How can I tell you what year this is of your lord, when you have no understanding of the Year of the Ox?"

"I *know* what year it is. Just tell me the day."

"Are you sure you know what year this is?"

"Yep," Standard said. "This is the Year of the Ox, and you're about as stubborn as one."

"Very good," Lin Sang said and saluted Standard with a mock bow. "You begin to understand how meaningless time is. You understand how worthless arbitrary nomenclature is. Besides, you are much better at answering questions than you are asking them," he added cheerfully.

"I could have done without that remark," Standard grumbled, and turned his face to the wall.

They left him alone again. Preparing the room took the better part of the afternoon. When someone entered or departed the room, Standard could glimpse the uniformed guards in the hallway. Aside from his drugged break, he had never left the room consciously. He gingerly lifted himself and the drainage tubes until he could see out the window. All he could see were the personnel trucks that occasionally drove up and divested packages of men, and those were five stories below. He was glad he hadn't been able to learn how the gnome had gotten through the window.

The war was far to the south from his private world. As time dragged by, broken only by the regular lapses of floating that marked the beginnings and ends of the uncon-

scious interrogations, he cared less and finally not at all about the question of loyalty. He reconciled his conscience with the thought he had not yet been brainwashed. Then he would wonder for hours whether his mind really was his own.

The new inhabitant's head was completely swathed in bandages. When he finally felt like talking to the new man, Standard found him totally uncommunicative. He wondered idly if under the bandages skulked the gnome.

If nothing else, the presence of the other man brought attendants to the room. They skirted Standard with a general display of indifference and spent a few minutes each day listening for a heartbeat in the new patient and taking brainwave readings, an event which never failed to excite them. Satisfied, they would change the bottles and drainage pans and, infrequently, the bedding. They never changed the dressing surrounding his head, though, and Standard began to wonder if the man had a head at all.

Which was pretty ridiculous, he told himself. If he didn't have a head, how could they take brainwave readings?

Tiring of the effort to guess the man's injuries—since there was no way to determine if he was correct or not, and Lin Sang seemed no more inclined to inform him of that than he had of the date—Standard altered his attention to the window and spent his time counting the strands of wire.

It became progressively more difficult after the first dozen wires, because his eyes would start watering from staring at it and they would swim out of focus. Then he would have to start again at the beginning, riveting his eyes to keep their place. It took him nearly a week to count all the vertical wires. He relaxed for a day, letting the noises of the hospital break around him, pleased with himself. Out of bland curiosity, he wondered if the number of horizontal wires was the same as the verticals, disregarding the fact that the window was taller than it was wide, so he began counting those. A quarter of the way through he forgot the original number of verticals and went back to counting those again.

There were more horizontals than there were verticals. After establishing that, there was little he could find to do except count the sounds of the ambulance doors opening and closing outside. Some days, he counted into the twenties, on other days, increasingly infrequent, the doors slammed as high as the fifties. After half a month had slid by, he became

aware that the slammings were becoming less each day. He needed a new diversion.

He occupied himself by watching his silent partner's breathing. The breathing was shallow and there would be long, irregular intervals between the inhalations. Since he could not talk to the man, he felt no great amount of sympathy. At least the man wasn't aware of the slow drag of time.

He devised a game. The meals, though meager, came twice a day without fail. Standard would save something, a bean or a shoot or some rare vestige of meat, and hide the tidbit under his pillow so that the gnome would not steal it if it should return. Then he guessed how many times the silent man would breathe during the day between breakfast and dinner. If he was too high, he saved the hidden food until the next day for a new guess. If he was low, he would eat the stored morsel after the lights were extinguished.

The food was always threatening to spoil, so he regularly guessed low, sometimes a hundred, sometimes a more realistic figure to give his comatose partner a sporting chance. Once he had guessed five and dared the patient to exceed it. The man had responded by hitting a record high that day, miffing Standard.

He had a week's morsels stashed away when he decided to get even, and instituted a new rule. If the man died, Standard intended to give the man a farewell ceremony and eat all the food immediately. Dinner was late that day and he hoped it would be soon. Besides, the man's shallow breathing was beginning to interrupt his sleep.

The man did not die, but Lin Sang did.

Lin Sang entered the room one day and sat at the end of Standard's bed. His eyes were puffed together and deep lines were etched at the sides of his drawn mouth. He spent several minutes looking at the silent man without saying a word and finally turned to Standard.

"Long time no see," Standard said cheerily.

"I have been employed by more pressing matters," Lin Sang said. There was a haggard slur in his voice. "Hopefully, you did not think I was not interested in your welfare. I am happy to see you are progressing well."

"As well as can be expected," Standard said.

"To be honest, you are quite healthy enough to leave your bed and resume moderate activity." The wrinkled cor-

ners of his mouth lifted slightly. "But to have released you would have meant transportation to my country. I doubt if you would have enjoyed the consequences."

The comment threw Standard off guard. "You aren't saying you've kept me doped up just to keep me out of a prison camp, are you?"

"No, not precisely. Let us say I found you more useful here than you could have been elsewhere."

"You mean the information you've pumped out of me?"

Ling Sang smiled brokenly. "We had all the information you knew long ago. Your knowledge of your own armies was surprisingly paltry. Quite sincerely, what information we were able to dredge out of you was no more helpful than what we monitored from your broadcasts."

"I don't believe you," Standard said. "That doesn't make sense. Why did you patch me up and keep me alive if you weren't interested in what I could tell you?"

"Not for what you could tell us, but for what you could do for us."

"I'm not doing anything for you!" Standard insisted. "Just what do you think I'm going to do for you clowns?"

"You're doing it for us now." Lin Sang peered at Standard. "You have an audacious will to live. It is like a charged cloud, permeating this very room. I thought it was so strong that it could help other patients recover, so we placed that patient with the head injury with you as an experiment to see if your will to live could be transferred to him also. Apparently, it has worked. He grows stronger each day. Do you believe this?"

"Hell, no," Standard said. "That's the damnedest hunk of hogwash I've ever heard."

"You're right." Lin Sang smiled. "Well, how about this? Do you believe you have three eyes? One of them is at the base of your brain where the spinal column connects. Long in your evolutionary history, it was a real eye and could see light and shadow, but now it's buried deep in your neck. But it's an eye, nonetheless."

"This is more of your Oriental inscrutability," Standard grunted. "If it's inside my head, and I can't see with it, what good is it?"

"A number of things you could not do without. It controls the sexual maturation for one thing, and it keeps the

mind functioning rationally for another. It's about the size of your fingernail, but it's very important."

"Bullshit," Standard said. "What's this got to do with your keeping me here?"

"I really had no intention of telling you," Lin Sang said abstractly. "Perhaps you will learn yourself some day. My real reason for being here today is to bring you some good news."

"I'll bet," Standard said. "Okay, get it over with. What is it?"

"You will be released tomorrow."

Standard's mouth hung open. He did not dare jump to the conclusion that was racing through him. "You mean I'm going to be released from this hospital?"

"Yes," said Lin Sang. "The transfer will take place shortly after daybreak. First, you will be bathed and given a fresh gown."

"Hold on a second," Standard said. "What are you telling me? Are you taking me to a prison camp?"

"No, no," Lin Sang said impatiently. "You are being released to your people in exchange for some of our people."

"What?" Standard cried. "An exchange? When did this happen? Honest to God, are you on the level?"

"Much has happened," Lin Sang said. "I do not have time to tell you all, but I thought you would be pleased."

"Oh, Christ, am I!" Standard whooped. The enormity of it struck him like a barrage. This could mean that the war had reached a settlement point. Maybe Australia had not gone under. If Australia had not fallen, could that mean that all the information he had dribbled out of his unconscious had really been as worthless as Lin Sang said it was?

"Hey." Standard jerked his head toward the silent second bed. "What about him. Does he go, too?"

"Yes, he will be exchanged also," Lin Sang said. "He, you, and about thirty more of your people."

He stood to leave. That was when the strangled gurgle ruptured from his throat. He clawed at his chest, sinking to his knees. The guard heard the hoarse cry and bolted into the room just as Lin Sang convulsed on the floor. The guard called an orderly and they carried him out stiffly and did not bother to clean the tile.

Standard received no bath and no meal in the morning, but he was not particularly hungry and in no mood to com-

plain. He had seen men die on the battlefields, but never the way Lin Sang had groveled and it unsettled his appetite. Death itself was obscene to him, but a man scrabbling and making a mess of himself on the floor was the ultimate obscenity, stripping away every remaining vestige of dignity. Death was the last great insult.

The exchange took place uneventfully. Several nurses unhooked him from his receptacles and the orderlies carried his stretcher to the elevator out of the building. For the first time, Standard saw the burnt windows in the surrounding buildings and the deep trenches cut in the lawn of the hospital by the ambulance trucks.

In the middle of the lawn, two Allied soldiers took his stretcher and placed him in a van that was decorated with the blue and white world symbol. Racks had been welded to the sides of the truck to accept the stretchers.

"What the hell has happened?" Standard asked anyone.

"The bloody war is over," the man at his feet said.

"Over? What do you mean 'over'?"

"Finished, kaput. It's all over."

Standard hesitated to ask the next question. "Look, anyone know who won? Did we beat 'em at McDonnell?"

"They ain't saying. It don't sound too good to me."

One of the drivers thrust his head into the truck and said, "How's everything back there? We're packing up now. Anybody need a medic?"

There was a rumbling grunt from inside. "Where the hell were you when we could've used you?"

Standard twisted on his cot. "Hey, buddy. Tell me something."

"Yeah. What do ya wanta know?"

"Just tell me one thing," Standard said. "Who won?"

The driver looked at him levelly. "I thought you knew. Nobody won."

"Nobody won? A draw? Both sides just up and quit?"

"You'll hear all about it when we get you down south," the driver said. "But that's about it."

He closed the panels heavily. Minutes later, the turbines churned over and they felt the road winding under them. They were silent until one of the men began sobbing.

"Ain't that a kick in the ass!" the man at Standard's side said. "I get buggered up and some goddamn politican figures

the war is costing too much so they call the whole fonking thing off. Jeezuzkeyrist."

Standard shrugged. "I don't much give a damn why they stopped it. Just so's it's over."

The man at his side glowered. "Yeah, maybe so." He turned his attention to the sobbing soldier. "Hey, shut up your goddamn bawling so we can enjoy this ride."

Standard counted the ruts in the pavement as they bounced to the heliport and wondered what had happened to the man with the bandaged head.

VI

THE TIP OF the electron pencil shimmered a delicate blue. Quinn adjusted the clasp on his briefcase. The blue arc enlarged to a cutting distance of six inches. There was a hushed whining sound as the molecules of the air surrounding the pencil were disunited, the electron force nullifying the valence cohesion.

Jeannine watched his adjustments with mounting anxiety. "Quinn, what if there's a bomb inside his arm? Won't it explode?"

"There's no bomb," Quinn said. He lifted the arm to avoid cutting into Jeannine's carpeting and prepared to separate the limb. The elbow seemed as good a spot as any to begin with. Graystone's X-rays had indicated a few blood vessels, but nothing too major, just a few capillaries. There was no cauterizing effect to the electron pencil, just a clean and instant separation, but Standard would lose only a negligible amount of blood with any luck at all. That is, the chances were fairly good that he would not die immediately.

"But what if there *is* a bomb? Or something else?" Jeannine insisted.

"Nothing's going to happen," Quinn asserted. "But if it does, you know what to do. Just drop your head between your legs and kiss your sweet little fanny goodbye."

She shook her head emphatically. "I'm worried, Quinn. I don't believe Rim ordered you to do this. There's no reason for cutting a man's arm off just because you *think* he's dangerous."

"There's every reason in this world for disarming a murderer." Quinn sucked in his breath sharply. "Now look, kid, you're getting out of line. Rim wants to know what this arm does, and it's my intention to find out. I can't locate the equipment around here to do a thorough exam, so I'm going to take this arm to the equipment. Afterward, maybe you'd like to keep it for yourself."

"I don't understand." She frowned.

He looked at her icily. "Why, after we get through checking it, you could tuck it under your pillow at night. When the urge strikes you, you could simply switch it on and enjoy yourself. Handy, don't you think?"

"That's not funny," she said.

"Maybe not, but it might keep you off the streets at night." She winced. "I have you to thank for that, Quinn."

"Of course. It's all nasty old Quinn's fault, isn't it? Honey, you were a natural-born hooker when I met you. All I did was take advantage of your latent talents." His voice hardened. "Now hold this arm up to me unless you want your rug cut to threads."

She stepped across Standard's prone form. "I still don't think Rim ordered this," she said, reaching for the arm.

"Does it matter? Who are you worried about? Yourself or this ape?"

She paused and shrugged. "You're right. I'm being silly." She smiled and wrapped her arms loosely around Quinn's shoulders. "Just in case it *does* blow up, how about giving me one last kiss?"

He opened his mouth angrily to blurt out his annoyance, but at the same moment Jeannine compressed the nerve pellet in her bracelet. The hydroxytryptophan injected directly into his spine. Quinn's eyes bugged out and his knees buckled. She stepped to the side and straight-armed him in the chest. He went over backward, hitting the floor hard. The electron gun skittered from his grip, shaving the pile from the carpet as it rolled across the floor.

She twisted the clasp on the briefcase. A puff of fabric followed the spurting beam as it lanced across the room.

Quickly, she spun the control clasp in the opposite direction until she felt it click into lock position.

It would take several minutes for Standard to regain consciousness, but she knew Quinn would be out for hours. The pellet she had fired at Standard was the same kind most girls carried with them in the city to ward off the especially insistent chance acquaintances. But the one that Quinn took was the real thing, packed with enough tryp to put a man out of commission for half a day. Two could kill, and she felt sorely tempted.

She tried to arrange the fragments of her swirling mind. Something was drastically wrong here. Quinn had always been arrogant and demanding, but why did she choose this particular time to rebel against him? And why had Rim not stopped him? Or stopped her, if Quinn was correct in wanting to cut off the arm. Rim had been powerful enough to stop the war and reunite the world, and he had been young then. Why didn't Rim know what was in Standard's arm?

It was like watching a vidiscreen play with interference from an insane asylum. On one channel an acrobat was tumbling her thoughts and at the same time a macabre maniac was tossing questions between the acrobat's gyrations. Too many questions without logical answers. Ever since she had met this man Standard, she had been confused and her emotions had been running backward. She did not *think* she loved him, but why else had she saved him? And she knew Rim was the only humane and just force in the world, so how could it allow Standard's arm to be separated?

When she had first met Quinn, she was barely sixteen, hustling the lakers along the shore bars. He had been better dressed, out of place with the rough and generally filthy boathands, and with more money to spend than any of them, so he had won her favor almost immediately. She chided herself afterward for being so naïve, but then it was too late and Quinn had given her the apartment.

She assumed she was going to be Quinn's girl. Her father had never returned from the war and her mother had taken off with one of the lakers. The thought of having her own home, even if it was under a "kept" arrangement, pleased her. It wasn't all bad. A few of her friends had made similar arrangements work well for them. After a time, they might complain they felt the possession, but even that had a sense of security about it. Her biggest worry was that

Quinn would become overly possessive and not allow her to even leave the apartment without escort.

She had nothing to fear. It turned out exactly the opposite. Quinn was not interested in her as a full-time mistress. Precisely why he had bothered to establish her in the apartment escaped her at first. He would encourage her to continue in her rounds, occasionally even pointing out likely dates for her.

Slowly, she understood. Quinn was using her as bait. The dates he selected for her somehow slipped out of sight. Quinn said they were recruits, but Jeannine suspected they were fugitives because she never saw any of the men again.

In time, Quinn told her more. She almost laughed in his face when he told her that Rim, the cryptic name of his organization, had ended the war. No organization was powerful enough to control whole nations, but Quinn insisted.

He had let her meet the Rim. Then she believed.

Standard's groaning brought her mind back to reality. Jeannine withdrew another pellet from her bracelet and watched Standard cough and roll slowly, fighting down the nausea. He managed to keep his stomach where it belonged and looked up. Jeannine was pointing the pellet at his face. "Oh, Christ. Not again," he said.

"Just mind your manners," Jeannine said. "He was going to cut your arm off, so I stopped him. But that doesn't mean I won't stop you again if you get nasty."

"In that case, thanks. Although with the way things are going, it's probably just as well if I got the fool thing taken off once and for all." He settled back on his haunches and pressed his eyes closed to clear them.

"You could've gotten hurt, you know," he added. "That was a pretty nervy thing."

"I didn't take any chances," Jeannine said calmly. "He didn't know what hit him."

"Yeah, well, I wasn't just talking about your boyfriend. I meant what could've happened if you hadn't stopped him." The effects of the nerve pellet were wearing off quickly. The girl was standing only a few feet from him. One good lunge should knock her off her feet before she could fire the pellet. He calculated the distance and knew he could make it, but was not entirely convinced that there was an immediate threat.

She cocked her head. "What do you mean? Is there really a weapon in your arm? Would it have exploded?"

"What is this?" Standard asked amiably. "Question and answer time?"

"It's serious talk time. *Is* there a weapon in your arm?"

"I guess so." He smiled brokenly, the scar tissue tugging at his mouth. "That's not much of an answer, but it's about the best I can do. I'm pretty sure I'm packing a weapon in there, but I don't know what it is, and I don't know how to use it. I suspect you don't believe that."

She looked at him thoughtfully. "I don't have much choice, do I? It doesn't make much difference. It's not my place to pass judgment on you."

Standard mulled her reply. "That opens up all kinds of conversational avenues. Since this is talk time, how about answering a question for me? Why did you help me? Your boyfriend may be a little unhappy when he comes to."

"I wish you wouldn't keep calling him my boyfriend. He's not a friend."

"Okay, he's not your friend. Then who is he? I seem to recall seeing him on your phone last night. Now, don't tell me he really is your doctor and he was treating you for a headache when I came in."

"No, he's not a doctor," Jeannine said. "His name is Quinn and he is my superior. As for helping you, I'm not sure why I did it. Maybe I'm in love with you. I don't even know why I'm talking to you at all."

"This morning didn't seem too loving to me. What changed your mind?"

Jeannine pouted her lips. "A lot of things happened since this morning."

"You can say that again. You mind if I get up? I'm getting cramps in my legs. You remind me of some Amazon huntress, standing with that gas thingamajig aimed at my skull."

"No tricks," she said, stepping back cautiously.

"You're a fine one to talk about tricks. Since we've met, you've been more fun than a memory circuit in a motel room. But you're growing on me, kid. Damned if I know why. Maybe it's the masochist in me."

"I told you to be nice," Jeannine warned, juggling the pellet. "Stop being witty and try to be serious."

Standard steadied himself against an inflated wall and appraised the girl. If he was going to make his move, now

was the time. She had saved his arm, but she was also the same one who had gotten him into the situation in the first place. Either Quinn or the girl was working under the Rim's directives, and not necessarily willingly.

He gambled on the girl and nodded lazily. "Okay, we'll talk seriously. What do you want to talk about?"

She curled into a chair the color and texture of raspberry gelatin, keeping the pellet trained on him. "Let's talk about you."

"I was afraid you'd say that. First you think you love me, and now you want to have a serious talk. Next thing, you'll want to take me home to your mother."

"I'd like to," she said quietly. "But I don't know where she is."

He let that pass and pointed at Quinn's form in the corner. "What about him? This isn't the most private spot in the world for a heart-to-heart talk."

"Don't worry about Quinn," she said. "He won't be waking for three or four hours, at least. I gave him a shot of tryp."

"It sure has a soothing effect," Standard agreed. "Did you give me some of the same stuff?"

"Of course not. You've only been unconscious for a few minutes. You got a little sniff of club. All the girls carry it for protection."

"Protection against what? This is the age of complete sexual freedom. Maybe you're not as free as you pretend to be?"

"Oh sure," Jeannine sighed. "Complete freedom. Has it ever occurred to you that there are time when it just isn't convenient for a girl to be passionate? Have you ever thought there might be times when I just don't *feel* like being mauled in a gutter or in a rest room in a bar?"

"I guess I really haven't thought too much about it," Standard admitted.

Jeannine sniffed. "You really are an ape."

"People have told me that," Standard said. "Look, just why did you save me since you have such obvious distaste for my social poise?"

"Because you've made such a mess of everything already and you're just making it worse. I don't know what you're supposed to be doing, but if you don't accept some help, you're going to destroy everything."

He looked at her and pressed his shoulders into the wall.

"Maybe I'm not the epitome of finesse in bed, but what do you expect from an ape?"

"Don't be coy," she said. "I'm not talking about making love. I'm talking about your mission."

"And what mission is that?"

"Quinn is sure you have a weapon in your arm. He couldn't learn anything from the doctor he took you to, so he was going to cut it off." She squirmed on her chair frustratedly.

"I already told you I'm as much in the dark about it as you are. Speaking of that doctor, is he a member of your friendly group, too?"

"Graystone? No, he's legitimate, I think. Quinn called him last night and set up the appointment. Mike, are you a killer?"

Standard masked his face with mock innocence. "You're just babbling sweet mysteries to me, baby. My feeble simian brain just can't comprehend what you're telling me."

She was on the verge of tears. "Please, Mike. It's terribly important to me. If I've made a mistake in helping you . . . please tell me."

"Okay, I'll be serious. Give me that pellet first." He crossed the room and reached for her hand.

"Don't, Mike. I'll fire."

He seized her wrist and forced it backward. The pellet popped sharply and sprayed the ceiling with the numbing mist.

He held her hand, looking down on her. She stared at him with large frightened eyes. Frightened not only because of him, he realized.

He released her and strode back across the room and prodded Quinn with his toe. He was stone still. Standard rifled his pockets. He withdrew a wallet and a flat case of burnished metal.

"Be careful of that," Jeannine whimpered. "You're pointing it at yourself."

"Oh?" he said and inspected the case. It fit easily into the palm of his hand like a deck of playing cards with evenly rounded corners. The burnished metallic surface was featureless except for the small hole centered in the edge nearest him.

"Just what am I pointing at myself?" he asked.

"It's a needle gun," Jeannine said. "It's one of Rim's inventions."

"Good for him. What do I press to make it fire?"

"Nothing. You will it to fire."

"Very nice. All I have to do is point this thing at you and want to fire, and you'd be nailed to that chair, right?"

She unfolded herself from the chair and came to him, massaging her hand. "Do you want to do that?"

"I guess not," he said as Jeannine wilted into his arms and began sniffling. Standard let her wet his tunic with her relief and held the metal object at arm's length. Half believing, he aimed the case loosely at the wall and willed it to fire. There was a faint tremor that tingled his hand and a section of polyplast puffed.

My god, it works! he thought absently.

The girl was still snuffling noisily, huddled in his chest, and had not heard the soft splintering sound of the needle impact. He wrapped his free arm around her and inspected the case again. It worried him. If it really was a thought-controlled Rim needle gun, how much use could it be against the Rim itself? It was a good trick, but thought-control was nothing new. He had a rudimentary form of it in his prosthetic.

Unless it did something more. A thought-aim device, for instance. There was an atrocious ashtray to his left across the room. He held the case to the opposite side of the room and willed it to strike the ashtray.

There was a melodious fracturing sound as the needle fragmented it.

Jeannine jerked and blinked her tears away. "What was that?"

"Your ashtray," Standard said, balancing the gun case and letting the air in his lungs whistle slowly out between his teeth.

"I wish you hadn't done that," she sniffed. "It was my only glass ashtray. They're hard to find, original five-and-dimers."

"Sorry, I didn't know you collected antiques. I wasn't watching where I was aiming. I wanted to see if it'd go where I told it to go."

"Of course it would." She smiled slightly and blew her nose. "I told you it was a thought-controlled gun."

"From now on, I'll believe you," he said respectfully.

"I'm glad." She smiled. "That makes me feel better. I don't feel as much a traitor now for tryping Quinn. Perhaps Rim wants you to stay alive. That's how I had the strength to save you."

"Well, don't start getting religious on me," Standard said. He slipped the gun into his pocket. As long as it behaved itself, it might be useful.

"Why shouldn't I?"

Standard grinned sheepishly. "Because I'm supposed to kill the Rim. That's what I'm doing here. I want to wipe out the Rim before it wipes out humanity."

Jeannine pushed away from him and cocked her head. She looked at him quizzically, shaking her hair.

"But that's silly. The Rim isn't wrecking the world. It's the greatest, most wonderful thing that has ever happened to the world. It holds humanity together, Mike. That's what Rim means. It's like a cup full of water. All the people in the world make up the water, always flowing and just sloshing around. If you tip the cup, the water will spill over and then it's no longer one. It's just a big mud puddle doing nothing. Government is the cup that holds people together. The cup gives the water its shape and meaning."

"Very poetic," Standard said. "What's that got to do with Rim?"

"The rim of the cup, of course. It doesn't do anything to the water, it only puts a definite limit on the cup. Rim doesn't interfere with people unless they're disrupting the social fabric. Then Rim would stop those people for their own good."

"We already have Policontrol and it's taking care of Unstables now. Why have another outfit doing the same thing?"

Jeannine tossed the question off with a flip of her hand. "Policontrol only takes care of individuals. Rim can govern whole countries."

Standard sucked on his tooth. "A topolgist would disagree with you about a rim defining the limits of a cup. He'd say it was only a part of the cup's surface and not a limiting mode."

"Well, maybe that's what a topologist would say, but what does he know about people?"

"Not much, I guess. Maybe I don't either, as far as that goes." Standard wrinkled his forehead. "I've got this old-fashioned notion about people being the government. If you

control the people, you control the government. And if you control the government, you have to say you're controlling the people. People aren't little bugs that can be pushed around and squashed or told what to do by some high and mighty social overseer who tells them just how far they can go and what they can't do."

"Rim stopped the war," Jeannine said sharply. "People started it and Rim ended it because those people didn't know how to stop it."

"You don't know that for sure. That's just a guess, a coincidence," Standard argued. "Hell, even a slavemaster has to do something decent once in a while, even if it's just to stop beating his drudges. So what if Rim *did* stop the war? Maybe there was a damned good reason for the war."

His hand was twitching again. Excitement made the nerve flaw jumpy.

"You don't really believe that, do you? Look at yourself. Your face is all cut up, your arm is missing and now that horrible metal thing is hopping like a rabbit. You don't really believe it would have been better to let the war continue, do you, Mike?"

"How do you know there *wasn't* a good reason? Look, you were just a kid. You don't remember how things were. We were on the edge of starvation, the whole world's population going crazy. You sit here in your marshmallow apartment and what do you know about overcrowding? Hell, maybe the war happened so we could get the population down to a manageable level so we could get a second chance to work it all out before everything blew up in our faces."

She closed her eyes gently. "I don't think you're the type to believe in destiny, Mike. I don't think you believe in a God, or mankind, or anything else."

He rocked on the balls of his feet, slowly jogging up and down. "You're wrong. I believe a whole lot in man. How the hell do you expect this world to find anything better if it's constantly held back by Rim? How do you expect it to progress?"

"That's a dumb argument," Jeannine said. "Rim knows what's best for man. Rim can guide us."

"*Damn* it, girl," Standard spat. "That's not progress, that's stagnation! Rim is a *man*, not some god that knows the future. All Rim knows is what is already known by the human race. It knows nothing about what is going to be needed

tomorrow or what is going to be created a year from now."

Jeannine shook her head and smiled. "You say Rim is a man, but you keep saying 'it' as though Rim is something more than a man."

He caught his temper, slowly reeling it back. "Yes," he said carefully. "Rim is more than just a man. He—it—is something more. That's why the Rim has to be stopped, Jeannine."

"I still don't understand," she said.

He was not entirely sure he understood himself. Was Rim really the tyrant Condliffe said it was? No way of asking him, with Condliffe and the whole world-saving crew on the moon. There was no evidence, just the gnawing feeling he had in his bones when he walked the streets.

He turned his back to the girl and softly punched the wall. "Maybe you're right, Jeannine. Maybe I don't give a damn for humanity. Maybe I don't care if this world goes up in smoke. Maybe all I care about is what I've got right now and to hell with the rest. But that's important enough. I don't want to see you get hurt. Rim is using you like a pawn in the middle of some big game, and I don't like to see that happening to you."

She touched his back, letting her hand slide across his shoulder. "That's nice of you, Mike. But even if you're right about Rim, what does it matter if I'm being used? I *believe* in Rim, Mike. I don't believe in you."

He caught her hand behind his back. "What if I said I loved you?"

"I still wouldn't believe you," she said. "You started out to kill Rim long before you met me. And you don't care what happens to the world. Why do you have to kill the Rim?"

It was improbable and stupid to begin with and getting dumber by the minute. A telepathic overlord of the world. In his own mind, regardless of what Condliffe had said, he doubted it.

In the lunacy of the gelatin-colored apartment, his mind shifted back to the Allied post hospital where he had recuperated. From the briefings he had received he could patch together what had happened.

"Come here, Jeannine," he said. "Let me explain a couple of things."

The city was quieter now. Jeannine sat with her legs

curled under her, listening to the hushed murmuring from beyond the windowed balcony that blended almost in cadence with Standard's voice. Again, she was struck by the soft burring monotone. Less than a day has passed since she met him in Harold's bar, but she felt, inexplicably, drawn closer to his battered hulk than she had to any other man, even knowing what his purpose was with the Rim.

Standard was stretched out on his stomach, picking tufts from the carpeting.

"After they installed the new arm, I never saw them again," he was saying. "It took me a couple of years to get used to it at a rehab center. All the time, they were worried Rim might pick up an inkling of the plan, but Rim was already in the States by then. The guys at the hospital didn't know anything about the arm. They thought it was just another pross. I was the only one left on Earth who knew anything, but I'll bet Condliffe and his boys ate their guts out worrying."

"So you think this—what did you call him?—Lin Sang tried to tell you about it first?" Jeannine asked.

"Just before he died, yeah. I was too dumb to understand what he was talking about."

"Well, Condliffe didn't understand, either."

"No, he didn't understand," Standard agreed. "Some doctor named Adamski found out about it first, I think. Then Adamski died, too. By the time anyone knew what was happening, Rim had already left."

"And you're sure Rim and the man with the bandaged head are the same?"

Standard nodded. "Some kind of freak accident. He should be dead, but he's not. Instead, he has a power now. He can kill without coming into actual contact with a person. At first, it was only at close range, like Lin Sang in the same room. Then he got a little stronger. Adamski was burned to death in his laboratory, a hundred yards from the hospital. There's no way of knowing how powerful he is now."

Standard crossed his arms and rested his chin on the floor. There were two routes to take when reality reached the limit of sanity. Either resist or take the final plunge. Standard felt he had taken the latter. He was relaxing in an apartment with an unconscious Rim agent, calmly spilling every detail he knew of his mission to another Rim agent.

"But that patient was only one man," Jeannine objected. "The Rim is an entire organization."

"It is now," Standard said. "He's had time to collect people, just as he's collected you. Even God has to have angels to carry out some of the more menial tasks. But it's still one man. And no matter how powerful he is, or what abilities he has, he's still a mortal man."

"But why you, Mike? Why do you have to be the one to kill Rim?"

He shrugged. "It only takes one man to kill a man."

She readjusted her legs. "Why kill the Rim at all? This man Condliffe is a soldier, so he believes in killing. And the doctors who built your arm weren't trying to help you. They're just using you to kill. These are the kind of men who led us into the war. Is this the way to the progress you talk about?"

"There are lots of ways to progress," Standard said. "I'm no wizard. Maybe war has some good purpose. Planes, rockets, atomics, lasers. If it weren't for what they learned from patching up all those casualties, they never would have learned how to make an arm like this. Disregarding the weapon that's supposed to be in it, it's a pretty good arm."

"If it wasn't for the war, you wouldn't need that arm."

"Pointless argument." Standard shook his head. "I could've lost my arm in a machine shop just as easily."

He was correct, of course. The conversation itself was pointless. She uncrossed her legs and wondered how she could explain to him the way Rim planned to change the world. It was an understanding for which she had no words, only an inner feeling that now had dispelled the doubts she had harbored only minutes earlier.

"I think you're wrong trying to destroy Rim," she said simply. "Rim could have killed you already if it wanted. It could have made you split your head open when you slipped in my bathroom, or made Graystone run a scalpel into you, or let Quinn cut off your arm. Or Rim could have made the needle gun backfire. But none of those things happened. Rim isn't a killer. It doesn't want to hurt you. Doesn't that mean anything to you?"

"A benevolent tyrant is still a tyrant," Standard said. He looked up from the carpeting. "And there's still two dead men in Australia you aren't counting."

"One could have died accidentally, and the other one

you would have killed yourself if you had a chance." She spread her hands in exasperation. "What can I say to convince you, Mike?"

"You can't," he said quietly. "Let Rim convince me."

She gazed at him and slowly rose to her feet. It was true that Rim often worked through people, that it sometimes took time for Rim to enter and warm even the most complacent mind, but having heard Standard openly admit his goal, did she dare to take him to Rim? Was this why Rim had let her save Standard? Did Rim *want* her to deliver Standard?

She parried. "But if I take you, you'll try to destroy Rim. Even if you become convinced that Rim is good, you have no control over your weapon."

"I don't think just meeting the Rim will set it off. It takes something special, a certain sequence or some emotional balance to set it off. Will you take me?"

"I don't know. Can I trust you?"

"That's a stupid question. Can I trust *you?*"

He stood and caught her face in his hands. Strange he had not noticed the gold coloring in her hair before. Was it a trick of the pastel lighting or was it a trick of his mind? How much control *did* Rim have?

He looked at her upturned face. "Are you with me or against me, girl?"

"Both," she said. "Neither. I want to help you. Don't you know that by now?"

"Not for sure, no." He reached down and tapped the bracelet on her wrist. "I'm thinking I should use one of your tryp pellets on you and leave you here to explain to Quinn. But then I'm thinking I'll wait and see how things develop."

"When you decide if you trust me, will you let me know?"

"I'll have to think. Maybe you should convince me." She pressed herself to him.

"That's what I like, a woman with no complications," he said. He enjoyed the contact of her body, her breasts softened against his ribs and the leisurely movement of her thighs.

This was not all Rim's doing. This was an involvement that he was allowing to happen. He knew he was out of command of the situation, that he should be the seducer, not her. He placated himself with the thought that she had more practice, but dismissed it from his mind immediately.

The men that had preceded him were unimportant and he preferred not to think of them.

That was a dangerous sign, he realized. Circumventing his pride and ego could dull his instincts, and vulnerability could end his mission as quickly as a guillotine blade. But he enjoyed the closeness of her warmth, the incongruity of her hair against his scarred face.

The phone was buzzing. He wanted to tell her to forget it, but she was out of his arms and across the room before he could stop her.

VII

THE STREETS WERE quiet in the working class district, with most of the windows glowing with the multicolored reflections of the adult rated vidi programs. Dactil brought the airwagon to a sliding halt outside the apartment building and sat looking at it as the turbines cooled.

"Anyone familiar with this place?" he asked.

"Yeah," Pejor said. "I used to have this beat. Ordinary kind of place. Little bit run-down, about half occupied. The gal lives on the top floor and it's pretty well fixed up."

"You've been up?"

"Yessir, couple times. She has the whole floor. Or at least she's the only one who pays rent. The other apartments are empty. Has a male visitor about once or twice a week."

"You seem to know quite a bit about her," DeAmico said.

Pejor flushed. "Aw, you know how it is, Sergeant. After a while, you get to know the people on your beat."

Dactil pushed his door open. "Well, let's go see who's visiting her now. You have your weapon, DeAmico?"

DeAmico patted his holster. "Of course. I hope using it won't be required. We'd like to interrogate these people."

"I hope it won't be necessary, either, but that's out of my hands. All we do is round them up," Dactil said. "What is it you people call us? The dog catchers?"

"I've heard that," DeAmico said. "On the other hand, I've heard you refer to us as the pushbutton patrol."

"That's not exactly the way I heard it," Jaffe said. "Privy peepers is what we used to say back in the academy."

DeAmico shot the patrolman a glance. There was a pointed rivalry between the Analytic and the Interception departments that dated back to the foot cops and the detective squads. He let Jaffe's remark pass.

The four of them fell into a loose cadence and crossed the lobby floor. A warm fishy odor from the dirty shoreline permeated the walls and mingled with the cloying smells of the herbals and the drugs in the apothecary.

"There's only two of the elevators working now," Pejor said, punching an up button. "They closed down the rest of them because there aren't enough people left."

"How about staircases? Any other ways out?" DeAmico asked.

"Two inside stairs alongside the elevator shafts in case of emergencies. No outside exits. You wouldn't catch me living in a firetrap like this."

The elevator announced its presence with a dull ringing sound. Pejor slipped his police identification in the pay slot and the door breathed open. "Think we should guard the stairs, Lieutenant?"

"No reason. They don't know we're coming. Even if they tried to run, so what? We could beat them down to the lobby with no sweat," Dactil said.

DeAmico frowned. Dactil's concern seemed too casual for his liking.

There was no voice on the phone. Instead, the screen coalesced into a gray vision of men entering a cramped quarters. Standard squinted at it over Jeannine's head and slowly recognized it as the elevator.

"What the hell's this?"

"Policontrol," Jeannine said simply and snapped the phone off. "They're coming up here." She found a handbag in one of the wall crevices and began tossing small items into it.

"What makes you think they're coming up here?"

"Quinn had a spy camera installed in the elevators for me. Whenever someone punches for the tenth floor, it automatically rings my phone."

"My compliments to Quinn. Anyone that sneaky can't be

all bad. Why the hell would they be coming up here? Aren't you legal?"

"Of course I am," she said sharply. "Medicals, license, diploma. It's a regular thing. They always come here without notice. I recognized one of the cops. The last time he was here, he brought his viditaper hoping to shoot a few juicy scenes for his department dinner. I'm afraid he was disappointed. Now it looks as though he brought his department over for a first-hand look."

"I don't think so," Standard said, scooping up the electron case. "It's going to be a little sticky explaining Quinn there in the corner. How many ways are there out of here?"

"The elevators." She shrugged. "There are some stairs that go down to the lobby."

"Nothing outside?"

"No." She closed her handbag. "Maybe we can hide on the roof until they're gone."

"That's the first place they'll look once they block the stairs. No, we have to get out of his building. How does this trick suitcase work?"

"The left clasp. Turn it clockwise for power. What are you going to do?"

"Slow them down." He grabbed Jeannine's hand and pulled her into the hall. He put his ear to the elevator doors. One was quiet, but the other whispered toward them. He spun the clasp and watched the blue shimmering flame touch the metal door.

The metal fumed and heated, turning an incandescent white. It dribbled down, flowing into the panels of the split door. He flicked the gun off, the metal cooling and forming a sloppy weld.

"Let's go," he said and pushed Jeannine toward the stairs.

They pushed open the staircase door and Standard dropped the briefcase, glancing around. He spun the dial to minimum power and aimed the rod at the bannister. It heated and he kept the rod trained on it as he put it on the floor. The plastic carpet began to melt, turning black and filling the stairwell with tentacles of treacly smoke.

"You'll burn the place down!" Jeannine cried as they plunged down the stairs.

The elevator creaked to a stop and the inner doors slid open but the outer hallway doors remained closed.

"Can't you even operate an elevator, Pejor?" Dactil grumbled.

"Goddamn old buildings," Pejor said. "They should tear them all down and start over again." He kicked the door futilely.

Jaffe wrinkled his nose. "You smell something burning? Like something hot?"

Pejor put his hand on the door to shove it open and shrieked. He yanked his hand back and DeAmico could see the burnt flesh peel away. "Jesus," Pejor screeched. "That thing's red hot!"

Dactil shouldered him aside and wet his fingers. They sizzled instantly as he touched the door. "Get this thing down," he barked.

"Down where?" Jaffe asked numbly.

"Down *down!*" Dactil yelled and slapped the five button. "That little girl up there welded that door closed and she's probably running her tail off down the stairs right now. If we can get down fast enough, maybe we can still stop them." He looked at Pejor clutching his hand. "How bad is it, kid?"

"Hurts, but I'll make it," Pejor said, clenching his teeth.

"Good man. DeAmico, you and Pejor get down to the lobby and watch for a quarry down there. I don't think this is any girl's game. Those two guys—what did you call them? Standard and Quinn?—may be with her. So stop them. This has gotten serious."

DeAmico wanted to point out that the mission had been serious when they left headquarters, but he nodded his head in agreement.

The elevator sank to the fifth floor. Dactil hopped out, grabbing Jaffe. "Don't forget we want those people for interrogation," DeAmico yelled as the doors closed.

Dactil frowned at the comment. "Don't take any chances, Jaf. You go up one staircase and I'll go up the other. Do whatever you have to if you run into them. Meet you in the girl's apartment otherwise."

Jaffe nodded and sprinted down the hall. Dactil pounded up the stairs, his breath coming hard and strained. He really should stay in better shape, but there was damned little to do nowadays. A good chase like this made life a little worthwhile. He unclipped his ram pistol and charged up the stairs.

"Don't worry about the building," Standard said. He pulled Jeannine down the stairs after him. "The cops will be up there in a couple of minutes and they'll put it out."

"You really don't care, do you?" Jeannine panted, trying to keep her feet on the stairs as Standard dived down them. "All your talk about saving humanity and you set a building on fire."

"Be quiet," he snapped. He heard the door open and heavy footsteps coming toward them. He pulled the needle gun from his pocket just as the head of the policeman cleared the flight of stairs. The policeman saw them in the same instant and swung his pistol up at them.

Standard stumbled against Jeannine, knocking her sprawling down the stairs. He careened after her as the policeman's autoram howled and chewed a line of pulverized plaster up the wall. A mental image of the needle gun refusing to respond flashed in Standard's mind as he willed it to fire.

The needle ripped into the patrolman's thigh and tore out a blossoming chunk of flesh. Dazed, the patrolman crumpled to his knees trying to aim the pistol. Standard vaulted over the bannisters, the steel arm coursing in a tight arc that connected with the autopistol, fracturing it and tearing it out of the policeman's grip.

The policeman whirled from the impact, Standard driving his fist at the exposed head. He connected with the policeman's temple and dropped him on the landing.

Jeannine was clambering to her feet. She saw the widening batch of blood and covered her mouth, her eyes wide and afraid.

"Come on, we're going out the back way," Standard said, taking her hand.

"My God, you're an animal. A brutal, inhuman animal."

"Him or us," Standard snapped.

Dactil reached the top stairs, breathing hard. He slid the door open cautiously and looked down the hallway. Smoke was curling out of the far staircase and the door to the girl's apartment was open. He glanced at the crude weld on the elevator as he passed it and stopped at the open door.

He pushed it open farther with the barrel of his pistol and saw the body in the corner. His eyes shot around the room, taking in the bulbous furniture and garish colors. He stepped

in and turned the thin man over and felt his chest. The heart was beating steadily, though feebly.

Satisfying himself with a glance inside the bedroom, he flicked on his callcom. "DeAmico, you down in the lobby yet?"

"We're here," DeAmico said. "Anything happening up there?"

"When the ambulance arrives, tell the meds to get up here, too. I found one of your guys. Thin guy. Looks like he's been stungassed."

"That'd be Quinn, I think," DeAmico said. "Hold him for Official Impersonation. I called some more men in from Policon to give us a hand. As soon as they get here, I'll be up to take a look at your find. Any trace of the girl?"

"Not yet," Dactil said. "Anybody on your stairs, Jaf?"

Dactil and DeAmico both heard the answering silence. "Jaffe, you hear me?"

"Looks like you were right about their trying the stairs," DeAmico said.

"Watch out for them," Dactil barked. "And the hell with your interrogation. You see them coming down the stairs, you *stop* 'em. Understand, Sergeant?" He emphasized *Sergeant* and ran to the staircase. He kicked open the door and coughed his way through the smoke.

Two flights down he found Jaffe bleeding on the stairs. He whipped his belt around the gaping hole in Jaffe's leg and tightened it. The blood was still pumping regularly, but it seemed there should have been more than there was coming out of the wound. Dactil yanked the callcom from his pocket and yelled into it.

"DeAmico, where the hell is that ambulance? Jaffe's up here on the eighth floor hit bad. Get those reinforcements here on emergency alert and have this whole goddamned area cordoned off, you hear?"

"On their way," DeAmico answered. He clicked the frequency on his callcom. "Emergency, Control. One of our men is seriously injured. Suspect Standard is hostile and armed. Block this area."

He heard the acknowledged bleep of Emergency Control's computer and flipped back to personal frequency. "Pejor, cover that other staircase. Stop anyone who comes down."

"I heard it all," Pejor said. His hand was oozing and alive with pain.

DeAmico was gaining a healthy respect for the "dog catchers." It was a lot easier sitting behind his console and having coffy served to him while passing interim judgments than it was getting shot at and nearly having your elevator chopped down.

That struck his analytic mind. Standard might be desperate, but he wasn't stupid. Anyone who had the capability to weld a door shut almost instantly, also could have severed the elevator cables just as easily. But Standard had not. Why not?

He knew the answer before he even glanced at the floor indicators over the elevators. The second elevator was registering on the tenth floor. Standard had backtracked, had gambled that they would have tried to stop him on the stairs.

Gambled and won.

He flipped his callcom. "Lieutenant, are you still with Jaffe?"

"Yeah. When's that ambulance coming?"

"Couple minutes. Listen, I know where Standard is. The other elevator has just gone up to the tenth floor. They must be trying to make for the roof."

"The roof?" Dactil yelled. "Oh my God, how dumb can you get! They must have an aircar parked up there. DeAmico, we don't have time to wait for those reinforcements. Get in the wagon and bring them down."

"Check," DeAmico said. "Hold the fort, Pejor. We've been outfoxed."

He ran across the lobby and outside. As he cleared the doors he saw the small aircar lift itself from the building roof and bank over the lake. He spun the turbines and dropped the wagon into grav gear, slamming his thumb down on the accelerator. The wagon bolted forward, sinking him into the seat. He angled the control bar and heard the auxiliary drive kick in, a screaming shrill that shattered against his eardrums.

The night was moonless and the small craft was flying without its lights. DeAmico flicked on the pinar screen and swept the sky. He located the aircar immediately, as it was flying over the open water of the lake to the southeast. It was still accelerating, but had almost reached its maximum. Even so, its maximum was proving to be considerably more

than the old wagon's. DeAmico switched on the narrowband radio and beamed it at the receding craft.

"Standard, this is Policontrol. Bring your car around and
land or we'll be forced to bring you down."

He waited for the reply he did not expect. The pinar
showed that the aircar had gained speed. It was cracking
the sound barrier now and the paddy wagon was hopelessly
subsonic. DeAmico switched back to broadband and tried
to reach Dactil but he was already out of the lieutenant's
callcom reception range.

Another thirty seconds and Standard would be out of De-
Amico's cannon range. DeAmico did not like the decisions he
was rushing toward.

He flicked on the narrowband. "Last chance, Standard.
Heave to or be blasted out of the sky."

There was no response.

"We know the girl's with you. If you have any concern
for her safety, now is the time to show it."

He waited, watching the coordinates flitter on the pinar
screen. He touched the activator switch and closed his fingers around the gunnery control.

"I'm sorry, miss," he said and squeezed.

The bright lances of flame quivered the wagon and knifed
into the darkness. They were a ruler line of destruction
across the pinar screen. He looked out the window and saw
a small sun suddenly nova in the distance. The blip that
marked the aircar on the pinar screen vanished instantly, to
be replaced by a dwindling spot of wavery disturbance.

DeAmico slowed the groaning wagon and turned it back
to land. He had never shot a man before, not with a pistol,
not with a disruptor cannon, and it left a metallic taste in
his mouth. It really meant no more than sentencing a man or
allowing him to be executed, but it was different, so much
more personal this way. He tried to analyze his emotions as
he flew back to the shore.

It still did not seem entirely real, killing a man over a
space of several miles. He still did not know how it would
feel to cut a man down with a rampistol. Maybe he would
have to put in for a transfer to Interception. That would be
the only way to learn if he enjoyed the feeling.

He could see the blinking lights of the ambulance as he
lobbed in over the shoreline. They were ushering Jaffe into it
as he brought the wagon to a stop in the street. Dactil was

standing by the doors of the apartment, talking to his superior.

DeAmico saluted as he dropped out of the airwagon. He recognized the man as high in Policontrol command, one of those almost legendary faces which would appear on a briefing tape from the computers.

"What happened out there, Sergeant?" the legendary face said. "We saw the explosion from here."

"He wouldn't respond to my order to halt, sir," DeAmico said. "He was trying to outrun me. I didn't have any choice but to shoot him down."

"You did a good job," and Dactil nodded in agreement. "I understand you have a good record in Analysis. Turns out you're a good man in Interception, too. Maybe we should discuss it more in the morning when you file your report."

"Thank you, sir." DeAmico flushed. "I've been considering a transfer."

"Fine, we'll talk about it tomorrow." He turned to Dactil. "You may as well clean up here, Lieutenant. That looks like it pretty well takes care of it for the night. Compliment your men for me."

They watched him enter his patrol car and motion to the driver.

"How's Jaffe?" DeAmico asked as the Politcontrol car sped away.

"Lost some blood, but the meds think they can patch him up. He had disability coming anyway."

DeAmico nodded. "That's good. Look, I'm going to grab a ride back with the Interrogation boys. I want to be around when they bring that skinny guy Quinn around. I've got a few questions for him myself."

Dactil rubbed his hand across his face. "The meds are still up there. Why don't you go on up? I'll wait for you and you can go back to headquarters with me."

DeAmico looked at the lieutenant suspiciously. Before he could turn to the apartment doors, the elevator opened and the medical team wheeled the cot into the lobby.

He watched them roll it toward him and a rising alarm clutched his spine. Quinn's head was covered. "What the . . . ?" he stammered.

"He's dead," Dactil said shortly.

DeAmico spun on him. "You said he had been gassed!"

"That's right," Dactil said. "He was alive when I reached

him. The meds got here right after you took off. By the time they got to Quinn, he was dead."

"That's impossible," DeAmico said. "Stungas doesn't kill."

Dactil shrugged. "Enough of it does."

"Sure, a double belt of it can, but it kills instantly, not ten minutes later." DeAmico was suddenly furious. "Good God, man, don't you understand? There may be a whole conspiracy revolving around that man. We *needed* that man for questioning."

"Watch your tongue, Sergeant," Dactil said. "The way I figure it, Standard stopped back in the room before he got away in the aircar. He must have hit Quinn with another dose of tryp to keep him quiet."

DeAmico bit the inside of his lip. "You're right, I guess."

He watched the med team load the body into the ambulance. Jaffe was being rigged for intravenous and Pejor was letting a nurse wrap his hand.

"Let's go home, Sergeant," Dactil said and slapped DeAmico's back.

They flew lazily over the city, DeAmico still trying to collect his thoughts and put them back into order.

"Everything's so damned neat and tidy," he grumbled. "Standard and the girl are dead. Quinn's dead. All the witnesses are dead. That's too neat. There's something more here. Something underneath all this. We don't know any more now than when we started."

"Maybe so," Dactil said. "That's not my job. That's your job to worry. We just go out and clean up dirty little cases. I'd say we did a pretty fair job of cleaning this one up."

"Yeah, I guess so," DeAmico said, watching the skyline pass under him. Perhaps Dactil could be satisfied with eradicating the obvious, but DeAmico had been trained to look beneath the surface for the mainstream currents. He still did not have the answers he wanted, and now he had nobody to give him that information.

With one exception. The doctor who had filed the original complaint. How much did he know about this, whatever *this* was?

"If you don't mind, Lieutenant, would you drop me off at Analysis? I've got a date with a computer tonight."

Dactil nodded and grinned lightly. "Yeah, I expected that. I didn't think you were really cut out for Interception."

VIII

FOUR PEOPLE in the back were playing Quod, the apparent randomness of their moves surpassed in frenzy only by the shrill decibel level of the tally board. They were grouped around the square playing table, each one stabbing at an individual control panel in total disregard of cadence or turn-taking, the center translucent cube glowing with minute bursts of colored light that held its position and sound.

The bar was filled with noise. Besides the players' own shouting and roaring, each flash of light carried its own distinctive sound, a piercing resistor-induced screech that rattled against the stemware, growing louder with each accumulated flash.

Graystone enjoyed games. Sitting in his side booth he watched the play, hoping to understand the purpose of what seemed to him to be complete abandon. Having watched for better than an hour, he was beginning to associate the players with their respective colors and sounds.

He had the heavy blonde sitting closest to him pegged with the speckles of lavender light, accompanied by something that approximated a high C note. The shaggy man at her elbow was splattering red and an unidentifiable chord throughout the barroom. The second woman, dark, with pendulous breasts that constantly threatened to add their own impressions to the control panel, had chosen an amber light with a sound that was vaguely similar to a mid-range F, while her escort, still in his tramp freighter overalls, was pouring tiny bomb bursts of green into the cube with a note that Graystone knew was totally out of his experience.

Associating the sounds and colors with the players had taken the better part of two drinks, since the object of the game seemed to be pressing the same coordinates as an opponent. When it occurred, by accident, Graystone was positive, the center cube would blaze with a hot white

light where the opposing light flashes coincided, the tally board recording the kill with a remarkable sliding howl.

How they decided who scored what, Graystone was at a loss to know. Scores were transferred back and forth instantly, one moment the red column indicating a long string of kills, the next instant the amber column suddenly showing more kills for which there hadn't been time to push an adequate number of buttons.

Perplexed, he turned his attention from the game and swirled his drink, watching the viscous eddies in the opaque black fluid caused by the ice. Graystone drank sparingly now, the bootleg liquor during the wartime rationing having ruined his taste for it, and generally relied on either the bartender's recommendation, which was always suspect and tempered by an understandable desire to sell the slow movers, or the gaudiest sign for his choice. Nearly all the old fermented and distilled potables had disappeared.

The particular drink he was twirling had been advertised as a Judas Ghost, promising, if one was to believe the commercials, visions of varying degrees of decadence. Instead, it tasted like the coal sludge it resembled. A few more swallows and he felt his stomach would metamorphose into an appropriate carboniferous clump.

There was an uproar at the end of the bar and Graystone glanced up to see the Quod cube awash in amber light, the pendulous brunette gleefully pounding the game table.

"Holy sweet Jesus!" the shaggy man was exclaiming. "A grandslam burn!"

The tramper was appreciatively watching the animated bouncing. The blonde feigned exaggerated defeat and sighed "Lucky bitch, ain't she?" under her breath.

"Aw hell, Mirabelle," the tramper yelled, "she ain't lucky. She's just *good.*"

"Yeah, by God, she looks pretty good to me," the shaggy man agreed. "And you oughta know."

"You bet your sweet biscuits I know." The tramper leered. "I'm telling you, pal, this bird is the movingest thing on the whole front. When she gets going, woowie, she just doesn't know when to quit."

"I was going to say you looked like you were losing a little weight."

The brunette giggled her approval and good-naturedly punched the tramper in the gut. The tramper provided him-

self with a handful of bosom and jostled the woman's legs under the table. "Hey, isn't it about time for a fresh round of lox?"

"Hell, yes. Who's buying this time?"

"Well, balls, it was my broad who won. *You* buy, you cheap bastard."

"*Thought* you'd say that. Hey, Harold," the shaggy man shouted. "Bring us another bottle of lox, will you?"

The bartender nodded his head in recognition, extracted a bottle of milky liquid from behind the counter and tore the cap off. He sauntered back to the game table and handed it to the tramper. They had started a new game before he returned to the bar.

Graystone signaled to him. Harold saw him and changed his course.

"Bring you another Ghost?"

"No, thanks. I'm fine with this one. What is that lox they ordered?"

"That stuff? Legalized moonshine, as far as I'm concerned. Synthetic gin is what it is, and when you start synthesizing gin, you know it's got to be pretty rough. They bottle the stuff in about an hour."

"Lox is a funny name for it."

"Aw, that's an old spacer term the trampers picked up. All the tramp freighters like to pretend they're heading out to Mars. They think it's narcotic, but it's just unfiltered. After a couple slugs of the stuff, you wind up with one helluva headache that lasts most of the week. Guess that's why they think it's narcotic."

Graystone chuckled. "How does it taste?"

"Like not much of anything. Old rocket fuel, more than anything. You like to try some?"

"Well, I don't know," Graystone said, tempted. "I'm on a vacation, but I'm supposed to meet a man later tonight and I suppose I really should remain relatively clear-headed. A small business transaction, you know."

"One wouldn't hurt you," Harold said. "Tell you what. Try one and if you can't stand it, it's on the house. Fair enough?"

"Oh, why not?" Graystone said expansively. "This *is* a vacation."

He was eager to tell the bartender his vacation plans, but Harold had already turned away.

The electronic howling was mounting again from the end of

the room as the two couples slammed their boards. If possible, they were going at it with even more detachment.

Graystone flicked on the booth vidiscreen and spun through the channels. Automatically, he flipped past the homosexual network, pausing at an adult cartoon show until he realized it was a rerun of Freddy Fornicator and that he had seen it before in a phone booth.

He had found a newscast when Harold returned with the drink.

"Hey, I know him," Harold exclaimed, his eyes on the screen.

Graystone followed his gaze. A scowling face was frozen on the vidi. Graystone recognized the face immediately, at the same time feeling something enormously familiar about the background. He was trying to decide what it was that was so familiar about the almost blank wall behind the face when the picture shifted to a view of a street choked with police cars.

"Turn it up," Harold said. "See what they're saying."

Graystone obliged.

". . . was the scene earlier tonight as Policontrol officers tried to apprehend the killer identified as Michael Standard. It was from the roof of this building that Standard and his accomplice attempted to escape. The area is quiet now. The police have left and that moment of terror has passed for the occupants of this normally peaceful building. Channel Forty-four newsman Sid Rombauer spoke to one of the people who live here."

The screen snapped to a heavyset woman clutching her bathrobe around her.

"You were awakened in the middle of the night, isn't that correct?"

"Yes, I was. I heard this sound like machine gun bullets in the hall and I woke up. I didn't know what it was so I woke up my husband Harry and told him to listen."

"That sound was the gunfire that nearly cost Patrolman Jaffe his leg. A deadly exchange that could have imperiled everyone in this building if it had not been for the effectiveness of the Policontrol squad which was sent here to investigate."

The picture hesitated, then shifted to a tight-jawed man at a desk, who was professionally shuffling papers. "Thanks, Sid. Sid Rombauer at the scene earlier tonight. That about

105

sums it up. One person murdered, two destroyed themselves trying to escape, two policemen injured trying to bring this mad killer to bay. I'd say that we owe a vote of gratitude to our area Policontrol, wouldn't you, Gorse?"

The team newscaster nodded and paused dramatically. "I certainly would, Alex. It's interesting to note that the officer who managed to shoot down the killer's escape ship was actually on loan to the Department of Interception. Normally, we understand, he works with Computer Control."

"I think that all points up how thoroughly trained all members of our Policontrol are. Speaking of well-trained, we have a message here from the friendly people who make Soyagood, the breakfast cereal that is *soy* good you can serve it for dinner. Here's how."

The screen panned across an idealized collection of coolies harvesting soya beans. Graystone deadened the volume as a heaping mound of gruel smothered with rice and chili powder was superimposed. The announcer was begining to say something about "Amercian-style Cantonese."

"Murder?" Harold's face contorted. "What did they say about murder?"

"I don't know," Graystone said. "I didn't catch all of it."

"Oh, God, if that bastard hurt her . . ."

"Hurt who?"

"One of my best girls. Jeannine. Nice gal. That damned ape Standard came in here yesterday and started hustling her. I tried to tell her to stay away from him, but you know women. Mind of their own, even if it is fuzzy. I knew he was trouble as soon as he walked in here. So off she goes with him anyway. Then she doesn't come in today. Damn, if he's hurt her, I'll . . ." He stopped confusedly, not knowing what he could do to a dead man.

"Why do you think she is necessarily in danger?" Graystone soothed.

"Hell, man, that was her apartment building!"

Graystone clucked his tongue. "If you were concerned about her, you should have called the police."

"I wish to hell I had," Harold said. He peered at the screen, expecting more information. A basset hound was floating, barking and ears flapping in simulated non-grav, followed by a honeymooning couple. Harold grunted and turned back to the bar, leaving Graystone without collecting the credit chit.

Graystone searched the dial for another newscast, found none, and settled for a concert with attendant floral patterns on the homo network. He tested the lox and shivered involuntarily. Any similarity between it and grain mash was as imaginary as its reputed narcotic effect.

Interesting. The picture of his recent patient on the newscast had not surprised him. Graystone had been confident that it was only a matter of time before the man became notorious. The girl . . . hadn't the fake agent Quinn mentioned something about a girl? Graystone wondered if it was the same girl as the bartender's.

Graystone watched a large rose slowly explode and re-form itself into a field of pastel petals and sipped the lox. He shivered again and poured the lox into the glass of Judas Ghost. It made a dirty liquid like thinned motor oil. It combined the worst qualities of taste of both.

This business of gents running around, especially armed ones, worried him. He had hoped he had left it all behind when he walked out of his office with Quinn's chit, but here it was plaguing him again. He was realistic enough to know that there was more to the affair than two or three people. He also knew the police would be looking for him since he had filed the Unstable report. Thankful though he should be for Policontrol's efficiency, he wanted no part of the police.

He swallowed more of the coal tar. Quinn had posed as a member of Policontrol, but had definitely not been. That certainly put him in the criminal ranks. Standard had been his enemy, but did that make him a good or socially correct man? And Policontrol had destroyed Standard. Where did that put Standard? For that matter, where did that put Policontrol? That was the question that frightened Graystone.

He downed his drink. There seemed to be two factions fighting each other somewhere in the gray zone between the underworld and the police.

A buzzing sensation was working up his spine from the hot spot in his stomach. His ears felt a growing numbness and he understood why the trampers drank the lox. *Well, my friend,* he told himself, *you have better things to do than brood about criminals and embalm yourself with this masquerading anesthetic.*

He still had to meet the man at the dock and complete

their transaction. Damn that silly credit voucher Quinn had given him . . . it was drawn on a foreign bank and there was a two hour delay in verification.

Still, he reflected, money was money, even though ten thousand was not precisely a princely sum. But it was sufficient to cover the rental on the beautiful little power catamaran, old to be sure, but refitted with a crystal computer to handle the sails. A delightful boat, with inlays of real teak in the miniscule cabin, its twin hulls glistening with a new polyplast coating, the laminated mast and boom wonders of sculptured wood, formed long before the forests had died, making the boat a charming antique, almost a museum piece.

But it was what was inside that had taken almost all of the money.

The two hour delay would have given the lease company time to outfit it as Graystone had specified, generously larded with irradiated meats and succulent fruits in the cooler. Some of them *fresh* fruit.

He chortled gleefully, winding his way to the bar and paying his tab, congratulating himself on the shrewdness of his bartering. He also congratulated himself for not having more of the lox. Already he was having problems in navigation and he was not even on the water yet.

The leasing company had asked five for just the boat alone and an additional seven thousand for the black market food. After a long session of skillful haggling, Graystone had talked them into including both the boat and the food for only ten. And what food! Real steaks and chops smuggled in from New Zealand, fruits from South America and from a botany garden in Quebec, and, incomprehensible in its wonder, a contraband cask of lager.

He was virtually drooling as he walked carefully toward the lakefront, anticipating the sweet charms of his vacation.

The yacht rental was spread out before him, the moon glinting on the masts, an armada of lighted toothpicks like the raised spears of a Roman legion, swaying slowly to a lingering rest. The sight excited him. The very thought of his own sailboat thrilled him.

To be blown along on the wind, cut free from any reliance on the mechanical frailties and limitations of the motorized world, a bird adrift. The crystals would compensate for his

course, setting and trimming the sails, adjusting the center-boards, relaxing the halyards, tightening them as he steered each new tack. Away from the madness behind him, the petulant women patients, the hypochondriacs, and the frightening intrigue of the past day.

The man was waiting for him at the beach, smiling broadly.

"Did it clear the banks?" Graystone asked.

"Without a hitch. The boat is loaded and everything is ready for you to cast off. Remember what I told you about operating the boat?"

"I believe so," Graystone said. "All I have to do is catch some wind and it takes care of itself."

"Yeah, well don't forget about the centerboards and the rudders. When you beach the boat, make sure you haul them up so they don't scrape. And keep it pointed upwind when you beach so the thing doesn't fall over."

"Yes, I remember," Graystone said impatiently.

"Don't forget to turn the computer off, too. And watch it in a hard wind. There's so much sail area on that old boat that the wind could topple it right over on its nose. The computer should take care of that, but if it looks like you're getting into trouble, just turn the switch off and slacken the sails."

"Yes, of course. Slacken the sails," Graystone said. "Well, really, I don't plan to do much hard sailing. What I really intend to do is sail up the lake and find some nice secluded beach where I can relax. My work schedule, you know, has been rather pressing lately." He burped quietly.

"Sure, Doc," the dockhand said. "Have a good trip and be careful."

"Oh, I shall, I shall," Graystone said. The boat was moored at the end of the floating dock where they had brought it around. The sails were draped loosely on the boom, waiting their erection to catch the placid night air. He jogged down the dock, feeling the planks grate and shift under him.

The leasing agent turned back to the grounded yacht that he used for his office. Not a bad night's work. The old fool's money had been burning a hole in his hip when he had arrived, so the agent had done the merciful thing and had relieved the itch. Five thousand rental for the old barge would make the company happy. With a little luck, who

knows? Maybe the decrepit thing would sink and then they could collect the insurance on it.

He would have to split up the remaining five thousand. A thousand to his buddy at the packing house, another half thousand to lease the gravtruck to haul the sour food in from the south side. And a little for himself. Hell, the inconvenience of making calls in the middle of the night was worth something, wasn't it? And the old man thought he was getting a bargain, so why disappoint him?

Three and a half grand for himself. Not bad at all. He settled himself on the rotting hull and watched the ancient catamaran angle out into the lake. There was a good breeze on the water and the running lights would not take long before they disappeared.

That was good because the extra thousand the couple had slipped him to surprise their uncle felt comfortable in his pocket. That was going to be a real kick when the doc found them aboard. The girl was a cutey, but how did she manage to get tied up with that character with her? Big and hairy as a damned ox with his hand shoved into his pocket. Maybe, the rental agent mused, the girl would be ready for some civilized company when she got back, and that reminded him to close the office. The doc might not feel too humorous, and turn back.

The rental agent liked the feel of the bills wadded in his pocket.

Graystone pulled up the mainsail, tying it firm to the mast cleat. It caught the air and billowed out, flapping massively. He balanced on one of the forward hulls and carefully stepped to the bows, leaning over the separation between them to snap on the sheets to the jib, then sliding back across the flat raised deck of the cabin.

He ran through his mind the steps the dockhand had given him. He dropped the double centerboards and the rudders, seeing them cut into the water, churning a small whirlpool of foam. He settled into the shallow depression behind the cabin, found the crystal controls under his hand and depressed the button. The computer read the breeze, swinging the boom and letting the sail grow taut with the wind. The boat glided into the bay.

The immediate silence astounded him. Movement to him was always associated with noise: the whining gravdrive in

an aircar, the monotonous growl of the streetwalks. Even thinking was filled with sound, because the act of thinking immediately brought to him visions of computers with myriad wheels and pulleys zipping down endless corridors.

But this was new, this was unfamiliar. This was only the lapping of the water against the hulls and the dimming sounds from the shore. A great awareness overtook him. He had spent his life healing anyone who walked through his door. He had been an intern during the big push to train general practitioners in the government's attempt to alleviate the glut of specialists and, because he honestly believed his calling was to serve his fellow men, he had bowed to the official suggestion. Long ago he had wanted to be a surgeon, but even the memory of that had become diffused and lost over the years. He contented himself with the knowledge that he was best serving his country, and during the war had taken pride in his belief.

He had opened his office in an area that was declining even before great lake cities had swollen and formed the sprawling conglomerate of Chidyland. His second wife, before she had left him too, had constantly upbraided him for not moving his location to one of the new growing complexes, but by then he had established his clientele and knew them and they knew him.

So he had stayed and she, as his first wife, had left him. The loneliness at first had been oppressive, but he lost himself among his patients and found comfort there.

And even earlier today he had felt pride when he had reported the violent man as Unstable. He hated death, but in an obscure way he was almost relieved to learn the man had been killed by the police. The man had represented an unknown in Graystone's world, a hint that the doctor's life was enmeshed in an undercurrent of force that did not belong.

So even then Graystone had known his position in life and had wrapped himself in that narrow blanket.

Perhaps the violent man had unsettled his thoughts. Perhaps he had kindled a spark of skepticism. Perhaps it was only the slippery sound of the water and the stillness of the air captured by the boat moving before the wind, but he suddenly became aware of a new kind of security. For that moment, security to him was being the only man on Earth, afloat on a raft in the middle of the ocean.

He pondered the illogic of the thought and tried to let it slough away from him, but it persisted, clinging to his awareness.

A mile out, a freighter moved its ponderous weight through the night, its rows of cabin lights giving the illusion of a city block bearing through the water. The sight of it snapped him from his spell.

He was becoming chilled. He had not considered the drop of temperature on the water. It had been warm and muggy on the land, but the night air blowing across the lake had turned uncomfortably cold.

Graystone locked the rudders and swung open the cabin door to find a jacket, savoring the anticipation of a creamy banana or a tantalizing tangerine. He crouched into the cabin and snapped on the light.

The man was spread across the foam bunk, a girl curled into the walkway between the hulls. The sight of him shocked Graystone, a crawling fear that gave way to pained anger.

Standard was crunching calmly on a Jonathan, the sweet juice wetting his mouth and dribbling down his chin.

"It's a good apple," he said. "Didn't know you could still get stuff like this. Must have cost you plenty. I wonder where you get vacation money so quickly?"

"What are you *doing* here?" Graystone blurted. Appalled, he watched Standard chew into the core, swallowing the seeds.

"Right at the moment, I'm trying to decide what to try next of your fruit," Standard said blandly. "But you mean what am I doing on your boat, right? That's pretty simple. I needed a boat that couldn't be tracked on the cops' pinar screens. Wood and plastic don't show up very well, and when I saw this old derelict being loaded up with supplies, and then when I found out who was renting it, why I just sort of invited myself aboard, knowing you wouldn't mind, Doc."

In the dim light, the pupils of his eyes seemed to vanish, leaving only slits of milky grayness peering under his brows.

"But I thought you were dead," Graystone stammered. "The news report said the police had killed you!"

"Come on, Doc," Standard said. He swung his feet off the bunk and began rummaging through the refrigerator. "Haven't you heard of an autopilot? I just set the controls and aimed it over the lake. By this time, the cops have prob-

112

ably realized that, if their computers are worth a damn."

"But you can't do this! And who is that girl?" Graystone eased himself against the hatch.

"She's a friend," Standard said. He glanced up. "Tell me, Doctor. Are you a friend?"

"What do you mean?"

"I'd like to know why you're suddenly leaving town, and I'd like to know who sicced the cops on me."

"I am on vacation," Graystone said peevishly, "although I can't see that that is any of your concern. As for who called the police, I haven't the slightest idea, but I'm sure the action was well advised."

Instantly, Graystone remembered. The annoyingly familiar picture on the vidiscreen came back to him and he recalled the setting.

It was his own office.

He sank to the flooring. "I called them, inadvertently. I called Policontrol to check on that man Quinn. They must have arrived after I left and played back my call computer. I think Quinn monkeyed with my machine, so they didn't find him but you instead. So it's all a misunderstanding, don't you see?"

"Uh huh," Standard said. He pulled an orange from the cubicle and bit into it, chewing the bitter skin slowly. Graystone felt the vacant eyes staring at him.

"What do you intend to do with me?" He fidgeted. "Murder me like you murdered Quinn?"

Standard stopped chewing. "What makes you think I murdered Quinn?"

"It was on the vid."

Standard stared at him and slowly resumed his chewing. "That's interesting. That's very interesting."

"Are you going to deny murdering him?" Graystone said suspiciously.

"Yep," Standard said. He squeezed the orange, sucking the juice noisily. "We gassed him, or more precisely, my girl-friend here gassed him. But Quinn was alive when we left him."

Graystone snorted. "Now I suppose you're going to tell me that the police killed him."

"No, I'm not going to tell you that," Standard said thoughtfully. "The cops didn't kill Quinn. But neither did I."

"You're talking in riddles." Graystone shook his head.

"Yeah, I guess so. Don't worry about it. But I still want to know just where you were going."

Graystone spread his hands. "Nowhere in particular," he said resignedly. "I intended to find a secluded beach and simply lose myself for a while."

"Sounds quaint," Standard said. "Instead of a beach, do you have any objections to an island?"

"Since you have assumed command, does it matter?" Graystone said stiffly.

"Not a whole lot," Standard said, wiping his hands on his tunic. "I just like to keep a happy ship. Now you must have sailing charts aboard this scow. How about digging them out for me?"

"They should be under your bunk," Graystone said.

Standard unrolled them and spread them out, frowning. He bent and shook Jeannine's shoulder. She woke slowly, then started as her eyes focused on Graystone. "Who . . . ?"

"That's Graystone, the *real* doctor," Standard said. "How are you feeling now?"

"Exhausted," Jeannine said. She pushed herself upright in the cramped cabin, pushing the hair back from her face. "Do you always run wherever you're going?"

"Only when the cops are looking for cars and I'm in a hurry," Standard said. "Look, you told me once that Rim was to the north. We're going to sail north with Graystone, but you're going to have to pick out the right island. Think you can do it?"

"I don't know," Jeannine said. "Quinn flew me there once, but I'm not sure I can find it on a map."

"Well, try hard. Maybe if you think hard enough, Rim will put the answer in your head. Rim seems to be calling all the goddamn shots, anyway."

"What do you mean?" Jeannine asked.

"You're smarter than that," Standard growled. "Rim has been dealing the cards since I stepped foot in this country. First meeting you, then getting my arm bummed up to give a good excuse to have it examined. When I need a way to get north without being detected, zip, here's Graystone with a stocked boat made out of wood. That's pushing coincidence a little too far, baby. I might as well have phoned Rim and told him I was coming to kill him."

Graystone glanced back and forth, perplexed by the conversation.

114

"That should prove to you that Rim doesn't want to harm you. When are you going to understand that?" Jeannine said.

"I was almost to the point of going along with that," Standard said. "Until the doc here told me something he had heard on the vidi. The cops think I'm a murderer, honey. Quinn is dead."

"Dead?" Jeannine's chin sagged. "He can't be dead. I only gave him a knockout dose."

"Exactly," Standard said. "You didn't kill him, and I didn't kill him. And I sure as hell don't think the cops killed him. So that leaves Rim. Still think Rim is such a nice guy?"

"Would one of you mind telling me just what this is all about?" Graystone interrupted.

"She can tell you," Standard said, pointing over his shoulder. "I'm going on top and sail this barge. You two can chat while she's fixing something for me to eat. I haven't eaten all day and I'm starved. Come to think of it, I've had a sample of her cooking. Why don't you get something together, Doc, and bring it out for me? You can take a look at my arm while you're at it, too."

He shoved his way out of the cabin, kicking the hatch closed behind him.

"Impetuous young man, isn't he?" Graystone said. He turned to Jeannine. "Whatever have you been talking about?"

Jeannine sighed. "His shoulder is bothering him. It keeps making his arm twitch and he thinks you caused it."

"That's not very likely. But even so, it shouldn't matter very much, even if I had caused the trauma." Graystone found a pan in the galley shelf and filled it, dropping ground leaves into the water. "I didn't order any coffee, but do you think Mr. Standard would tolerate tea?"

She shrugged. "He probably won't even notice the difference."

The microwave boiled the water in seconds and Graystone rummaged through his larder of fresh meat. "I suppose I shouldn't ask, but how did you become involved in this?"

"How much do you know?" Jeannine asked, watching Graystone prepare the food. It surprised her how raw everything appeared.

"I know that he's an assasin, and that his arm is a weapon. A rather lethal weapon, at that."

115

Jeannine looked up suddenly at the words. "You know about his arm?"

"Oh, yes, of course," Graystone said, pouring the tea.

"You know how it works?"

"Certainly. It's really quite simple," Graystone said.

Standard swung the boat eastward, driving from the luminous horizon behind him. The water was calm, slurring between the hulls. The steady offshore breeze filled the sails, pressing them solidly. He checked the compass, guessed their speed, and estimated the time of their next tack. The girl still had not identified the correct island, but he was unconcerned. Rim would pull him toward it regardless what he did. He had been under the control of Rim from the outset, and now believed it fully.

There was a cluster of islands to the north, almost where the lake ended. Running from the apartment building, Jeannine had told him, and the rest had fallen into place. Neatly. Painfully neat. Before, he had felt he was a pawn in Condliffe's game, but he now the stakes had expanded. He was dangling between the Rim and the world.

Why kill Quinn, Standard thought, *and keep me alive?* He nearly expected the answer to boom out of the clouds.

The hatch cracked open and Jeannine slid beside him on the deck. "Here's some food," she said. "And you don't have to worry. Graystone fixed it."

He locked the rudders and took the tray, tearing into it. "You have a nice talk with the doc?" he asked between mouthfuls.

"There's something you should know, Mike," Jeannine said. "Graystone knows how your arm works. He told me."

Standard almost gagged on the food. "What!"

"Your arm is like a separate brain all in itself. The information on how to make it work is held inside, in the form of coded nucleic acid. When the time is right, the nucleic acid acts as a motor impulse."

"Shut up!" Standard snarled. "I don't want to know. I *can't* allow myself to know!"

She leaned against the railing. "Don't you see, Mike? It doesn't matter now. Rim knew how it worked the instant Graystone examined you. So you can't possibly kill Rim now. He'll know what to expect."

Standard shook his head angrily. "No. Rim can't read a strange mind over that kind of distance."

"Do you doubt that Rim can read my mind?" Jeannine asked quietly.

Of course! *That* was why Rim had arranged Standard's meeting with the girl. Rim could pick her mind as cleanly as a bone in a hammock. All it required was to get close enough to Graystone, and that had been arranged, too. Lord, he had walked into it blindfolded.

He stared at her with an expression of pain and confusion. "You led me right into it," he said. "You're like a monitor. As long as you stayed with me, Rim knew exactly where I was and what I was doing."

"Yes," Jeannine said. "That's why I work for Rim. He's always in tune with me. He watches over me, Mike. He can watch over you, too."

"No. Not me." Standard said. He shook his head dumbly. "I want no part of Rim. Rim is a tyrant. He's out to enslave the world."

"Rim is the last hope of the world," Jeannine said. "He brought the world out of a war that could have destroyed it, and he is holding it together now until it can cure itself. Someday Rim will be able to remove all the hate and greed in the world. That's not enslavement, Mike. That's love."

"No," Standard said. "If Rim is going to remove all the hate in the world, he's going to have to remove me, too."

"He can do better than that," Jeannine said. "He can make you whole again. He can repair the world, and he can re-make your arm, Mike. That's why he wants me to bring you to him."

"I don't believe it. Why me, girl? I'm trying to kill him, remember? With Rim's power, he could blot me out in an eyeblink. Why keep *me* alive?"

She moved closer to him. His gray eyes were almost luminous in the dark and she knew that Rim's power was coursing through Standard even now. She had guessed from the start that she could fall in love with this broken man, and now she realized why.

She ran her finger over his scarred face, touching his lips. "I'm falling in love with you, Mike. You are the greatest single man in the world."

"Greater than Rim?" Standard said, his anger slowly becoming a memory.

"Rim is more than a man," Jeannine said. "But of all the men in this world, you are the most wonderful."

"My God, what have you been drinking with the doc?"

"Don't joke," she said. "Mike, you are the Rim's father. Without you, there would be no Rim."

It stunned him, but deep inside he had suspected it. "Oh God," he breathed.

"In the Chinasian hospital where you were held, Rim depended on you for strength. He was so terribly wounded, Mike. He had no vision, or hearing, or touch. For a long while, he didn't know if he was alive. So he borrowed your mind so he could find his way back to reality. And when he had, he discovered something more. This great power of his. But without you, he would never have lived and would never have become what he is now."

He bowed his head, clenching his teeth. "How long have you known?"

"Rim told me while I was asleep. It came to me like a dream, but it wasn't a dream."

His arm was quivering, the violation of metal and artificial nerves revolting against his flesh. She placed her hand on it and leaned forward, brushing her lips across his face.

"Do you want me, Mike?"

He looked at her, letting his eyes fall over her dark hair and the large defensive eyes that peered back at him. He liked the feel of her and wanted her to stay on the gently moving deck with him. It would be easy, peacefully warm to fall asleep against her, to call an end to a doomed mission.

Except that he was still Michael Standard. And all the questions had not yet been answered.

He moved his arm around her. It would be good to really be able to feel her, her softness, her smoothness, not just the sensation of pressure that the arm transmitted. Good to be able to feel her with both arms.

Could Rim really do that, replace the mechanical contrivance with living tissue, give back the arm he had lost in a futile war? There was no longer any reason to doubt Rim's power. Rim could do that.

"Go inside," he said softly. "I need time to think, Jeannine."

IX

THE MORNING BROKE slowly in a blast of red that turned the sails to copper. It brought a rising column of clouds in front of them that grew out of the horizon and paced the sun as it climbed the sky. The water, table calm and flat throughout the night, began to show riffles of air. The weather was coming from the north, running directly into them.

Standard estimated his pattern of tacks and started his crisscrossing into the wind, squinting into the glare as he angled into the sun.

Jeannine heard the increased pounding of the wind-driven waves against the bow and came out on the deck. "What's happening?" she asked.

"We're running into some weather," Standard said. "Take a look."

She looked to where he pointed and saw the mounting thunderheads. "It looks nasty. Is it going to trouble us?"

"Don't know. It may veer off, but I don't think so. You'd better ask Graystone if this tub is rigged for lightning. Otherwise, we won't have to worry about Rim."

"I'll ask him. Is there anything else you need?"

"Yeah," Standard said. "I'm hungry. See if you can pry any more food out of him. And see if he has any shades. I'm going to burn my sockets out looking into those whitecaps."

The wind was building by the time she brought the food, forcing one hull up and churning a ribbon of foam. He ate hurriedly, shoving the food into his mouth, and wished he had more time to savor the fruit.

"Is there anything else?" Jeannine asked, wiping the spray from her face. "Can Graystone or I do anything to help you?"

"What I need is a couple of those trampers you know to sit on that far hull and hold it down," Standard said. "You're too light to do me much good, and Graystone is probably

119

too old to do anything more than peel grapes. So the answer's no. You can't help me. Go inside and have a nice talk with him and keep out of my way."

Jeannine squatted on the deck and collected the bowls. "We talked last night. He's a nice man."

"I'll bet he is," Standard said. He tightened the mainsail and angled as closely into the wind as the boat could hold. "What'd you talk about?"

"We talked about you and we talked about the Rim," Jeannine said. Her hair was hanging loosely in wet strands. "He said if my description of Rim is correct, he doesn't see how you can possibly win in a fight."

"That's encouraging," Standard said. "If your description was as muddle-headed as your thinking normally is, I'm a dead cinch to come out ahead with Rim."

"You may have said the word," Jeannine said. "Dead."

Standard grinned. "One of us or the other. Sorry, Jeannine. You just haven't convinced me yet."

The storm hit shortly after noon, the wind hitting them like a solid wall, shredding the tops of the waves and breaking the water across the deck. He slapped the sunglasses tighter to his face and was drenched in moments as the twin hulls chopped into the waves, sending plumes of water pouring into the boat.

When the storm struck, he was almost relieved. It gave him a chance to lose his thoughts in the bursting whitecaps. He canceled the computer and slacked off the sails, looping his feet under the hiking straps as the boat heaved and bolted on the waves. The storm passed in an hour, leaving the lake chopped and churning and Standard in a tense calmness. It had reminded him that he was still alive.

He spent the afternoon watching the neon blue reflections of the polarized light glinting off the tops of the whitecaps and sailed into the evening. As the winds settled, the anger in him returned and grew.

Jeannine stayed with Graystone, sampling his hoard of food, laughing at the fruit and fresh meat. In the middle of the afternoon, she had fought across the pitching deck to Standard and had brought him lunch.

"I can't get over that fresh meat," she told Standard. "It's so repulsive looking."

"Cooks up pretty good," Standard said and chewed into a

chop. "On the other hand, you can take a good-looking pre-pack breakfast and turn it into something repulsive to eat. I guess that takes skill. Not many girls can do that, you told me."

After that, Jeannine stopped talking to him. It suited him. He felt there was something he wanted to say to her, but since he was unsure of what, he preferred not to talk. His face was becoming seared from the sun and wind, but he pushed away the lotion that Graystone offered. He was alive and he was still Mike Standard. That was all he needed. He waited until they doused the lights in the cabin and locked the rudders, snapping the computer back on after replotting their course. The hull was hard, but at least it was smooth and he was damned if he was going to sleep inside the cabin with them.

Someone had covered him with a tarpaulin and his breath had condensed under it, soaking his face. Annoyed, he pushed the tarp back and peered around him.

Fog was curtaining the still water. It was resting a slight foot off the surface, as though a section of dull gray sky had dropped over the boat during the night. Lying on the hull, he could see under the layer, like looking edgewise into a white mirrored sandwich. It was thick and opaque, a low ceiling roiling over the lake.

He knelt, letting the wet tarp slough off his shoulders. His head in the fog, he could only see to the stern. Beyond that, his vision was lost in the cotton swirls.

The morning was cool and he was soaked from the condensation. He kicked the tarpaulin to the deck and stood on the hull. As he stood, the sunlight flooded his face.

The fog was less than five feet thick, a solid barrier over the water that stopped at his shoulders. Standing, he could look over the fog blanket. It drifted around him, a clinging cloud that covered the lake as far as he could see until it merged with the washed horizon. He was struck with a sensation of having been decapitated, his body a part of the nebulous fog and his head, a hollow orb that the fog curled into, only floating on the coiling blanket.

There was no way of knowing how far they had drifted during the night. With the stillness of the morning, the night had probably been calm also and they could not have drifted far.

He turned to the cabin to awaken Graystone and the girl, and then he saw it. Poking up out of the fog off the stern, less than ten kilometers away, was the island, a protuberance of gray floating in the hazy white swirls. It could have been any island within a radius of a hundred kilometers, but he knew, inexplicably, that he was looking at the island of the Rim.

He pounded on the cabin as he slid over it and threw the hatch open. Graystone was snorting heartily, blinking his heavy eyes, but the girl had stirred instantly.

"What's happening?" she asked.

"It's the island," Standard said.

She was alert and on her feet. "Are you sure? How do you know it's the right island?"

"Call it a feeling. Take a look at this and tell me if I'm right." He pulled her to the cabin top and pointed over the fog. "Out there. You see it?"

"Yes. Yes, I can see it."

"Well?" he said impatiently. "Is that the island or not?"

She stared across the fog. "I've only been on Rim's island once, Mike. And I was flown there that time by Quinn. It was when I was just starting to work for Rim and I met *him*. Quinn took me there and we only stayed a few hours. It's hard to tell from here if it's the right island."

Graystone pushed his head out of the cabin and looked up at them. "What's the commotion all about? Have we sighted land?"

"Yeah, we've sighted something, but Miss Birdwatcher here isn't sure what it is," Standard grumbled. He glanced frowningly at her and saw her face. Her eyes were wide and intent on the distant shape.

"How far away is it?" Graystone asked, unbending on the deck.

"Quiet," Standard hushed him. He was watching Jeannine as she strained against the mist. "What is it, girl? Do you see something familiar?"

His question brought her back, as though her mind were refocusing, trying to remember him. "Mike," she said quietly. "The Rim is there."

"How do you know?" Standard asked. He said it carefully, not wanting to risk jolting her back into reality too rapidly.

She looked at him and he saw the mixture of awe and fear. "Rim is calling me."

He felt the chill run up his spine and reassured himself that it was a cold morning. "Okay. Doc, why don't you see if you can get some breakfast going for us?"

"Certainly," Graystone said. "Jeannine, would you like to help me?"

"No," she said, her voice sounding empty in the fog. "I want to stay out here." Her voice trailed off, tangling itself in the white swirls.

Standard slid down from the cabin. "I'll give you a hand, Doc. I want to check something inside, anyway." He guided Graystone through the hatch and closed it behind them. He listened for a moment for Jeannine's footsteps over them, but she was motionless, her attention riveted on the island.

"What is it you wanted to check?" Graystone asked, pulling out pots.

Standard was unrolling the charts. "This isn't making any damn sense at all. I've got a feeling in my bones that Rim is out there, and Jeannine feels it even stronger. But take a look at this chart," he said, jabbing his finger to a fringed spot in the northern lake. "That's where Jeannine said the island was. We started off Chidy way down here in the south. How the hell did we cover so much distance?"

Graystone looked over his shoulder. "Isn't it possible? We sailed nearly all night long the first night, and all the next day in some rather stiff wind. We could have drifted several miles last night also."

"Sure, it's possible to sail that far in thirty hours. With a crack crew and some damned good weather, it's possible. No offense, Doc, but you and Jeannine don't exactly qualify as Chris Columbo's rowing team. We had some stiff wind yesterday, but it was all against us. We weren't making much time tacking into that storm. I can't see how it's possible that we could've sailed this far."

"Yet you seem positive your Rim is out there on that island."

"Yeah," Standard said, rubbing his chin. "That's what has me worried."

Graystone was cracking eggs into a skillet. "It's foolish to worry about something you cannot control. Either ignore it entirely or accept it."

Standard grunted and smirked. "Thanks a lot. Jeannine told me what kind of odds you were giving me. Think it's pretty hopeless, huh?"

The doctor watched the egg whites cloud and firm. "If Rim can do everything Jeannine says he can do, then I think your best course of action would be to join your comrades on the moon. It is impossible for you to win. This confusion you are having with the island is a fair indication of your impotency. If Rim is on that island, then he has either moved the island closer to us, or he has moved us closer to the island. In either event, that makes for a rather formidable foe."

Standard peered out the porthole. The fog was beginning to lift, and he nodded his head. "You're a civilian, Doc, so you've never been told. All but two of the moon lifters were destroyed in the war. I can't get off this planet if I wanted to. The only way I can get off Earth is for Condliffe to bring back one of the lifters and get me, and he's sure as hell not going to step on this planet as long as Rim is still alive."

He turned to Graystone. "I'm marooned on my own world, Doc. If I can kill Rim, then it'll be a world worth fixing. If I lose, then it won't matter. I don't want any part of the world Rim is making."

"But you don't really know what kind of world Rim is building. All you have to go on is what Condliffe told you and for all we know Condliffe may be another Hitler or Napoleon. Perhaps Condliffe, and not Rim, wants to tyrannize the world." Graystone said.

"You're a doctor," Standard said. "You should know the statistics, what's happening to the birth rate, the maturation rate."

"Those are only statistics. Of course I am aware of them. But there can be any number of causes, not merely some superhuman trying to control the destinies of man."

Standard did not answer, but stared again out the porthole.

Graystone turned back to his skillet. "I believe I feel sorry for you, Michael. You're so eager to rush headlong off the side of the cliff."

"I don't have any choice," Standard said.

"That's why I feel sorry for you."

They heard the shuffling on the cabin roof over them and Jeannine slid to the deck. Standard had the hatch open before she could reach it.

"Take me to the island, Mike," she said. "The Rim is tired of waiting."

"I'll take you to the island, but you're not coming ashore with me," Standard said. "You're going to stay on the boat with Graystone. It's my game this time, baby. I'll have to go alone."

"No." She shook her head emphatically. "You shouldn't go ashore at all. Something has changed. Something terrible is going to happen. If we both go to the island now, this may be the last time we'll ever be together."

"I thought Rim was leading me on this far so he could meet me and try to change my mind," Standard said coldly.

"He was, but this isn't quite the right time. I can't explain why, it just isn't." She stammered, groping for an explanation. "Everything is so mixed up now. If you go ashore, Mike, you *must* take me. Maybe if I'm there with you, it . . . it won't be so bad for you."

"Listen to her, Mike," Graystone said. "I think she knows what she's talking about."

Standard turned angrily. "Since when do you have a vote in this?"

"It's my world also," Graystone said. "I'll be going ashore with you, and I think it would be wise to have Jeannine with us."

"Like hell you're coming ashore with me! Jeannine might be helpful to me to point out the way, but I sure don't need you. Once we get off this boat, you turn it around and go find that beach you wanted."

"You're overlooking something," Graystone said. "I can be of enormous use to you. We've established that Rim cannot read every mind singly, but needs a reference point. It appears that he can communicate directly with Jeannine, and can make some kind of impression on your mind. But he seems unable to read my mind accurately thus far. If he could read my mind, there would have been no need for Quinn to personally report to him. There would have been no reason to force our meeting again on this boat."

Standard glowered at the doctor, not willing to admit the validity of the argument. Finally he tossed up his hand. "Oh, what the hell. Okay, you're coming with me. Jeannine's coming with me. Maybe we ought to drag the boat along with us, too."

Graystone smiled. "You do have moments of lucidity, Michael."

The wind was rising gradually, scattering the fog. As they neared, Standard scanned the island. There was no movement that he could detect, no pinar nets or buildings, only the rocks and a covering of trees. He was beginning to mistrust his own feelings and Jeannine's tentative identification. It did not seem a likely throne room for a ruler of the world.

He saw the sunlight glint from something in the forested center. Glass. Hidden in the trees was a building.

The beach was a rubble of stones, boundaried by the heavy bush. He lifted the boards and drifted in close, guiding with a paddle. There was no sound from the island. It was as dead and lifeless as the vanished fog. Even the ever-present gulls had disappeared.

"Strange," Graystone said under his breath. "There doesn't seem to be anything alive on the island."

"Spooky," Standard agreed. "That's what Rim will do to the whole world. Sap the life out of everything that lives."

He dropped over the hull and waded ashore, pulling the boat behind him. Jeannine slid into the water and splashed beside him onto the beach. They stood for a moment, Standard balancing the needle gun in his hand and listening intently. Graystone dropped off the deck and helped him drag the hulls out of the water.

"Well?" Standard asked.

"I'm not familiar with this part of the island," Jeannine said slowly. "The main dock should be on the other side. There's a paved road that runs from it up to the house."

"House? I expected more than that."

"It's more than a house," Jeannine said. "You'll see."

"Shall we split up?" Graystone asked.

Standard grunted. "I think our chances for a surprise attack have hit rock bottom. No, hell, we'll just walk on up to the house and knock."

He pushed incautiously into the brush, flicking aside limbs and stepping over decaying trunks. Jeannine and Graystone followed him across the rockstrewn beach into the willows and scrub pines. The ground sloped upward to the high point where Standard had noticed the reflection. The underbrush became denser, coiling around their feet and driving sharp branches through their clothes.

They stumbled into a cleared area that curved away from them on both sides. Standard recognized it immediately. It was a perimeter boundary, still showing the grooved treads of the land buster that had cleared it. He stepped onto the pulverized sawdust of the cleared brush and stopped. Graystone ne..rly bumped into him.

"What is it, Mike?" he asked.

Standard peered into the brush at the other side of the devastated band. "This clearing," he said. "It looks like it runs all the way around the island. It's probably mined. Not with explosives, but with detector devices."

Graystone tugged his lip. "Curious. Are you thinking what I'm thinking?"

"Yeah. Seems like a pretty ordinary warning method for a god."

"Precisely," Graystone said. "I imagine we should be on our guard from now on."

"Uh huh," Standard said. He turned abruptly and stepped back into the brush. He picked out a limb and aimed the needle gun at it loosely. It obeyed his will and clipped the limb in half. Then he stepped back on the sawdust of the clearing and tried it again. There was no response. The needle gun was no more effective than a chunk of steel inside the barrier.

"Well, children," he said, dropping the gun in the sawdust. "It looks like inside this barrier, we're in the direct control of Rim. Cheers."

"More direct than you suppose," Graystone said, nodding across the barrier.

Standard could have sworn there had been no one near them a moment ago, but now a seven-foot giant was standing before them on the other side. He was dressed in an ultraviolet white uniform that dazzled even in the heavy shade of the forest.

Standard dropped to his knees and scooped up the needle gun.

"Don't do it," Jeannine cried. "It'll backfire."

He was not listening. He threw himself sideways off the sawdust into the brush and visualized a spreading blot of red on the giant's chest. He fired and the gun came alive in his hand.

The needle slammed into the invisible field and hung suspended in the air for a second as the straight-line force be-

hind it piled up and blasted the gun out of his hand. It disintegrated in a rod of shrapnel that chopped off the brush behind him.

It was like holding a white-hot poker. The sensory pads in his metal hand overloaded and shorted, the sudden heat shriveling the plastic flesh and peeling it back from his fingers.

He could cope with pain. He had taught himself in the Chin hospital and later when Condliffe had sawed another three inches off his stub to house the arm apparatus. The worst thing about pain was the fear of disability, the thought of being maimed for life. Overcome the fear and any amount of pain could be endured until the body went into total shock, and even shock was partially fear.

He fought to his knees, his jaws aching from the effort of clenching them, and felt the jagged cracks on his teeth that he had broken.

Graystone helped him upright. "The Rim seems to take care of his own, wouldn't you say?" Graystone asked unnecessarily.

"Yeah, I'd say that," Standard grunted, waggling his arm to cool it. He still retained full control, but there was no way of guessing if any internal damage had been caused.

Jeannine had crossed the sawdust boundary and approached the giant, a quizzical expression clouding her face. The giant had barely moved, but instead watched Standard passively. He seemed unperturbed that Standard had tried to kill him. As Jeannine stopped before him, the giant turned his attention to her and smiled loosely.

"Hello again, Miss Brochet," he said. "Tell me, do you still have those orange lights in your apartment?"

She frowned, peering into his relaxed face. "Drog? Is that you, Drog?"

"Of course," the giant said. "I hope you and your friends are well."

"Yes, very." Jeannine smiled. "They're all well. Someday you'll have to visit me, if you've forgiven me yet."

Standard glowered as he stumbled across the sawdust with Graystone. The conversation was obviously for his benefit, to emphasize his impotence.

"There's nothing to forgive," the giant said. "You opened life to me. Naturally, at first I reacted the same any man would who felt he had been shanghaied. I tried to fight my

way free, to destroy everything around me. But then I slowly became aware of what total freedom really was, and then I began to accept my position."

Jeannine nodded, well pleased with herself. "That's good, Drog. The Rim must have great confidence in you now to give you this duty."

Standard grimaced at Graystone. "Do you ever get the feeling you're going to throw up?"

"Well, they are old friends, apparently," Graystone said. He felt himself sharing Standard's cynicism.

Jeannine turned quickly, angrily, to them. "Yes, Drog is an old friend. But more importantly, he is an inner agent of Rim. In time, Mr. Michael Standard, you may begin to appreciate what that means."

"I can hardly wait," Standard said dryly.

"We are keeping the Master waiting. He asked me to bring you to him. Follow me and I'll lead you to him," Drog said abruptly. He crashed into the underbrush, glancing warmly back at Jeannine. "It *is* good to see you again, Miss Brochet."

"Thank you, Drog," she answered.

"What the hell are you?" Standard snapped. "The queen bee for this whole damned outfit?"

Jeannine did not answer him. Standard felt a slow fury building inside him and knew there was no way he could fight what was happening. The Rim had him in its power like a gnat in the palm of a hand. Whatever Condliffe had planted in his arm had better work. There was going to be no second chance. There might not even be a first chance, what with the way things were rapidly disintegrating into a shambles.

Only Graystone seemed at ease as they broke their way through the underbrush and into the scrub forest. He hummed to himself, exuding the air of a Rotarian on Sunday walk, except his analytical mind was absorbing every twig and pebble. Carefully, cautiously, he was creating conclusions.

They broke out of the woods onto a circular plaza with the texture of crushed pearls. In the center was a glass cube, a shade over ten meters square, totally transparent, the trees on the opposite side showing clearly through it. Just as clearly, the cube was empty: an enigmatic presence squatting in the center of a rough island.

Graystone squinted at it. Whether Standard noticed it, Graystone was unaware, but as they neared the cube Gray-

stone saw the outlines of the trees on the opposite side shimmer slightly. For a second, they seemed to blur out of focus. He meant to ask Standard if he too had seen it, but the next action caught him entirely unprepared.

Drog led them to the cube. Without hesitating, he walked into a wall. *Into* the wall. It flowed away from him momentarily like a water drop separating from an oil slick, then closed behind him. He smiled at them from the opposite side of the glass, motioning them in.

They followed Drog through the wall. First was Jeannine, who had not even broken stride. She stood beside Drog and nodded to Graystone and Standard.

"Amazing," Graystone exclaimed.

"After you, Doctor," Standard said.

Graystone stepped into the wall. He expected some sensation, some evidence of a discharged force field, but there was no feeling whatsoever. He had just walked through a wall. It was as simple as that.

Standard followed him gruffly. "Damn good trick," he grumbled. "But not worth a damn for keeping prowlers out."

"Don't be too sure about that," Jeannine warned. "Remember what happened back on the beach. If you had an ordinary arm, you'd be missing it now."

Standard let the comment pass. He and Graystone were silent, trying to adjust their eyes to the interior of the cube. The light was dazzling, a mind-jolting brilliance that flooded out of the very walls around them. In the penetrating glare, it took long seconds for Standard to realize the glass wall he had just walked through was not transparent at all. There was no indication of the wooded island outside, only the intense incandescent light that bombarded him.

Half-blinded, he tried to retain his bearings. They were in a long hall that stretched for a hundred feet before them, made of the same luminous material as the plaza. The light glittered off a million surfaces, bouncing around him. It was nearly impossible to see where the walls met the floor. He reached for the wall and found it as difficult to feel as to see. There was a mushy resilience that gradually turned hard, but even so, the solid wall was farther behind him than the short steps he had taken to walk through it. And the hallway. A hundred feet long in a ten meter cube?

"Come," Jeannine said, taking his hand. "You are in the

vortex of life now, Mike. For the first time in your life, you are experiencing reality as it actually exists."

"Fine," Standard said, his mind swimming. "Give me that old illusion I've been living with if this is reality."

"That's why you are here," Jeannine said. "To find the truth."

Drog was already walking down the hall toward the far end. They fell into step behind the giant. *Reality exists on the other side of the wall,* Standard kept telling himself. But where was the wall? A coldness was seeping into him, tying knots around his spine. Jeannine's eyes were wide, her mouth parted as though she were listening to an inaudible voice.

"It's more beautiful than I remember," she said. "Oh yes, yes."

Graystone had stopped humming.

Standard forced himself to keep pace with Drog and Jeannine. Graystone was lagging behind, also stunned by the light. Standard's eyes were beginning to water and lose focus. The tears were running down his face, dripping off his chin as he staggered toward the far end of the hall.

The room was swimming for Graystone, throwing his eyes out of kilter as though he had been hit with a crunching concussion. He knew Standard was being affected too from the way he lurched before the doctor. For an instant, Graystone reflected on the physical properties of light to keep his mind clear, but the battering impact of the light drove all thoughts away. It was more than light, he knew instinctively. It was a shattering, pounding force.

But it was more than that, also. Because Jeannine seemed to revel in it, almost bathing in it like a crackling stream of water. And Drog seemed utterly insensitive to it. Graystone knew what it was, the answer hanging on a shred of his brain, balancing on the conscious, but the crushing light held the answer in limbo.

Drog and Jeannine stopped at the wall. Staggering, Standard almost ran into it.

"You can go no further, Mike," Jeannine said. "Drog and I will go on to meet the Rim. But you and Graystone must wait until the Rim is ready to see you."

"Wait, hell," Standard said, dragging the words out of his throat. "If you're going in, I'm going in. I've got some business to attend to."

"No, Michael," Jeannine said sweetly. "You're tired now. Rest for a while, and then you'll be admitted. Believe me, you will see the Rim, but not yet. It won't be long, I promise you."

He was having difficulty standing upright. The tears coursing down his face were mixing with sweat from the effort. The steel arm hanging from his shoulder seemed to weigh a ton, a millstone trying to drag him to his knees.

"Sorry, baby, but it's my show now," he said with a tongue that was as dry as the sand outside the cube. "Get out of my way, kid. I'm going in."

He took one step sideways, twisting his body and swinging the ponderous arm like a leaden pendulum. Drog was more intent on his daydreaming than on blocking the blow. Standard plowed the steel arm into Drog's chest. With an explosive gasp, Drog racked backward, his eyes wide with surprise.

Standard twisted back, hauling the arm back around. There was a dull snap as it caught Drog's jaw. The giant spun slowly, a ballet turn that sprawled him across the floor.

Someone was moving toward him. Standard saw the figure materialize out of the glittering light, another giant block of man rushing to stop him. In the glare, Standard had completely overlooked the white uniform standing close to the wall.

The guard was almost on him, reaching for his head. Standard ducked, coming up sharply under the guard's arm, driving his steel fist into the glittering area directly below the guard's belt.

Standard felt the blow jam into his shoulder as the three hundred pound guard stopped cold, his mouth gagging open, his lips curled back. Standard grabbed his steel fist and stood violently, bringing his clenched fists up. They hit the guard under the chin, jolting his head back.

The exertion was clearing his mind. By God, Condliffe was right! Fight a mental giant with brute force. It was working.

More guards were running toward him from across the hall. But they were long seconds away, running toward him as though locked in slow motion.

He glanced back at the wall that separated him from the Rim and made his decision. By the time the guards reached

him, he could be through that nebulously sparkling wall, putting an end to his mission.

He spun on the wall, driving his fist at it, preparing for the numbing blow. It had been a glass wall outside and he was determined that it was a glass wall inside.

His fist struck the wall and he lost his balance. There was no resistance. It was as though he had struck air. He fell forward, wildly wagging his arms to stop himself, and suddenly found himself imprisoned.

The wall, like a mass of gelatin, closed around him. He was suspended, one foot touching the floor, his body hanging in an impossible angle. For a moment a vague figure moved closer to him on the other side of the wall before the glittering light closed around him, blocking his sight, sealing his mouth.

In the dim sparkle of his mind, Graystone tried to follow what was happening around him. Drog was bleeding from his ear and the other guard was moaning on the floor, and Standard had bolted through the wall.

But not exactly *through* the wall. *Into* the wall was more accurate, because Graystone could see Standard's foot dangling outside. It was twitching spastically, trying to extricate itself from the shimmering morass. But it was firm, locked in the wall.

"Help him!" Graystone yelled, but Jeannine was standing dumbfounded.

She faced Graystone painfully, her face drawn in deep furrows.

"I can't," she whimpered.

"Appeal to your Rim," Graystone cried. "Good lord, girl, the man is suffocating!"

"The Rim does as he chooses," Jeannine said. She pressed her knuckles to her face, holding back her fear.

Graystone sputtered, immobilized by his frustration. He was jostled stiffly aside as the running guards reached the wall. Both stumbled to a halt, staring at Standard's protruding foot.

Graystone felt a command riffle through the hall, an order that emanated beyond his hearing.

Immediately, one of the guards grabbed Standard's now still foot and pulled. The wall again took the consistency of gelatin. Standard began sliding out like a rotten wisdom tooth. His second foot became visible and the other guard

grabbed it and helped tug. Slowly they pulled the limp body out of the wall.

With a drawn sucking sound, Standard oozed out, dropping brokenly on the floor. Graystone pushed past the guards and reached for Standard's pulse and saw Standard's chest heave just before one of the guards caught Graystone by the collar and unceremoniously tossed him back.

Graystone collected himself and rose painfully to his feet. The light was still dazzling him and now his neck hurt. He was having serious misgivings for having insisted on coming ashore.

Jeannine was bending over Standard, stroking his face. "Is he all right, Doctor?" she asked.

"He's alive. Your associates did not give me much opportunity to examine him," he said ruefully, rubbing his neck.

"You'll have to forgive them. They didn't understand you were a doctor," she said. She touched the livid scar on Standard's cheek and stood away. The guard who had yanked Graystone off his feet leaned down and lifted Standard off the floor. "Go with him," Jeannine said. "See if Mike is all right."

Graystone squinted around. Drog was leaning against the wall, glassy-eyed, his jaw hanging crookedly. "Perhaps I should have a look at Drog, also. Michael may have hurt him badly."

"No," Jeannine insisted. "You mustn't stay here now. Take care of Mike. Drog will be all right. Please, Doctor."

The guard stepped away with Standard. Graystone hesitated, then decided he had seen enough of the Rim's will and tagged after the guard before he was lost in the shimmering light.

Graystone had the distinct impression he was being led through a maze. The guard turned, angled, ran up stairs and down ramps, turning again, until Graystone had lost all orientation. He followed doggedly, trying to keep pace.

They rounded another corner and Graystone saw a gray rectangle hanging before them. The sight of it, not shimmering or vibrating, was a balm to his throbbing mind. The guard stepped through the rectangle and Graystone followed, stepping over the low sill.

It was a doorway and he found himself in a small cubicle,

all the walls, floor and ceiling a sheened gray substance that gave softly under his heel.

The guard placed Standard on the floor. Soundlessly, he turned and stepped through the rectangle into the glittering white light. The portal closed around him, blocking the glare and leaving only the soft gray light.

Graystone inspected Standard, found him breathing normally, and settled back. There were no seats in the room, no features of any kind. Even the doorway had vanished without a seam. The floor was gently resistant to his touch, exuding a faint warmth.

He paced around the room. It was smaller than the deceptive light indicated. He counted off four steps in each direction. Barely enough to allow two men to sleep on the floor. Graystone was thankful he was not susceptible to claustrophobia and tried to guess what Standard's reaction would be when he awoke.

X

IT WAS A perfect morning to stay sleeping. Sunlight was dribbling through the bedroom windows and he buried his face in the pillow, not wanting to acknowledge the morning. The scent of honeysuckle was drifting in with the sun, carrying a bird's chattering with it. He wanted to stay here, in this half-awake state, feeling the softness of the day, knowing it was not intruding, not demanding of him.

He burrowed deeper into the pillow, feeling soft foam on his arms. Someone was calling him, telling him to wake. The voice came lazing in with the sunlight and honeysuckle, gentle and sweet, and he recognized it as Jeannine's.

With a start, he realized he was feeling the pillow with *both* arms. He had his real arm back, real flesh and blood.

He bolted out of bed and found himself looking at Graystone. They were in a dull gray room and he interpreted it as a cell instantly.

"The hell . . . ?" he said uncertainly, looking for Jeannine. There was only the stark gray walls. He caught his breath and peered around more closely.

"How do you feel?" Graystone asked.

"I'm okay," Standard snapped. He flexed his steel arm, sensing the coldness of it. "How long have we been here?"

Graystone glanced at his watch. "About three hours. They brought us here after they pulled you out of the wall. Are you sure you're feeling well? You woke very suddenly."

"I was having a dream," he grunted. "Just a dream." He frowned at the sheen walls. "Dammit, I should've stayed asleep. It was a helluva lot better than this."

"At least it's better than that terrible glare," Graystone suggested.

Standard stood and walked around the cubicle. "Rim doesn't have much imagination when it comes to architecture, does he? Have you checked this room out, Doc?"

"Yes, it seems to be exactly as it appears. The gray light seems to be generated by the walls and the ceiling. It's becoming rather monotonous."

"I'll buy that. Where's the door to this closet? How did we get in?"

"Actually," Graystone said, "I think you're standing in front of it now. It was there when the guard carried you in. Then he went back out and the door dematerialized. Or the wall materialized in its place, whichever you prefer."

Standard felt the rubbery wall. "Everything has this spongy feel?"

"Apparently so," Graystone said, punching the floor.

Standard slumped back to Graystone and sank down on the floor. "Looks like a temporary dead-end, huh? You're pretty good at guessing games, Doc. Any idea where we go from here?"

"I've been thinking about that," Graystone said, tapping his chin. "Tell me, Mike, do you notice anything inconsistent about all this?"

"In what way?"

"I'm not really sure. It's more of a feeling than anything I can really nail down. Finding this island, as an example. You admitted that it would have been impossible to have actually sailed this far in such a short time. Yet, suddenly, here it is. And not even Jeannine is entirely positive she recognizes it."

Standard scraped the floor with his foot. "Doesn't matter

much. Wherever we are, we're here and it's getting nasty."

"Think for a moment," Graystone said, jabbing his fingers for emphasis. "Let's assume that there is an island here, and that there is some sort of building on it. But that's all. All the special effects, the dissolving walls, that terrible light, may all be an illusion."

"Getting swallowed up by a wall is real, and it's damned uncomfortable," Standard said. He slapped the cell floor. "And I don't care what you call it, the floor is *firm*."

Graystone fell silent, lost in thought.

"Look, what does it matter?" Standard said. "If it is partially illusion, that just makes the Rim's power all the more awesome. I couldn't breathe in that wall, Doc. So what the hell is real, anyway? You're dead no matter if Rim kills you with his mental powers or with a club. Dead is dead."

"You're correct, of course," Graystone said. "We're very limited in what we can really perceive. In a way, you could say that televid is all an illusion. Obviously, little people aren't chasing around inside the set. Nevertheless, for what it is, it is certainly real, in the sense that it exists."

"My point exactly," Standard said gruffly. "Anything that can kill you is real, no matter what it is."

Graystone looked at him quietly. "Do you still think you can fight the Rim?"

"Who knows? For a minute out there when I was slugging those fancy guards around I thought my vision started to clear. Here's something else . . . when I went into that wall, I thought I saw someone on the other side."

"The presence of Rim." Graystone nodded. "I sensed that, also." He curled back against the wall and sighed. "I'm not sure if you can win, Michael. But if this is an example of the Rim's powers, then heaven help us if you lose."

They waited for something to happen until they fell asleep from boredom. When they awoke, they found a tray of food and wine in the cell. They cleaned the platter, an innocuous assortment of bland sauces and pastries, and cracked open the wine.

"Well, Rim has *some* taste," Graystone commented, inspecting the label. "It was a fairly decent year, 'Seventy-eight."

He tasted it and smacked his lips, passing it to Standard.

Standard downed half the bottle and handed it back. "Yeah, not bad." He belched.

The drug hit quickly. Standard felt it coming and tried to warn Graystone, but the doctor had already taken a generous swallow. The floor tilted up and met Standard's face.

Oh hell, another goddamn dream. This time he recognized it and eased himself to see what Rim had concocted for his entertainment. *It's just a damned illusion, right?*

He was walking in a sunlit glade, the light shining through the delicate trees and forming patterns of gold and green on the soft moist leaves under his feet. It was the day of the morning he had dreamed about earlier. People were laughing at the edge of the woods and he walked to them in the small valley. Jeannine was there, shining like the golden leaves, letting the sun play on her hair.

"It's beautiful, isn't it?" she said. He looked around. It was the same world he knew, but something drastic had changed. It was gossamer soft, with a sweet scent of the honeysuckles that flowed with the sound of quietude. It was so gently quiet that he knew he could have heard a war on the other side of the world if there had been one, but the world was at peace.

"Sure," he said. "Everything's beautiful in a dream."

"It's more than a dream. This is the way it can be with Rim."

They walked together and stopped at a cool stream that flowed crisply around a rounded bank. A deer was lapping water not far from them. Standard selected a flattened stone and skipped it across the water, startling the deer.

"It's still a dream," Standard said. "Anything's possible in a dream."

"But it's a very real dream." Jeannine smiled. "You and I exist. Those people really exist."

"Maybe so, but all this embroidery," Standard said, waving his hand and noticing it was flesh again. "These trees, this stream, none of that exists. It's just my imagination, like having my arm here. Rim is only dipping into my memory and forcing me into this illusion. I know damned well I had my arm shot off, so it doesn't exist any more and Rim can't bring it back no matter what. Sorry, baby. Nice try, but I'm not falling for it."

"You try to be so hard," Jeannine said. She sat beside

Standard and rolled a pebble into the stream. "I wish you would try to understand. Rim is grateful to you, but it pains him to see you rejecting him. You helped him stay alive once. You were so strong and you had so much will to live that he borrowed some of it. It helped him overcome his own injuries. He was hurt very badly, Mike. So badly I don't even understand it."

"Lin Sang started to explain it," Standard grunted. "Something about glands and a screwy mysticism."

"That was the only way Lin Sang could understand it, but it's more than that," Jeanniné said. "Something fantastic happened deep inside Rim. He became the end chain of the human possibility. He is almost an angel now."

Standard stretched back on the grass. He knew he should resist the pleasantness of the dream, but the sunlight felt good on his face. "So what can Rim give me? Illusions? A lovely trance? What about the real me, lying in that cell? How can Rim keep me alive, with transfusions and vein feedings? Is that what he's offering the world, Jeannine? Everybody drugged into sleep with their minds wandering through a fairy tale existence while their bodies slowly rust away?"

Jeannine shook her head. "You still don't understand. Come with me; I'll show you something."

Standard crawled to his feet as Jeannine danced away. They walked across the grassy veld into a small woods. Rich fruit was hanging from the trees, fruit unlike any Standard had ever seen. He wondered how he had culled it from his imagination as Jeannine plucked a blue apricot and tossed it lightly at him.

"Try it," Jeannine offered. "They're very good. And they're real."

He bit into it, crunching its firm pulp. "How do you mean it's real?"

"It *is*," Jeannine insisted. "You *aren't* in the cell. You really are here with me, and you really are eating real fruit. Everything you are doing, you are really doing."

Standard toyed with the fruit. "How can that be? Nothing like this exists."

"I told you before, this is the way it *can* be. You're partially correct. All this doesn't exist exactly as you see it. We're still on Rim's island. The people we saw are really the guards and the stream is the lake. You may be eating a

hickory nut right now, and of course your arm is still metal. But Rim is only starting to remake the world. For the time being, he can give us this, a better appearance of reality. But it doesn't matter, Mike. If we accept it, it will be like this for us as long as we want. Then someday the whole world will *really* be this way, and we won't even notice the change. It will be this way for everyone. It's like a preview that we can enjoy now."

Standard finished the fruit, whatever it was, and leaned against a tree. He thought deeply. "What about progress? What happens to the human race in the meantime?"

"We live together," Jeannine said. "When the time is ready, we'll learn how to travel beyond the stars and create new worlds." She nestled against Standard. "Maybe we could be among the ones to make a new world grow."

"You can't make babies in a dream." Standard chuckled.

"But it's not a dream. Love is real," Jeannine said and turned her face up to him.

They made love on the grass. Nude, they splashed in the stream/lake, throwing water on each other and letting the sun dry them, intrigued with the shifting light patterns. It was easy to love in this world, Standard felt. Easier than he had ever loved before. It was as though a missing part of him were being replaced and now, accepting it, it seemed to fit well and made him feel whole again.

She bit his ear playfully. "It *is* better this way, isn't it, Mike?"

He watched a cloud drift across the blue-shot sky. It was actually real. He still possessed his own thoughts, his own emotions. He thought of the war, the pain he had known and had inflicted, the devastated lands. He thought of his own doubts, of his mission to kill the Rim, of Condliffe hiding on the barren lunar landscape. He tried to think of what he wanted in his life, and was annoyed to find that he had never decided on an answer. He closed his eyes and felt the grass tickling his skin. "Yes," he said at last. "It is better this way."

Jeannine pressed him tightly. "I'm happy, Mike. Will you talk to the Rim now? He would like to see you again."

"Sure." Standard nodded. "I'll talk to him."

The sunlight dimmed and formed the sheen walls around him. Graystone was still sleeping off the drug and one of

the walls had parted to allow the white light to flood the cubicle.

Standard stepped through the portal, surprised to find the light pleasant and comforting. He could see the corridors winding away from him clearly. The portal closed behind him. He glanced back to see that even the wall had vanished. Only an open corridor remained.

He scratched his head, wishing Jeannine had stuck around to guide him to the main hall again. Shrugging his shoulders, he wandered down one of the corridors. It rambled aimlessly, over short stairs and rises, around columns and veiled curtains of light. It reminded him of something he knew and he was beginning to feel uneasy when he stumbled onto the great hall he had originally entered.

The familiarity dawned on him. He had been wandering through the woods of the island. The trees, the thickets. It was as Jeannine had said. It was real, all right, but with a special veneer applied by Rim. Lounging around the room were a dozen guards, all radiating the glossy white light. They watched him warily as he entered the hall. Standard glanced over them, noticing that Drog was missing. None of the guards spoke. Two of them became so bored watching him they rolled over and fell asleep.

If the corridors and columns are the woods, he told himself, then this hall had to be a clearing, probably the same glade he had walked through with Jeannine in his dream. Close by, then, had to be the glass cube they had seen when they first walked up the beach. A glass cube that could bend and distort the light to look transparent one moment, then opaque and shimmering the next.

He guessed the cube was actually the inner chamber of the Rim, and rather than being enmeshed by the wall, he had simply run straight into it. The guards were probably sunning themselves in the clearing, perhaps under the illusion they were in the grassy glade. In a lopsided way, it was real, with solid obstacles hidden in a mental cloud.

And he knew why he had not been allowed entry at first. Graystone was correct. This was not the Rim's island, only a temporary meeting place. It helped explain the absence of vast groups of guards and the people Rim had already taken under control. He had not been allowed to meet the Rim because the Rim had not yet arrived. The Rim was still physical. Travel was still physical.

Standard frowned. The illusions were impressive, especially if Rim had created them at long distance. The thought bothered Standard.

But the Rim was here now. The illusory wall began to glow with a golden gleam. It spread toward Standard, opening a growing split in the wall. He looked through it, recognizing its actuality as a sliding panel. It opened into another chamber about ten meters square, awash in the same brilliant light. This time, Standard could adjust his eyes to it. In the center of the chamber was a raised dais and seated on the dais was the figure of a man.

The Rim beckoned Standard inside.

Standard entered, squinting at the Rim's face, trying to place him. The light in the chamber emanated from the Rim's head, swathing his face in ribbons of light. It stung Standard's eyes to peer directly into the Rim's face, the source of the brilliant light.

"It's good to see you again," the Rim said. It was an unspectacular voice, soft, but with an edge of determination.

Standard nodded. "The last time I saw you, your head was wrapped in bandages. Now you have it wrapped in light. I was trying to see if I could recognize who you were."

"It's unimportant," the Rim said. "We didn't know each other in my former life. All that matters is what I am now. For that, I wanted to thank you."

Standard squatted on the floor. "The same way you thanked Lin Sang?"

The Rim seemed embarrassed by the question. "That was unfortunate. I wanted to end the war, but to do it, I needed more strength. I couldn't bring myself to borrow more from you, so I borrowed from Lin Sang. Unfortunately, I borrowed too much. But that was before I learned how to control this power. Besides, wasn't one man's death an even exchange for peace?"

"Yeah, I guess so," Standard said. He was really not particularly concerned for Lin Sang. He had been an enemy, hadn't he? He fidgeted on the floor. He had not considered the original source of Rim's power, and it disturbed him. But it was logical: things aren't created out of nothing. There had to be an exchange of energy, and Rim had learned how to tap the living life forces in the people he collected.

"Jeannine has shown you a fraction of what I am building," the Rim said. "The beauty, the joy this world can be.

To build it, I need support, Michael. I need people who will help me build. I would like you to join me."

Standard frowned. "I'll tell you honestly, I'm considering it. But there's a few questions I'd like answered first. Tell me those, and I'll let you know."

"I expected questions from you," the Rim said. "Ask them."

"Okay. First, why did you kill Quinn? Still practicing control?"

"That's a very understandable question," the Rim said. "Very well, if it will ease your mind. I killed Quinn because he disobeyed me. I wanted you brought here, so that I could talk to you. But he did not believe you were capable of rational thought and felt you would be too great a threat. So he tried to destroy you and destroyed himself in the process."

"Very neat. How much power did you gain from him by killing him?" Standard asked quietly.

The Rim studied his face carefully. Standard could sense him thinking carefully. The Rim laughed shortly, more nervousness than humor. "I won't mislead you, Michael. I could, but you deserve more than that. I need your help willingly." The Rim stood, the light crackling around him. "I gained enough power to bridge the contact between myself and Jeannine. She became my focal point and I led you here through her."

Standard grunted. "I suspected as much, but it's nice to hear you admit it."

"As I said, I intend to be honest with you."

It wasn't all bad. If it was partially a dream, still it was pleasant. Hell, more than pleasant. The Rim's world beat anything in the real world by a flying parsec.

"Next question," Standard said. "Why me? What do you want of me?"

"That's quite simple," the Rim said. "I know your potential. Your mind is still shuttered and closed, but I know what you are capable of doing. You wouldn't be happy in this fantasy world. Your mind is too closed on what you think is reality, so until that reality occurs, I wouldn't insist that you stay here. I'd rather have you free in the world. My long-range eyes and ears, so to speak."

"You have something more in mind than just letting me wander around."

"Yes, I do," the Rim said. "I want you to contact Condliffe somehow and persuade him to return to Earth."

"So that you can eliminate him?"

"So that I can convince him, just as you are being convinced."

Standard mulled. What the hell, he had no real allegiances to Condliffe, or to anyone else, for that matter. And it could be one helluva kick having a power like the Rim backing him. "Sounds interesting," he said.

"Think of what you could do, Michael." The Rim smiled behind the glaring halo of light. "There are a thousand things to be done before this world is the way you saw it in your dream. It would take a very powerful, relentless man to accomplish them. I need you, Michael. Together, we would be unstoppable. I can channel the power to the universe into you when you needed it. You would be a god. And when you had it completed, you could rest in the new world you had created, not just for yourself, for all of mankind."

Standard stood. The thought appealed to him and he liked it. As he stood, he felt the weight of his metal arm. "What about this? Can you give me back my original arm?"

"Perhaps in time," the Rim said evasively. "For the moment, that steel battering ram may be useful to you. When Condliffe returns, I'll be able to delve into his mind and see how it functions. Then we'll deactivate the weapon."

"Aren't you taking a helluva risk? I mean, I don't have control over the weapon. The thing is automatic. It might blow up and kill you any minute now," Standard said.

"I don't think so," the Rim said coolly. "You've been threatened with death, pummeled, beaten . . . in the last few days you've gone through nearly every human emotion possible. Uncertainty, despair, doubt. For a while, I thought that love was the key, but even that had no reaction. And here you are now, talking to me, and nothing has happened. My next thought was that rebellion against Condliffe would activate the weapon, but you are seriously considering my offer and still I'm safe."

"Yeah, I can't argue with that. The thing doesn't even itch." Standard said, dangling the arm.

"So it is inconsequential now," the Rim said. "Eventually, I'm sure we'll find the key, but perhaps we'll know how to disarm it before then."

"I take it that's why you're not too keen on my staying on the island with you?" Standard grinned.

"Of course," the Rim said. "I am a realist, too."

"I think you've sold me," Standard said. "What happens to Graystone when I leave? He's a pretty good old coot, even though he caused me some real grief."

"He can stay here or leave, as he wishes," the Rim said, shrugging his blinding shoulders. "He is getting on in years and won't be of much use to me. If he decides to stay, I'll make it pleasant for him."

Standard joggled on his feet. With the Rim's power flowing through him, what couldn't he do? He was becoming anxious to try it.

Lordy! Michael, the archangel of the world.

"I think you've made a deal, Rim," Standard said. "You tell me what you want done, and I'll do it. My way, right?"

"Within limits." The Rim smiled evenly. "We're two of a kind, Michael. We both know the inadequacies of this world and we both know that some things will have to be destroyed before they can be rebuilt."

Standard grinned. "Yeah, I noticed a few inadequacies in Policontrol. They gave me a pretty rough time. Maybe they need some straightening out."

"In due time," the Rim said. "Our new world won't need a police force after it is created. You'll have the time to correct it after we have dealt with Condliffe. I can give you a life-time three times longer than the average. Nearly two centuries, Michael, to do what must be done."

Standard chuckled. "I'll knock myself out for the first century, then ease off and relax for the second. Yeah, you've got a deal. Sounds good to me, Rim."

"Fine," the Rim said, relaxed. "You'll stay here for the time being so that I can learn your mind. After that, we'll be able to contact each other mentally. It will be a two-way contact. Since I already share some of your mind, we'll be able to function almost as one."

"That settles it, then," Standard said happily. He rubbed his hands together and looked around. "Where's Jeannine? I kinda want to say goodbye to her. I've learned to like that kid."

"So have I," the Rim said. "I'm going to keep her with me. She has served me well."

Standard felt an alien tingle run up his arm. He ig-

nored it, glancing around. He saw the shimmering white wall part, and Jeannine entered. He blinked quickly. She was dressed in a flowing white gown that mingled with the glaring white light that glittered around her face. She crossed in front of him, mounting the dais with the Rim. Together they looked down at him, sharing the cutting light.

"I'm proud of you, Mike," she said. Her smile was a radiant burst of energy that charged through his mind.

"Wait a minute." Standard grimaced. "What's going on here?"

"I told you, Michael," the Rim said. "She will stay here with me. Already, she has become part of me." He draped his arm around her and the light was like an electrical shock.

"This isn't exactly what I had in mind," Standard stammered. He felt the tingle in his arm again and stepped closer to the dais. "Somehow I thought you and me, Jeannine . . ."

"We can still be together, Mike," she said. "Through the Rim's mind, we can still love and know each other."

"Yeah, but . . ." He moved across the floor. Jeannine was a part of the Rim, like a steak becomes part of a man after he has eaten it. Standard understood where the power would come from for him to live a second century.

Suddenly he understood Condliffe's key. For one brief imaginary instant he had known love and held it in his arms, and now he was seeing it lost to him in reality. He felt the arm throb at his side.

"What's wrong, Michael?" the Rim questioned.

"I can't share her," Standard said, feeling the agony in his voice. "She did her job too well, Rim."

The Rim held out his hand. "Stop it, Michael. Control it!"

"I *can't!*" Standard cried painfully. The arm moved upward of its own accord, leveling itself at the Rim's head. He imagined two centuries of virtually unlimited power and the coming reality of the dream, the grassy slope, the chiming stream. "Oh, damn you, Condliffe," he sobbed. "Damn you!"

The Rim instantly poured out a volcano of power, a devastating bolt of mental energy that shattered the walls. Standard felt it hit like a booster rocket, slamming into his psyche. He staggered backward, quivering from the blow, but knew the Rim was not yet in tune with his mind. Another giant

blow struck him. The Rim was lashing out desperately, casting raw explosions of power at him.

Dimly, Standard saw the guards crumple outside the broken glass walls. Rim had exhausted them of their life forces.

Standard's arm grew rigid, tensing itself. The Rim saw it and blasted another current of power.

Jeannine gasped, tumbling from the dais, her eyes suddenly glazed and staring fearfully into space.

It was real. She was gone. The concussion fractured Standard's shoulder. Like a five-fingered projectile, the weapon struck the Rim, exploding his head in a shower of blood, throwing stained shreds to the wall framework.

He picked himself up from the gravel floor, numb with agony. Everything had disappeared in Rim's fight for life, every iota of energy had been drained. The light, the shimmering pearl walls, had fallen back into reality, leaving only the bent framework of the cube. The bodies of the guards were strewn around him, contorted into grasping, clawing positions. In the woods, Graystone was dazedly propping himself against a tree.

Standard knelt over Jeannine's body, seeing the blood from his handless arm dribble over her gown, mingling with the livid stains of Rim's draining corpse. He touched her lips with his fingers, his real ones, the only ones he had left, then pressed her eyes closed.

What were left of the bones in his right arm were mashed, the remainder of his steel arm dangling from the ruined plastic and flesh. Blood continued to ooze from his shoulder where the joint had been fragmented and broken through his skin. He stood, the pain blackening his eyes momentarily.

"I'll keep it this way, Jeannine," he said and stepped across the clearing into the world he had created.

ACE DOUBLE BOOKS . . . more for your money